Moments

Book #3 in The Condemned Man Series

by Kevin Byrne

NEVER STOP NEVER QUIT
Portland, Oregon
NeverStopNeverQuit.com

Dedication

This book is a labor of love and is dedicated to our continuing fight against the devastating effects of multiple sclerosis (MS).

- I wrote and edited this book, over the course of two-and-a-half years, using voice-to-text technology, as MS has crippled my hands to the point of making typing and writing virtually impossible.
- There is nothing on the market today with the ability to cure my MS or send it into remission.
- It is debatable whether or not my current medications are slowing the progression of my MS, or even giving me an extra year when, before, I only had a month.
- There is no known way to recover function I have lost, or will lose, due to the damaging effects of my MS.
- There is no way to predict, identify, or isolate early-onset MS, and eradicate the disease before it affects the next generation.
- Not yet...

One hundred percent of the costs to write, edit, and create this book was borne by me. I offer *Moments* through retail book outlets at minimum possible price points which will earn near-$0 in royalties. This story is my gift to you.

To request this book in additional formats, please send a note to: Moments@NeverStopNeverQuit.com.

Why give this story away? Solely for the opportunity to take this Dedication to highlight my need for your donation to our fight. We can't do it without your love and support.

Please consider making a tax-deductible donation to the National Multiple Sclerosis Society at: Main.NationalMSSociety.org/goto/Eleanor. I fundraise under my daughter's name so that maybe her generation will no longer hear the words, "You have MS."

To give a tax-deductible donation to the NEVER STOP NEVER QUIT charitable foundation, please reach out to me directly at Kevin@NeverStopNeverQuit.com.

With love and thanks,
Kevin

This book is published by NEVER STOP NEVER QUIT, a charitable foundation whose mission is to raise funds, support treatment, and promote awareness in the fight against multiple sclerosis. One hundred percent of the profits from this book will go toward that fight.

Because it is a fight.
For more than 2.5 million people
with MS worldwide, the fight is not over and it
won't be over until a cure is found.

It will never stop...nor will we
It will never quit...nor will we
This is why we fight!

Never Stop... Never Quit...®

For more information, please go to: NeverStopNeverQuit.com

Table of Contents

Chapter 1 - Voice: Angela 7

Chapter 2 - Voice: Angela 22

Chapter 3 - Voice: Angela 49

Chapter 4 - Voice: Dominic 76

Chapter 5 - Voice: Angela 85

Chapter 6 - Voice: Dominic 94

Chapter 7 - Voice: Dominic 116

Chapter 8 - Voice: Dominic 127

Chapter 9 - Voice: Dominic 159

Chapter 10 - Voice: Dominic 187

Chapter 11 - Voice: Dominic 214

Chapter 12 - Voice: Angela 234

Chapter 13 - Voice: Dominic 241

Chapter 14 - Voice: Dominic 254

Chapter 15 - Voice: Dominic 268

Chapter 16 - Voice: Dominic 281

Chapter 17 - Voice: Dominic 300

Chapter 18 - Voice: Dominic 313

Chapter 19 - Voice: Dominic 342

Chapter 20 - Voice: Dominic 360

Chapter 21 - Voice: Angela.. 368

Chapter 22 - Voice: Dominic 378

Chapter 23 - Voice: Angela.. 455

Chapter 24 - Voice: Dominic 461

Chapter 25 - Voice: Dominic 470

Chapter 26 - Voice: Dominic 489

Chapter 27 - Voice: Dominic 497

Chapter 28 - Voice: Dominic 500

Chapter 29 - Voice: Angela.. 505

Chapter 30 - Voice: Dominic 512

Chapter 31 - Voice: Angela.. 535

Chapter 32 - Saturday, October 9, 2024.. 540

About the Author 543

Acknowledgments 544

Moments 545

The Condemned Man Series 546

Chapter 1 - Voice: Angela

Rule Number 1, my love: Never search for a time that didn't exist. The repercussions will be severe.

Thursday, February 28th, 2019, was the day I met Dominic Bandall. A sense of elation ran through my mind again and again. "This trip is going to change my life!" From the day I received Dominic's invitation, I held on to that thought. That this was by far the greatest understatement of my life does nothing to quell my need to describe the adventure I am going to tell you in the very same manner today. I was actually going to meet the legendary Dominic Bandall.

The flight attendant broke me out of the trance I had been in since we took off. "Ladies and gentlemen, we have begun our final approach into Kona International Airport. Please bring all seat backs and tray tables to their upright and locked position."

The hours seemed to have flashed by in an instant; my lost time was spent gazing out the window. Beneath us, there was nothing but deep blue ocean stretching out until it blended into the soft blue sky that swept around and wrapped back over us.

"Please ensure that approved portable electronic devices such as tablets and cell phones remain in airplane mode until—" I scanned my area for any contraband, but realized that my plush first-class seat meant the rules of the masses didn't apply to me. While I had been focused on the view outside the window, the remnants of my last meal—fresh seared ahi tuna steak with steamed baby carrots in a honey, lime, and cilantro soy glaze—had been cleaned up by an attendant. My magazines, newspaper, and notes were stacked neatly next to my new leather portfolio—a case subtly embossed across the bottom with *Bandall and Bandall, Attorneys at Law*. Every time I looked at the inscription, I wondered if Bandall and Bandall was somehow going to be part of my future. I pulled out the letter I had received two weeks earlier. To think that a girl like me would ever get an invitation like this. Mom would have been so proud!

"Other larger devices need to be safely stowed until we are at the gate and the pilot has turned off the—" The attendant's words faded away once more as I was captured by the cryptic words in my letter. The letterhead was subdued, professional, and quite eerie once you understood what it represented. The law offices of Bandall and

Bandall had once loomed over the top of New York City, towering over a part of the world that no longer exists:

One World Trade Center, 94th floor, Suite 105

New York, NY 10048

And now, the head of that firm had suddenly resurfaced...only to call on me, a student, just a kid really, in my last semester of law school.

February 17, 2019

Ms. Angela Grant

c/o New York Law School

185 W Broadway

New York, NY 10013

Dear Ms. Grant:

It is with sincere humility that Mr. Dominic J. Bandall, Esquire invites you to his office in Honu'apo, Hawai'i. The purpose of this meeting is for you to conduct a series of interviews with Mr. Bandall. All travel arrangements and lodging expenses will be handled by the law firm of Bandall and Bandall. As an alumnus of New York Law School, Mr. Bandall has taken the liberty of contacting your professors and the dean of students, and they have agreed to allow you to use these interviews as part of the final project required for graduation.

When I first got the letter, I must have read it six times before I was able to tear my eyes away from the page. Even today, when I read the invitation, it still sends chills down my spine. Right away, I had so many questions. One of the first was whether Dominic Bandall was my guardian angel. I always felt someone was looking out for me—that I had a secret benefactor. Mom always thought the college scholarships I won and the work programs I was accepted to resulted from my hard work, perseverance, and the "grace of God." While my good grades undoubtedly helped, I was always convinced someone was helping me. After graduating from college, I needed to take time off before starting law school, in part because college had been a rough time for me. I took my mother's illness and death hard and went through periods in which I felt utterly alone. But oddly, every so often I got a feeling of warmth and security, one I could never quite define. I wasn't even sure it was real, but with this new windfall, I felt it again. It couldn't be my imagination. It couldn't be a coincidence.

I was given hardly any information about the trip and had no idea what to expect. In a note that was included with the letter, I was instructed to contact Michael Girard—one of Mr. Bandall's representatives in New York—to make arrangements for the trip. As I later found out, Michael's mother had been a legal administrator at Bandall and Bandall before she was killed on 9/11. Actually, every person in the law firm died on 9/11—everyone, that is, except Dominic. I assumed Dominic felt a debt of allegiance to Michael.

Michael did not shed much light on the trip. "Dominic does not travel to New York anymore," he told me. "He doesn't travel anywhere these days. He prefers to remain in Hawai'i, possibly because of his frail condition." I asked about his "frail condition," but either Michael didn't know, or he didn't want to share it with me. As I would soon find out, having a limited understanding of what was going on was something I would regularly have to deal with on that trip.

When I met with a few of my professors and the dean of students, I hoped to find out more about Dominic and the invitation, but they didn't seem to know any more than I did. The only new thing I learned was an odd tidbit: most people do not like to challenge or contradict Mr. Bandall. Michael had told me the same thing, but he had added another seemingly random piece of information: "He almost always prefers to be called Dominic, except when he's in a formal legal venue." That was pretty much all I knew.

As I said, limited understanding.

When the plane finally touched down in Hawaii, I took a moment to soak in the fairy tale. It was the most magnificent sight! Even from the airport, even from the plane window, it was just fantastic. Trees—the deepest shades of green I had ever seen—swayed gently in the background, interrupted only by the blue waters and sky. The perimeter of the Island was outlined by a gathering of majestic white clouds that appeared to increase in size and number with each second.

"Storm's coming." I was jolted out of my trance by the woman sitting next to me. Over fourteen hours sitting next to each other and not a word had been spoken by either of us until we landed.

I smiled at her. "Really? They're beautiful. The clouds, I mean."

"Have you ever seen a Hawaiian thunderstorm?" I shook my head no and her eyes lit up. "Oh, you're in for a treat! They are the most magnificent storms you've ever seen."

"I don't know about that. I grew up in Philly and have lived in New York for a few years now. Nothing compares to our storms." Those of us who live on the East Coast really take pride in them. Hawaiian storms may be incredible, but I wasn't yet ready to hand over our cherished title.

"Well, dear, you just wait and see. You are in for a treat," she said with a smile. I remember thinking, *To have so much pride in Hawaiian storms, she must be Hawaiian. And why the sudden burst of conversation? Was she nervous about something, or maybe happy...excited? Like going home?* I would never know because as soon as that distinct ding sounded, she bolted for the door. No carry-on, just a purse clutched in her hand. Yep, I figured, probably nervous anticipation about something—a feeling that I could, at that exact moment, very much relate to. I grabbed my new briefcase and matching carry-on luggage—all purchased by Michael and compliments, of course, of Mr. Bandall—Dominic—and got off the plane.

Once inside, I wanted to get my bearings and review my arrival instructions again. Just as I was looking for a place to sit, I was greeted by a very large and impeccably dressed man. I can't describe what it means to look Hawaiian, but this guy did. He offered me his hand.

"Angela?" I nodded. "Hi. My name's Sage. Here, let me take your bags. Can you please follow me?"

So far, everything about the trip had been unusual—this encounter was no different. I thought to myself, *Who is this guy? Why is he here at the gate? I mean, don't they have the same security as everywhere else...where you kind of need a ticket to be at the gate?* Before I could ask him anything, Sage reached for my bag and said, "The luggage you checked has already been collected and will be at the transport location." He added that he worked for the airport but had been asked by Dominic to meet and assist me.

Sage and I walked in silence across the terminal—silence except for my little gasping sounds as I tried to keep pace. We finally turned in to an area marked "Private Aircraft."

"Another plane? I thought we were there—I mean, here." My flight had been comfortable enough, but also long—the idea of getting on yet another plane was not at all appealing.

Sage must have thought me quite pitiable, but he just smiled and said, "It's just a quick flight to the other side of the Island, Angela. We can drive if you really want to, but this way is a lot quicker. Besides..." he swept his arm across his body, unfurled his hand, and gestured to what sat in front of us. Out on the runway was a small silver-and-blue helicopter, flanked by a woman, the pilot I guessed, wearing a dark-blue flight suit and gold-rimmed tinted sunglasses. Her hair was cropped in a short bob, the perfect accent to her formidable appearance. The helicopter didn't look large enough to hold one person, let alone a pilot, me, Sage, and my luggage.

"Are we all going to fit in that thing?"

Sage chuckled. "Oh, I'm not going. It's just you and Kalena. Don't worry. She's a good stick. Here, let me introduce you." As I would soon learn, everyone called each other by their first names; it was informal and friendly. After introductions, Kalena explained that we were going to a small ranch outside of Honuʻapo, near the south end of the Island. "It is just outside of the Kaʻū Forest Reserve, and it's isolated, so it is hard to get there by car."

Kalena conducted a safety briefing, then Sage gave me a helmet and walked me around to my seat...in the front! He helped me buckle my seatbelt, closed the door, gently tapped on the window, and waved goodbye. I got the impression he was okay with staying on the ground. I wouldn't have minded hanging back with him.

Kalena walked around the helicopter once more for climbing into the seat on the right side. She plugged her helmet into the console, then reached across and plugged mine in.

"Can you hear me?" she asked. I nodded. Kalena chuckled. "You have to say something."

I giggled. "Sorry about that. Yes, I can hear you just fine." Kalena went through another round of safety briefings, describing the possible emergencies we might encounter while in the air. Oddly, her enumeration of every catastrophe imaginable didn't frighten me; it was comforting. She was confident and knew what to do in every scenario. After that final briefing, she looked at me and stared hard into my eyes in a way that felt intimidating. I wasn't sure whether she was expecting some sort of response from me or just trying to gauge my comfort level. Either way, it made me uneasy. Trying to break the awkward moment, I nodded toward the clouds and said, "A storm is coming. Looks like we are in for a treat."

Smiling, Kalena pulled out a checklist and continued to work through the preflight procedures. I watched as this gloved wonder blurred both hands across the instrument panel, adjusting knobs, tuning frequencies, and entering coordinates on the computer, all the while explaining each step. She then pointed at a ground crew member standing well outside of the rotor area on the runway, and yelled, "Clear!" loud enough that I could hear even though she wasn't using her microphone. He looked down both sides of the aircraft and then gave Kalena a thumbs up. With the trivial press of a button, the engine started, and the blades slowly began to turn. As the spin picked up faster and faster, the helicopter developed the slightest harmonic shake.

Kalena looked all around and above. "So, have you ever flown in a helicopter before?" I shook my head no. "Hey! Remember, you have to talk because I can't stare into your face to get your answer."

I felt a little foolish. "Sorry about that. No, I've never flown in a helicopter before."

Kalena quickly returned to her calm and comforting manner. "This little trip will be easy. The clouds are of no concern to me. It will be some time before the storm builds up and moves down to the south end of the Island. We'll be down at the ranch well before that. You'll have a delicious smoothie in your hands in time to watch the storm hit."

Then she added, "By the way, Dominic doesn't drink. He doesn't seem to mind if other people drink, but it just isn't for him. He says it clouds his mind. Also, he says the nighttime is when he does his best thinking, and he likes to go to sleep with a clear head. None of the people who work for Dominic drink in his presence, not out of mandate, but out of respect for him."

"That's okay with me. I am no good after more than one glass of wine with dinner. Anyway, I hear the mango is out of this world!" I giggled with anticipation.

Kalena nodded in agreement, a slight smile peering out from under her tinted helmet visor. After a quick conversation with someone through her microphone, she yelled out, "Here we go!" and pulled the helicopter straight up into the air for what seemed like forever. I felt like I was on an amusement park ride. Then, in an instant, she pointed the face of the aircraft back toward the ground, swapping vertical lift with horizontal speed. The moment was breathtaking! It occurred to me that I was so glad I hadn't told the airplane pilot that it was my first time on a jet.

I looked down just in time to watch the coast of the land slip away underneath us. Now there was nothing but blue water and the sky ahead. It was the same view I had from the plane when we were nearing the Island, but now the comfort and security of a massive airplane—one that had sheltered me and narrowed my view through one small portal—was replaced with only a thin piece of glass. Faint images of the tiny helicopter's airframe bordered the perimeter of my vision, including the control panels in front of me and the blur of rotor blades above. Kalena said something about our altitude and speed, but I was too lost in the waves of the water as they rippled far below to pay close attention. Then, after making a slow turn, she pointed to a huge volcano directly in front of us. She told me it was Mauna Loa, which means "long mountain." I hadn't noticed it from the plane. Maybe I had been too lost in my daydreams. Also, I hadn't had the pilot's view I now possessed...thank goodness. We were headed straight toward it. After a brief history lesson, which did not ease my apprehension of being so close to this massive, active volcano, we turned our attention back to the coastline. The beaches were unlike anything I had ever seen before. Compared to what I was used to—sandy, almond-colored beaches dotted with candy-cane-striped umbrellas and happy beachgoers—this jagged coast looked menacing. The waves were shooting up fifteen, even twenty feet when they hit the coastline. As I learned, every time Mauna Loa erupts, the Island changes its shape, extending to wherever the flowing lava meets the ocean. The hardened lava, crusty and dark gray, was the first thing I saw in Hawaii that wasn't a luscious shade of blue or green, but it was magnificent nonetheless. As we flew down the coast, I hung on every word Kalena said about the history of the Island.

We then turned toward the luscious green terrain of Ka'ū Forest Reserve and I suspected the ranch was close by, sparking a sense of disappointment that my amazing experience was about to end. We appeared to be following a makeshift dirt road that ran across miles and miles of deserted grassland. After another radio call, Kalena slowed to a crawl and dropped the aircraft down to just over the trees that appeared to have crawled from the lava and once again regrouped.

All at once, another incredible view opened up. What lay below was the strangest assemblage of beauty. The tender stalks of wild grass growing out of the dirt now outnumbered the strips of dark lava flow that seemed to point toward the top of the volcano, now in the distance. No human could ever replicate such beauty.

The only hint of civilization I could see was Dominic's white ranch house in the distance. The parcel of land on which it sat was roughly the size of a New York City block. I could tell that every effort had been made to incorporate the grounds and the house organically into the natural beauty of the Island.

Kalena brought us down on an airstrip near the far end of the ranch. With her checklist out again, she went through what she called shutdown procedures. Once she was done and the rotor blades had stopped spinning, she turned to look at me and smiled. "Not a bad job to have, huh?" I nodded yes, then shook my head no; I wasn't sure what she expected me to say. She unplugged my helmet, unbuckled my seatbelt, and then slapped my leg. "Come on! Let's go meet Dominic."

Chapter 2 - Voice: Angela

While we were flying in, the one-level house seemed small compared to the vast swath of land it sat on, but once I saw it up close, I was surprised at how big it actually was. I couldn't help but wonder just how much of the island Dominic owned. There was not a soul in sight. It almost seemed like the home and grounds had been abandoned moments before we arrived.

Either feeling no need to knock or knowing no one would answer, Kalena opened the unlocked front door. "Go ahead in. I'm going to head back to my bird and grab your bags. Just make yourself comfortable. I am sure Dominic will be here momentarily."

Kalena closed the door behind her and left me alone in the largest room I had ever seen. It was a massive entryway with ceilings that must've climbed twenty-five feet high or more. There were three massive hallways: on the left, on the right, and in the back. The bare walls gave no indication of what was at each of the destinations. My nose twitched, recoiling from the strong odor that filled the room. My guess was that it had been painted not too long ago, maybe as recently as that morning. The room had no furniture in it, so there was nowhere to sit, but that didn't matter; my fear of possibly leaving footprints on the pristine bamboo floors kept me glued to the spot where Kalena left me. Anyway, I was quite content to examine my surroundings from where I was standing. Wide expanses of freshly buffed floors ran in every direction, ending only when they bumped into the bare walls. The walls were painted off-white and the textured ceiling, which may have been bamboo as well, was painted a very light pale blue. There were no old nail holes on the walls. Nothing hung from the windows. Only the simplest of fixtures covered bare light bulbs.

I immediately had questions. Why do such a renovation like this, why remove every piece of furniture and strip the room completely bare, while you are hosting an out-of-town visitor? Was there some kind of story behind it? What did it look like before? I looked outside to the luscious green and blue. I thought to myself, *What a difference between inside and out! If life existed in the house before, it sure doesn't seem to any longer.*

"Pardon the appearance, but I'm in the process of remodeling." Echoing in the bare room, the voice behind me was unexpected, but it did not startle me. I felt it was him. I wanted to act confident, so I replied without turning around.

"My first question is, what made this room so grotesque that you felt the need to strip it of everything?"

"Grotesque? Why choose such a hostile characterization?"

I turned to see Dominic Bandall standing just a few feet from me. I didn't know where he had come from. Of course, he had entered through one of the hallways, but it was impossible to know which because he was at least twenty feet from the nearest entry. He looked frail, as if barely able to stand on his own feet without the walker that was propping him up.

As surprised as I was by his state, I had to answer his question and explain my admittedly bold comment. "This room is grotesque, Mr. Bandall. While on my picturesque, albeit short, helicopter flight to your house, I witnessed the greatest majestic panorama I have ever seen. I assume this was intentional, just as everything in your career has been. Yet, when I walked into your house...what a stark contrast! There is no beauty here. I can only conclude that there is some reason you intentionally removed all the character from this room just before my arrival. Is there something you are covering up...or should I say, is there something you are trying to cover up? I mean, the smell of new paint is obvious." The whole time that I was making my case, I paced the room. When I was finished, I turned to look at my host. "Does my explanation satisfy you, Dominic?"

To this day, I'm not sure if my attempt to act confident and to use words that sounded lawyerly came across as professional, arrogant, or naive to Dominic. Either way, I was immediately welcomed by the friendliest little old man I had ever met in my life. A formal introduction never occurred—there was no need.

"I am going through a reset. This happens every once in a while. It coincides with changing priorities in my life."

We chatted about nothing extraordinary for a while. I was hoping to figure out why he flew me all the way to Hawaii. It made no sense. On one side, there was the master lawyer, a superstar who had brought down the likes of River City Ironworks and the Priel Foundation. And on the other, there was me, a young student working her way through law school. The only connection I could make between the two of us, aside from the law, was our shared alma mater. I had no clue what he wanted from me or what I could do for him.

"A storm's about to roll in. Let's go look! I used to pine for a good New York thunderstorm until my arrival on this Island. I realized very quickly what a truly powerful storm is. But enough of all this for now."

The magical roller-coaster ride continued when we got outside. Out on the lawn, under a large white tent, were two sturdy wooden chairs facing the rolling clouds, but instead of sitting in them, we stayed on the porch. As we chatted, I noticed that Kalena's helicopter was gone. "I meant to ask you earlier," Dominic said, "I hope your flight was okay and all of the arrangements we made were satisfactory."

"It was great. Everything was just first class. And so were all of the people you arranged to help me. I cannot thank you enough for your efforts."

"Oh, no need to thank me! It's just a standard part of being a good host." Dominic was clearly accustomed to different standards than I was at that point in my life.

As we watched storm clouds overtake the mountain, I decided to broach the reason for my visit. I figured that if he was reaching out to me as a lawyer, he probably expected me to act like a lawyer. I collected my thoughts and checked my emotions before opening, "With all due respect, Dominic, as much as I am loving watching this weather, I assume the reason you brought me here was not to compare the ferocity of storm cells in New York with those on this island. I wonder if we could discuss the interview...my interview of you, Dominic J. Bandall, Esquire. That is, unless you have something else in mind." I hoped I was portraying the confidence I thought he would expect, but I was afraid my trembling knees were giving me away. I wasn't very good at the game yet.

I had to wait through an uncomfortable pause before he finally replied.

"Agreed. You are right. We should begin! Let's go to my office." Dominic walked inside in a slow, unsteady fashion. As I followed him, I noticed our route along the polished bamboo floor was covered with faint black rubber marks from the wheels of his walker. I didn't see these marks anywhere else in the house. Either those floors had also recently been refinished or Dominic rarely walked in those areas. He explained that he and his wife, Sharon, had purchased the land in 1979. At first, they lived in a modest cabin and planned to build a big house after they stopped practicing. It wasn't until 2002 that Dominic finally built the couple's dream home, a year after Sharon's death.

From my position behind Dominic, I was able to observe his manner. Each of his steps was deliberate: one foot lifted slightly off the floor and placed down a few inches in front. Only when his new footing was secured did he shift his weight forward, push his walker along, then finally raise the second shoe. Slow. Deliberate. He held the handle of the walker with one hand. His other arm appeared to be limp, hanging listlessly over the other handle. Clearly, he took great care with his appearance. Clean-shaven and manicured, he was dressed in a dark-blue-plaid vested suit cleverly tailored to mask the obtrusive braces on his legs. During my visit, I never once saw Dominic look anything less than perfectly groomed. I wondered how he did it. Did his staff help him? I just couldn't imagine that he could dress and make himself ready, especially with impeccable results like that.

After traversing a hall and passing several closed rooms, we finally reached a doorless office. It was as grand as, quite possibly larger than, the main foyer. Its centerpiece was a beautiful oak desk. Gray marble tiles covered the walls. The planked wood floor gleamed. Wheel marks indicated that he spent most of his time at the desk, presumably working at the computer.

What caught my attention, though, was his massive library. There were all of the law books I expected an attorney with his background to have. There were books on landmark cases in tort law, civil procedure, constitutional law, civil rights, contract law, criminal law, and property law. There was also a massive collection of books on international law, including constitutions, charters, treaties, and the founding documents of at least sixteen different countries, as well as the Charter of the United Nations. A full bookcase was devoted to various articles of convention. There was the 1926 Slavery Convention and the International Covenant on Economic, Social and Cultural Rights of 1966. I had never heard of the 1971 United Nations treaty: Convention on Psychotropic Substances, nor could I imagine why Dominic would have it. There were books on crime, human rights, diplomatic relations, education, the rights of women and children, and so much more. It would take me two lifetimes to read just the titles of all those books. The books on the last row of the international section were shelved carefully, each in its own place, in contrast to the other books that were crammed in and stacked on top of each other. Peering more closely, I saw it was a collection of books on terrorism, war, and organized violence.

Again, I had many questions. Why books on these subjects? Did it have something to do with 9/11? Was he still mired in the memories of that soulless day? Perhaps the tragedy broke him; he looked so unhealthy. His sunken eyes! Maybe he didn't sleep well. Perhaps I hadn't given enough consideration to his experience with 9/11. All of it suddenly made sense to me. For the first time, I noticed his bruises and scrapes, only the most recent of which were bandaged. They may have revealed a man who had lost the ability to sustain his fight. Had he asked me here because of something to do with 9/11? It seemed unlikely. I was ten years old when the Towers came down, and I was far separated from the dangers that befell people in New York; Washington, DC; and Shanksville, Pennsylvania. I didn't even know anyone who died on that day. My mind raced through all those considerations, but none of it was clear to me. I tried to maintain my composure by regulating my breathing and coaching my emotions into place.

"You're not a very good poker player, Angela. I can see your anxiety. I am guessing it has something to do with the books you are looking at." As Dominic was talking, he slowly made his way to his desk. "You see, there are five senses: sight, smell, hearing, touch, and taste. Every person interprets each of these senses differently. Touch and taste often require interpretation. Jagged, sharp, smooth. Terms like these have no real meaning until one physically impresses upon an object and experiences the sensations themselves. Sure, we learn that fire and burning red embers are hot, but it's not until we physically endure the stinging pain that we fully understand what a burn feels like. In terms of taste, you will never understand the incredible flavor of a food until you eat it. For example, until you place a strip of delicious spiced gusht-e-qaaq—a sort of jerky from northern Afghanistan—on your tongue, you will not be able to fully comprehend the rich, dominant spices. And yet, one only need be present in the moist, salty air of this Island to feel the temperature drop and know a storm is coming. Before tasting the deliciously spiced jerky in the city of Taloqan, Marco Polo knew the difference between the sweltering summer heat and the bitter cold winters he endured when he first came across that beautiful Afghan city in 1275.

"The other three senses—sight, smell, hearing—can not be defined in various ways by different people. An object can be 'seen' only one way, if you will: the manner in which a point of light refracts through or reflects off a surface. People may interpret the energy in different ways, but everyone starts out with the same basic information. Odors are merely the result of a specific combination of elements in the air. Sound is the pattern formed and frequency created by vibration of those elements. These things can be scientifically measured. Everyone will have the same data to begin with.

"The emotions I just saw you display have a different understanding. Thoughts, like our sense of sight and our sense of sound, are unique and specific patterns of energy. With thoughts, however, it's all in your mind. No one can know which ideas and emotions are occurring inside your head. That is, not until your body happens to respond to your reflections and translates them into energy that can be seen, heard, smelled, touched, or tasted. In other words, only your body can betray your thoughts."

Everything he said seemed plausible, if not scientifically accurate. What I couldn't understand was why Dominic was sharing that physics lesson with me. His mind seemed sharp, his voice steady, but I could see that safety, most likely preventing a fall, was a big factor for him. I suddenly understood he was a proud man, determined to move about on his own. It made me feel for him.

"I asked you here to talk about moments. Moments are energy. The sight, sound, and smell of every moment exist, even if we don't experience all of them together in one particular instance. The energy in moments cannot be created or destroyed. Energy simply moves on to a different combination, thereby creating a different moment. That's the best explanation I can give you." He had lost me. I could not understand what he was talking about. On top of that, I had forgotten my notebook and couldn't even take notes. I hoped I could remember enough about what he said to be able to write it down later.

"Angela!" he snapped. Once again, apparently, I physically betrayed my thoughts. Perhaps he sensed I was struggling to understand what he was talking about. He continued, "I tried for a long time to fully consider the scientific theory behind moments of energy. When I was a student, I dedicated a lot of effort into figuring it out. When I discovered there was little information, and certainly no definitive facts about it, I switched my focus to this,"—he gestured to the massive library—"the law. Law is a collection of interpretations and judgments, but are they rooted in historical fact? Most are. Some, however, are misinterpretations, incorrect assumptions of thought and intent, or flat-out falsehoods. For almost fifty years, my focus has been the law, first as a student and then as a practicing attorney. All the books and documents you see here? I use them all to help me practice law. I sense you are puzzled by the odd assortment in my library. We will get to that in time. Before we talk about where I am now, I feel it's my responsibility to share my journey with you."

Dominic leaned back into his chair. He started to say something, but couldn't seem to find the right words. He leaned toward the side of his chair, then slowly swirled himself around. With his chin safely crooked between his index finger and thumb, he appeared to drift off. He was lost in thought so long, I reached over and placed my hand on his arm. "Dominic? Are you okay?" He turned his chair back toward me and gave me a look as if he had known me my whole life and was thinking, *Where have all the years gone, Angela?* It was odd.

"I can see moments in time, Angela."

"What do you mean?"

"I can see the moments that existed before. Patterns of energy form whenever time existed. As I said before, energy is neither created nor destroyed; instead, it is something that is always changing.

It is in eternal motion, every moment a unique pattern. I can recall those specific arrangements and am able to replay them in my mind. I know what happened in the past.

"We usually know about the past from what others have told us. The problem with this is that we always have to rely on another person's impression or maybe even fabrication of what factually occurred. I can recall the past without having to rely on someone else's version. I am able to see former times firsthand."

I could tell Dominic fully believed what he had just told me. Looking at him and feeling the greatest sense of pity was just a horrifying experience. I had extensively researched the man. I knew about his hardships and his accomplishments. I had read about the tragedy he experienced on 9/11. He lost everything that day: his wife, all his colleagues, his company. While I was on the plane, I tried to imagine what his life had been like since then—the day his public days ended, and his private sentence began.

"Please don't look at me like I'm crazy. I assure you I am not." He was firm and calm.

"I don't think you're crazy, Dominic." I leaned forward and laid my hand back on his forearm. "I don't believe that at all." I was being careful not to reveal what I was really thinking.

"I am quite certain that right about now you are trying to assess my mental capacity. Keep in mind, Angela, I am not on trial and there is no need to assess my competence. If, during our time together, you start to think that any of the information I disclose implies I have committed a criminal act or that I had criminal intent, may I direct you right now to the Reform Act of 1984, US Code Title 18, section 4241. This does not apply, nor is there anything having to do with insanity for which I would require defense. I understand right from wrong."

I reiterated, "I don't think you're crazy, Dominic," only this time, I said it more emphatically, leaving no room for doubt.

"So, what is your reaction? What do you think?"

We spent the better part of the afternoon discussing my response to his claim to be able to see moments in the past. The word "insane" never came up once, but that was precisely what the whole thing felt like to me. Pure insanity! To make the situation even more surreal, in the most casual way, Dominic revealed that he had been trying to help me for many years. I was right about having a secret benefactor! He told me he had been providing me with valuable opportunities to help me move in positive directions, yet he made sure his help never interfered with me doing the hard work myself. Apparently, he was elated when I decided to pursue a career in law. Then, he told me he had made the decision to invite me to his house two years ago, that he realized I was the perfect person to document his life story. It was chilling to have my suspicions confirmed after so many years.

"So, I ask again, Angela, what do you think?"

Rather than answering the question—one I still hadn't formulated an answer to—I said, "What do you expect me to think? What am I supposed to do with this information?"

"That is up to you, and you alone. I want to tell you my story. But I can offer neither direction nor sound recourse on your reaction to any of it."

I started to grow irritated and frustrated. I had no idea what the hell Dominic was even talking about, and then he laid that burden on me. It was as if I was supposed to make a ruling on this man's legacy, a man legendary in a field I had yet to become a part of professionally, a man who had endured immense suffering in his life, both physical and emotional, a man who had been stalking me for years under the guise of providing me with support...and then he expected me to believe he had this crazy ability? I searched for a word softer than crazy: Delusional? Senile?

"Angela," he said, "in just a month, your schooling will be over and you will be a lawyer. However, I hope you understand your education is far from complete. You have so much still to learn. My desire is for you to learn effective methods of analyzing data, pinpointing your inquiries, and determining the optimal way to move a case forward. But first, I need you to listen to me and try to understand."

I decided to play along with the cat-and-mouse game we seemed to be playing. I grabbed a pad and pen from his desk and began. "Mr. Bandall—Dominic—I would like to begin this interview now. Is this agreeable to you?"

"Yes, Angela, let's start."

"Today's date is Thursday, the 28th of February, 2019. Dominic, I'm here at your invitation to interview you. I intend to use the interview as part of my final project for New York Law School.

This evening, I would like to start by reviewing some pertinent background information. Upon completion of our first interview, I would like to stop for today. Using the information you provide, I will develop a strategy for the rest of the interviews. Is this acceptable?" I looked down at the scribble of notes I had been taking. Satisfied that they generally described my opening statement, I looked back up for a response. With what appeared to be a slightly arrogant grin, Dominic agreed.

I was trying hard to be professional and to appear confident, but my mind was racing through the predicament I found myself in. How was I going to interview him seriously when it seemed clear he was going to focus on something that seemed delusional to me? Dominic patiently waited. As I was gathering my thoughts, I realized there was a recording studio of sorts off to my left. I don't know how I had failed to notice it before. There was a video camera mounted on a tripod. Carefully taped-down wires ran to boxes of recording equipment. The camera faced a leather Chesterfield club chair with a simple boom microphone next to it. And, along the wall, there were shelves of books. Some looked like typical law books, but there were also dingy textbooks and softcover workbooks. I was close enough to see that none of the books were in English. I would later discover they were written in Arabic, Pashto, and Farsi, and some were in Turkic languages. The tracks of Dominic's walker made it clear that he regularly traveled back and forth between those books and his desk. The tape holding the cables down was fresh and clean, indicating the recording equipment had just been put there.

I finally decided on my approach. To appeal to what I hoped would be the rational side of someone used to presenting evidence and methodically debating ideas, I was going to challenge Dominic's claim. Of course, I fully understood that I faced the risk of creating an adversary.

I took a calming breath. "Dominic, you claim to have the ability to see what you describe as 'moments in time.' You claim you can go back and relive events that have occurred in the past."

"Close enough. You are correct, Angela."

"Thank you, Dominic. What perplexes me here is how to continue with our interview when the discussion will be rooted in something you see as fact, yet everyone else, including the entire scientific community, would label as nonsense. Why would I spend my time on something that my instructors at school will not support?

And how can I document something I do not believe...something I know is false?"

"What if I could prove my claims? What if I can prove to you that I have the ability to experience all the energy that has been created from a moment in the past?"

"How do you propose to do that?"

"Okay, fair enough. I have an idea. A parlor trick, if you will. You can give me any real moment in history, one that we both agree has occurred, and I will tell you precisely what happened. I will convince you that my ability is real."

I sighed deeply and leaned my head back against the chair. I didn't want to offend him, but I didn't care to indulge him either. Have you ever had the feeling that you've played along with something for entirely too long? My hope for a quick and graceful exit from this whole charade was fading fast.

Dominic was very patient while I considered his proposal. So tolerant, in fact, it occurred to me that perhaps he *needed* me to do the interview—that my involvement was somehow pivotal to his plan. I just didn't know what his plan was. In fact, all I had was a concise description of his so-called ability and his proposal to prove it. Fear of the consequences of conducting the interview lost out, but only narrowly, to my piqued interest. I closed my eyes and carefully repeated Dominic's proposal aloud to make sure I correctly heard and understood what he had told me.

I finally settled on the event I wanted him to use to prove his ability: my university graduation. That date was seared into my memory for many reasons. There was a tangible list of facts, such as my school, class size, my class standing, graduates, speakers, and notable people in attendance. I was sure plenty of other details were available online about things like the weather. My mom was there. It was the last time we celebrated an event together; she got sick and passed away less than two months later. I have a photo I love of us standing on the field after the ceremony…me in my cap and gown, clutching my freshly minted diploma. Mom had her arms wrapped so tightly around my waist I could barely breathe. She had no intention of letting me go. I had no intention of trying to get away. As soon as Justin snapped that photo, he boasted, "Two beautiful ladies. Perfect!" I remember thinking nothing could be better, that that was as good as it gets…and what transpired during the following hours, days, and months proved my feeling was accurate.

"Okay. My graduation day from La Salle University and—" Dominic cut me off before I could continue.

"Perfect. We both know that is an event that occurred and that is all the information I need. All your questions will be answered, but we cannot start until tomorrow morning. My ability to see the past occurs during the night, while I am asleep."

As quickly as the day's events spiraled into a frenzy, so did they end. Dominic announced his retirement for the evening. After pressing a button on his desk, he assured me my needs had all been attended to. Hy'ing, one of his staff members, entered the room just as Dominic rose. He gently lifted my hand and kissed it. "Angela, thank you so much for a wonderful afternoon. Please have a relaxing evening. I look forward to our continued discussion tomorrow."

As I watched him slowly walk out of the room, I felt somewhat shocked. He was as charming as he was forceful. At times he seemed aloof. His insight, keen observation, and rational deduction contrasted so sharply with his strange claim to be able to see moments in the past. I've never met a person like him, before or since that day.

Hy'ing waited until Dominic left the room before reviewing the details of my accommodations, told me my dinner was already prepared and invited me to dine with her and the other staff members. I graciously accepted her invitation and followed her out of the room to the dining area where two other members of Dominic's staff, Robert and Wen, were already seated. They told me they did maintenance work on the property and supported Hy'ing, Dominic's personal assistant, when necessary. I suddenly realized thirteen hours had passed since I last ate, so I was thrilled when Hy'ing presented me with a feast of traditional Hawaiian food. She described each item. The menu had been harvested from the Island or caught offshore. There was poi and laulau (I wasn't a fan), kalua pig, poke, lomi salmon, chicken long-rice, and delicious pineapple for dessert. It was one of the best meals I ever had.

Apparently, word that I had asked all those questions of Michael back in New York City had made its way back to Hy'ing. She was happy to answer questions but wanted to be clear about a few things. First, she told me no one knew exactly why I was invited to the ranch. Second, none of the staff knew what the years-long project was that Dominic had been working on. When they were hired, each had entered into a contract and nondisclosure agreement. Everything associated with his current research and everything in his office was not to be disturbed under any circumstances. Other than Hy'ing, no one could even enter his office. To ensure there was no continuity of the cleaning staff, Hy'ing rotated them regularly. Hy'ing was the one who had installed the video camera in his office just the other day. When I asked about the peculiar law books in Dominic's office, all three of them cut me off simultaneously. Apparently, this was a subject they contractually could not discuss with me. Their allegiance to Dominic was based on more than just the contracts they had entered into. All three staff members, I discovered, were children of Bandall and Bandall employees killed when the Tower went down on 9/11.

Dominic was loyal to all his employees. He cared for them in life. He cared for their families in death. Wen said she thought this allegiance was driven by the guilt he felt after being the only one in the firm to survive. Apparently, his arrival at the office had been delayed the morning of the attack. Robert said he thought Dominic simply considered his employees to be family. Whatever the reason, the respect, care, and loyalty between them was mutual.

I knew it was not appropriate to ask them about Dominic's claim to be able to see the past. I doubted any of them knew about it, and even if they did, they would probably not have discussed it with me. But, there was one thing I did ask them: why every room I passed, except for his office, appeared to have been repainted and emptied. The rooms not completely empty were sparsely furnished. All the furnishings were new. Wen told me that until a few weeks before, the house was richly furnished, primarily in a kind of Middle Eastern style. Every so often, Dominic would strip, repaint, and refurnish certain rooms. Some changes were extreme, but others were so subtle it was hard to detect what, if anything, was different. In the most current renovation, the rooms remained empty; the staff assumed he was still mulling it over. Even the back-kitchen area in which we were sitting contained only the essentials required for daily operations.

With a full belly and an overloaded mind, I decided to turn in for the evening. Hy'ing escorted me to my bedroom. The room, painted a soft rose color and newly furnished two weeks before, was larger than any apartment I had lived in. There was a king-size bed covered with a floral-patterned quilt and pillows, a large-screen television and entertainment system, a magnificent bathroom, and an equally grand walk-in closet. Hy'ing told me that my clothes had been put away, and then she opened the closet to reveal that it was full of brand-new clothes in my size, suitable for any activity I might choose to partake in. A mini exercise area was in one corner of the room, and in the other was an office area with a huge desk. There was a bar, snacks, and a refrigerator with several containers of the fresh fruit smoothies Kalena had mentioned. I jumped at the opportunity to try one. Heaven! The far wall was mostly glass. Privacy shades were drawn, and with the press of a button, Hy'ing unveiled the incredible view. Every majestic scene from the Island seemed to fit in that one sweeping frame: the forest reserve up close, the rocky lava shoreline beyond, and then the ocean, black as night itself. Apparently, the eastern-facing view was one of the best on the Island.

"When would you like me to program the shades to open tomorrow?"

"Thank you. At sunrise."

We were scheduled to start tomorrow at my convenience. Hy'ing urged me to rest for as long as I wanted. There was a button—like the one in Dominic's office—on my desk should I need assistance. After giving final instructions, Hy'ing bid me a good night.

My mind raced through all of the things I wanted to do. I wanted to research my graduation in detail and discover what information was publicly available because I expected Dominic to look it up too. I also wanted to do further research on Dominic's health. I had been taken aback by how frail he was and how severely disabled his arms and legs were. I wanted to see if there was information that would better explain what happened to him.

That was the plan. Instead, I sat on the edge of the bed and stared out the window, lost in the delicious flavors of my drink. After finishing it, I put the glass down on the nightstand, closed the blinds with the button, and leaned back to rest my head on the pillow.

Thus ended February 28th, 2019, the day I first met Dominic Bandall.

Chapter 3 - Voice: Angela

There's a special place in my heart for the song "You Belong to Me." It created a bond that ran three generations deep in my family. My grandmother adored the song when it first came out in 1952. When my mother was an infant, my grandmother sang it to her every night. When I was a baby, my mother lulled me to sleep with the same melody. I always looked forward to having a daughter of my own so I could share the song with her while I rock her in my arms.

I heard the shades open at sunrise that first morning at the ranch. I lay in bed watching the lace curtains swaying from the breeze coming through the open window. I could picture images of my mother holding me at different times throughout the years: first carrying me, her baby girl; later wrapping her arms around her "grown-up" baby girl. I could hear Jo Stafford's voice as I watched the sunrise from that tropic isle. I thought how wonderful it would be to remember moments from the past as if you had been there, to see other people's memories. I was almost jealous of Dominic. Even if he couldn't actually do it, simply believing he could must have been comforting and given him a tremendous feeling of warmth.

The sun had fully risen before my body would even entertain the thought of moving. I thought about doing some further research on Dominic but decided there wasn't much point. I was sure I had already read just about everything on his background, starting from when he was a schoolboy in the Bronx, the boy genius who exceeded every academic standard, through his near-perfect performance in law school. The cases he had tried were already part of both undergraduate and law school curricula. Dominic's self-proclaimed focus was simple: justice. His firm had been focused on obtaining justice for those who had been wronged. They brought both civil and criminal lawsuits. Their vetting process for accepting clients was extreme and lengthy, often taking more time than the actual trials did. There was never a guarantee that Dominic or Sharon Bandall would accept a case. Instead of high-profile cases, they tended to choose humbler victims of injustice: the underprivileged, the overlooked, the disadvantaged. I realized that nothing I could learn that morning would offer more insight into whatever was coming next.

Deciding I would indulge the old man by letting him tell me about his fantasy, I quickly showered and dressed. Choosing one of the modest island-style sundresses provided for me, I checked myself in the mirror and hoped I looked professional. Before leaving the room, I made sure my briefcase contained everything I needed for a full day of interviewing, including pens, notepads, and my digital voice recorder. I pressed record: "Be sure to find out who picked out these clothes. These color combinations look fantastic on me! I could definitely get used to this."

I was about to go to the kitchen when I noticed a note taped to my door: "Angela, good morning. Ring the call button on your desk and we'll have breakfast brought to you—Hy'ing." A service button wasn't really my style, so I went down to the kitchen where I found Hy'ing with another incredible local Hawaiian meal. We exchanged pleasantries while I dove into breakfast. She told me Dominic was ready to begin whenever I was. Figuring there was no time like the present, I pulled out my recorder and asked Hy'ing for permission to record our discussion. This is the transcript from the recording I made on that day.

> "March 1st, 2019. I'm speaking with Hy'ing, one of Dominic Bandall's staff members here at his ranch in Honu'apo, Hawaii."

Hy'ing smirked at my formal approach.

"Hy'ing, thank you for agreeing to speak with me this morning."

"It's my pleasure, Angela."

"Before we begin, I must ask, are you the one who picked out the incredible clothes for me?"

"I am."

Hy'ing recoiled. For the first time, she seemed almost shy.

"Dominic showed me some photos of you. Nothing intrusive, mind you. Just some university photos. I also spoke with Michael in New York because I wanted to make sure to get colors that would show off those beautiful blue eyes of yours and styles that would enhance your athletic build. You know, you kind of look like a Polynesian dancer. You're going to make quite a few women very jealous during your stay."

Then I was the one who was shy and blushing.

"Thank you very much. Can you tell me your full name for the record?"

"Sure. My full name is Hy'ing Wei. My father was born in China, but moved to the United States in...I think it was 1985. He had become friends with Sharon Bandall when she and Dominic went to China to research a case. My father was a lawyer in Shanghai. Sharon very much wanted him to join their firm. Even though my father couldn't legally practice in the States, Sharon thought his experience in Asian tort law would be beneficial to them. He accepted her offer and moved to Hawai'i. I think Sharon was the one who introduced him to my mother here in Hawai'i."

"Now, you mentioned yesterday that many of Dominic's staff are the children of his law firm employees."

"That's correct. Children or siblings. While so many people lost much that day, Dominic lost everything, except, of course, his life. In the year after 9/11, he offered employment to every direct relative of his employees. We're not his surrogate family. He's not our replacement family. We are just family. Even those who chose not to accept his offer to come work for him are in his care and are held close in our hearts. That's why he requested we never use last names, or even Mr. or Mrs., ever. No one in my family would ever call me Hy'ing Wei. I'm just Hy'ing. Maybe we take it a little too far, but it's something we feel strongly about. It's a sense of pride, I guess."

"That is wonderful."

I realized I was being treated like a family member. I wasn't sure why.

"Now, you mentioned yesterday that all of you have a confidentiality agreement with Dominic. Is that agreement preventing you from talking to me about why Dominic invited me here?"

"Not at all, Angela. Dominic was clear when we began planning your visit several weeks ago that you can talk to all of us freely and that you have complete access to anything in the house. His

> personal affairs are the only limitation with us. Our communication with you falls within the same confidentiality agreement we have with Dominic."

I had no idea what she meant.

> "The only reason we might not tell you something is because we don't know about it. Even though I am Dominic's personal assistant, there's an awful lot about him I don't know. In fact, he told us practically nothing about you or why he had asked you here, but he did make it clear that you were part of the black hole we lovingly refer to as Dominic's World. Here's how we see it. If he wants to keep his private affairs private, that's up to him. As long as it doesn't have a negative effect on us—like put us in danger or something—it is not our concern. Something tells me though, Angela, you may know a lot more about his private affairs than we do by the time your visit is over."

I stopped recording. I didn't want to hear any more just then. Before, I was merely curious. Now I was beginning to feel a bit unnerved by the thought of uncovering secrets Dominic kept hidden from those closest to him. But I had another question to ask. I motioned to Hy'ing that I was turning the recorder back on.

"Does Dominic usually eat with all of you? I only ask because he didn't eat with us last night."

"Dominic chooses to eat by himself, either in his room or his office. When I asked him why one time, he said he doesn't want to subject anyone to what he thinks is the unpleasant sight of him feeding. He is self-conscious about his disabilities—not because of vanity. Occasionally, this illness he has apparently had since he was a child rears its ugly head. As you can see, he is really quite disabled now.

"About the only thing he allows others to see is when he shuffles about on the walker. I make sure that his mobility aids—you know, his walker, his wheelchair, and all that—are there for him when he needs them and functioning correctly. I'm responsible for arranging his room, clothes, and bathroom, but no one assists him in the morning.

"Personally, I think he's embarrassed by his eating problems. Whatever it is, his disease is an awful thing. I don't really know much about it. Maybe in a few days, you'll be able to educate us. Well, anyway, it's definitely time. Let's head to Dominic's office. I'm sure he's ready for you."

I stopped the recorder and followed Hy'ing through the hallways once again. Dominic looked up and smiled when I walked through the door. The sweet gentleman was back. It was a sight much better than the sad old man from last night. He inquired about my evening and whether my room was comfortable. I gave him a glowing review of his staff, the room, my new clothes, and the beautiful sunrise he had afforded me. Dominic chuckled, claiming he couldn't take credit for the beauty of the morning. As if he was trying to brush off his comment, he stood up, leaned over the desk, and grasped my hand to give it a firm shake. For the first time, I noticed just how deformed his hands were. His fingers were mangled and bent, almost as if they had been violently broken and had never set correctly. He seemed unable to extend either arm. They were curled at the wrist and twisted inward at the elbow. He seemed to have a similar problem with his legs, although at least they appeared to be straight, maybe the result of the brace he was wearing under his trousers. I wondered what hurt more, the deformities or the brace. Once again, I felt pity for him.

"Don't be alarmed, Angela. I have grown quite used to my body in this state. Although it's unsightly, I've become adept at most common functions." He swiveled in the chair, stood up, and grabbed the walker. "But, before we talk about my arms and legs, we've got some work to do." Dominic slowly paced around his office, retracing the route drawn by the wheels.

"Is it okay if I record this?"

"That will be fine."

When I pressed the record button, he repeated himself.

> "Don't be alarmed. I am used to my body like this. Although it's unsightly, I've become adept at most daily functions. Besides, we've got other work to do before we talk about my arms and legs."

He winked at me.

> "No sense in missing anything, is there? Now, where would you like to begin? I suppose, for posterity's sake, we could start by reviewing everything we discussed in our first meeting yesterday."

At this point, my curiosity and frustration quickly reached the levels they had the day before, triggered by his admittedly reasonable suggestion to repeat what we had discussed in our first meeting.

> "Let's discuss what you told me about your ability, as you put it, to see moments in time. By any chance, does it have something to do with why you asked me here? What exactly is the purpose of this ability? How do you use it? And why discuss it with me? Do others know about it? Or am I the only one? If I am, why me?"

I raised my hand before Dominic could answer. I didn't want to hear that everything would become clear in due time.

> "Yesterday, we decided that for proof of concept, you would tell me about my graduation day from La Salle."

"Ah, that is the kind of focus and direction I was hoping to see, Angela. It is a valuable trait for a lawyer to have. You want me to prove to you that I can see moments in the past. Or, to better phrase that, it seems to be your intent to disprove my claim."

"That sounds about right."

"Very well, Angela. La Salle University, the 18th of May, 2014. The weather was beautiful, allowing for an outdoor ceremony at McCarthy Stadium. The nice part about the sunshine was that the inclement weather rule didn't have to be invoked, meaning that each graduate did not have to limit the number of their guests to five. But that wasn't a concern for you as you only had two guests: your mother and your fiancé, Justin."

Dominic had done his research. But those were easy facts to obtain. I was careful not to provide any visual clues as to the accuracy of his information.

"If you so choose, I can keep giving you details like this, but you will assume they came from research such as photographs, newspaper clippings, contacting people who were there, etcetera. None of that will convince you of my claim, however. My goal is to gain your confidence. Instead, I suggest we move to an interrogation style of interview, where you ask the questions and they will either validate my claims or endorse my insanity."

That made sense to me, so I changed my approach.

"Dominic, can you tell me where I was seated?"

"The graduates were seated in two sections that were separated by an aisle. Each section had twelve chairs across and was twenty-five rows deep. You were in the group on the right, four rows up, in the second chair from the center aisle."

I frantically jotted down notes.

"You were seated with your classmates who were graduating from the criminal justice program."

"And what did I wear that day?"

"The traditional black La Salle cap and gown. Your tassel and hood were dark blue and gold—the university colors. You wore silver-and-pearl drop earrings. Based on the way you lit up and smiled with every compliment you received, I assume there's a story behind them."

"They were a gift from my mother. She gave them to me for my sixteenth birthday. They were given to her as a gift on her sixteenth birthday."

"From your grandmother?"

"Yes."

It seemed as if Dominic was trying to extract information from me, looking for signs to direct him or confirm his fortune-telling.

"Under your gown, you wore a practical and very pretty tan blouse with a pair of black slacks. You

> wore simple black flats...also practical. Shall I continue?"

These details felt a bit too personal. I could tell Dominic thought so as well.

> "No, but thank you. So, what did I do after the ceremony was over?"

I wanted to focus on details that were not so easy for him to have looked up.

> "Your mother wanted to treat you to dinner at your favorite restaurant. You made a half-hearted attempt to avoid the pomp and circumstance, but there was no denying that it made you happy and that you were excited to celebrate at that little seafood spot in Rittenhouse Square. It was your favorite and had been since you were a little girl. You savored every bite of those fish tacos! Justin smiled when you said you didn't want anything to drink: no beer, no wine. I think it was his comment 'a little too much pre-graduation celebrating last night' that started the argument."

I stopped writing and lifted my head.

> "As your words with Justin became sharp, your mother grew visibly uncomfortable. But as much as she didn't want to sit there while you two argued, she was not going to leave you alone with him. You and Justin appeared highly aggravated. He didn't blink an eye when you slammed your engagement ring on the table. All he did was pick it up and walk away. Tell me, did you ever see him again after that night?"

I thought, *No, but it seems you did. You managed to track him down.*

> "No, Justin and I never spoke again. There were a few 'never-agains' that weekend. I never went to that restaurant again. I never went to any restaurant with my mother again because she died soon after that. Between her death and Justin, there were too many dark memories."

Dominic returned to his desk and sat down. I thought maybe he had grown tired from all that pacing, but instead I think he wanted to sit and focus all of his energy on our conversation.

"Did you ever talk to Nikki again after that weekend?"

The soothsayer struck a nerve.

"How do you know about...?"

"Your mother asked what was troubling you. As always, she was there to listen to you. You spent the rest of the evening telling her about Nikki. The way her eyes lit up listening to you and watching you—her only daughter, her only family member—describe the love you shared with this girl, well, it was truly an amazing scene. After telling her about the day you first met Nikki—in a collaborative group assignment in your first-year Legislation and the Regulatory State class—you described how the two of you became inseparable. It was clear that was the first time you had told her about Nikki."

"I have never spoken about Nikki to anyone except my mother. Did you contact Nikki?"

"No, Angela, I have not reached out to her. If you would like, I can uncover any details you might want about her."

"No."

There were so many emotions building up inside of me. I grew frightened about the direction the interview had just taken, but my curiosity outweighed my fear, annoyance, and confusion.

"Please continue, Dominic."

"Even when your relationship with Nikki grew stronger, you never told anyone else about her— only your mother. I do find that odd. If your mother questioned your decision to keep your relationship a secret, she didn't let on. Instead, she sat quietly, keenly focused on you, your story, and the way you were feeling. You told your mother that the two of you shared every aspect of your lives, your loves, and your hopes and fears for the future. You were best friends, yet neither of you was willing to tell another soul about your bond. Although you never introduced Nikki to Justin, she knew everything about him, including the hesitation you felt about your relationship. Justin, on the other hand, didn't realize Nikki even existed.

"You told your mother that you and Nikki often studied together. A few days before graduation, you were both elated to learn the two of you were going to graduate number one and number two in the program. There was less than a quarter of a percentage point separating your grade-point averages.

"The night before graduation, you and Nikki shared a bottle of wine. You told your mother she lived in a small apartment off campus. Nikki wasn't going to be at the graduation ceremony because she was taking an early flight to California. She was doing a summer internship before starting at Stanford Law, and apparently it started that following Monday morning.

"The way you spoke to your mother...it chills me now just to think about it. It was Nikki, you said, who first expressed her attraction to you. It was amazing to hear you describe your night with her...the hesitation, the fear you felt. To avoid the possibility of rejection, both of you had shelved your feelings for three long years. It was a world neither of you understood; both of you were sure the other would be repulsed by the attraction. For one night, though, you finally allowed yourselves to express your love and passion. Your mother asked you if you decided to open up about your feelings because you knew it would be the last night together. You said you weren't sure, but whatever the reason, you felt an intense connection with her, a oneness shared in every possible way."

I was glad the recorder was only capturing our voices. I could feel streams of tears pouring down my face as I listened to Dominic. It was at that moment that I stopped trying to determine if he was a charlatan, insane, or a demigod with powers beyond comprehension. It didn't matter. Assess the validity of his ability? Offer a ruling? Never again.

"When we got back from the restaurant the night of my graduation, my mother cared for me as if I were a six-year-old child again. She tucked me in and sang me to sleep with our favorite lullaby. Did you see that?"

"I did. The moment I searched was your graduation day, from the time you lay curled in Nikki's arms early that morning until long past when you cried yourself to sleep that night."

"My mother. Was she still proud of me?"

"I can't tell you what she was thinking. I can, however, tell you where you inherited your dismal poker face from. Your mother couldn't hide her emotions either, nor do I think she wanted to. She was so proud, yet also sad. After you fell asleep, she sat at the foot of the bed and watched. I'm not sure why she looked sad, but I can imagine the possibilities. Possibly she was reflecting on your father, and how the two of them had shared so many beautiful nights together when you and Nikki were only able to share one. Perhaps she was recalling memories of a different love. After tragedy ripped love from your mother, she was able to love and be loved again. Just as you will. Regardless, that one moment of sadness was dwarfed by the length of time her heart rejoiced because of you."

"Will you please—now—go back to my night with Nikki?"

"No, dear. That moment belongs to you. A long time ago, I made a decision that moments that are not mine are sacred, and for me to intrude on them, there has to be a damn good reason."

I finally smiled, although it was a weak one. Dominic had finally unnerved me, just as quickly company frayed heart.

> "Besides, that night when you talked to your mother about Nikki, you provided me with enough information. I was able to experience everything you told your mother. I felt your moment through the emotions you expressed and your body language—you were not holding back, even though you were telling these private things to your mother. I saw how your eyes lit up; the passion you felt was so clear to me. In other words, there was enough for me to see and hear and extrapolate, so there was no need for me to intrude on your moment. Sharon had the same effect on me. Every day, for over thirty years, I could never hide the love I felt for her. I have enough love for her to last me the rest of my days."

That made me smile.

> "Angela, what are you thinking right now?"

Dominic leaned back in his chair. He had a dispassionate expression that gave me no insight into what he was thinking.

"I am thinking...how is this possible?"

"The simple answer is, I don't know. I can see into the past. I can see your past if I want to. I can see exactly where you were and what you did. I can see you and everything around you. I can even experience the sounds and smells that existed around you. In my dreams, I can connect to that permanent link of energy in our world. I don't know how. A long time ago, I learned to control this connection. I was taught how to carefully select what I choose to peer into. The consequences of making mistakes are severe."

"You learned this? From whom?"

"All in due time, Angela. My life is full of its own moments. I am at a point where I want to share my true history, the true moments, with you. I want you to know the truth, regardless of whether the truth can be proven or not."

"Why me, Dominic? Why tell me? What if I don't want—?"

"When I look at you, I see images of myself, both the person I once was and the person I am today. We both want to make a difference and are willing to make the necessary sacrifices. In you, I see someone I admire, someone I always wanted to be. I'm not as strong as you are, although I would love to be. As you move through life, I can only provide you with the knowledge I have accumulated during mine. It's my hope that the benefits of this will exceed any negative consequences of the burden of my story."

Needing to digest all of that, I stood up and ambled along Dominic's wheel-marked trail. I tried to imagine what things were like for him, imprisoned as he appeared to be to the life inside that office. He spent his days surrounded by knowledge—written down on pages, bound in books, stored on shelves. Everything was somber, muted, black, brown, gray. He kept notes on faded olive-green legal pads. He paced the brown wooden floors with a gray metal walker that left black tracks. Everything looked dull, worn, and faded. But, I realized, that was only one aspect of his world. He had an escape. At night, he had the power to dream the vibrant colors of the past. And, for some reason, he had decided he wanted to pull me into that world.

> "If we're conducting the interview over there, by the camera, I'm going to need a chair."
>
> "Excellent. Why don't we begin, then?"

Dominic reached across the desk, turned off my recorder, and began pulling papers from his desk drawer. *Oh boy*, I thought, *here comes the famous confidentiality agreement.* But I was wrong. It was a detailed itinerary, including the exact hours we would do the interviews, eat lunch (in the office, while working), and even when we would take personal time (in the evening). He told me I was to coordinate with Hy'ing about my breakfast and dinner. Later on, Hy'ing told me she was surprised about the working lunch, reiterating how Dominic always dined alone and had ever since he moved to the Island in 2002.

Dominic also explained his interview protocols. His exact words were, "I like to talk," and during our time, he wanted to do just that: talk. He would not answer questions or tolerate interruptions.

Our sessions were to be filmed. I was not to take notes. I was not to use my recorder. Dominic wanted to tell me a story and he insisted on my complete attention. If I would endure his drawn-out storytelling, as he called it, the video recordings were mine to keep at the end, to do with as I pleased. Those were his conditions. No discussion, no negotiation.

Dominic pulled out one more piece of paper and a pen and slid them across the desk. It wasn't a contract that time either. Instead, it was a lunch menu listing a fantastic selection of seafood dishes in various mango sauces.

"Order your lunch and then let's get started."

Both of us chuckled in nervous anticipation. I took a deep breath and stepped into the unknown.

Chapter 4 - Voice: Dominic

Today is March 1st, 2019. My name is Dominic J. Bandall, and this is session number one of Angela Grant's interview of me.

For you to understand how the events of my life have unfolded, how we ended up here, it is necessary to start at the beginning. I need to tell you how my ability was realized and how the unusual nature of events, and the manner in which they transpired, created this most extraordinary circumstance.

Childhood memories, at least the ones people hold most dear, are rarely based on their own recollections. Instead, memories often come from stories they have been told by others or from photographs and home movies. The things they think they saw, felt, and heard are usually just echoes of those snapshots. But for me, I have the rare ability to experience events as if I had been there.

To make sure that everything I am about to tell you is factual—not "to the best of my recollection," but the real events as they actually occurred—I have spent the last two years carefully reviewing all of the relevant events in my past.

Let's start on October 9th, 1949.

May Bandall was pregnant. She was not due to give birth to me for another three weeks, so she convinced Tony, my father, that it would be safe to leave her at home for the afternoon while he went to a baseball game with his friend, Rob. His beloved New York Yankees were playing the Brooklyn Dodgers at Ebbets Field.

Even though that Sunday was game five of the 1949 World Series, and Dad was a lifelong Yankees fan, he refused to leave my mother's side. But the tickets were a present from her—a thank-you and an expression of much-deserved appreciation for the way he had helped and supported her during the pregnancy—and when she absolutely insisted that he go, Dad finally agreed. Taking extra precautions, he asked their neighbors to check in on her while he was gone. You know, young people today don't realize how different things were in 1949. Once you left, there was no way for anyone to reach you if something happened. There were no smartphones or pagers. We didn't even have a telephone line in our house until 1952.

It was right before Dad and Rob left for the game that my mom's water broke. I was on the way! Without hesitation, Dad turned to Rob and handed him his ticket. "Here you go, Robbie. I'm sure you can find a taker." Dad was not disappointed about missing the game, or if he was, he didn't show it. He would have been a great poker player.

Rob, who of course understood Dad's decision, took the ticket, yelled, "Good luck, May!" and bolted out the door to track down their mutual friend, Saul, who was just returning from an overnight shift at the loading dock. Rob had to move fast. It was close—having to track him down, then take three subways to get to the stadium—but they made it just in time.

Ebbets Field was a monument of beauty. I remember the stadium seemed to get bigger and bigger as you made the short walk from the subway station—the platform was so close, you could almost climb into the ballpark from there—and by the time you reached the gates, you were just in awe. With less than thirty-four thousand seats, it was minuscule by modern standards but a massive sprawl for the middle of Flatbush. And it was cramped! The seats were pushed right up against the edge of the playing field.

Play was starting just as Rob and Saul walked in. The sun was just preparing to set on a beautiful fall afternoon. Blazing rays from the sun practically blinded him, but that didn't stop Rob from staring hard at the majestic green-and-brown ball field before them. The look on his face when they walked to the bleachers...it was pure rapture! It was the look of total bliss when someone experiences what may be a once-in-a-lifetime event. That is one memory I particularly cherish. In fact, I almost feel envious of Rob for his true experience of that moment.

In the top of the fourth inning, Joe DiMaggio hit a towering fly ball deep into the left-field stands—a home run that gave the Yankees a commanding six-one lead over Brooklyn. When Rob saw Saul reach up and pull in the home-run ball, he wore that same rapturous look. The Yankees won game five and ended up winning the World Series.

Dad heard the game from the waiting room at Parkchester General Hospital. When DiMaggio hit the home run, Mother swore she heard him yell all the way from her bed in the delivery room.

Mother and I came home from the hospital the next day. Rob was there to greet us and help Dad carry everything into the apartment. Because I arrived early, Mother and Dad had not finished fixing up my room. When they left for the hospital, my room was nothing more than a storage closet stuffed full of boxes of gifts, hand-me-downs, and a random collection of baby furniture. However, by the time we got home, Rob had unpacked, set up, and organized everything. And that was not all. He had even filled the refrigerator with groceries and had a casserole his wife made warming in the oven for the tired new parents. That was just one of many meals prepared by the neighbors in our close-knit community. Before hastily retreating to give us some time alone, Rob had one more gift. He handed my dad DiMaggio's ball and said, "Saul and I both want you to have this." Joe D. was Dad's favorite Yankee.

Alone at last, Dad looked at Mother and then at the baseball. "This is great, but I already have everything I need to keep me happy right here." He placed the baseball next to me and softly whispered, "Happy birthday."

* * *

While I was growing up, that baseball taught me how to use my ability, even before I knew I had it. I took every opportunity to take the ball out and ask Dad my favorite question: "Where did I get this baseball?" Whenever I asked him, our conversation was the same. Even though both of us knew the story so well, we always wanted another go-around.

"Your Uncle Robbie gave it to me, and I gave it to you." There was a pause as a grin etched across Dad's face.

"No, silly! Dad, how did Uncle Robbie get the ball?"

"How do you think he got it?"

One day, I felt the need to tell him the version I had seen so many times in my dreams.

"You know! It was at the Yankees game. The World Series. On the day I was born. You couldn't go because when you were about to leave with Uncle Robbie, Mommy's water broke. It was 1:32 in the afternoon. Uncle Robbie took Saul instead, and had to listen to how Saul had just gotten off a gosh-dang double shift and had to work another gosh-dang double shift in the morning, and how he was so tired and how he was going to be really tired tomorrow, and how this was going to put a stitch in his wife because he didn't tell her he was going to the game. Uncle Robbie didn't mind the outburst. He never minded. He was just excited to see Joltin' Joe and eat a soft pretzel."

I was just warming up.

"In the third inning, after the Yankees scored five runs, Rex Barney was run out of the game. Jack Banta was brought in to step things up and save the game, and the series. By the top of the fourth, he was really slowing down the Yankees. He got Tommy Henrich to ground out to Jackie Robinson.

"Then Yogi Berra hit a firecracker right to first base that Gil Hodges couldn't drop even if he tried. But then Joe DiMaggio came up. After putting two balls in the dirt, Joe mumbled, 'Come on Jack, give me something I can hit!' That's when Joe sent the ball high over the left-field wall. Saul reached up and caught it. He was so excited! He told Robbie he would see if one of the boys at the shop would buy it, but Uncle Robbie took it from him and said, 'No, Tony's getting this.' And that's what he did! He gave it to you, and you gave it to me, and said, 'Happy birthday!'"

My dad looked at me funny; the source of my vivid imagination was a puzzle to him.

"Well, I guess I've told the story enough times." I was six years old and had seen that game over three hundred times. Joe DiMaggio had the most beautiful swing I had, and have, ever seen.

I continued to tell him the story.

"And Joe was surprised he could pull the ball that much because he had all that cramping in his left shoulder. When they were sitting in the dugout, Yogi laughed at him and punched him in the hurt shoulder and said, 'I sure wish I had your problems, Joe. I just want to hit one out of the infield.' And he did! In the sixth inning. His ball went in almost the same direction as DiMaggio's, but it didn't go far enough; Marv Rackley was able to pull it in, but it allowed Rizzuto to score from third base and make the game seven-one.

"After Yogi batted, DiMaggio hit a lazy ground ball that didn't make it past second base. Yogi laughed so hard when Joe returned to the bench. He said, 'How's that cramp?' and hit him on the arm again. DiMaggio shook his head and laughed. 'Keep it up, Berra. Keep it up.' That was all he said. And that was enough because the Yankees won the game ten-six."

Dad loved it. "I don't know what's better, Dominic: your memory or that imagination of yours. It seems that Joe 'the Clipper' DiMaggio gave you some great advice when he said, 'Keep it up!'"

* * *

The moments that occurred on the date of my birth, October 9th, 1949, saved me because they rooted my childhood dreams in reality. Reality is my salvation, allowing me to avoid falling prey to the danger of fantasy and an overactive imagination.

That day contains many of my favorite memories, not so much because of the story of my birth, or even that incredible game, but rather seeing the love my parents and their close friends had for each other. I looked forward to one day sharing such a bond with someone.

Why don't we take a pause here, Angela? It's been a long day for both of us.

Chapter 5 - Voice: Angela

The entire time, Dominic was very much in control. After we finished lunch, Dominic made his way over to the improvised studio and sat down in front of the camera. Following his lead, I slid my chair to the side of the camera so that I was not in the frame and he and I were facing each other. After reiterating his interview rules, he pressed the remote record button and launched into his story.

As I listened, I noticed Dominic was very much the same person, the same lawyer, I had learned about in law school. He was still devoted to the art of convincing others to accept and believe his version of events. And he was good at it. He was a powerful and influential lawyer who won some very big cases. When he was in a courtroom, his unrelenting words would often create a clamor and buzz among a previously serene jury. He was a master at turning even the most challenging cases into indisputable wins for his clients. Years ago, he represented a group of investors who accused a man named Julián Gate of embezzling over $500 million from them. In a matter of days, Dominic had gathered so much new evidence and put together such a convincing case, he got the SEC to agree to investigate. In another case, his firm represented a homeless man, James Bell, who had been accused of setting fire to a restaurant on the Upper East Side. In one afternoon, Dominic presented evidence so compelling, it proved not only Bell's innocence, but the culpability of the establishment's owner.

While Dominic was a master at convincing juries of his version of the facts—his trick was to present his case in the form of a story— I did not feel he was not using this technique with me. There was no reason to believe what he was telling me. He knew there was no way for me to corroborate his version of events—no one to confirm that he watched my mother holding me while I slept in her arms, no one to substantiate conversations he said took place in the dugout of a 1949 Yankees-Dodgers game. It's so easy to base your argument on events that cannot be backed up somehow. When you don't have corroborating evidence, nothing can be considered factual. That was the basis of my education to date. Fiction. Fantasy. It was fiction, however, clouded and interspersed with historical fact.

After Dominic said we should call it a night, he rang for Hy'ing. He asked her to make sure I had dinner, to be there for me if I needed anything during the evening, and said that our day of interviewing was to start promptly at eight the next morning.

I told Hy'ing I wanted to eat dinner in my room that night. I wanted to review my notes and do some research in preparation for my next meeting with Dominic. I just picked at my meal. When I looked up details of the Yankees-Dodgers game, I discovered everything occurred precisely as Dominic said it had. Of course, I was unable to find anything about conversations between Joe DiMaggio and Yogi Berra, but I did not expect to.

My graduation day was a different story. I knew those details inside and out. I can still feel the skin on my face pulling taut when my smile fought to break new bounds. I remember Mom's kindness—how she listened intently as I went on and on about my hopes and dreams, and about Justin. And, of course, I remember Nikki. I remember waking up in her arms, and the sweet smell of her skin. I wondered if Dominic saw us as we giggled and scampered around the apartment because both of us were running so late—she for catching her flight and me for my graduation which I was in danger of missing altogether. While rushing around and shrieking, "My dad is going to kill me for leaving this place a mess," Nikki ran into the coffee table and knocked over the second bottle of red wine, thankfully still corked. We both stopped and looked at each other, neither of us willing to speak our thoughts. After one last prolonged hug and a kiss, I left. I took the bottle with me, vowing that if I were ever brave enough to be honest with Nikki, we would drink it together. But, I've moved on. The bottle, which once sat on my bookshelf, is now tucked away somewhere, still sealed tight.

Dominic. What he had just told me convinced me his powers were for real...that he could without a doubt see into the past. After that, I no longer saw him as a sad and distraught old man who believed he possessed some kind of crazy power. The skepticism I initially felt was replaced with belief, awe, and curiosity. He had completely changed my mind, just like he did to the jurors on many of his cases. It was as if, suddenly, the truth was just there...right in front of me. After that day, I never again wavered from my belief that he could indeed see the past, and see it in minute detail. I'm sure some of those jurors believed it was their careful analysis of the evidence that led them to such conclusions, but I wasn't naive enough to assume that. It was Dominic and the way he told me that story that changed my mind.

Yes, I now believed him, but I had no idea how it was possible. I wrote one word on my notepad: "How?" How did

Dominic have the ability to see moments in the past? How did he realize he had it? How did he learn to use it? How does he choose which moments he wants to explore? What has he done with his ability so far? What does he do with it now? Does he have to control his powers in some way, and if so, how? I tried to imagine Dominic's world...what life is like when you have the ability to experience the past, witness it as if you are right there, even when you are not. I wondered what I would do with a power like that.

It was alarming to realize Dominic's powers meant that all the secrets in the history of the world, including those that people died over, or killed to keep hidden, are not safe from his ability and therefore, are not secret at all. Think about Jimmy Hoffa. So many people want to know who killed him and where he is buried, and think about the people who want that information to remain hidden. If you had that power, would you unwrap the mysteries of D. B. Cooper or the Zodiac Killer? Or Amelia Earhart or JFK? Or even find out exactly what happened to Jesus Christ on the day of his crucifixion? There are so many ways to use an ability like this, but what I wanted to know was how Dominic was using it. He could use it to become a billionaire, he could find kidnapped children, he could influence political elections. Oh, the possibilities were endless. But, it was clear to me at the time that he had done none of these things. The question remained: How had he used it? How was he using it? Maybe he was more interested in discovering the specifics of how things happened, not so much which events did or did not occur. Details like that can be used as evidence in a lawsuit, but what case was he trying to prove? I knew if I asked him these kinds of questions, he would give me the same line: "I'll get to that." Although I believed, or hoped, he would, I was still bursting with curiosity and not happy about having to wait.

    Thinking about all of that kept me awake for a long time that night. Had he invited me to Hawaii not only to tell me about his ability to see the past, but to somehow share it with me? Give me an entrance into his world? And if so, what would I do with such a power? Where would I go in my dreams? Who would I visit? Just as I was finally starting to doze off, thoughts of Nikki on graduation day flooded my head. Had she felt as lost as I did? Did she stroke her hand across her face to catch a lingering scent of my body pressed against hers all night long? Maybe the secret is in the desire of the dreamer. The last thing I remember wishing was to see the life that became hers, in the way I always dreamed it would.

When I awoke the next morning, I still had thoughts of the previous night in my head. I felt melancholy, but in my typical optimistic fashion, I shifted my thoughts to what the new day would bring. That did not mean I had lost focus on my burning question: How?

When I walked into the kitchen, Hy'ing smiled and said, "Hi, Angela. How are you feeling this morning? You looked tired last night, maybe even troubled. In fact, Dominic did too. Did you get a good night's sleep?" It was apparent she was used to worrying.

"I am fine. Don't worry. It is just that Dominic is a complex person. He gave me a lot to think about. I suspect there is a lot more to come, things that may be more complicated than what he has already told me."

Hy'ing changed the subject and urged me to eat. And exercise. "You should use the exercise equipment we set up in your room. Also, we have some amazing running trails crisscrossing through the reserve. I'd be glad to point them out to you later. Maybe we can go for a little run tonight. I'll show you some of my favorite routes."

"It's been four days since I last worked out. I would love that!"

"Great! Now, your breakfast. Try to eat." Hy'ing went back to doing paperwork. I heard her murmur to herself, "Here we go again."

I made my way down to the office slightly before eight o'clock. Dominic was already seated in his chair and ready to begin our session. There was a new overstuffed leather armchair for me so I wouldn't have to slide my seat back and forth each time we filmed. I took my place.

"Dominic, all the information you gave me yesterday...it has left me with so many questions. There is so much I want to ask you about before we get started today. I need to understand more about your ability. Can you tell me how it started?"

Dominic raised his hand, palm facing me. "Stop right there. Yesterday we talked about the construct, nay, the rules of these interviews." Before I could get out an objection, he continued, "I have already assured you everything will be clear by the end of our time together. As clear, that is, as everything is to me. I guarantee I will answer all your questions, and I will do so to the best of my ability. The truth is, I have no idea how else to do this. I cannot apply the way I learned—the way everything was explained to me—to this situation. If

I answer any of your questions now, you won't have the necessary context to understand what I want you to know." He leaned forward. "In addition to my ability to capture moments in the past, there is one other skill I have honed: my ability to develop and tell a story in such a way as to convince my audience that what I am saying is the truth. Believe me, Angela, this is the only way. At the moment, I can't offer you anything more than that. It is my only condition."

I realized I had no choice. My questions would just have to wait.

For the next week, I filled my mornings with beautiful sunrises and worked out in my room. At night, Hy'ing and I explored rugged trails and dined on the delicious food provided by the Island. During the daytime, however, I sat on the edge of my seat, listening as Dominic shed more and more light on his world with each moment he brought to life again.

Chapter 6 - Voice: Dominic

Today is March 2nd, 2019. My name is Dominic Bandall and this is session number two of Angela Grant's interview of me.

My parents were living in the Parkchester section of the Bronx at the time I was born. Built in the late 1930s and early '40s, Parkchester was still a relatively new development when we lived there. That kind of housing gave returning vets like my father an opportunity to transition to normal life...to civilian life. My father, Anthony Bandall, married his sweetheart, Mabel—my mother—after returning from the war. Eager to put the years of fighting behind them, they lived a happy and simple life. I cannot recall a single time growing up when my parents fought or even spoke sharply to each other. In a letter my dad wrote to Mabel from Europe, he told her that if he made it back home alive, he would make her feel like the most treasured woman in the world. And he did, happily keeping his promise to her throughout the rest of their lives.

Dad had a successful career in construction, first during the postwar boom in New York City, and later with the development and renovation of South Bronx and Harlem. As soon as he could, he moved us to a cozy house in Pelham Bay. Mother's job was raising me and making our house a wonderful home. Tony and May did it right!

Both my parents died in 1996, within days of each other. I was in my mid-forties. Their life together was only love and peace. The only times I ever saw any indication of stress or disagreement between them were on account of me. They suffered because I was sick as a kid. They suffered because of my long history of disabilities and ailments. I also want to tell you they never knew about my ability because I never told them. In fact, I didn't share it with anyone for a long time. You, Angela, are only the fourth person to know. I often thought of telling them but decided against it because I was not sure how they would have responded. I don't know if they would have blamed themselves. It may have been too much for them to deal with. Sharon was my guide, my confidant. But that's getting ahead of myself....

Keeping me safe and healthy was my parents' primary concern, but once they were sure I was, they were able to focus on helping me become a good and successful person. My mother was proud of me simply because I was "her beautiful boy." To her, that was all that mattered. My father loved me unconditionally as well, but he saw things somewhat differently than my mother did. He didn't just look at who I was, but also at what I could be. To him, I was smart, but I was also creative. He was amazed by my ability to remember nearly everything I heard, saw, and learned. He couldn't believe I would know about or remember the subtlest conversation I must have overheard and little stories he or Mother had told about some random event. He was also impressed with my imagination, especially my ability to embellish stories of past events with what he called "creatively imagined details." He simply thought I was making things up, even when the "imagined" details I described were accurate. Dad never asked me how I knew those things. He never wanted to stifle my imagination. The very first time I shared my ability was on my parents' sixth anniversary, in February of 1952. I was nearly two and a half. When the war in Europe ended in April of 1945, Dad's unit had been preparing to join the Allied forces in the Pacific as part of a land force for the invasion of Japan. He was a sergeant in the infantry, serving under General Patton in the US Third Army. Because such a great number of tanks were of little value in the Pacific Theater, the infantry was reorganized: they were to fight, consolidate the remaining troops, reorganize, fight again, reorganize, fight again, and so on...until there was no more enemy left to fight. In August, after Truman changed that approach, they had different plans for Dad. His role was to help process other returning soldiers through Fort Hamilton in Brooklyn. He did that for one year, until it was time for his discharge from the Army.

When Dad first returned to the States on January 15th, he wasted no time starting a new life; he proposed to my mother on the same day. Their wedding, a remarkable celebration, was a combination of a welcome-home for Sergeant Bandall and a celebration of their new life together as Mr. and Mrs. Bandall.

Mother and Dad would celebrate every anniversary by spending a quiet evening alone, reflecting on their life together and revisiting their beautiful wedding day in February of 1946. When I came along, those quiet evenings faded away—as most quiet evenings do when babies arrive in young lovers' homes. By the time I was two, I was a captive audience to Dad and his stories.

Oh, how Dad loved to tell stories! We would often sit together in the evening and look through our photo albums. When Dad was the one turning the pages, we rarely made it past the first page because his stories began with the first photo and ended only when Mother would finally reach over us to close the album.

"All right, you two. Story time is over. Say goodnight to Dominic."

That was Dad's cue. He would look me squarely in the eyes and, in the best impression of Mother he could muster, he'd say: "Goodnight to Dominic."

Mother would continue the ritual. "Say goodnight to Tony."

"Goodnight to Tony!"

For their anniversary in 1952, Dad had a special treat for all of us. He reached up to the top shelf of the bookcase and took down their wedding album. It'd been three years since they had looked at it. Dad talked about their wedding often. He said it was the day he realized what his life was meant to be. We sat down on the floor of the family room and Dad opened the album. Then, a most unusual exchange took place. Dad pointed to the first photo. "This is us, Mommy and Daddy, on our wedding day. Isn't Mommy's dress beautiful?"

"Yeah." Even though I loved to talk—every bit as much as Dad did—I was still too young to articulately express myself.

"And do you know who that handsome man is?" he said, pointing to himself and smiling. He was wearing a drab army jacket—olive wool, four-button, adorned with the infantry braid, rank, and the medals that he had earned in his three years of service. I placed my index finger on the man in the photo and said, "Dada." Then I pointed to each of the other people standing with my parents and rambled off their names: "Uncle Robbie. Aunt Cindy. Grandma. Poppa. Nanny. Father Reardon."

Unsure of what they had just witnessed, Mother and Dad looked at each other quizzically.

"We shouldn't be surprised, Anthony. You've told him these stories many times. He remembers them. It makes sense that he can repeat what you said!"

"Gosh, this boy is smart!" Dad boasted. He looked at me, beaming with pride.

As we continued to look through the album, every now and then he would ask me questions about certain photographs to determine if I had previously heard anything about them. I knew all the answers, recognized all the people—by name—and repeated the conversations that had taken place at the time the photo was taken.

The only thing holding me back was not yet having the words to adequately describe what I could see.

The last photo we looked at that night was of the two of them dancing their first dance together as husband and wife. "May, what was that song we danced to?" On cue, I sang a song in the same manner any toddler would easily recite their favorite nursery rhyme:

> *Symphony*
>
> *Symphony of love*
>
> *Music from above*
>
> *How does it start? You walk in*
>
> *And the song begins*
>
> *Singing violins start in my heart*
>
> *Then you speak*
>
> *The melody seems to rise*
>
> *Then you sigh*
>
> *It sighs, and it softly dies*
>
> *Symphony*
>
> *Sing to me*
>
> *Then we kiss*
>
> *And it's clear to me*

When you're near to me

You are my symphony

My symphony

Dad looked confused. Mother giggled, "Anthony! I can't believe you forgot our song. It's Freddy Martin. He is on the radio all the time. Even Dominic knows that one."

Dad just looked at me and smiled. "Geez, you're smart."

* * *

I was one and a half the first time I got sick. When Mother came in to get me from my crib that morning, I was unconscious. They rushed me to the hospital. I was barely breathing and not moving. The doctors told my parents I experienced a bout of cerebral hypoxia, that my brain had been deprived of oxygen. They could not explain the cause of my illness and said I might recover and maybe I could regain partial or even full function.

Eventually, I got better, but had lost some function in my left leg and hand. It took more than a year before I was able to even attempt to crawl or walk. Back then, there were no facilities that provided the type of rehabilitation I needed, so Mother took charge.

I have tried to reach back to see if I could determine what caused the attacks. Of course, I had no luck because I was trying to recall something that no one knew, something that never took place. I suffered five more episodes of cerebral hypoxia before I was eight years old. I recovered each time and gradually regained most of the function in my legs and hands. Most, but never all. My doctors said that if the episodes continued, or if I didn't get the right treatment, their cumulative effects could render me severely disabled by the time I was in my late teens or early twenties.

They wanted to run tests and then, depending on the results, try some procedures that were being used to treat critically wounded veterans. These procedures were considered highly experimental. Dad flatly refused. Mother pleaded with him to let me get the treatments. But no, Dad had seen too much in the war. In the European Theater of Operations, he learned that some things are more important than just living. He told Mother, "I watched men live, May. I watched men try to live—to not die—but at what cost? It often meant they had to give up everything they once lived for: their happiness, peace, and dignity. It makes no sense. I am not willing to take the risk of trying to help Dominic if it means possibly hurting him, damaging the very parts of the body and brain we are trying to save! If Dominic is going to live, not just survive, his body is going to have to learn how to fight this illness without those procedures. He will live, May. He will."

The doctors had proposed six different procedures they believed might help me. If the first didn't work, they would try the next, and so on. In the sixty-plus years since then, not one of those procedures turned out to be successful. Had my father agreed, I would have been dead or severely crippled in a matter of years.

Instead, my parents focused on living, and they taught me how to thrive. Aside from those disabling episodes, I was a happy boy and my childhood was normal. My life was balanced between family, friends, and school.

I excelled academically in those early years. My parents credited that to my uncanny ability to remember, recall, and repeat the things I learned. According to my teachers, the only problem was my tendency to let my imagination fly. As they saw it, I often pretended to know more about their lessons than they did. Dad did not see this as a problem at all. In fact, he encouraged it because to him, my ability to see beyond what was in front of me—the ability to extrapolate and expand—was one of my best traits. He would say, "In order to lead men, you have to know men. To do that, you need to understand more than what you see."

My father believed I would grow up to be a great leader in politics or in business. Mother saw me as a teacher, perhaps of history, as I absorbed it so well and expressed what I had learned in such a compelling manner—almost as if I had been there myself. Or maybe, she thought, a teacher of literature. Or a writer so I could fully use my imagination, most especially to dazzle lovers of fiction. As a boy just shy of eight years old, I was simply interested in experiencing everything I could without a concern that it was "learning."

One of my goals at that time was to learn to spin tales as grand as Dad's. We would try to top each other. One night, he would tell me the story of the day he met Mother. The next night, I told him about the time he followed her while she was strolling along the pier. When he saw her wipe a bit of sweat from her brow, he ran over to her, introduced himself, and offered her his handkerchief—a piece of an old sock he kept in his pocket! "That's right, Dominic. Gosh, she was beautiful back then. Just as beautiful as she is today."

Other days we would talk about baseball. Dad told me about the time his father took him to his first Yankees game. He described the smell of the ballpark, the fresh-cut grass, and the starched Yankee pinstripes. "They were almost blindingly white. Never saw anything quite that white." The next night I would tell him about the day Yankee Stadium first opened. It was April 18th, 1923. There was a deafening roar from the crowd when Babe Ruth hit the first home run, a shot into the bleachers in the third inning.

"You know I was there, son?"

"Yeah Dad, that was the first ball game your dad took you to."

"That's right," he said as he gently patted me on the head. "It was a great game."

Like Dad, I loved to tell stories. Another night, I told him about that day we moved to Pelham Bay. When we first pulled up to our new house, Mother and Dad beamed with pride. My response was disbelief. When I looked down the street and realized every family had their own house, my mouth gaped wide open. Having lived my entire life in a small apartment cubed into a big apartment building, in an even bigger complex, having this much space was just unbelievable. Houses for only one family, houses with two floors, driveways that had an additional house at the end! Yes, I soon discovered the little houses were garages, but that did not diminish my astonishment—a separate home for a lawnmower and tools! Almost every house had a tree in the front yard. Years later, I remember feeling the same sense of surprise when I discovered that, in neighborhoods outside of the City, people had even bigger yards, with even more and bigger trees. At least they were bigger than the puny poplar tree to which I staked a claim in Pelham Bay.

While Dad and his cronies unloaded our few belongings from the truck, I took a stroll down the block to explore my new neighborhood. That is when I first laid eyes on Elizabeth. She lived with her father on the same street as ours. Her long sandy-blonde hair, olive skin, and smile caught my attention immediately. She was the most beautiful creature I had ever seen—an angel in my new heaven. I realized right away she was no ordinary little girl. No, even while she was taking her place on the sewer cap serving as home plate, this girl was the picture of grace and elegance. She was the only girl playing in an otherwise all-boy game of stickball.

As I walked up to them, she noticed me. Without a pause or the slightest bit of hesitation, she blurted out, "Hi, I'm Lizzy. Wanna play?" Then she looked down at the brace on my leg. "Oh! Sorry about that," she said, before turning toward the pitcher and letting the first pitch rip over the second baseman's head. I watched in awe as she rounded first base—a teal-green 1955 Chevrolet Nomad (which I later discovered belonged to her father)—tagged the second-base sewer cap with her foot, peeled past the steel trash can that was third base, then bolted home. She announced her home run with a massive leap in the air followed by the loud thump of her tennis shoes striking the sewer cap.

Lizzy turned to me and tried again. "Hi, I'm Lizzy."

"I'm Dominic. We just moved in over there. That was a really nice hit." It was all I could muster. Obviously, my sophisticated self hadn't yet been created. But, boy oh boy, was I hooked. Absolutely everything about Lizzy was amazing. She was the girl of my dreams, even before I had begun to dream about girls.

* * *

Once, when my parents thought I was out of earshot, Mother told Dad the "sad tale" of Lizzy's parents, Stephen and Rebecca Strauss. They moved to the neighborhood about seven years before we did, when Elizabeth was just an infant. Lizzy was five when Mrs. Strauss was stricken with cancer. Mr. Strauss took such great care of his wife and child and practically lost his job to stay home with them. As Mrs. Strauss grew sicker, she worried that she was becoming too much of a burden on her family; eventually, the anxiety and stress of it all became too much for her. One night, she took a handful of amphetamines which gave her the courage to walk down the Avenue, up into the El, and lean as far as she could over the tracks, just as the subway train was pulling in.

Elizabeth's father hired a nanny to take care of her during the day and when he had to leave town on business. I could tell Mother was moved by the love and care Stephen Strauss showed for his family.

* * *

When I got home from the game—I cheered them on and stayed until it was over—Uncle Robbie was cooking steaks outside on the grill and was talking with my dad. "Wow, Tony, they got just about everything you could want up on the Avenue. A butcher shop, fresh produce, and ice-cold beer—all within spitting distance of your house."

"You are right. It has everything this little family needs. Dominic's got a great school, and yes, it is absolutely within spitting distance. With the IRT, I can be anywhere in the City within an hour. And, Yankee Stadium is only one transfer away! Yessirree, Bob, we sure got it made."

That was the end of summer, 1957. In a matter of days, I became close friends with a bunch of neighborhood kids. In less than a month, I would start third grade at my new school. Many of my new friends were going to be in my class. Having known each other most of their lives, they had a close bond, but they welcomed me warmly and made me feel as if I had always been part of the group. Rich, Patrick, Jimmy, Dennis, Billy, Laurie, Bobby, Karen, Milt, and, of course, Lizzy. After that summer, we were inseparable. We were the neighborhood gang. After that first stickball game, I felt as if nothing would ever come between us.

I could barely contain my excitement that evening as Dad and I nuzzled together in my new bedroom, ready for our nighttime stories. I told him about all my new friends, and about how Lizzy hit the stickball almost as far as the second sewer cap. I told him I'd met seven kids who were going to be in my grade, but because they broke each grade into two classes, I didn't know if I'd be in the first or the second class, but Billy thought I'd be in the second because that was the class all of them were in, and the teachers liked to keep the neighborhood kids together. I told him how Lizzy could also throw a perfect strike, one so fast it was put past the batter before he could even begin to swing. I also told him that Bobby said his history teacher told amazing stories after every chapter they read.

My frenzied recap of the day made Dad chuckle. "I'm sure you'll fit in perfectly!" I shared how Lizzy had the brightest blonde hair, but she said a lot of the highlights were from the sun and it would get darker in the winter and then light again in the spring. I was over the moon.

Dad's shoulders bounced slightly as he tried to contain his laughter. "So, who is this Lizzy girl?"

Sensing he was making fun of me, I mumbled, "Oh, she's just some girl who lives on the block," and quickly changed the conversation. "Dad, can you tell me a story about when you were in the Army during the war?" He looked at me with a disapproving scowl. "No, not about war and killing," I said. "About your friends. Did you have any friends over there?"

"Sure, I had friends when I was over there. I had lots of friends. Thing is, in the war, a lot of the time, your friends don't stick around. Here, you can keep pals for a long time. Look at your Uncle Robbie. I met him on the first day of school, in third grade–just like you did today. When you're my age, you may still be friends with some of the kids you just met." A slight smile formed as he anticipated his next zinger. "Who knows! Maybe you and little Lizzy will get married and someday you'll be having the same conversation with your son."

"Dad!" I yelled as I jabbed him in the stomach.

Angela, I've experienced many moments throughout my life, moments that belong to other people, many of whom are now long gone. But the story I just told you is my own moment. Every time I relive it, I know exactly how I felt when it occurred. Yes, I was embarrassed when Dad joked about marrying Lizzy and so I shrieked and play-punched him. But that is only part of the story. What Dad didn't know was that I wanted to ask him if he thought we really could get married! I wanted to see if he thought Lizzy and I could be as happy as he and Mother were. Instead, I hid my feelings, mainly because I didn't understand my emotions. Kids are not used to thinking about those kinds of things.

"Why can't you and your friends stay together?" I asked him, deliberately stepping past the Lizzy subject.

Dad started to spin his story. "Well son, army units always reorganize their strategy based on where they are going. When we were in the desert, in North Africa, there wasn't a lot of need for infantry guys like me because they used tanks, trucks, and tracks to get where they needed to go. I usually rode in the back of a truck. Now, once we got into Europe, it was a whole different story. Infantry soldiers were a lot more valuable there. We were able to go into places that tanks couldn't. We could walk from house to house, down roads, and in between them. They organized us differently so there were a lot more infantry and a lot fewer tanks. Every time they reorganized, they split us up and sent us into different units."

"Did you have friends like Uncle Robbie when you were over there?"

"Sure, I did. Steve. Corporal Stephen Bean. We used to call him String Bean because he was six feet, four inches tall and only weighed 155 pounds. We went to basic training together here in the States, and we stayed together the longest of any other pair of grunts I knew."

Dad continued as if he were in a trance.

"We served together in North Africa, the Sicily Campaign, then sailed into Normandy after D-Day to support the breakout offensive. After the Battle of the Bulge, they started to reorganize us once again as we prepared to move into Germany and end the dang war. String Bean was sent to Germany with a group called Task Force Baum. We were never reunited again. The war in Europe ended less than two months later." Dad's eyes started to well up.

"Did you ever see String Bean again?"

"Sure, I did. After the war ended, before I was shipped home, we met up once in Berlin. When we were both back in the States, and he was living in Teaneck, we used to see each other all the time. String Bean stayed in the Army, got reorganized again, then got married and moved to California."

The long day finally caught up with me. I was starting to feel drowsy, and Dad was clearly done talking for the night. He tucked me in and gently kissed me on my forehead. As he began to close the door to my room, I asked him, "Dad, can we make plans to see Uncle String Bean?"

Dad tried to reassure me. "Sure, son." I fell asleep with visions of he and Uncle String Bean in Berlin, celebrating the end of the war.

When Mother came to wake me up the next morning, she found me unresponsive. Having been in that situation many times before, she knew exactly what to do. Although her heart was breaking, she was calm and methodical. Her process was to shake me three times, slap me hard across the cheek, yell my name, and shout for me to wake up. She then screamed for Dad, who hadn't left for work yet because he was working an overnight shift on the Cross Bronx Expressway construction project the previous night. To shock me into consciousness and to reduce any possible swelling, they wrapped me in cold soaked towels and drove me to the hospital.

I woke up a day later with my entire left side paralyzed. Dad reluctantly agreed to electroshock therapy. He refused to allow the doctors to do anything involving my brain. He limited treatment to my arm, leg, and spinal cord.

I have never searched for those moments in my dreams, nor will I ever do so. I'm not sure I could watch myself endure all that pain without losing my sanity. After three days of electroshock and physical therapy, I got up and was able to take a few steps. I had regained almost all function in my left arm, but my old lower-leg brace was replaced with a new one that now went up over my knee. Dad stood by cautiously, prepared to catch me if I fell. He tried to support and encourage me. "You lug that thing around for too long and you will have legs like Popeye. Okay, maybe just one Popeye leg, but you'll be able to kick a football clear across the field!"

"Thanks, Dad," was about as much as I could say. Something wasn't sitting well with me during the time I was recovering in the hospital. As much as I struggled, I couldn't determine the cause of my angst.

Break time! I'm famished, Angela.

Chapter 7 - Voice: Dominic

Today is March 2nd, 2019. My name is Dominic Bandall, and this is session number three in Angela Grant's interview of me.

I was taking four walks a day at that time as part of my physical therapy. I would walk down to the Avenue and then cross over for a few blocks. It wasn't long before I felt stronger. Dad was right; I was beginning to feel like Popeye.

No one on the Avenue was a stranger. The Avenue, if you don't know, is the main street under which our subway ran...well, still runs. Even today, everyone knows who everyone else is.

In my neighborhood, everyone—adults and children—was very friendly and always greeted each other. As children, we were instructed how to greet neighbors properly. If you didn't know the other person well, it was usually a brief greeting, something simple like, "Good morning." If you didn't know their name, you greeted them with respect. "Good morning, ma'am!" If you were friends, it was, "Good morning, Mrs. Paulson!" and the greeting was usually a bit longer: "Hey, Dominic, how's it going? Did you hear the Yankees game last night? Think they got another one in them tonight?"

Children always greeted adults first, but we were taught to keep it brief in case they were busy.

We all knew who Giuseppe was, but no one talked to him or knew all that much about the man. People would call him "that crazy old kook," and parents told their kids to stay away from him. I met Giuseppe and got to know him during my rehabilitation walks.

Every morning, I would see Giuseppe heading up the stairs to the train station and late in the afternoon, when I was finishing my last walk, I would see him return and travel down the same stairs. Where he went or what he did when he got there, I had no idea. I noticed he wore the same suit every day—it was not clean. In fact, it looked as if it hadn't been cleaned in months.

One morning, I ran into Giuseppe just before he was about to start up the stairs to the train station. He paused and looked at me...longer than I was comfortable with. It was almost as if he was sizing me up. Something about the way he was looking at me was so unnerving, I couldn't even whisper hello. Instead, I looked away.

"Good morning there, boy. That's quite a bit of hardware you're lugging around."

Mother would've rightly told me that being afraid is no reason for poor manners. "Yes, sir. Good morning to you as well."

"So, what are you trying to do there? Turning yourself into your own train car so you don't have to pay the fare?"

"No, sir. Sometimes I just get hurt in my sleep." Giuseppe looked surprised, then suddenly sat down on the stairway so we were about eye to eye.

"Hurt in your sleep? You don't say."

"Yes, sir."

He was making me quite uncomfortable, but I was too polite to just walk away. I blurted out, "My mother wants me home now, sir. I have to get on my way."

"Well, we know a mother's patience should never be tested. You take care of that leg, all right?" I could tell he was trying not to frighten me or make a bad impression. He stood up to leave and nodded his head slightly at me.

"Yes, sir," I said.

"Giuseppe."

"Yes, Mr. Giuseppe."

As he started up the stairs, he yelled back, "Just Giuseppe, my boy. It's just Giuseppe." I hurried home.

Because my mother always asked for a full report on my morning walk—how far I went, how my leg felt—I told her everything...except, of course, that I had talked with Giuseppe. I don't think she would've reacted well to my encounter.

When it was time for my afternoon walk, I told Mother I wanted to try going a bit farther. While she was cautious, she also encouraged me to push myself. Mother told me I could stay out for an additional thirty minutes but had to be home well before supper. Dad would be home from work and able to join us, and she was baking a ham. If ever she wanted me to be home on time, she had only to say we were having ham!

Moments after the 4:45 subway pulled in, I saw Giuseppe come down the subway stairs. I was standing at the end of the street, peering out from the side of the corner café. It was a great hiding place because I could see Giuseppe when he came down the stairs, but he couldn't see me. I felt a sudden wave of anxiety when I realized I didn't know if he would go straight or turn when he got to the bottom. Just then, he made a sudden left turn and, before I could run away, he was right in front of me. "Hey there, boy!" Again, there was something unsettling about him. He had been courteous, and not at all unfriendly. His manner and tone, even his kind of odd personality, were almost comforting. I was confused! In a matter of moments, I went from feeling distressed, to panicked, to disarmed, to finding the guy somehow comforting. Except for his clothing, which was so disheveled, he seemed to be a normal guy. His suit looked like it had once been a good one.

"Good afternoon, Giuseppe!" I tried to sound confident.

"That! That, right there, is a sign of a future scholar, my boy. Customs are a fine thing to uphold and so is having good manners. However, all too often we adhere to certain rigid standards that prevent us from tailoring our discourse to suit certain situations. Well done! You passed the first lesson with flying colors." I wasn't sure what he meant by "the first lesson," but decided it was just part of his oddness. He smiled, gave me a thumbs up, then continued on his way. I thought that maybe Giuseppe wasn't unique after all. Feeling rather foolish, I headed back home for supper.

That night we feasted on Mother's delicious fresh ham. Although we were all eating together, each of us was off in our own separate world. We heard a report on the radio that President Eisenhower would suspend testing of nuclear weapons for up to two years if the Soviets would agree to certain conditions. The mention of nuclear testing caught my dad's attention. Having served with General Eisenhower in the war, he trusted him as a soldier. Dad believed the president always had our best interests at heart. And, when I say "served with Eisenhower," I mean he served in a unit that was many, many, many levels below the general's command in the ETO. That's the European Theater of Operations. Nuclear weapons frightened my dad.

"Dad, what do they mean by nuclear?"

"It is a powerful material they use to make bombs."

"Oh, like the bombs they made to end the war?"

Dad had given me a quick and simple answer because he was trying to listen to the radio. The thing is, that half-baked response was just not Dad's customary style with me, and he knew it. He laid down his knife and fork, gently wiped the corners of his mouth with his napkin, then took a long sip of water.

"No, Dominic. Nuclear and atomic weapons are very different. I don't know the engineering differences between them, but

I know it has to do with the level of their power—the level of their intensity.

"Here, look at it this way. You know what I do in construction, right?" I nodded yes. "My job is to build things, but sometimes, to create something, you need to get rid of whatever is already there. For instance, if you are building a road, sometimes there is something in the way of where that road is going to be constructed. Maybe it's another road, trees, or boulders, a hill, or even a mountain. We have choices: we can try to build the road over it, around it, or even try to dig a tunnel through it. But no matter which option we choose, we will have to destroy something before we can build that road.

"When men are at war, the concept is quite similar. We are trying to build something. Typically, we are trying to engage a population to improve the way of life there. For those who want to construct a new society, they have to destroy the one that is already there. Of course, there are many opinions about what constitutes a better society and what should be destroyed and what should be built. Just like with construction, destroying as little as possible should always be the goal. Keeping destruction to a minimum is cheaper, quicker, and requires fewer resources.

"In war, there are lots of ways to destroy things. In that sense, it's a lot like my construction job. You try to do the job with just a few people. If you can't, you get more manpower, more or better equipment, and so on. Perhaps you use tools to scrape away, break, and remove whatever is in your way. Sometimes you have to blow things up. In my job, we might use sticks of dynamite. When I was in the war, we used hand grenades and other kinds of charges. When more destruction was needed, we increased the power of the tools we had. Tanks. Planes. Bombs. Rockets. And after all of that, at some point, we would have to send men in to build or rebuild."

I didn't know where Dad was going with all this. Mother must've felt the same way because she stopped clearing the table and sat back down with us.

"The first big difference between construction and war concerns the end results. In construction, we usually want to build something entirely new or at least different from what is already there. We remove trees, hills, and mountains to create asphalt roads. Sometimes we dig up roads of asphalt to create buildings made of steel and stone. Sometimes we remove buildings made of steel and stone to construct a building made of bricks and glass.

"In war, when we are trying to build something new, we try not to completely destroy whatever is there. We want to maintain the infrastructure—that's the basic physical skeleton of something. Infrastructure may be the people, their industry, resources, homes. Instead of total destruction, in war, we try to remove only the things that we oppose. This could include the government or part of their government. It may be select leaders. It may even be their military. It may be all or some of these things. The goal is to rebuild in the way we want while maintaining as much of the infrastructure as possible.

"When we dropped the bombs on Hiroshima and Nagasaki in 1945, the destruction was absolute. We destroyed everything there. We killed every living creature. What we saved, however, was the rest of Japan. We had to completely rebuild the cities of Hiroshima and Nagasaki, but we were able to keep the whole of Japan. We did not have to destroy their government and their leaders, although we demonstrated that we had the ability to do so if we had wanted to. In the end, we were able to maintain some of their infrastructures.

"A bullet destroys a person. A hand grenade destroys a vehicle. A bomb destroys a building. Atomic bombs destroy entire cities. Nuclear weapons destroy nations. In war, we use weapons until we have destroyed enough to achieve our goal. At the time the United States dropped atomic bombs on Japan, we were the only country to have that kind of weapon. If the Japs had had one and had used it against us, we might have retaliated and destroyed a lot more of Japan. Now the Soviets have atomic weapons and nuclear weapons.

"When the United States dropped the bombs on Japan to end the war, no one was happier than we were—the American soldiers who were in Germany at the time. We knew that if we were sent to invade Japan, most of us would not come home. My heart hurts every day for all the people we killed with those two bombs. I can't imagine what it was like to be in the center of Hiroshima on that horrible day. But, I am at least grateful we could rebuild their country and ours. If we go down this route again, using weapons we now have that are even more destructive, there will be nothing left to rebuild...anywhere."

My mother wiped a tear from her eye. "Oh, I'm sure glad President Eisenhower has put an end to all that nonsense."

I asked Mother if she would put me to bed that night, sensing Dad was in no mood to tell stories. I didn't want to hear any more that night anyway. I went to sleep that night wondering what it was like to be in the center of Hiroshima when that bomb hit.

Unfortunately for me, I would soon find out.

<There is an extended pause as Dominic closes his eyes and sits silently in reflection.>

I will never again revisit those moments, nor will I inflict the details of their horror on another soul.

Let's take a break right here, Angela.

Chapter 8 - Voice: Dominic

Today is March 2nd, 2019. My name is Dominic Bandall. This is session number four of Angela Grant's interview of me.

Okay, now where were we? Ah...yes, 1957. In the waning days of summer, I would discover so much about the boy I was then and about the man I would later become.

As I just mentioned, the dream I had that night about Hiroshima was disturbing. It was also very confusing. When I had my dream, I didn't understand what I witnessed. And when I woke up, I didn't realize the events I had just dreamed about were my own recollections of something that had occurred on August 6th, 1945— more than four years before I was born. Yet when I woke, what stayed with me was a vibrant and busy city that was wiped out in one horrific flash and the sight of strange, almost alien-looking people.

Not only do I have the ability to dream about moments in the past, but I am able to obtain a perfect map of the energy created in whatever moment I reach for. Hiroshima was a beautiful city, a bustling mix of traditional Japanese culture within a city thriving in the modern days of 1945. I watched as the densely built-up areas along the Motoyasugawa River were torn apart and leveled. The moment of the bombing did not happen in a single point of time and space; it occurred over an excruciating infinite of so-called instances. Even to this day, I still carry the weight of each detailed memory in that horrid collection: the last moment a child blinked before his innocent features vanished; the fisherman who, while lashing his boat to the dock in the harbor, quickly turned in the direction of the falling bomb, sensing something horrible was coming; the houses, trees, and people slowly torn apart. Each scene felt as if it lasted for decades, yet they all occurred within that flashpoint. Everything that wasn't obliterated burned from the fire and heat. What remained stood as a crippled reminder of the horrific power we unleashed.

Witnessing that scene when I did was both a blessing and a curse. While I was old enough to know what destruction was, I was still too young and naive to understand the meaning of true horror. But, that naivete didn't last long. I soon discovered that by reading the subtle clues that reveal a person's feelings and thoughts—by studying their faces, looking deep into their eyes, carefully watching their body language—I could feel their pain as if it were my own. That night, I took the first step by realizing there were no quick deaths. Instantaneous spans a lifetime.

I never physically endured the horrors of August 6th, 1945, but I hold the painful memory deep in my psyche, just as if I had been there. I can recall the images, both the ghastly and the majestic. I remember a picturesque city, then the total force of that bomb, blinding flashes, piercing wails...yet my body was not harmed. I know what it feels like to stand in a blast area so intense its heat will first char the flesh from your bones and then pulverize your remains to dust. These are the memories my ability leaves me with: horrible nightmares of moments in which I am not physically present but retain experience as if I were right there. However, at least my knowledge of and involvement in these moments is not accompanied by fear. I am not afraid when I experience moments of horror because I don't have to worry about things that typically accompany a ghastly event. I don't have to think about how long or to what degree any agony or fear might continue. I don't have to worry about what kind of suffering may yet come. All of that has already been determined. It has already happened. When I awake, all I have is the memory. When I dream, I am introduced to the entire moment— beginning to end—all at once. I understand the concept now, but when I was a child, I feared its intrusion.

Mother rushed into my room when she heard me screaming. I couldn't explain what I'd seen. All I could say was, "I had a horrible nightmare, Mother. Everything was destroyed. Everything! And all the people...they just disappeared." Mother tried her best to console me. "It's okay, dear. You just had a bad dream, that's all." She decided that the best thing for me was to get up and do my physical therapy exercises and then take a long, cold bath intended to reduce any brain or spinal column swelling I may have incurred. I continued that elevated work for a few weeks. The duration and distance of my walks increased.

I didn't see Giuseppe for nearly two weeks. At first, my avoidance was more intentional than circumstantial. I stayed away from the Avenue during the times I thought Giuseppe would be there. Before long, however, my new friends became the most significant factors in how I spent my time. Lizzy was usually my main distraction. She joined me on my walks and offered to teach me everything about the neighborhood. In a matter of days, I knew who lived in which house, which mothers made lemonade for the kids, and which places should be avoided at all costs. One morning, when we were about a mile away from home, Lizzy stopped, turned, and said, "You see that house on the corner? Stay away from it. Everyone does. Even on Halloween, none of us go anywhere near that house." That was more than enough to pique my attention.

"Why? What's wrong with that house?"

"Crazy old man Giuseppe. He lives there. He is alone now but he used to live there with his wife and two little girls, one of whom was about our age. The younger one—I think her name was Penelope—she was rushed to the hospital one day. She was dead by the time they got her there. No one knew how or why she died. The doctors said that it was natural causes."

"Wow."

"I know. And that was the day Giuseppe went crazy. He began accusing bosses in the neighborhood of killing his daughter. He told the police he knew what they were doing, he knew about their corruption, and that they murdered Penelope to keep him quiet."

Lizzy's animated storytelling turned somber and cold. "That was about five or six years ago. I don't remember much about it. My father told me the story. He said crazy old Giuseppe got worse and worse. He told me Giuseppe started going to the coffee shop where all the old guys hang out. Giuseppe said to tell the mob guys that he knew what they did and he was going to prove it. Then he started going downtown to City Hall. He used to work there as some sort of lawyer for the City. Well, I guess he still worked there when this all first happened. Anyway, he kept on trying to convince them to shut down the coffee shop where all the old men hung out."

I tell you, Angela, that is still just about the best description of organized crime and corruption I ever heard, all provided by an eight-year-old kid. Lizzy knew so much about the story, I suspect she had heard it more than once. At that time, the Bronx was an interesting place to grow up. Organized crime was commonplace in some of the older neighborhoods, like ours. While they conducted their illegal activities in other parts of the City, they chose to live in communities like ours that were quiet and residential. To put it mildly, they were not happy about the allegations Giuseppe was making.

Lizzy continued. "About two years ago, Giuseppe's wife and other daughter disappeared. No one really knows what happened, but last spring, Giuseppe went to the coffee shop and threw a trash can through the window. He told them he was going to get his revenge and he was going to see that justice was served for what they did. Giuseppe got arrested. I guess he lost his job. And, what's weird is that he still goes down to City Hall every day like he's going to work. Have you ever seen him, Dominic?" I just shook my head because I didn't trust myself to speak. I was worried that anything I said would reveal my secret. What would Lizzy think if she discovered Giuseppe and I had spoken to each other?

"Got it. Stay away from that house." My non sequitur puzzled Lizzy, but at least it changed the subject. Fortunately, it was time to head back. Lizzy and her dad were coming to a barbecue at our house and we didn't want to be late.

The next morning, I retraced the steps of my old route. I was curious to see if Giuseppe was still taking the subway downtown. Somehow, when I awoke, I actually knew a lot more about the day his daughter died than Lizzy did. Her name was Phoebe. The doctors said her heart stopped while she was sleeping, but they didn't know why. No other explanation was ever provided.

Giuseppe saw me standing on the corner of the Avenue, with the unmistakable look of a kid scouting out for someone. He shouted when he saw me, "Ahhh, there you are! How's that leg coming along, boy?"

"Fine, Giuseppe. The doctors say that they should be able to take this big brace off by the end of the week. I have to go back to wearing my smaller one, but that's okay because I'm kind of used to it."

"You better make sure you know what you're dreaming about, Dominic. If you don't learn how to use your ability, no brace in the world is going to save you."

"Excuse me, sir?" I was dumbfounded.

"Remember what I told you about your potential to be a scholar?"

I corrected myself. "Right. Giuseppe. Excuse me, Giuseppe."

"That's better, Dominic." I couldn't remember telling him my name, but because everyone knew everyone else in the neighborhood, I decided it wasn't all that strange.

"I'm talking about your ability. You know things. You see things that most people cannot. But, I need you to know that if you try to see something that never existed, your body will go into a deep, dark hole from which it may never recover."

For some reason, what he was telling me made sense. Even at such a young age, it all made sense. I had always felt there was something different about me. Not wanting to reveal that I knew what he was talking about, I asked him what he meant by "seeing things."

Giuseppe then proceeded to tell me what he meant and why I was special...that was the day my world started to come together. He told me I had the ability to see the past when I slept and that I could control what I saw and what I heard. But there was a caveat: to use this ability, I needed to have the real desire to see and hear moments in the past.

I had never told a soul, and I didn't want to confirm anything he was saying. "How do you know all of this about me?"

"Because I have seen you do it. I've watched you drift off to sleep while your father is telling you a story. Then next time the two of you discussed the story, you knew things about it he had not told you. In fact, you knew details he himself could not have known."

He looked at me long and hard. "Tell me about that last story he told you before you got sick. I have been thinking about it. When was the last time your dad saw String Bean?" Hearing him say that name sparked fear in me; until then, I could somehow rationalize everything he had said, but there was no way Giuseppe could know about String Bean unless he knew him, or knew my dad, or worst of all, had been in my room that night. As much as I would have liked to just walk away, my desire forced me to stay.

"They saw each other in Berlin after the war ended. No wait," I corrected myself, "they saw each other in New Jersey when the Army sent them home. But he is in California now."

His lighthearted mood seemed to have suddenly vanished. He bent his knees until he was looking directly into my eyes. In a slow, clear voice, he directed, "Now listen to what I have to tell you, Dominic. It is imperative to do exactly as I say: What your life will be from this day on depends on what you do. Do you understand?"

I nodded yes. I did not understand.

"I'd like you to go home now. I prefer that you not tell your parents about our conversation, at least not today. When you prepare for sleep tonight, I'd like you to think about the last time your dad and Corporal Stephen Bean spoke. Try not to think of anything but that. Don't try to pinpoint a specific place or a time. Don't think about when they were in Berlin, Teaneck, or anywhere else. Just think about the last time your dad and String Bean were together. Can you do that?"

I told Giuseppe I would do as he requested. I'm not sure why I agreed. Perhaps because I was brought up to always respect my elders? Because I was afraid of what might happen if I didn't follow his instructions? Or because I had a sense that what he was asking me to do was important, although why, I had no idea? Whatever the reason, I did exactly as I was told. He sent me on my way with a few pleasantries and promised we would talk again the next day.

From the time I left Giuseppe until I drifted off to sleep that night, I focused on that one thought: the last time Dad and String Bean were together.

Mother was rather cheerful the next morning, maybe because my somber mood appeared to have lifted and I finally had a healthy appetite again. As I scarfed down my oatmeal, I told Mother I was going for an extra-long walk because I wanted to get my strength back in time for school. Of course, I just wanted to find Giuseppe.

I bolted out the door and walked down the Avenue. When I turned the corner, he was waiting for me.

"Good morning. You have no idea how glad I am to see you. How was your evening, Dominic?"

"Fine, thanks." I wanted to get to the matter at hand. Apparently, so did he.

"Did you do what we talked about? Did you remember the last time your dad and Bean talked?"

"I did, Giuseppe. I had a dream about my dad and String Bean. But they were out in the woods. Maybe like a place where my dad was during the war. Dad was walking to a campsite when a truck drove by with String Bean in it."

Giuseppe nodded as if affirming what I was remembering.

"I know you have a perfect memory of your dreams. What exactly did they say to each other? What were their precise words?"

"Dad said some bad words when he saw String Bean in the—"

"No. No. I'm not asking you to paraphrase, Dominic. I need you to tell me exactly what they said."

"Okay then, Giuseppe, here's what Dad said: 'Hey, Bean. Where the fuck are you headed off to?' And then String Bean said, 'I have no idea, Tony. The captain is putting together a party to make a run up toward the line. He says the big guy wants a quick force, so I guess he's leaving you and the rest of the dead weight back in camp. We're not bringing much, so I guess we'll be back tonight or early tomorrow.' Then Dad said, 'Well, if you travel the countryside, see if you can find me a good piece of strudel. Try not to kill all the Krauts by yourself. I have been waiting a long time to cross that river. See you soon, buddy.' And before he drove away in the truck, String Bean said, 'Wilco. Will be back before you can say "Heil Hitler"!' I'm not really sure what they were talking about."

Giuseppe paused, then took a deep breath. He pulled a piece of paper from his pocket and handed it to me. "Dominic, I wrote this after my own dream last night."

> Hey Bean, where the fuck are you headed off to?
>
> I have no idea, Tony. The captain is putting together a party to make a run up toward the line. He says the big guy wants a quick force, so I guess he's leaving you and the rest of the dead weight back in camp. We're not bringing much, so I guess we'll be back tonight or early tomorrow.
>
> Well, if you travel the countryside, see if you can find me a good piece of strudel. Try not

to kill all the Krauts by yourself. I have been waiting a long time to cross that river. See you soon, buddy.

Wilco. Will be back before you can say "Heil Hitler."

I was staggered...almost speechless. All the weird things I somehow knew—the memories of other people's lives, the stories about DiMaggio and the Babe, the time I gave Mother the recipe for peach cobbler that her grandmother had taken to her grave—they began to fall into place. Giuseppe obviously knew a lot about all of it. All I could get out was, "So can you see stuff as well?"

"Let's walk." As we walked down the Avenue, Giuseppe began to tell me his own story. He told me he was just about my age when he realized that if, before he went to sleep, he concentrated on something that had happened in the past, he could fall asleep and dream about it and remember it in detail when he woke up. He told me it didn't matter if the event was his own or someone else's. It was as if he was there when the moment happened, a third-party onlooker, present everywhere at once, witnessing everything happening in real time, even if it was hundreds of years ago.

"What memories have you seen?" I asked him. He ignored my question.

Giuseppe told me you have to be sure the moments you want to discover are real events, not just someone's made-up story or something you think may have occurred. He explained that when you try to see something that never happened, it makes the body fail. This, he told me, is precisely what happened the night I went to sleep thinking about Dad and String Bean in Berlin and why I was unconscious the following morning when Mother came into my room. It was not at all lost on me that Giuseppe was saying my father's story wasn't true.

After watching my moment the night before I got sick, hearing my dad tell the story of String Bean and him, Giuseppe had enough information to dream about the moment I first heard a story about the man nicknamed String Bean. I was four years old when Dad first told me about his friend.

Now follow me here, Angela. If something happens, there is always a first time it occurred. There is always a last time, although both may indeed be the same. A second, or third, or fiftieth time may not exist...yet, or ever.

In the two weeks we did not see each other, in addition to the first time Dad told me about String Bean, Giuseppe also found the first time he told anyone a story about String Bean—it was in basic training when they were together. He saw the day Dad and String Bean met, as well as the day they last spoke. Before we even made plans to experience the same moment, Giuseppe already knew how the events transpired.

While the information Giuseppe gave me answered many questions and helped me understand so much about myself, it left me with a thousand more questions. I interrogated him, one question after another. Giuseppe barely had a chance to answer one before he was hit no inquiries. I guess you could say that was the day I became a litigator.

"How does it work? Are there others with this ability? How did you learn about everything? Will my ability go away? Will it hurt me? What can I do with it? Can I tell other people about it? Why did you reach out to me?"

Giuseppe gave me only one definitive answer: "Yes, this ability can hurt you. If not controlled, it will kill you. Of the twelve other people I have known of with this ability—and that doesn't include me and you—those who did not recognize their gift, or were unable to control it, all suffered terrible repercussions." That sounded much like me at the time. He told me that all too often, the unforgiving nature of this ability takes over before people can learn to use it correctly. Giuseppe told me that, if he had to guess, the reason this happens is similar to why a child suddenly stops breathing during the night. For no other reason than this, the muscles powering their lungs and diaphragm will fail.

Children have a highly developed sense of imagination. Sometimes, it develops before they can speak or remotely comprehend what they hear and see. Considering that most children are told stories that have no basis in reality—fairy tales of wonderment and bravery, magical creatures and far-off adventures, frightening warnings and danger—it is no wonder they sometimes have trouble differentiating between what is real and what is not. "I don't know how any of us ever even make it to our first birthday!" Giuseppe uttered in amazement.

When Giuseppe was a child, his grandfather told him all about his ability and how to use it safely. His grandfather was a doctor who did not have the ability to see moments in the past, but had learned all about it from treating a few of his patients who did. He explained what happens to you when you try to dream about a moment that never actually occurred...when you reach into darkness. He said people have different reactions. For some, the consequences manifest physically, while for others, they affect the mind. For those with physical responses, the symptoms can be tissue, muscle, or nerve damage to the arms and legs. Sometimes the results are even worse.

To make sure Giuseppe wouldn't hurt himself by making that mistake, his grandfather taught him how to determine what was factual and what was fiction. And, I must point out, Angela, determining this is not as simple as you may think. You cannot imagine how often what we believe is historical accuracy is, in fact, not that at all. We learn about the past in many ways and it is easy for the truth to be hidden. Stories, especially those that have been handed down for hundreds and thousands of years, become modified—they can be the product of someone's creative imagination, faulty memory, or deliberate falsehood.

When Giuseppe was in his late teens, his grandfather passed away. For ten years, Giuseppe had someone to guide him; now, suddenly, he was left to navigate life alone. He told me that he studied everything his grandfather had taught him. He thought about the many stories his grandfather shared and did the necessary research to determine their validity. It was while reviewing his grandfather's stories that he first saw what occurred during the Civil War, the westward expansion, and countless other events throughout history. I then asked my new friend, "So, what do I do now?"

"The next steps are up to you. Some people use their ability in ways that are not noble. For example, they use it to take advantage of others. There's a lot of things you can do when you know the truth about the past. Perhaps you learn where Mrs. Hinkle is hiding the spare key to her house. Perhaps you can get the combination to the main vault at Commercial Bank. Or, in your case, since you will be starting third grade next month, maybe you can look at the test your teacher has prepared and will be giving you in the first week of school.

"What you do with it will be your choice, but remember that there are always repercussions for ill-gotten gains. Justice will eventually prevail. For myself, I've used my ability as an opportunity to learn. What I learn from the kind of dreaming I do—living the moment as if I am experiencing it myself, watching the event unfold live—it just cannot compare to any other way of learning...not reading a book, watching a movie, or having someone tell me a story. Is that your experience as well?"

I nodded. "Mother and Dad always talk about my ability to remember all sorts of details from stories I've been told, even when they don't remember telling me those details."

"That is exactly right, Dominic. The ability to see moments of the past...well, it unlocks those events, and once unlocked, they stay with me forever. I can never close them back up." At the time, his words seemed to me like an oversimplified answer, but after more than sixty years, I can't come up with a better explanation for you.

Giuseppe and I planned to meet again the next day.

Before departing, he said, "You know, I was lucky because I had my grandfather to help me and keep me safe. I want to help you and want to make sure you do not forget what I told you. Do not make the mistake of trying to recall events that never occurred. And, I am telling you, if you do, the consequences will get worse each time. What was first a toe will then become a foot, then a leg."

Until that moment, my health problems had been a mystery to me, my parents, and my doctors. "I know you have already had your share of problems from making this exact mistake. How much more will you be able to handle? I am sorry to say, I am not sure you will be given many more chances. So, it is absolutely imperative you make certain any history you attempt to experience is factual."

Like I had for much of the day, I nodded my response, but it wasn't enough for Giuseppe.

"Tell me you understand," he insisted.

"I understand, Giuseppe. I must make sure that moments I try to visit in my dreams actually occurred."

"That, right there, is the mark of a potential scholar, my boy!" Appearing content with his first lesson, Giuseppe walked away.

I made my way home, my mind reeling with a new wealth of knowledge. Mother was none too happy that I had been gone half the day. While she understood the value of recovering on my own, she was afraid when she wasn't there to protect me. Knowing she would never understand everything a little boy needs to grow up, but not wanting her protectiveness to stifle me, Mother said, "Just make sure you are using caution, dear," and then let the matter rest. She never understood just how seriously I would heed her words, something I regret she never knew.

Later that night, Dad and I were alone in my room. He was eager to share a bedtime story, especially because we had missed the last few nights when he was supervising the late-shift construction project. When I was tucked in, he said, "So what do you want to talk about tonight, Dominic?"

"Dad, what I want to know is why didn't you tell me the truth about String Bean?" I could tell he knew immediately to what I was referring. He frowned, looked ashamed, and promptly excused himself.

"I'll be back in a moment," he said as he hastily left my room. He finally returned with a leather box. "This contains some of my favorite treasures from my time in the Army. There weren't a lot of memories from over there that made me happy. I wasn't proud of most of the things I did. There weren't a lot of things I wanted to keep from my time in the war, but I did keep some. This one," he handed it to me, "is the campaign medal I was awarded. You see here? It says EUROPEAN-AFRICAN-MIDDLE-EAST CAMPAIGN. This is what they gave us for winning the war in Europe.

"And this one, called the World War II Victory Medal, is what they gave us for being victorious over our enemy." It was a beautiful bronze medallion of Lady Liberty, hanging from a red fabric stream and surrounded by a bright double rainbow that flowed down both sides of the fabric. I gingerly held his medal in my hand, expecting it to be much heavier than it was. I turned the medal over and read the back. In the center was the inscription:

FREEDOM FROM FEAR AND WANT

FREEDOM OF SPEECH AND RELIGION

Dad told me it was awarded to those who served in the military between 1941, when Pearl Harbor was attacked, and 1946. "Everyone who served—whether alive or dead, deployed overseas or stateside—deserved recognition. Some took part in terrible combat, while many more did not have to bear that burden. Yes, everyone deserved recognition."

I reached in the box and picked up the one remaining medal. "This is called the Bronze Star," Dad said. "I earned it on Christmas day in 1944. It was the last offensive by the German forces before we pushed all the way into their homeland, what many now call the Battle of the Bulge. Our unit was in Belgium, just outside of Bastogne. We were effectively holding off the Krauts. We had stopped and formed a perimeter and were waiting for resupply. As infantrymen, we were really good at securing perimeters for the tanks. Anyway, I was part of the team guarding our battalion command post at the time we were attacked. They kept on coming all night long. We didn't lose any troops, but we killed a lot of Germans that night." My dad hung his head and closed his eyes.

I asked my dad if he personally killed any Germans that night. He reached into the box and pulled out a long knife as he told me, yes, he had. That bayonet, he explained, had been attached to a German soldier's rifle. When the soldier charged at him in the dark of night, that blade was the first thing my dad saw. With their bayonets fixed and their weapons ready, they faced each other. One of them was going to spend that Christmas night on the other's knife.

Dad heaved a deep sigh. "There but for the grace of God, I made it through and made it home to your mother." Dad never told me exactly what happened that night. Either he just didn't want to tell me, or maybe he was worried that I would try to find out for myself, in my dreams, what he had done. I never did search for his moment on Christmas day in 1944. Some experiences are better left buried. The memory that was formed on the tip of that bayonet's edge, still stained with a man's blood, will forever be one of those.

Dad saw the opportunity to change the subject and exclaimed, "Ah, this is what I was looking for!" He pulled out his dog tags and handed them to me. I marveled at the two oval disks, each with a notch on one end, dangling from a ball chain. I read one of them:

BANDALL, ANTHONY T

13268144 T42 A

SUSAN BANDALL

198 E GRAND AVE

NEW YORK NY P

Seeing my dad's name embossed on the tag made me glisten with pride. I wondered how many sleepless nights my grandmother had while he was serving; Dad always carried this necklace with him, a note that said, "Contact me at this address if anything happens to my boy." I started to hand the tags back to Dad when the other caught my eye.

BEAN, STEPHEN N

17384592 T42 O

HELEN BEAN

16 FRONT ST

TEANECK NJ P

I looked up at my dad with curiosity. He explained that he and Stephen, who became close friends early on in the war, each gave the other one of their dog tags. They agreed that if one of them should fall, the other should give one of the tags to the slain soldier's mother. They also agreed that if neither of them made it, then the tags should be given to the next of kin. It was a token of their brotherhood. Dad explained: "String Bean never made it back home. He never made it to Berlin. The mission he was sent on failed. I don't know what happened to him. All we were told was that his task force had been overrun. A week later, I was told that a few of the soldiers had been taken prisoner, or were classified as missing, and that the rest were returning to our unit. Bean's body was never recovered. I wanted to keep my promise to give his dog tag to his mother when I made it back stateside. She refused it. She wanted nothing to do with it and couldn't bear the eternal reminder. I'm so glad I didn't have to part with this treasure."

Dad held me in his arms as he sobbed softly. His story touched me so much, but I also felt angry at him for lying. I asked him—no, I insisted—"Please don't tell me another story of a moment that didn't happen." Dad heaved mightily, wiped his eyes, looked me in the eye, and vowed never to do it again.

Dad's honesty meant everything to me. Until then, I'd felt certain that he always told me the truth. He was so honest, he didn't even like to tell me fairy tales or any story that included made-up material. Mom was the same. Because of my parents' decision to present me with a strictly realistic, fact-based view of the world, as a child, I missed out on tales of knights in shining armor who slew dragons to save fair maidens. Thankfully, however, what I missed out on in fancy, I made up for in longevity; I stayed alive and am still here!

I have often wondered why my dad offered up the truth about String Bean so immediately. His knee-jerk response—telling me such a painful story and showing me the dog tags—has always made me wonder if he knew about my ability and therefore knew right away that he had to fess up. Or, was he so wrought with guilt that confessing the truth was his only option?

* * *

In 1993, before my dad had grown weak and frail, Sharon and I took my parents to Europe for their anniversary. We had a grand time touring the countryside in Spain, France, Belgium, and Germany. We visited some of the places that Dad had gone to during the war, almost fifty years earlier. For him, the trip gave him a much-needed and long-overdue sense of closure, one that allowed him to finally let go of some of the pain. I remember this one remark Dad made: "How beautiful the countryside is when it isn't on fire!"

For most of the trip, I let my parents decide where they wanted to go and what they wanted to see, but when we got to Germany, I took over the planning. Once we were there, we drove to the rural town of Gemünden. When I pulled into a small church with a cemetery, Dad said, "Son, I think Sharon and your mother would agree that we have already dragged them to enough cemeteries on this trip." I told them to be patient. As we walked into the cemetery, I pulled out a piece of paper and read it aloud.

> On the evening of 26 March 1945, Task Force Baum waited behind a hill in the American bridgehead east of the Main and south of Aschaffenburg. Two companies of tanks and infantry tried to punch a hole in the German frontline at Schweinheim. The attack was scheduled for thirty minutes, but they

encountered heavy resistance and lost two tanks. It took hours until Baum's task force could move out in the early morning hours and finally break through the German lines. The task force made good time along the Reichsstraße 26 through the Spessart Forest. They passed through the town of Lohr and later destroyed German trains. Baum didn't know that the area was the assembly area for a German division. About 0800 hours, the column reached Gemünden. The German troops were surprised by the arrival of the Americans. The town was bombed a day before and had no telephone connection, so no warnings were received. Despite no warning, a company of German combat engineers gave heavy resistance. A bridge was blown, and Task Force Baum lost three tanks and a platoon of infantry, which was captured by the Germans.

I continued to tell my family the rest of the story, although my father already knew it, probably too well. Task Force Baum pulled out in search of an alternate route to Hammelburg where there was a POW camp they intended to liberate. Here in the town of Gemünden, I explained, was where twenty infantry soldiers from Dad's unit were killed. Eighteen of them were repatriated back to the United States after the end of the conflict, and two of them were lost in the fog of war. I could see Dad's eyes starting to well up.

I continued, "The grateful townspeople of Gemünden, unsure of the proper procedure for returning the bodies of the two dead American soldiers and afraid of possible retaliation for safeguarding the bodies from German troops, buried them in this cemetery. They are buried here in unmarked graves in a part of the cemetery reserved for the most notable and influential citizens of Gemünden. The soldiers' sacrifice is quietly noted in church records."

As we walked over to the plots, I told my dad I had been able to determine from the church records the location of the grave that probably held the remains of Corporal Stephen Bean. Of course, I already knew this was the right grave. I had already seen the battle and Bean's death firsthand. I had borne witness to the tender care offered by the townspeople, people who had seen more than their fair share of blood, as they laid String Bean to rest.

I told Dad I had arranged for the excavation of the two bodies with an American committee that handles the identification and repatriation of American soldiers killed during World War II, as well as with the German government. The bodies were later returned to the United States, where they were identified as the remains of Corporal Bean and Sergeant Kevin O'Malley. Dad could not fight back the tears and asked Mother if she would get him his handkerchief from the car. When she was out of earshot, Dad stood up straight and looked me in the eye.

"Are you certain this is String Bean?"

"Yes, Dad. I am sure."

"How did he die? Did he suffer?"

"No, Dad. A sniper shot him in the head...here, just under his helmet"—I pointed to the spot—"as they approached the bridge."

Dad kneeled at the plot and placed a hand gently on the grass. In true infantryman fashion, he whispered to his friend, "Welcome back, fucker. Where's my strudel?"

Sharon never asked me what my father meant by those questions or how much he knew about my ability. I guess she believed some things should stay between a father and his son. The truth is, I don't have a goddamn clue how my dad knew to ask me those questions. I simply reflected on the story he told me about String Bean before I went to sleep that night in 1957 and decided to never tell a story of a moment that didn't happen.

Chapter 9 - Voice: Dominic

Today is March 2nd, 2019. My name is Dominic Bandall. This is session number five of Angela Grant's interview of me.

I didn't stay angry with Dad for long after that night in '57. Instead, I focused on getting as much information about my ability from Giuseppe as possible. For the next few days, I spent every possible moment with him. I know now that what I learned during that time saved my life. I practiced the techniques he had developed and refined after years of trial and tweaking. He made one thing very clear: I did not have many opportunities to fail. Making an error was not an option.

"Never go back to a time that did not exist. That is Rule Number 1, Dominic. Rule Number 1 is clear." Giuseppe kept telling me this. I knew what he was talking about because I had already made that particular mistake when using my ability and had experienced the powerful repercussions of doing so. "As horrific as the consequences of your mistakes have been, they pale in comparison to what you will experience next time, or the time after that. I've already told you, what happened to you is not uncommon. I have seen the same result with others. Use your brace as a physical reminder to never forget this one simple rule."

I knew that Giuseppe's grandfather had taught him how to use his ability safely, but I still wanted to know how he had managed to get through his life without ever searching for a nonexistent moment. He told me, "For a long time, my boy, I have to say, a lot of it was luck. How, as a child, I never fell into the trap of trying to search for Saint Nicholas making a nighttime visit, I'll never know. But, my grandfather's efforts definitely had a lot to do with my ability to focus on reality and helped me not to dream about events that did not occur. He knew what he was doing. It is all about Rule Number 1. It is that simple."

I had to ask him, "What about those other people with our ability? Where do they live? What do they do?"

"There's no one left anymore but us, my boy," Giuseppe replied in a cold voice. "They all suffered from illnesses—body failures—very similar to yours, but obviously, they got it much worse than you did. Anyhow, their deaths should not be a concern of yours. Instead of burdening yourself with them, focus on controlling what you think about, focus on reality and events you can verify are real.

Just remember, you have that one simple rule to follow. Use me as an example of how to excel with our ability."

His advice ended up becoming my salvation.

My formal lessons with Giuseppe began eighteen days before school started. Instruction, instruction, repetition. That's the best way for third graders to learn and that's the way Giuseppe taught me. He would give me specific tasks to do as I got ready to drift off to sleep at night, and in the morning, we would review what I learned. Looking back, I am sure he was surprised that I even showed up in the morning several times to meet him. A little kid with this powerful gift who does not yet have the ability to control it...well, he probably expected me to promptly hurl my body off a cliff. And honestly, he would not have been wrong to worry; not yet knowing how to harness my ability was quite dangerous. My tremendous power was also frightening and made me feel strangely helpless.

Giuseppe started by asking me to think about one event I knew had, without a doubt, occurred. I chose the moment I was born: October 9th, 1949. I focused on that moment before falling asleep that night and the following morning, when I reported back the details of my dream to Giuseppe, I realized all I had was a snapshot. I could remember certain details—where each person was in the delivery room, the awkward position mother was in while she was in twilight sleep, watching as I was pulled out of my mother's body, and even every sight, sound, and smell—but only at the precise moment the clock on the wall said 3:52 that afternoon. That was it. I saw nothing more.

"Moments," Giuseppe explained, "are defined by those who experience them." He meant that what I dreamt about, the moments I chose and the parameters of those moments, were up to me, the dreamer. In choosing to dream about the moment of my birth, I had searched for a very specific event at a particular snapshot of time. If, for example, I chose to dream about what my mother did on the day I was born, my dream would be affected by my understanding of what constitutes a day: twenty-four hours, sunrise to sunset, or something else. If I were to search for what my parents did on the day I was born, my dream would be scattered because Dad was in the waiting room and Mother was in the delivery room. Dates, of course, are human associations to a particular moment—arbitrary, many times inaccurate representations of what happened. Giuseppe taught me to focus on the moment, rather than a date or a time potentially associated with it. Scattered searches would cause, at best, confused experiences. At worst, I would risk encountering another dangerous abyss.

I used the moment of my birth to practice these techniques. After several days, I was able to define the precise moment I wanted and then experience it. So that we could compare notes, Giuseppe would also revisit the same moment I had chosen. He would review my dream and evaluate the impact of the parameters I had set. Soon, I was able to perfectly duplicate Giuseppe's experience of my moment. We discussed my mother shrieking in our apartment when her water broke, and how she grimaced during her pains of labor. We discussed what the doctor told her when he was giving her anesthesia: "It is a mixture of morphine and scopolamine. It will keep you sedated during the delivery." We both experienced the fantastic look of bewilderment on my father's face when he first came into the delivery room, and his smile when he saw Mother and his new son. I still cherish seeing Dad's joy and wide smile when he looked into my mother's eyes. The look on his face made it clear there was no place he would rather have been. His happiness was standing there with her, face-to-face.

After a few short but intense sessions, Giuseppe was pleased enough with my progress to feel comfortable sending me off into the new world of my new school. That meant I would have to assume the responsibility of following Rule Number 1 all on my own.

My final test entailed choosing a factually verified moment in the past of which I knew no details. The event I chose was the day the Declaration of Independence obtained its first signature. He instructed me to focus on one thing about the event I knew to be true. I knew for certain that the document had been signed.

On the Friday before school started, Giuseppe and I strolled through the park and discussed the results of my test. I gave him a detailed description of that momentous event. I described the dark chamber in which John Hancock stood and the almost rushed way he had signed his name. I also reported my discovery that the document had not actually been signed on July 4th, and that it had not been signed by all the signers at one time.

Proudly puffing up his chest, Giuseppe boasted, "Well done, boy! With a lot more practice and a little bit of luck, you just might see this experience through." Even then, in the early days of my ability, I felt an incredible surge of gratitude and the desire to show my thanks.

I asked Giuseppe again, "So what happens after this?"

"Just like I told you, Dominic, it is all up to you."

"No, that's not what I mean. What I mean is, what do *you* do now? You told me about the other people with our ability and what happened to them. Why do you do this? Why did you reach out to me and is there something you want me to do? Everybody wants something."

Giuseppe smiled with the satisfaction of a well-worn man finally proven right. "Dominic, I have been inspired by your potential from the first moment I saw you. The fact that you made it this far without a guide is surely an indication of your potential to use your special gift carefully and effectively. The thing is, much like we have a unique ability, there are others who possess powerful capacities of their own, and some of them do not use those gifts for good. It is important for you to know that we can be exploited by people like that."

"What kinds of abilities do they have?"

"Power, and the willingness to wield it over others; the strength to influence what people do in order to advance their own interests."

"What...who are you talking about?"

"The people who try to levy their power like this are criminals. I know people like that. In fact, they live right here in our neighborhood. And I have been a victim of the terrible things they have done. But what's important is that you know that those of us with this ability can be exploited, especially by people less scrupulous."

I listened attentively but I really didn't understand what he was talking about.

"I have tried hard to find out more about them when I sleep, but I am held back by the need to stay within the confines of moments I am certain occurred. Also, each time they find out I have more dirt on them, they see me as a bigger threat, and they push back harder. Even though these dangerous people are an ever-present threat to me and to others, I am committed to putting an end to their crimes and getting justice."

The more Giuseppe spoke, the incongruous his story sounded.

"I investigated and researched every lead to determine precisely what these lawbreakers had done, what they were still doing, and what they were planning. Then I made a bad mistake. I failed to accept the extent of their power. I saw them sitting in the coffee shop and I got so mad, I just couldn't help myself. I confronted them. I damned them for the things they had done in our neighborhood, their corruption, and vowed to right their wrongs.

"Soon after that, I was accosted by a group of them—a gang—and they gave me a severe beating. When my wife arrived at the hospital, she was so upset and frightened, so much so, I could tell she was struggling to find a reason to stay with me...to remain true to the life she had wanted with me. I was just mortified, not only because she was so scared, but because without my impetuous request for her to marry me, she wouldn't have had to be dealing with any of that. That night, as my daughter lay sleeping in her bed, she became the first member of my family to fall victim to the rage of these criminals."

"Was that Phoebe?"

Unprepared to hear her name, he winced. "I haven't heard anyone say her name for so long now. Yes. She was the first. But she was not the last. I had so much rage inside of me, but I needed to suppress it in order to focus on nailing these people. Getting justice became my reason for living. On the day we laid our beautiful little girl to rest, my wife and I reaffirmed our commitment to do just that.

"When they caught wind of the progress I was making, they retaliated, this time with greater ferocity. Their plan that time was to take everything from me. And they did. They had already taken my daughter. That time, they took my wife and my littlest child. That time, they left nothing behind but a reminder of their influence: a handbag and its scattered contents."

Giuseppe filled in many of the holes in the story Lizzy had told me. It's easy to see how a man could strike fear in the hearts and minds of others when the only thing they see is a body that once stood strong and tall crumble when faced with horrible transgressions. The neighborhood feared Giuseppe; I began to pity his circumstances.

He continued. "As much as I have lost, it hasn't diminished my desire for justice. I am as committed now as I ever was. In fact, my need is greater now than ever. Justice is needed and must prevail."

I tried to complete the rest of his thought, "...and you want justice for your family, for what they did to your family."

"No. That would not be justice, that would be revenge. There is no way that I can prove what they did to my family. I've seen their faces, but I can never get any of their names. I've seen their wicked acts of cowardice, their vengeance against me, but I have no proof. Obviously, I cannot use the moments I see in my dreams in a court of law. They would never hold up. I need to prove they committed these crimes, with hard evidence so the charges will stick.

"But I tell you, boy, that is not an easy task and the dangers and pitfalls of their world are many. Because these men live in a world of rumor, innuendo, deceit, and lies, it is difficult to investigate them. To find truthful moments—so I can safely seek them out in my dreams—takes days; to then prove that an event took place takes weeks; to figure out the correct path to follow, that takes months. This is what is causing me so much trouble. It is their camouflage. It allows them to hide. This is the web in which I am getting snared.

"Dominic, do you want to know why I sought you out? Recruitment. Recruitment of an ally who can augment my ability. In a short time, your capabilities will far exceed mine. That is why it is so important for me to train you." So now I knew; Giuseppe had not run into me by accident.

He continued, "School was everything to me. Formal education was how I learned the fundamental skills: logic, how to reason, how to listen, communicate, and how to use inference. However, I need to warn you about what they teach you. You will find that sometimes, what you learn in school, especially regarding history and science, is not always based on the truth but instead on someone's interpretation of the facts. You are the only one who can discover the truth about historical events. With your ability, you can do that. Your goal is to uncover the accurate events in history and present the evidence in such a way that it categorically proves the generally accepted version is wrong. Once you do that, your version will be, forever after, deemed the true and real history. That is justice. What people do with this information is not our concern. That is where the law comes into play. I've dedicated my life to preparing and presenting information so it will be considered factual by our legal system. Once my job is completed, enforcement rolls over to the executors of the legal system. That is justice. I need your help to find the evidence that will prove the facts.

"Don't worry if this is too complicated for you to understand fully right now. Just go and learn. In time, we will fight for justice together. For now, use them to learn what is true by yourself." After that last vague instruction, Giuseppe sent me on my way.

I never discovered what "them" referred to.

Even though I was too young to understand the enormity of the responsibility Giuseppe had laid at my feet, and there was a lot I didn't know about my ability and how to use it, I felt as if I had a general plan in place for my life. I will add that my youth and naivete ended up working in my favor. It made it easier for me not to worry about the horrid things I saw in my dreams. For one, I wasn't yet scarred and blackened by knowing how far the human race is capable of falling. And for two, when the opportunity to experience pure bliss presented itself, I was able to quickly put aside the harsh realities I witnessed in my dreams.

That day, as I turned the corner for home, that bliss presented herself! Lizzy was riding her bicycle, an adorable pink-and-white Huffy, with red and green streamers coming from the handlebars and a rose-petal basket in the front. She must've been riding around for a while, for there were dozens of black tire marks on the street between our two houses. These were, I soon realized, rubber residue her tires left every time she slammed on the brakes at full speed. Lizzy had become almost as awkward as me. We stared at each other, unwilling to move and unable to speak. This time, I broke the stalemate. "Hey, Lizzy. How's it going?" I was rather impressed with myself for my grand display of self-confidence, wit, and charisma.

Not one to be outdone, she tried to impress me with her knowledge of the Yankees...and, of course, that was just the kind of thing a kid like me considered important. She rattled off all sorts of statistics and said she thought they'd definitely make it to the World Series again that year. "The White Sox are only four games behind, but their roster is a mess. Dolby is in a slump, and Pierce gave up five runs in both of his last two games. Besides, the Yankees are on a tear. Berra's on a six-game hitting streak and the Mick is batting over three-fifty for the year."

She asked me if I wanted to come over and listen to the game that night. The Red Sox were in town, and Tommy Byrne was on the mound for New York. Even if I hadn't been so tongue-tied and had been able to respond, there wasn't a chance for me to get a word in. Even before the invitation finished coming out of her mouth, she had her next subject lined up: Did I want to go for a ride in her father's brand-new Chevrolet Bel Air convertible? "The one with a 140-

horsepower, straight-six engine. I can get him to take us for a drive when he gets home, but it can't be for too long because we are going to your house for supper. Remember?"

No, I did not remember that because it was information I hadn't yet been privy to. But nothing like that mattered to Lizzy, it definitely did not slow her down. "My dad is bringing the steaks, and your mom is preparing a garden salad." She continued to educate me. "My dad never serves vegetables when he makes dinner and your mother keeps telling my dad that growing kids need their veggies, but he never listens, so that's why she made a scrumptious salad, and she said she made extra for us to take home." After taking in a deep, much-needed breath, she continued, "My dad will be home in about ten minutes, so if you wanna go for a drive, you should make sure you're at our house." She kept talking as fast as her mind could find the words. "Well, I have to get going...'cause, look," she pointed to her knees, "I have to clean these scrapes from crashing my bike." And then...on to the next topic. She jumped off her bike, grabbed my hand and said, "You have to come here and see this." She walked over to her array of skid marks and knelt beside them. "Check this one out. I bet that slide has to be at least seven feet long. What do you think about that? I bet Jimmy or Milt never had a slide that long, huh? Milt will probably say he has, but I bet you it never happened."

I found perfection in everything Lizzy did. I was enchanted by her enthusiasm. I loved how she poured her heart into even the most ordinary task. She knew more about the Yankees and cars than any boy in our neighborhood. She could hit a stickball farther than any of them. Running, riding a bike, climbing a tree, or playing tag—no one stood a chance against Lizzy. Her eyes and her long blonde hair...I would get lost just looking at her. Sometimes, I would just stand there without saying a word, without moving...I didn't want to distract her from doing something I found particularly enchanting. There was nothing she could say that I didn't take as absolute gospel, nothing she could do that wasn't flawless and magical.

Dad always chuckled when I sang her praises, but he never ridiculed me. When I was around her, I was too shy to tell her how I felt. And anyway, I didn't even understand what I was feeling. Had Dad ever pointed out that I was infatuated—in love—with her, it would have completely deflated me. No, he never did such a thing. My crush was left to flourish in my heart.

That afternoon, as Lizzy continued her unyielding assault on the art of conversation, I just stood there, savoring being in her presence. Although I may not have understood I was in love with Lizzy, I sensed I might seem less pitiful if I acted like I was interested in things other than just her. I complimented her father on his new car as we drove around the neighborhood. I joined in the cheer when we heard on the radio that Tommy Byrne had shut down the first thirteen batters. I even managed to ask my father a question when we got to my house, although it was not well thought out: "Why did the steaks Lizzy and her dad brought have so much more marbling than the ones you get?" Dad let that one slide.

Later that night, while lying in bed, I decided I wanted to use what I had learned from Giuseppe not to impress him or receive a satisfactory evaluation, but to satisfy my own curiosity about the object of my adoration. It was truly innocent, childlike curiosity, mind you. What I wanted was to see Lizzy while she was sleeping. Preparing myself precisely the way Giuseppe had taught me, when I felt myself getting sleepy, I chose my moment: Lizzy the last night she slept. When I began to dream, my senses seemed especially sharp. I saw the order in her room. Everything was just so: every stuffed animal positioned so they all had a clear view of her, books placed neatly on the shelf...all except one chapter book lying on her nightstand, a bookmark holding the place where she had stopped reading. I could see every curve in her face, and around her eyes and lips. As she slept soundly and quietly that night, the child was innocent perfection.

When I saw Lizzy the next day, I felt as if I knew her better. I also decided I no longer wanted to keep my feelings to myself. I wanted to confess my fondness for her with the hope she might feel the same way. Our friendship would soon blossom into the incomparable bond that can form between two close childhood friends, the kind that can go so much further, the kind that can last a lifetime. But, before we could explore our friendship further, a chain of events darkened our close community and changed my life forever.

On Sunday, Lizzy and her father went to morning mass with my parents and me. That had quickly become our weekly custom after we arrived in Pelham Bay. For Mother, the tradition of going to church with the family on the Lord's day was essential if civility was to be maintained and children were to prosper. She tried to include Lizzy whenever she could. While she never intended to be a substitute mother to Lizzy, she believed that for certain things, Lizzy needed the support and guidance of a woman. Mr. Strauss appreciated any extra help he could get, although I'm not sure he was ever afforded an opportunity to refuse it.

After church, we walked down the Avenue on our way to our weekly Sunday breakfast. In front of the coffee shop, just past the steps to the subway, we encountered a disturbance. Four policemen were trying to maintain control of a crowd of onlookers who had gathered there. The cops were barking angry orders at several reporters and photographers who were covering the scene. No one seemed to be listening to them, however. Several neighborhood residents who often congregated on the Avenue were vying for the attention of the hungry newsmen, eager to tell them their stories.

We paid little attention, as we were more interested in a hearty breakfast to help us digest the longer-than-usual sermon Father O'Malley had just dished out. His "back-to-school" sermon included none-too-subtle warnings for all of us grade-school children—a combination of "trust unto the Lord all that he has created" and "do your homework, or else." None of the children were impressed with his assiduous efforts to prepare us for the mundane days that lay ahead, but parents appreciated the extra ammunition and handy verbal projectiles they could use in the next few weeks. "Remember what Father O'Malley said. Now, get in there and finish your homework."

As soon as we sat in the corner booth, Missy, the waitress, hurried over to our table with cups of hot coffee and glasses of cold milk. She considered us one of her Sunday regulars even though we had only been living there a short time. Dad asked her about the crowd down the block.

"Oh, you haven't heard yet?" She was more than happy to talk about everything she knew, especially the things we had yet to hear about. "You might be the only ones in Pelham Bay. I guess our little corner of the City is going to make the paper today. Heck, we may even make the front page! They had a shooting last night, right there in front of Russo's Espresso Shop." She pointed across the street. "You know Giuseppe? The crazy old fellow?"

My attention shot from the crowd outside to our waitress.

"Well, I guess he was up here late last night. He started yelling at all those nice old men in Russo's again. He screamed, 'I know what you did!' and 'I promise to get revenge and—'"

"No, not revenge. Justice," I said, interrupting her. My dad shot me an inquisitive glance.

"That's right, hon. Justice. He promised to get justice. So, you already know the story?"

I shook my head no.

"Of course you don't. Justice...it's all he ever hollers about. Well anyway, he got so hot and bothered that someone ended up calling the police on him. They came, but didn't do a thing. I don't know if they felt bad for him. Maybe they're tired of arresting him. It's a pity, y'know, because of everything that's happened to him, I mean."

What had happened? I wondered. What had Giuseppe done to make the police come? Had he finally found the proof he was looking for? Did he deliberately cause a scene to get the police there to deliver the justice he kept telling me was coming?

Our waitress, the town crier, went on to answer my unspoken questions.

"Well anyway, they brought him home and things finally quieted down over here, at least for a while. He must've been still pretty fired up, or maybe he was drunk, because he came back down here again, maybe about midnight." Abdicating her waitressing duties entirely, Missy put her order pad and pencil down, nudged Mr. Strauss to "skootch on over," and climbed into our booth. "I don't know what he expected all those guys to be doing at the coffee shop that late at night, but the place was closed up tighter than his whiskey bottle should've been. Sorry, hon," she reached across and waved at me, dismissing her comment.

"Anyway, there ain't much going on down here on Saturday night that isn't trouble, so if that's what he was looking for, then he came to the right place. Our delivery boys are the ones who spotted him this morning. Cops say it could've been a mugging gone wrong, maybe by one of those homeless men who ride the train all day. You know, the guys who ride until the end of the line, then at night get off to find a place to sleep. They say he was in the wrong place at the wrong time, that maybe the mugger got mad when the old man didn't have anything worth stealing. Probably not from around here because everyone knows that kook hasn't got a pot to piss in...not anymore. Sorry, hon." She was waving at me again.

"Well, whoever it was, he just shot that poor old man dead, right there on the sidewalk. Poor old kook."

I couldn't believe it. "They shot Giuseppe? Shot him dead?"

"Yeah, hon, he's dead all right. From what I heard, it was a pretty good shot. Giuseppe must've tried to get away because he turned and got hit clean on the side of the head. Made quite a mess all over the Avenue, from what I heard. Sorry, hon. Anyway," she said while shrugging her shoulders, "what are you folks gonna have for breakfast this morning?"

We just sat in silence trying to digest the horrific story. No one seemed in the mood for breakfast anymore...not after hearing about the side of Giuseppe's head spewed across the concrete.

"Well, I'm going to have some eggs. Sunny-side up with a side of bacon," Mr. Strauss announced, breaking the uncomfortable silence.

Mother snapped at him for being so nonchalant.

"Oh, come on, May! Maybe you don't know the stories about that codger. He's been crazy for a long time, well before we moved here. He was always crazy, but I guess he managed anyway."

Mr. Strauss told us that Giuseppe, in his younger days, worked as a lawyer in Manhattan. He was a federal prosecutor for over twelve years and had convicted some of the biggest mobsters in New York on racketeering, gambling, loansharking, and drug trafficking charges.

His convictions not only reduced crime in the City, but they also made him a legend. "He was a successful guy. The things he was doing were working for him...right up until his daughter died. Lizzy, what was her name?"

"Penelope."

I corrected her. "Phoebe." Everyone looked at me. "Yeah, someone told me that. I also heard Giuseppe was also trying to clean up our neighborhood because there was a lot of crime. They say he was close to solving a big case just when Phoebe was killed. They also told me that whoever killed Phoebe also killed the rest of his family because he was getting close to nailing them."

"Oh hon, now that's just crazy." Missy had quietly slid back into our booth again. "That poor kid died in her sleep, in her own house, in her own bed. They say it was no one's fault—well, maybe if his wife had her in a better crib—but really, she didn't do nothing wrong. That happens a lot, you know. Little kids dying like that. No, she didn't do nothing wrong. In fact, I think she was doing a bang-up job of taking care of her two little girls and her husband. And after little Phoebe died, she did all she could. But Giuseppe? He plain couldn't deal with it. He lost it and got worse and worse. That's when he started messing with them guys at Russo's. That's when things began to get really bad for him.

"And another thing. No way was the wife killed like Giuseppe said. She just finally got up the nerve to take her other daughter and get out of there. I heard she went to Brooklyn and her family helped her. Who knows what was going on in the crazy man's head? Maybe he just didn't want to face the reality of his daughter's death or maybe he just went crazy. And I mean it. He was crazy!"

* * *

Rule Number 1: Never go back to a time that didn't exist.

It would take me a long time to figure out the truth about what happened over the course of Giuseppe's life, but when I fell asleep and dreamed on that Sunday evening, I was able to find out how the events unfolded that caused him to die.

Russo's Coffee Shop was indeed closed that night, but it was not vacant. Three men were sitting at one of its sidewalk tables, casually sipping espresso and anisette, when Giuseppe walked up to them. He was just beginning to berate them when a fourth man walked out of the shop. At close to point-blank range, one bullet to the head, the man shut him up. Then, without saying a word, the three men casually finished the remaining drops in their cups, picked up their things, and all four walked into the shop, locking the door behind them. No one saw them again that night.

Despite what Giuseppe had led me to believe, after that night I knew he had definitely searched for a moment, or moments, that had never occurred, and it had caused him to lose his mind. By the time death called, he was indeed a crazy man. Of course, with my newfound knowledge about my friend, I had to accept the fact that other things he had told me might not have been true. As hard as that was to swallow, it didn't diminish the pivotal role he played in my life. Everything he had taught me—the lessons, the stories, his life and, yes, his death—were lifelong lessons that I couldn't have managed without. His death was also a brutal example of the compassionless and callous penalties for making that one terrible mistake.

Many years later, I would witness moments in Giuseppe's life...his bliss and his pitfalls. I'll never know the reason why Phoebe died or if she had her father's ability. If she did, had she made the mistake of breaking Rule Number 1? Did she die because she made the mistake of dreaming about a fairy tale her loving father had told her? That possibility would be enough to drive any father insane.

Searching for someone else to blame for her death may very well have been what sealed Giuseppe's fate.

It frightened me that someone like Giuseppe—a man with all the tools needed to use his ability safely—had broken Rule Number 1. Had it happened more than once? And if so, how often? Was Phoebe's death the catalyst that ultimately allowed or forced him to make the mistake he had meticulously avoided for years? Or was it something else? Was his understanding of how to navigate his ability ultimately crippled by the emotional scarring he had endured? I couldn't answer those and many other questions. When did Giuseppe's mind finally break under the weight of his delusions? Had he warned Phoebe not to search for moments that had not occurred? I knew that trying to find the moment he went crazy would not give me the information I wanted. Moreover, the moment itself, and my attempt to retrieve it, could destroy me. Giuseppe—a prime example of a man whose mind was destroyed—never let me forget Rule Number 1.

* * *

The death of the deranged man soon faded from everyone's minds. Giuseppe had no family—well, at least no blood relatives. He was buried in the potter's field on Hart Island. His house was sold at auction. All proceeds from the sale of the home and its contents went to his law school alma mater "...in the name of justice." That one instruction was all he left behind. After those matters were handled, there was never a reason to think of him again, at least for most people.

    I, however, remember.

    Let's call it an evening, Angela. We can resume in the morning.

Chapter 10 - Voice: Dominic

My name is Dominic Bandall. Today is Sunday, March 3rd, 2019. This is session number six of Angela Grant's interviews of me.

Though troubling for our community, Giuseppe's murder was, of course, no reason to delay the start of the new year. School started off with a bang for me. In math, my first class, I was assigned a seat all the way in the front of the room, right in the middle, with Karen on my left and Lori on my right. I was literally in the middle of a sea of girls...something everyone found very funny. Even though my buddies razzed me, I didn't mind where I was sitting. I only wished that Lizzy was there next to me. Apparently, I was the only boy who hadn't yet figured out how to avoid being the lone male centerpiece.

Social studies was my next class. When Mr. Price directed me to sit in the front, once again surrounded by girls, I couldn't believe it. My heart sank with a thud as I lowered myself into my seat. As I was rummaging around in my bookbag, I heard Mr. Price direct someone to sit next to me. I looked up and...Lizzy! Oh, I nearly leapt for joy! The thought of spending the entire school year right next to her...well, naturally, social studies became my new favorite subject. I still love it. It looked like it was going to be a good year for me.

I was relegated to the front of the room and surrounded by girls in my other classes too—science, English, and health. It took the boys about two weeks to realize that it was I, not them, who had won the lottery. I spent my days surrounded by girls while their days were spent dodging spitballs, passing around baseball cards, and watching me having the time of my life in the front row. Every giggle I elicited from the girls, every time one of them would lean in close to ask me a question about the lesson, every press of a palm against my shoulder—all of that cemented my standing as The Luckiest Guy in Pelham Bay.

I worked hard to do well in school, inspired in large part by the things Giuseppe taught me during our short time together. I was aware of what happens when you don't learn how to differentiate fact from fiction. I discounted anything I couldn't personally validate. Fear of the unknown was my strict teacher. Learning became my truth.

I remembered what Giuseppe had taught me: your teachers and schoolbooks will present what someone, at some point in time, wanted to establish as factual—but that doesn't mean everything happened the way they said it did, or that it happened at all. He taught me that I am the only one who can determine the truth about what happened in the past. To do that, I relied on my schoolbooks, not because I accepted them as fact but because they gave me a starting point, if you will, to do my own research. At night, my textbooks acted as a catalyst for a flood of new information—the rise of a second sun. The discoveries I made started slowly and innocently, as I had only the slightest grasp of what my mind could do.

Giuseppe had taught me that to determine what was fact and what was fiction, I had to find the first occurrence of an event, but only events I knew for a fact had occurred. I spent weeks reviewing specific things I had learned in school and in my textbooks, and then I would dream about them. To practice the process, I would, for example, start with the first time Mrs. Herndon taught me the addition and subtraction tables—something I knew for a fact had happened—and then go back to the first time she taught anyone those tables—she was a math teacher so I knew that had happened—and then back to the first time she herself studied those tables—which of course she would also have done. Each moment I was able to verify allowed me to safely explore the next moment. This fact-checking process inadvertently brought with it a vast amount of additional knowledge—information that dwarfed the contents of our simple third-grade textbooks.

I didn't limit my fact-checking to only one subject, or one topic; I did it in every class, with everything we were taught. Validating my teachers' "facts" was more important to me than focusing on any one subject. For the time being, the raw information in my textbooks was the limit of my curiosity.

I could spend more time discussing my education, but I don't think there's much of importance beyond what I have already mentioned. Last year, when one of my assistants was preparing a report for my foundation, he researched my early years in school. What he found was rather in-depth. He even found a scan of my last third-grade report card from that 1957–58 school year! My homeroom teacher had been Miss Luff. Miss Patricia Luff.

I have an interesting story about Patricia Luff. Years later, after completing her Ph.D. in child psychology, she wrote a book entitled *Prodigies: Identification, Development, and Exploitation in Our Public School System.* In it, she proposed a system for developing protocols that would ultimately ensure the educational success of our students. It was a superficial attempt to argue for the establishment of one centralized school system that could withstand the destructive nature of the counterculture revolution taking place during the late

'60s and early '70s. It never sold well. Years later, in the spring of 1982, Dr. Luff wrote an article for the *New York Times* entitled, "When Justice Needs a Hand," about my successful representation of public interests in the 1981 Abscam case. In it, she described how much of the information I discovered and gave to the FBI had helped convict thirty-three politicians, seven of whom were sitting members of Congress when they were indicted. Besides being an exposé on the eight people whose lives were shattered by the scam, Dr. Luff's article explained that my systematic, effective, and ruthless tactics—finding the truth, linking seemingly random connections, zeroing in on only what could be proven—validated her theory that schools should "groom prodigies" and "construct models of citizenship." It was difficult for her to connect "dots" she couldn't possibly have imagined!

I digress. Where was I? Still in 1957. I did not consider myself a prodigy. To others, I was still the new kid in the neighborhood. However, I was also known as a rare bird because of my uncanny knack for remembering things.

I was dedicating five to six nights a week to learning about and verifying the information I was being taught in school. Sunday nights, at the very least, were always set aside for Lizzy. In my dreams, I would innocently watch her as she slept soundly through the night. Sometimes, I would keep myself awake as long as possible so my designated moment for my dream—"the last day Lizzy went to sleep"—would take place on the same evening I was dreaming about her. I would also recall things she did during the day. I would watch the look of grit and determination on her face as she swiftly raced and beat the fastest boys, often by as much as three strides. Thursday—when she had two hours of after-school classical voice-training classes that her father insisted on—was the day she hated, and the day I loved, the most. She would much rather have been outside running and jumping or hitting a ball. I often asked her to sing a song to me, but I never received one. Had she agreed, I could have happily watched it again and again in my dreams for years without ever growing tired.

 I'm not sure how Lizzy would have reacted to my invasion of her privacy. I'm sure Giuseppe would not have approved and would probably have been quite angered. I was too young to understand how my behavior affected others. The way I saw it was, if I had verified that a moment was real, what harm could come from seeing it one more time?

The answer to my foolish question was something I was destined to discover.

In the fall, shortly after my eighth birthday, we were learning about the US presidents in social studies. As part of the project, Mr. Price assigned each of us a president; we were supposed to put together a five-minute presentation on them and present it to the class. Mr. Price made a big show of assigning presidents to students. He would call out a student's name, remove one of the thirty-four little portraits off the wall and hand it to them in a dramatic fashion. "Master Nickolossy, you are assigned Theodore Roosevelt, the twenty-sixth president of our United States." Mr. Price remained silent until he called the next name.

I remember thinking—no, I remember praying—that I would get Eisenhower. I knew Dad and I would have so much fun working together on a report of our favorite president. As each new president's portrait was untacked from the wall, I anticipated hearing the words: "Master Bandall, you are assigned Dwight David Eisenhower, the thirty-fourth and current president of our United States."

My heart pounded in anticipation as Mr. Price stood in front of President Eisenhower, removed his portrait, walked right toward me, walked right past me, stopped at the next desk, and said, "Miss Strauss, you are assigned Dwight David Eisenhower, the thirty-fourth and current president of our United States." I hung my head, barely able to look up when he announced, "Master Bandall, you are assigned Abraham Lincoln, the sixteenth president of our United States."

I boiled. "Lincoln? What the heck am I supposed to do with Lincoln?"

For the rest of the day, I was full of gloom. Not even Lizzy was able to break me out of it. As we walked home, she asked, "Hey, Dominic, you got Lincoln, right? You saw I got Eisenhower? Pretty cool, huh? He's even still president...I think! Hey, did your dad say he was in the war with Ike? Is it disrespectful to call him Ike? Does your dad know him? Maybe your dad can give me some ideas for my project. Can you ask him if he'll help me?"

I muttered an acknowledgment of some sort, said goodbye, and walked the short distance home by myself. When Dad asked me during supper how my day went, I instantly unloaded. "I so much wanted to get President Eisenhower, Dad. I know there's so much I could've done if I'd got him. But Lizzy got picked instead. She doesn't even know anything about him. She doesn't even know he's still president, and she doesn't know what he did during the war. But I know! I know from your stories and from all the stuff we've read. I should be the one to report on Eisenhower!"

Dad frowned. He seemed sympathetic to my plight. But, when I told him who my president was, he said, "Lincoln? That's wonderful! He's my favorite president." I looked up from my plate of mashed potatoes and gravy. "Yes, sirree! Lincoln was a great president. Did you know he was the one who freed the slaves? Yep, he did it with the...um...what's it called, May?"

"The Emancipation Proclamation," Mother said, using her napkin to discreetly hide her smile.

"That's right, the Emancipation Proclamation. He proclaimed all the slaves were free, even the ones down South. Now that was during the Civil War, when the North and the South were fighting each other. They were fighting because of slavery. Yep, Lincoln gave a great speech, although I don't really know what he said in the speech."

Dad got my attention. He could always grasp on to the tiniest of threads and spin them into a magical tale for me.

"Could you recite one of Lincoln's speeches for your project?"

"I don't know. The only instruction we were given was to do a presentation."

"Well, I think you should give a speech. Lincoln made some great speeches. You could do the Gettysburg Address. He gave that speech after one of the big battles in the Civil War. 'Four score and seven years ago.' That would really light a fire under the class!"

"Lincoln? He's one of your favorite presidents?"

"Not one of my favorites. He is my favorite." That was it. Dad's enthusiasm was all I needed to make Abraham Lincoln my favorite president as well.

I also asked Dad if he would help Lizzy with President Eisenhower. "She wants you to tell her a story about when the two of you were in the war together." Dad said he'd be glad to help Lizzy learn about his second-favorite president.

I began to do the research for my presentation. I read in my textbook about the Civil War and the Gettysburg Address, but there wasn't much value in those texts. The next day, I asked Mr. Price if he had any other books I could read on the subject. He gave me a few age-appropriate books on Abraham Lincoln and the Civil War, and with his trademark flair for the dramatic, he warned: "Be careful what you read in these pages of history. There is a danger in learning too much, Master Bandall." He was mocking my diligence and curiosity, but I heeded his warning for reasons far too frightening for him to comprehend: I had seen in my dreams the carnage and annihilation caused by war. I assured him I would exercise care. He sent me off with the books—children's books that turned out to be dumbed-down and creative renditions of some the darkest days in our nation's history.

While I wanted to obtain as much information as possible in the three weeks allotted, I knew I had to be careful not to venture into any moments that were not factual. I wanted Giuseppe, wherever he was, to know I was heeding Rule Number 1. I also wanted to make the best use of one of the most practicable facets of my ability: my powers of observation. I never missed a single detail—not a sound, sight, or feeling.

As I began to read the first book, the history it described, both the text and the little drawings and paintings, seemed to be presented in a highly civilized, antiseptic, and emotionless way.

A child born in a simple log cabin. A tall, slender president, delivering powerful speeches from a podium, looming over great crowds. A man driven to fight for the rights of all men, white and black. A president who led his country through a terrible civil war and who united our nation. A man who freed the slaves. A man shot and murdered in a theater, his loving wife by his side.

I didn't know how or where to look to determine what was factual and what was not. After the first book, I flipped through the pages of the second, then the third. They all gave short, bland accounts of a very complex period, and taught children about history without revealing the actual darkness of what really happened. As I drifted off to sleep that night, I kept thinking about the stack of books on my desk, and page after page of text and pictures I couldn't comprehend.

The next morning, I awoke refreshed and energetic. It was one of the first times I could remember feeling so entirely peaceful. Mother had prepared a breakfast of scrambled eggs, bacon, and fresh-baked bread, lightly toasted and slathered in butter. She knew I had worked late into the night and said, "A growing boy needs plenty of good food to feed his mind." And boy was I famished! I quickly devoured the entire breakfast.

After dressing, I brushed my teeth, made final adjustments to my ankle brace, and grabbed my bookbag. When I reached for the stack of books on the floor, I was suddenly overcome by a flood of data rushing throughout my brain. I knew every word on every page of the books, every detail, every image...and I had only skimmed them! That was the first time I realized the extent of my ability to remember and recall. I later found out that once I read, saw, or even overheard something, it was there to stay, seared forever into my memory. At the time though, I didn't understand what I had just discovered about myself, so I brushed it off, raced down the stairs, and yelled to my father, "Dad, what's a score?"

"What? Not understanding your question, Dominic."

"A score. As in 'four score and seven years ago.' I read it in one of the books. What does it mean?"

"It means twenty. One score is twenty years. When President Lincoln said, 'Four score and seven years ago,' it's just math. Four times twenty years is eighty years. Add seven more years and you get eighty-seven years. That's from the Gettysburg Address. When was it written?"

"In 1863." I had read it in every book.

"Yes, that's right—1863. So eighty-seven years before 1863 was 1776. That was when our founders wrote the Declaration of Independence, on July 4th, and when the United States became a nation. The president was using fancy talk to say 'eighty-seven years ago our fathers found upon our continent a new nation.'"

I let the accuracy of his single date slide but felt it necessary to correct his verbiage. "No, Dad! It is 'our fathers brought forth, on this continent, a new nation, conceived in liberty, and dedicated to the proposition that all men are created equal.'"

Dad laughed. "That's right. Geez, you're smart. You know, memorizing words is one thing—it is fine—but understanding what that stuff means is even more important." He planted in me something valuable that day. Over time, I would better comprehend the importance of understanding what I learned, not only for my own benefit but to share the information with others, to teach others. So, for the next two weeks, I did just what my father suggested: I tried to understand the meaning of everything I read.

Using Giuseppe's techniques, I began to try to figure out what had and what had not happened in Lincoln's past. I started with something that I believed to be a fact that had occurred: the president presented a speech in Gettysburg in 1863, at the dedication ceremony for the Gettysburg National Cemetery. It was four months after the horrific battle had claimed over forty thousand lives. I learned that Lincoln, opting for brevity on that cold morning, made massive cuts to his original draft. By the time Edward Everett, who spoke before Lincoln, finished his painfully long oration, Lincoln had discarded all but two pages of his speech. And, he ended up using just a fraction of that. In the solitude of his staging tent, the president read his speech aloud four times.

I discovered that when Lincoln left the tent, he did not get up on the stage as is usually claimed, but instead, walked out and stood on the ground among the masses—the weary soldiers and attendees who had come for the dedication ceremony. Standing in the crowd, Lincoln barely stood out, but when he began to speak, it was as if the ground began to shake. Everyone stopped what they were doing and listened intently. Though only two minutes long, Lincoln's speech ignited a fire in me, just as it did to so many others long ago. I researched some of his other great speeches, but none compared to the brilliance of the Gettysburg Address.

I couldn't bring myself to endure witnessing his assassination in my dreams. The depictions of this calamitous event in drawings and paintings—a man standing behind the president and pointing a gun at him, Lincoln's top hat comically jumping off his head, his arms and legs splayed in front of him—were enough for me to know I did not want to experience it. I couldn't face his assassination, so the Gettysburg Address became the focus of my presentation for Mr. Price.

On the day of the assignment, I felt much like Lincoln did: uncertain about what I would say and scrambling to revise my speech at the last minute. My plan was to follow Lincoln's playbook. I wanted to show the same oration skills he did when he faced his weary crowd, but in my case, my weary onlookers were bored classmates, eager to finish a project that had dragged on too long. I wanted them to stop everything they were doing and listen, just like Lincoln's crowd had. My goal was not to make the people rally and cheer but, like Lincoln, to make them so impressed with my words, they would want to pass the message on to others.

I began my presentation, focusing on the few scattered minutes while Lincoln was preparing his address. I described how Lincoln walked out of the tent, disregarded the stage, and walked slowly out into the thick of the crowd to deliver his speech. I walked between the desks, into the center of our classroom—then I repeated his speech, word for word:

"Four score and seven years ago our founding fathers brought forth onto our continent this new nation, which is conceived in liberty and dedicated to the proposition that all men are created equal.

"Now we are engaged in this most terrible of civil conflicts, testing how long that nation, or any nation so conceived and so dedicated, can endure. We are met on a great battlefield today; a battlefield of that war. We have come to dedicate this portion of that field as a final resting place for those who here gave their lives that that nation might live.

"But, in a larger sense, we cannot dedicate, we cannot hallow, we cannot consecrate this ground. The brave men, both men living and men dead, who struggled here, have consecrated it, far above our meager power to add or detract. Nor will men who will plow and seed these fields many years from now, nor the families who will reap their bounty, nor the children with whom stories of the struggle are but a faded memory. The world will little note, nor long remember what we say here, but it can never forget what they did here. It is for us the living, rather, to be dedicated today to the unfinished work, which they who fought here have thus far so nobly advanced. It is rather for us to be here dedicated to the great task remaining before us—that from these honored dead we take increased devotion to that cause for which they gave the last full measure of devotion—that we here highly resolve that these dead shall not have died in vain—that this nation shall have a new birth of freedom—and that government of the people, by the people, for the people, shall not suffer for the ground on which we stand."

My classmates seemed impressed by my presentation and were quiet as I spoke. Mr. Price, while satisfied with my presentation skills, objected to what he called my "artistic interpretation of history." He told me, "You cannot create your own variation of events when it comes to history. Leave those made-up versions to fiction. This part of our history is well documented, Master Bandall. You have read what happened and what the books teach us Lincoln said in his speech. There is no room for you to create your own version of words for the entertainment of your friends." Jimmy and Milt chuckled.

"I didn't make any of it up, Mr. Price," I told him. "The books you gave me are wrong." I explained that the speech in our textbook had been written by Lincoln *after* he gave the Gettysburg Address, while he was on the train going back to Washington. I explained that the speech didn't elicit cheers and cries, but rather somber reflection. And that he removed his silk top hat before beginning the speech. I repeated how he didn't stand at a podium but on the ground in the middle of all the soldiers and spectators. I finally told him there are five versions of the Gettysburg Address, all of which vary slightly from each other, but I assured him that not one of those five was the actual speech Lincoln gave that day.

None of my efforts swayed Mr. Price. His commitment to the textbook version of history, combined with my refusal to budge from the facts as I knew them, put my grade for the project at serious risk. And yes, I got a failing grade, but that is not what bothered me. What disturbed me was that a teacher, someone supposed to be fair and inclusive in their understanding of history, would be so inflexible.

That night, Dad did his best to comfort me. "Son," he said, "history is what is written in our books." I started to interrupt, but he cut me off. "Now, I know this will be hard for you to understand. What you read in history books is often what someone or a group of people has decided is the 'official' story—what they say is the truth. And also, it can be challenging to know what the truth is and what it is not. There are many reasons why there is a difference between the facts of what actually occurred and what finds its way into our version of history. The truth is, history gets modified and changed over the years for many reasons. Sometimes it is deliberate, and sometimes it is inadvertent. Sometimes, those who tell stories about the past have little or no firsthand knowledge of, or experience with, the events they are describing. Sometimes, people have personal or political reasons to not share some of the true versions of an account. Maybe they did something wrong for what they saw as the greater good, and would rather not share, or can't even remember it themselves. Often it is a different interpretation of what happened; sometimes it is propaganda. These are only some of the ways accounts of history can veer sharply from the facts.

"There are thousands of books on World War II, many of which say our fight was a noble, worthy cause against an enemy whose only agenda was to destroy us. That is true, for the most part, but let me tell you one thing: if the Germans had ended up being victorious in Europe, our history books would tell a very different story. Many facts about the war and its causes would have a different interpretation." In my mind, however, there was no interpretation of fact.

"Then why do we bother calling it history? Why don't we just call it stories? That's what history really is, isn't it?"

I didn't even know what argument I was trying to win.

"History is indeed storytelling, but to know if it is factual or not, you first need to understand who the storyteller is and what their motives are. There is a purpose behind every event we retrace and share. Some stories are told to entertain, some to explain or instruct, others serve up morals, others are for reference. It's up to the storyteller to determine the purpose. Some choose not to include the details of an event because specific details are easy to dispute, and they don't want uncertainty to detract from their intended message."

I must have looked confused, so Dad tried again. "With the Gettysburg Address, to many people, it doesn't matter which specific words Lincoln actually said that day. What was his message that day?" We both were silent until I realized Dad expected an answer from me.

"I don't know."

"The message President Lincoln wanted to share in his speech was the value of the sacrifices made by the soldiers who died on the Gettysburg battlefield. We didn't truly listen when he said, 'The world will little note, nor long remember what we say here.' Instead, we focused on the words, we focused on the details of the image we created, and we overlooked the meaning. And as a result, the unfinished work of those dead soldiers remains incomplete."

I began to understand that Dad was sharing his own feelings of discontent as one of the many soldiers who had suffered because of the mistakes people made. All men are created equal, but it's after that that we make mistakes. Equality gives way to hierarchy, which gives way to segregation and disunion.

I asked him, "So what am I supposed to do if something like this happens again...if I am in this same kind of situation?"

"You're a smart boy, Dominic. Probably smarter than I even realize. It's up to you to decide what's true. There is much to be said for learning the facts of what actually occurred in the past, but it's up to you to determine what is important, much like the authors of your textbooks did. As we have discussed, the facts of history are all too often passed over to send a specific message. Maybe the facts conflict with the meaning the storyteller is delivering. Maybe including something like a factual timeline dilutes the value of a message. And ultimately, if people do not trust that an event has been accurately depicted, it causes them to doubt those telling the story and creates fear.

"And son, maybe one day you can correct the historical accounts by proving that some of the so-called 'facts' are not facts at all. Unfortunately, though, once an account finds its way into the common record and into history books, it is exceedingly hard to undo it."

I understood what he was saying, but it made me realize that I had a big problem, one that made me feel rather hopeless. When he said I might uncover the truth of the past, I assume he was referring to examining documents, reading accounts, checking archaeological data, and things like that. But my approach to finding the truth was based on the firsthand knowledge I got in my dreams. If that kind of knowledge would never pass muster, if it were considered the same kind of dubious information every other child "learns" from their dreams, what was the point?

"So, the history books are wrong, but correcting them has no value?"

"Correcting history always has value to those who need the truth," he told me.

Only to those who need the truth. It was difficult for me to grasp why everyone didn't have my same need for the truth. This was 1957. To many, the American way of life was an ideal, a way of life that was envied the world over. To many, our government, our laws, our morals, would continue to prevail because we were right.

Many others think knowledge supersedes all power. I believe that to be true. The two realities emerge when information is defined. To some, knowledge is the elimination of uncertainty. To others, it's the grasp of the unknown, the embrace of conjecture, and the search for truth. Latching on to comfort while calling it truth only leads us down a vile path of cause and effect.

When I think about what I went through in those early days...well, it was astonishing. I had to learn all about the mechanics of my ability, all the while avoiding the potentially fatal repercussions of making a mistake. And Giuseppe! He taught me how to identify pitfalls, even as they were ravaging his own mind. And my dad...to this day, how much he knew about my ability is unclear. His love was my lifesaver.

You may think it's quite a feat that at such a young age I was able to avoid dreaming about anything but factual events. But it was natural for me because I was taught to keep my imagination in check and because my parents never filled my head with illusion. Also, I quickly learned how to differentiate between fact and fiction. What was once curiosity of how something happened soon became a question of whether it happened at all. Soon I had trouble separating the two different worlds: the world based on historical facts as they are documented in books, and the fact-based world to which my ability gives me firsthand knowledge. I wasn't sure which was a more truthful portrait of the past. I also knew the knowledge obtained from the dreams of an eight-year-old could never compete with the "authority" of the information contained in our history texts. So, for the time being, to preserve my sanity, I decided to turn to my schoolbooks, resort to rote memorization, and spew back information that would appease my teachers.

There is no better way for kids to gain favor with adults than by repeating information they have decided is valuable for you. I must admit, I enjoyed winning praise from my teachers for learning their lessons so well. I threw myself into it. I learned tricks to retain everything they taught me. I read the books and then experienced firsthand in my dreams the events they referenced, although first, of course, I used Giuseppe's techniques for determining if something they taught me was a moment that ever occurred at all.

It wasn't long before I discovered I didn't even need to read the books. To remember any of the content, all I had to do was flip through the pages, create an image in front of me, and then experience that moment in my sleep. Everything I learn in my dreams becomes permanently etched in my mind, available for recall on demand. All of it stays with me forever.

As a result of this newfound skill, I hardly had to participate in class anymore. I just observed. The next day, or the next week, I was well versed in whatever I had been taught. All I needed was the time and effort to create a moment I could then dream about. Over time, the moments I chose became less specific and were composed of more extended periods. The limit I had was the capacity to experience just one moment each night.

Chapter 11 - Voice: Dominic

Today is March 3rd, 2019. My name is Dominic Bandall; this is session number seven in my continuing interview with Angela Grant.

Within two years—by the time I was ten—I had mastered the ability to perfectly recall everything I learned. By that point, *savant* would have been a more appropriate description of me than *prodigy*. The only thing holding me back was the slow pace at which I was taught. I found the monotonous routine at school tiresome, but the painful lessons of the past forced me to develop and stick to a rigid protocol.

None of it was easy for me. In fact, I do not wish my ability on anyone else. I couldn't indulge in fancies of imagination. I was denied the ability to wish, for such gains are often unrealistic. To stay safe, my only option was to embrace nothing. Dad noticed my apathy and, to inspire me, he suggested that we once again tell each other stories, but of course, I couldn't indulge in that kind of imagination anymore.

There was only one remedy, and it was my salvation: Lizzy. I was still absolutely enamored with her. That first crush, that innocent puppy love, that beautiful time before your mind gets clouded...it is so precious. Within the naivete of youth, I spent most of my time focusing on Lizzy. She ate breakfast with us most of the time, as her father usually left early for work, so I would start my days by gazing out the bedroom window, eagerly anticipating her arrival. I would time it so I was magically at the bottom of the stairs just at the moment she walked through our front door. That morning, Lizzy smiled at me when I met her. "Wow, nice timing again, Dominic!" I think she was on to me but, fortunately, she never gave me flak about it. I always wondered if she was as shy as I was. That was the thing about Lizzy and me: we never had awkward conversations or even tenuous moments of silence.

We had a routine in the morning. After breakfast, on our way to school, we would talk briefly about our classes before switching over to Lizzy's favorite subject: what we would do after school. She had so many interests! There was nothing the girl didn't want to try. And she excelled at everything, be it stickball and basketball, taking center stage in neighborhood dance and theater performances, or scouring the park in search of the perfect spot to sit and read.

Although Lizzy always encouraged me to join her, my brace sometimes interfered. That didn't stop me from trying. I never could run as fast or for as long—but, then again, who could? Anyway, I was almost as content to just watch and admire her. Her self-confidence, her brazen disregard for the possibility she might not be the best at something, her victory in every encounter...well, all of it was mesmerizing.

On our way home from school one Friday afternoon, while Lizzy was going on about our packed schedule of weekend activities, I interrupted her. "I have to ask you something. Why are you so nice to me? The guys in our class razz me about you. They say I'm your pet project. I know they're only kidding, but is it true? I mean, the doctors say I'm always going to have to wear this brace, meaning that there are a lot of things I can't do. I know you spend a lot of time over at our house, and my mom takes special trips with you, but, you know, you don't have to be nice to me just so you can come over and stuff. Dad says neighbors do that kind of thing for each other anyway." It was awkward for me to bare my soul like that, but I couldn't stand the skepticism I had begun to feel about Lizzy's reasons for being my friend.

I was afraid that tantrum had just given her the perfect out, but she looked right at me and said, "You're such a doofus, Dominic! You're a doofus and all your buddies are even worse than you. Jimmy only makes fun of you because last summer I told him I wouldn't be his girlfriend. I like being around you because you are smart and you know so much. Sure, you can't run that fast but if I asked you who the fastest Yankee is, you would probably know the answer right off the top of your head."

"Well this year it's definitely Maris, but everybody knows—"

She cut me off. "Exactly my point. And you can probably tell me how fast Lou Gehrig was in 1926, or any other statistic. You know everything there is to know about the Yankees. You can probably name every bone in our skeleton, even though we only discussed it one time in science class, and it was over a month ago. I'm sure you can tell me exactly what happens on page ninety-two of *Moby Dick*. I don't know how you do it. I also like that you don't act as if you're smarter than everyone else." As Lizzy showered me with praises, I hardly listened to her. I just stood there lost in her eyes. Only later did I hear the beautiful things she said. "I like to watch you at your desk when we are taking a test. You sit there and pretend it is soooo hard, and after you finish, while everyone else is still working, you sit there and look like you're daydreaming. I wonder what you're thinking about. Sometimes I imagine you're thinking about me, about the time

I beat all the boys in dodgeball, about the time I pitched that no-hitter. Y'know, sometimes I play so hard because I want to impress you. I want you to be proud of me. When I have my singing recitals, you're the only one in our class who comes to watch me. I try so hard to get my voice, my words, and my tone perfect just so you'll be proud of me." It occurred to me that we were two sides of the same coin: freshly minted and equally valuable to each other, while on the surface, we looked so different. We continued walking without talking. Then she said, "Sometimes I do stuff hoping it will make you proud of me, or at least keep you entertained enough so you'll want to keep hanging around."

At that time, even though I was still dreaming about her sleeping, I was doing it less often. It's embarrassing for me to talk about today...to reveal that I intruded that way. Now, of course, I know my behavior was immoral. It was wrong and I'm ashamed of my actions. But, at that age, I had no concept—no understanding—of privacy. To me, privacy only meant something I chose to keep to myself. No one else had the luxury of privacy. All I had to do was to have the desire to watch something and I could see any man's darkest moments, their most embarrassing secrets. My childishness was the worst invasion of privacy of all.

* * *

Several months after Giuseppe's murder, I decided to take another look at that dark night. I wanted to know more about the man who had killed my friend. I researched everything connected with the moment: what the shooter did on the day before the crime, the day he came into possession of that damn gun, the instant he moved to kill Giuseppe.

I discovered that it was not a heat-of-the-moment killing. The men in the coffee shop planned the murder three days before they carried it out. They knew Giuseppe would go to the shop to rant and rave, to accuse them of killing his wife and child. The old men would laugh at him behind his back. They joked, "We gotta find the bastard who really killed that girl and give 'em a hundred bucks." To them, Giuseppe was crazy and his ravings were ridiculous. Ridiculous, that is, until he started detailing their other criminal activities.

I saw them sitting in the coffee shop discussing the situation. They couldn't figure out how he had such accurate information on them and knew so much about their activities. In one conversation, they mentioned the weeks they had spent trying to figure out who he was working with. But none of that mattered, they decided. Giuseppe simply knew too much. Their police contacts told them there were no signs of, or plans for, an investigation because no one was taking the crazy man seriously, although they figured that would not be the case for long. Giuseppe had to go. If there were a rat in their organization, they'd weed him out eventually, but Giuseppe had to go now. So, they hired a skell from Melrose named Gino and told him the hit had to happen three days later. He used a Smith & Wesson M&P .38 Special that had "gone missing" from a police evidence box. I must've watched Giuseppe's murder a dozen times before I was able to put the whole thing together.

Watching his death took a terrible toll on me...on my youth. But by that point, I had witnessed so many deaths and murders and wars in my dreams that I began to believe I was inured to the sight of blood. I'm sad to say, death no longer horrified me.

I learned several important things after researching Giuseppe's murder. I realized I had to avoid experiencing more death and suffering—to preserve my own sanity. I had seen enough of it in my short life to last a thousand lifetimes. If I had to witness death, I would look at it as merely a historical event that I would observe, note, and place aside.

I also discovered there were no boundaries for me, that nothing stood in the way of my ability. If I needed to find a truth, the world's energy was there for me to rifle through. Another person's privacy was never an obstacle; for me, other people's privacy did not exist in my search for the truth. I convinced myself that moments with Lizzy were different. I carefully formulated what I was searching for before I fell asleep so I could just sit beside her as she slept. I justified my behavior by convincing myself I was protecting her...that I was there for her security.

I also learned there wasn't anything I could do to avenge Giuseppe's murder. I was an eight-year-old boy with no hard evidence. I knew the police would laugh at me and scoot me on back home. And even if I did get hard evidence of the murder, I knew my parents would find out, and that was something I could not risk. They would fear for my safety, and I would fear for theirs.

My books and the sight of my love while she slept...those were the only boundaries I had in 1960.

* * *

Summer was fast approaching, and vacation plans were already being made. The gang had picked teams for the first week of stickball and parents were busy planning activities and schedules. Who would be making the kids' lunches? Who would be driving the kids to Orchard Beach?

All that remained of the school year was a week of final exams.

Because I didn't have to study, I spent my time in school daydreaming about Lizzy, my afternoons helping Lizzy cram for exams, and my nights watching Lizzy sleep. I would continue to carefully choose the precise moment I wanted to see: the last night Lizzy slept. The adjustment protected me from making more embarrassing intrusions, such as seeing Lizzy getting ready for bed. I made that mistake only once. I know how odd it sounds, but all I wanted was to see my friend sleeping peacefully.

The Sunday evening before our first exams, I planned to stay up as late as possible so my moment with Lizzy would be that same night. As I drifted off, I anticipated a pleasant night of watching my friend sleep, but when I awoke the following morning, I could tell right away something hadn't gone according to plan. Had I made a mistake and broken Giuseppe's rule? I tried to remember exactly what I had thought about right before I fell asleep. I was sure I had focused on the last time Lizzy slept. What I dreamed about, however, was entirely different. As Lizzy slept, her slow, relaxed breaths barely made the sheet rise and fall. After only an hour—an hour and three minutes, to be exact—the dream ended with a ferocious bang and crash that instantly woke Lizzy up. I didn't know what happened and was worried.

My concern increased when Lizzy didn't show up for breakfast. I grabbed a piece of toast to take with me, and as I headed out of the house, I assured Mother that Lizzy's absence was probably a case of pretest jitters. She seemed satisfied with that explanation, but I was not as confident. I rushed to Lizzy's house. Oh, was I relieved to see her sitting on the porch. She seemed ready to go, but when she looked up at me, she didn't get up.

Cautiously approaching, I called out, "Hey, Lizzy! Whatcha doing? You didn't come for breakfast. You okay?" I wasn't sure she heard me, so I walked up to the porch steps and placed my hand on her shoulder.

"Liz? You okay?" My touch startled her. Now alert, she turned her face away from me and muttered, "Yeah. Fine. Let's go."

That was it. She didn't say another word as we walked to school. Hoping to distract her from whatever was wrong, I was a chatterbox. I talked about Mr. Ross's history test and how I was positive Lizzy would ace it. I talked about next week's stickball matchup, and how excited I was to finally be on one of the teams because Milt would probably have to go to summer school for at least two classes, so they'd be down a man. I talked about going to the beach, about signing up to take singing classes with her in the fall. I kept it up all the way to school. Nothing worked.

When school was out, Lizzy didn't wait for me, as she always did. I saw her bolt out the door. She was so fast, I knew there was no way I could have caught up, let alone kept pace with her if I had.

It's strange…the thoughts that go through your head when you are a child. Here was my friend, clearly hurting. Something had changed her happy-go-lucky attitude into a sullen brood, and what was my response? I became defensive. Was she angry at me? Did she think I had done something wrong? I racked my brain but couldn't come up with anything. Maybe she was mad at me because she knew I would do better on the exams than she would…I didn't think there was any way she was in danger of summer school. In fact, I was sure she would get excellent marks, maybe even the second highest. But why should I suffer for being first?

That night, as I drifted off to sleep, my anger mounted. I needed something to make me feel better. For me, that was the 1949 Yankees and the incredible October game I still cherish today. But at the last minute, right before I fell asleep, I couldn't stop myself from thinking again about Lizzy. I wondered what had happened the night before. It was the most painful mistake of my life. She seemed so peaceful at first. I needed to know what had happened, so that night, instead of focusing on the last time Lizzy slept, my usual moment, I focused on Lizzy's night after she fell asleep on Sunday.

<Anguished tears begin rolling down Dominic's face.>

<Angela: "Dominic, are you okay? Do you want to continue, or should we call it a day?">

No, I don't want to call it a day. Continuing this interview is of the utmost importance. It is my penance for what happened on June 12th, 1960.

June 12th was Stephen and Rebecca Strauss's anniversary. They were married on a beautiful Saturday afternoon in 1948. After Rebecca died, Stephen had a rough go of it. He tried hard to maintain a grasp on the things he once cherished, but any hold was tenuous. As an outlet for his grief and rage, he began to drink a lot. He also began to take trips out of town. Those trips were the only way he could separate his fits of anger and rage from the rest of his life.

The sound that woke Lizzy up was her father stumbling up the last few stairs and sending a near-empty bottle of whiskey flying across the hall where it smashed into the wall. By her reaction, I could tell Lizzy had seen this behavior before and knew it was in her best interest to remain quiet and in her room. In other moments, once her father fell asleep in his room, she would quietly go and clean up any mess he left behind.

But that night, Stephen didn't pass out on his bed. "Liz, you awake?" His whispered slur was barely intelligible. He stumbled toward her and fell by the foot of the bed, breaking the right bedpost. "Sorry about that, Lizzy." Only one of them found that humorous. "I'll buy you a brand-new bed in the morning. I got myself another raise this week. Hey! Another big jump for us! Aren't you excited about that?" I could see Lizzy was scared. Maybe she was seeing a side of her dad she wasn't used to. "Know what day it is? It's our wedding anniversary. Mom and I would've been married for twelve years." His voice faded and drifted. "Twelve years...."

He stared at his daughter, head cocked slightly to the side as he tried to find his words. "You look so much like your mother. God, she was beautiful. My beautiful wife." Stephen stroked his hand gently down Lizzy's cheek, brushed her hair away from her eyes, and tucked it behind her ear. "My beautiful wife. My Rebecca."

That night, Stephen found a replacement for what had been missing since his wife died. At that moment, Rebecca Strauss was still very much alive. She was right there with him, sharing a bed, sharing their love. She was in front of him, beside him, underneath him.

The unspeakable horrors Lizzy endured that night were not moments inflicted on me in a dream. This wasn't history I was forced to witness. This was Lizzy. It was her moment to suffer. I was to bear witness to her anguish.

Lizzy stayed awake for the rest of the night. I guessed she was probably afraid her father would come back into her room. When I think of the moment, I try to imagine her pain and the hurt in her heart. Her father violated and desecrated her forever. She curled up in her broken bed and cried. There she remained as the sun rose on a new day.

When I awoke in the morning, there were tears streaming down my face. I didn't understand what had happened, but I knew I had to see Lizzy right away. When I got to her house, Lizzy was sitting on the porch, looking as dazed as the day before. This time, I cut to the chase. I had to make sure she was safe and that that monster was nowhere near her.

"Lizzy, where's your father?"

She told me she didn't know. She hadn't seen him for a day.

"Not since Sunday night? Since he left your bedroom?"

"What does that mean?" she demanded incredulously. I tried to put my arm around her shoulders. She pulled back and yelled, "Get your hands off me! I mean it! Get away from me, Dominic!"

I drew back, muttering apologies. "It's okay, Lizzy. It's okay." I was a scared child trying to comfort another scared child. "Let's go back to my house. Dad is still home; we'll talk to him and he can help us. He can help you." That infuriated her even more.

"What the hell are you even talking about? Nothing happened. Just go away!" Lizzy tore off.

That was it. I never saw Elizabeth Strauss again. Well, except in my dreams, I never saw her alive again. I ran home fast, falling twice on the way. I told Dad that Lizzy was upset. I didn't know why, but her dad wasn't home and I didn't know what to do. Dad told me to stay in the house, then flew out the door and ran down to the Avenue in the direction I told him Lizzy had run.

There was a crowd near the subway station when my father got there. Lizzy had stepped in front of a moving train in an eerie replication of her mother's suicide. Dad didn't stay to find out the details; he turned on his heel and went home to be with his family.

The few remaining days of school were canceled. The official story was that Lizzy was a troubled child. Her parents' anniversary had been a tragic reminder of Rebecca Strauss's death and it caused a break in her fragile mind. Lizzy missed her mother and wanted to be with her, so she left this world just as her mother had years before.

Neighbors gathered together at the wake and funeral to grieve and offer their condolences to Mr. Strauss. "Oh, it is so sad," and "Poor guy," and "How awful it is to have everything taken away." That is what everyone was saying, but I knew the truth. Stephen Strauss and I both knew the truth.

But there was nothing I could do; I had no proof. The accusations of a ten-year-old boy would not stand up against this man...a man who everyone saw as a saint, a wonderful father who did everything for his little girl. No one would ever believe he was the demon I knew him to be.

At the cemetery, after the priest offered a final prayer for Lizzy's departed soul, a line formed in front of Stephen Strauss. Everyone offered condolences and reassured him that, whatever he needed, they were there for him. Each person gave him a kiss and a warm hug and then placed a red rose on his daughter's closed coffin. Lizzy's classmates and other children brought up the end of the line. While I watched the line dwindle, I clung to my mother's side. "You know you do not have to go to the coffin, Dominic," she told me. "Anyway, no one was a closer friend to Lizzy than you were, and everyone knows it."

They had no idea what I did to Lizzy.

I hung my head in shame, released my grip from the side of my mother's black mourning dress, and took my place in the line. When I got to the front, Stephen Strauss and I stood face-to-face for the longest of moments. The last time I was this close to him, he was causing unimaginable pain to his daughter. Making sure no one could hear me, I leaned in and whispered: "We both failed her."

"What do you mean, child?" Mr. Strauss looked confused.

"I failed her as a friend. I violated her trust."

Stephen bent down to my level and gently said, "You didn't do anything wrong, Dominic. You couldn't have done anything wrong."

He wrapped his arms around me. I felt disgust, but I didn't pull away from him. Instead, I pressed my cheek against his and, staring coldly into the distance over his shoulder, whispered in his ear, "You failed her as a father. You violated her. And for that, you will suffer."

He lurched back like I had punched him with the weight of a thousand Dominics. I knew he wanted to interrogate me. He got only one question out—"What on earth are you talking about?"—but I kept my jaw clenched closed and didn't answer. Finally, I mouthed the words: "And for that, you will suffer."

Strauss flew into a rage. He grabbed me, tossed me to the ground, and cursed my name. Dad rushed over and scooped me up as everyone else rushed to the aid of the grieving father. When asked what had happened, Mr. Strauss refused to answer. As far as I was concerned, the words I had spoken were no longer mine. I had said my piece and did not want to discuss it anymore, with anyone. Whatever was left of my childhood innocence was lost on that day: June 16th, 1960.

At that age, I was aware of my immense power and the debilitating hold it had on me. That hasn't changed; it is just the same today. I knew I couldn't use the truths I discovered in my dreams. Nor would I even be able to tell anyone about it. Without corroborating evidence to prove my claims, all of it was useless. I certainly couldn't use it to avenge the deaths of Giuseppe and Lizzy. Searching for truth only exposed me to the potential dangers of its absence. If I do expose a secret, anyone who wants it to remain hidden will want to silence me. I realized then that my ability was more likely to kill than benefit me.

I learned that seeking knowledge just for the sake of knowing has its own price. Every night as I go to sleep and consider searching for a moment, I have important questions to consider: Do I want to know the truth? What will I do with it? What will be my course of action once I discover it? And, when I wake up, not only do I still have those questions, but I am also burdened by a mind filled with revelations of newly experienced moments.

You may be asking about the ethics, the morality, of what I do with my ability. The greatest regret, the most extreme sorrow of my life—witnessing the moments of Lizzy's pain—was my own creation. I violated the privacy of my friend's world to satisfy my own curiosities. My punishment is the knowledge I gained—I will never suffer enough for what I did to get it. I wonder how much Lizzy would have suffered if she had known about the many nights of my "innocent intrusions" into her bedroom.

I live in a world where my actions are checked only by myself and my creator. The vows I made almost sixty years ago still guide me today. I'm comfortable with the choices I've made since then. The final ruling on my past, the judgment, is with our Lord alone.

Chapter 12 - Voice: Angela

Dominic leaned over and turned off the camera. After that long monologue, we both sat in silence for almost fifteen minutes. I kept shooting glances at him, hoping he wouldn't notice. I was trying to determine the best way to describe him...to describe his soul. Tortured? Lost? Broken?

I wanted to let him make the next move. Three days of listening to him talk had been taxing on me, both physically and emotionally. I am sure it was much harder for him to live that story than it was to tell it to me. He had carried the weight of his secrets for so long. His ability had brought him both joy and horror, yet for so long he was unwilling to share the joys and unable to escape the horrors. I had no idea how he had managed to live through all of that, especially without being able to share any of it. How had he survived?

Finally, he broke the silence by telling me that because we had turned off the camera, I could use my recorder if I wished. I turned it on as he continued.

> "Several years later, I decided I had to do something about the deaths of my friends, Giuseppe and Lizzy. I needed to find justice for

them. I first needed to investigate Gino, the guy who killed Giuseppe. So, I searched for the last day he was awake. The last day he was awake...choosing that specific moment is a trick I learned a long time ago. Once I confirm that a person exists, or existed, searching for the last time they were awake leads me safely to the next step.

"Anyway, the last day Gino was awake was August 29th, 1963. He spent the morning with a couple of his buddies talking about the civil rights rally that had taken place in Washington, DC, the day before. That was when Martin Luther King Jr. gave his 'I Have a Dream' speech. They were outraged and disgusted by the march. I heard a lot of 'damn niggers' in their conversation. After a day full of drinking and cocaine, Gino and one of his pals went to work: they committed three robberies in Clason Point.

"The first was an elderly gentleman returning home from the community center. They stole six dollars and a cheap watch from him.

"Second was a cashier at a bodega. After stealing twenty-two dollars, Gino shot up the refrigerators with the sawed-off .22 he had inside his coat. They did over three hundred dollars' worth of damage.

"Their third job was to rob a man and a woman who were sitting in their car and stopped at a red light. Gino and his friend didn't realize the man was an off-duty cop. The officer pumped three rounds into Gino, killing him instantly. Gino's dirtbag friend got away.

"The other three men from the coffee shop died of natural causes late in life. Believe it or not, all of those guys were considered 'pillars of the community.'"

"What about Stephen Strauss? What happened to him, Dominic?"

"He's dead."

After hearing his story up to that point, it was hard for me not to see Dominic as the innocent, curious, and scared child he had portrayed himself as. But when I looked over at him, I didn't see fear...or even anger. I realized there was still so much more I needed to find out.

> "Of course, you know that Lizzy's death was not your fault, right? You have to know you did nothing wrong."

> "Angela, you are a law student, soon to be a full-fledged lawyer. But that doesn't mean your education is over. Like me, you always have more to learn. What I am trying to say is that you are missing something. Surely you know about privacy laws. Although they are constantly changing, especially because of the digital age in which we live, to assume that moments of energy are somehow exempt from the laws governing reasonable expectation of privacy shows a severe lack of knowledge."

> "Okay, I take your point. Agreed."

"The issue is not whether I have committed crimes—that's of no consequence to me. Nor am I concerned about the morality or ethics of what I have done. Every intrusion I have made since watching Lizzy on June 12th, 1960 has been done with a clear conscience. Still, I suffer so much over the many ways that I violated Lizzy. And it sickens me to think how my perversions might have developed had life turned out differently...had Lizzy and I made it to adolescence together. The fact that we were only children at the time does not excuse my behavior. Of course, what her father did to her was a big part of what ended her life, but it was me—my words—that pushed her to suicide. Do you dispute that?"

"I do not, Dominic."

"I've already talked outside of my script too much. Why don't we call it a day, okay?"

I agreed and turned off my recorder. I then asked him what he meant by "outside of his script." Dominic explained that he had planned our interviews for almost two years. So far, he said, he had managed to stick to his schedule and agenda, even including my initial questions about his mental competence. Everything had been going according to plan until his rant in our just-finished interview. His concern wasn't that going off script had eaten into our allotted time; he had two other issues. The first had to do with my education. I believe his comment was: "There's still so much you don't know." I found that somewhat condescending, but I had been warned early on not to challenge Dominic Bandall. Second, and more disconcerting to Dominic, was the problem of deviating from his script. He explained that as a trial lawyer, he had mastered the art of elocution and timing; he knew exactly how to pace himself and vary the tempo of an argument to keep a jury, a judge, opposing counsel, even the press, riveted. He knew that the slightest tangent or interruption could distract and confuse his audience. And, the last thing he wanted was for them—or in this case, me—to seek answers he was not yet ready to provide. He explained that for me to comprehend his complicated story, he had to tell it in a very particular way. And that was why he had a script, a perfect one. He assured me it would be perfect, if he could only keep his love for storytelling under control!

We broke for the evening. It was nice to finish while the sun was still shining, especially because Dominic had warned me that as we went "further down this rabbit hole," our days would get longer and longer. "Enjoy this time," he said, "because we're about to see just how many moments we can shove into the day."

As I got up to leave the office, I was already planning my free evening. Just as I was walking out the door, Dominic yelled, "One more thing! I took the liberty of having the exercise equipment in your room moved into an adjacent location. Before you arrived, Hy'ing told me you probably wouldn't want to have it in your bedroom. I didn't listen and told her she had no idea of what city-dwellers want."

"Word travels fast, I see!" I said. Hy'ing and I had discussed this just the night before.

"Seems like I owe her another twenty bucks. Have a wonderful evening, Angela." I watched as Dominic slowly raised his crippled frame and shuffled out of the office.

Thus began a peaceful, enchanting evening on the Island—the last one of my trip.

Chapter 13 - Voice: Dominic

My name is Dominic Bandall. Today is Monday, March 4th, 2019. This is session number eight in my interview with Ms. Angela Grant.

The summer of 1960 was an introspective time for me. Even though I had gotten to a point where I just wanted to be free of my ability and the dangerous problems it caused, there were certain times that summer when I was okay with it...mainly because it allowed me to revisit the many treasured shared memories with Lizzy.

Whenever I experience intense and highly charged moments for the first time, whether they are beautiful and peaceful or full of anguish and pain, it affects me in unexpected ways. It takes a tremendous toll on my body, akin to the most grueling of workouts. That summer, I kept myself safe by only choosing moments I had already experienced or that were my own memories. During those summer nights, I relived many times with Lizzy.

It was during the day that I experienced horror. The enormity of my loss of Lizzy and Giuseppe was soul-crushing. I longed to remain asleep, to never wake up. All I wanted was to remember my friends. I thought I had successfully gotten past my grief over

Giuseppe, but Lizzy's death was a jarring reminder that I had not; it was very much there, burning inside me.

Even now, as I reflect on those days, I'm both astonished and angered by the level of my immaturity. Instead of feeling grief for my friends who had departed, all I thought about was my own loss. In my self-pity, I saw only what had been taken from me.

Dad saw my despair and tried to help.

"Dominic," he said, "our family, Mr. Strauss, the whole neighborhood, is suffering because of what happened to Lizzy. We are shredded by sadness, but we are not torn apart. But that is what will happen if we don't take the necessary measures to protect those who remain behind." Apparently, Stephen Strauss could no longer bear to live in a house with so many ghosts. He moved out three weeks after the funeral, hiring an agent to handle all matters in absentia. My family never saw or heard from the monster again, though Mother continued to feel sorry for him. Every time she mentioned his name, it hit me like a punch, but I didn't have the heart to tell her what I knew.

Dad said it was important to focus on the survivors...those who were left behind. We talked about happier times with the Strauss family. As a loving father who cherished his own family, he genuinely felt Mr. Strauss's loss, and it meant a lot to him to talk about that with me.

Despite Dad's advice, I continued to think mostly about myself and my loss. "It's so hard, Dad, to even think about how to move on. I miss her so much. I lost so much."

With my self-pity becoming too much for him, he snapped back, "You haven't lost a goddamn thing! Dammit, Dominic, I'm tired of listening to you moan about what you lost and what happened to you. That is the same reaction I saw from soldiers in the war. They were healthy, they had not been injured, but they suffered terribly from the experience of watching their brothers die. Many a man lost the will to fight, lost the will to live. Do you know who was there to help them and console them in their time of mourning? Not a goddamn person, that's who. They lost their will to live. They were unable to function. They lost their way. As a result, many of them ended up joining their brothers in death. That behavior also caused their fellow soldiers to die.

"You didn't lose anything, Dominic. Lizzy lost everything the moment she died. You still have wonderful memories to relish and share. You didn't lose anything, you just don't get any more—at least not from Lizzy. Don't give up on yourself. Don't give up on the people who still need you. Most important, don't lose anything. If you do, you haven't lost it; you've thrown it away."

I never saw my father show that kind of anger. While he was standing over me, his face flushed red, his finger striking down on the table with every point, I looked up and saw a soldier who couldn't bear to see one more person give up and die. I saw my loving father willing to beat his point into me if that's what it took to save my life. I saw a father who, as he scolded his child like never before, stood there with his legs shaking from fear. I just lost control and began to sob. He immediately dropped to his knees and wrapped his arms around me.

He repeated, "It's okay, Dominic. It's okay." As my crying slowed, I waited for him to say something I needed to hear—that he was sorry. He did not. He consoled me, but clearly did not regret what he had said. He held me close until my tears dried. Those tears only stopped when I realized he was right. Everything my father told me was honest, accurate, and true.

I have never stopped grieving Lizzy's death. I am sorry for the loss—not mine, but hers. I am sad about not being able to experience more with my friend. I also made a promise that day. If I should lose, or better yet, *when* I lose the opportunity to experience more with a loved one, I will not add regret to my sadness. For if I do, I waste precious time.

* * *

When the school year began in the fall of 1960, I had no idea what my life would look like after Lizzy's death. I was only ten, almost eleven, and had no clue how to cope with it. I gradually came around to the idea that all of it was so unfair—so unfair—but it was reality. Once I acknowledged that, I realized I had no choice but to approach things systematically. Survival. Security. Betterment. These were the things I needed to focus on.

My dad was my security. He protected me. I trusted him and he was always there for me. I never revealed my secret to him—and still don't know if or what he knew—but he guided me in ways that befitted me as both a prepubescent boy who knew so little and a tortured soul who had seen too much.

A few days after our talk, I asked Dad if he would put me to bed, "You know, like you used to do when I was a baby." In my room, I asked him to tell me a story of the time he was most frightened. He closed his eyes for a minute and thought about my request. When he continued to hesitate, I suspected he had chosen a story, but couldn't decide if he should tell me, or if I was prepared to hear it.

Finally, he decided.

"Nicolas Bandall, your grandfather, my dad, was a troubled soul. He, like you, had a debilitating illness that caused severe leg deformities. He was very disabled, far worse than you are. Medicine then, in the early 1900s, was not what it is today. To survive, he had to rely on his wits.

"Dad was an investor at Goldman Sachs Trading Corporation. Though he was by no means wealthy, he supported us comfortably, mainly because the stock market was booming during the Roaring Twenties. In October of 1929, the market crashed, and it continued to fall for more than two-and-a-half years. At that time, I was a little bit younger than you are now. Today, people refer to the years following the crash as the Great Depression. That is a silly name because it was so much more than a depression. It was devastation. My parents' wealth was entirely on paper; all their money, their savings, were tied up in those stocks. When the stocks lost their value, we lost it all.

"To survive, Dad had to sell everything we owned. Sometime around 1931, he sold the last of our furniture and moved into a squatter's village where there were twelve other families. Mothers would care for other people's children during the day, and the men would queue up to see if they could get a job doing some kind of manual labor. Because of his lame foot, Dad was rarely chosen. Most of our sustenance came from the goodwill of the other people in our community.

"My parents made the most difficult decision of their lives when they sent me away to live in a boys town camp—government housing for juveniles—in Kings County. I lived there for two years. My parents visited me whenever possible, and occasionally I made the trek back to Manhattan to visit them. I finally left the camp for good on my thirteenth birthday.

"On December 16th, 1932, I returned home—well, the room in a shack my parents shared with two other families—late in the morning. I wanted to surprise them with decorations I had made to brighten up the place."

Dad stopped talking and I could see he was conflicted about continuing. I have to say, except for String Bean, my father was always honest with me—he never even shared those little white lies parents use to keep children feeling secure. It is one of his attributes I have always tried to emulate. I never asked him why he was so brutally honest with me, maybe because I feared his answer. Ever since that one fateful bedtime story years ago, I have always accepted, without question, everything he said. Had he chosen to stop talking, I would've accepted his decision. But he didn't stop. Instead, he closed his eyes and told me about an experience in 1932.

"As I approached the shack they called a home, the most unusual feeling came over my body. It was neither hectic nor agitated, but rather, the most intense feeling of serenity I have ever experienced. I called out to my dad. I was sure he was there, but I didn't expect a reply. I'm not sure how I would've responded had he answered.

"I opened the door, calling his name once again. This time my voice was calm, subdued. He was lying in his bed, just off to the left, about six or seven feet from the door. Even today, the image remains clear in my mind. He was lying on the sheets, lifeless. I softly called his name one last time. I wasn't searching for a reply, I just didn't know what else to do. Slowly and silently, I walked toward his bed. A pale blue blanket was pulled up midway across his back, a pillow was lying over his head, and his head was resting on one forearm. The image was pristine, innocent. The pillow and bedcover were magically white—a white I never thought possible. I stood over my father and saw a new man. After years of anguish, he was finally calm.

"I reached down and slowly lifted the corner of the pillow to reveal a most gruesome scene. My father's head, face down into the mattress, was submerged in a pool of blood and brain. His right hand was still gripping the revolver that was still pressed against his temple. Instinctively, I looked to the left to see where the bullet had struck the wall. The trajectory formed a straight line through the middle of his skull. I had to compliment his perfect shot. I looked down and sighed heavily, with absolutely no thought or other reaction. I suppressed nothing because nothing was there. I lowered the pillow back onto his head. I turned and sat down on the end of his bed, close to the body, my left hand on his leg, gently caressing the body's calf. I don't remember how long I was there. It felt like hours, yet could not have been more than a few seconds.

"I tell you, that experience was the most peaceful moment of my life. I never experienced such stillness, and I never hope to experience it again. I took one last deep breath and left my father's body, in search of my only remaining parent. As I walked toward my mother, the greatest sense of fear imaginable rushed over me. All my emotions ran cold, except for fear. I said, 'He's dead,' for I didn't know what else to say or do. Fear gripped and squeezed my heart, refusing to let go.

"Gradually, with my mother's unending love and support, my world was safe. In time, I opened up about my feelings. I learned how to embrace emotion again, simply by doing normal, everyday things. I even learned to laugh and to cry, to like and to hate. Fear, however, never released its hold on me. I grew up with it. I lived with it. I lived around it. That fear nearly destroyed me."

Dad finally opened his eyes. He looked down at me, smiled, and gently wiped a tear from my cheek. "Do you want to know when I stopped being afraid? When I lost my fear?" he asked me. I opened my eyes wide—much like yours are right now, Angela—as I waited to hear his answer. He paused. Much like me right now, Angela, my father's smile lasted longer than I expected. The pause wasn't to tease me; he was savoring the few extra moments he had of keeping the story to himself. Finally, he took a deep breath and continued.

"My fear released its stranglehold on me when I met your mother. We didn't know each other, nor could I have known anything about the life we would have together, but the moment I met her, I knew I no longer needed to be afraid all the time."

Dad told me Mother gave him a wonderful sense of security, especially during the years he was fighting overseas. He was sure he never would have returned alive had he gone to war alone, not with her blanket of protection but with the shadow of death over him. Life wasn't perfect and rosy. He experienced pain and loss, sadness and grief. But, by placing the hurt—the past, the current, and future—into perspective, he found solace.

I was very close to my father, but after he opened his heart to me with that story, I felt more love for him than ever before. Not only were we father and son, blood, but we also shared the intense bond of having been right there when our loved ones had chosen to die because they believed they had no other option. My father found his salvation in my mother. I wondered if I would find—no, *when* I would find—my own salvation. I decided then that until that happened for me, I needed to open up, and act as "normal" as possible...doing what was expected of me. I just didn't know how I was going to do that.

Before my tears started to flow again, I asked, "What do I do next? What steps do I take, Daddy?"

"You learn," he told me. "You learn everything you can. Start with what is required. After that, learn what you want. After that, learn what you need. Use this time in your youth to your advantage, Dominic. As a child, your needs are few. Your mother and I have decided what you need to learn...the essential things. Don't fight this, just absorb everything you can. We will make sure you have what you require. There will be plenty of time later for you to fret over what you think are your essential needs. For now, that will be my problem. Then, decide what you want to learn. Focus all your energy in that direction. That's your job."

We sat in silence, my father snuggling me. As I became sleepy, I pushed aside my vow not to intrude on another person's moment and, once I fell asleep, I dove once more into the moment when my father, Anthony Bandall, first met my mother, Mable

Geurin, down by the pier. I'd seen the scene many times before, but that night, for the first time, I saw the moment he had just told me about. I saw the fear lift from his face. My father would never again fall to the same depths of despair.

The next morning, I awoke with the simplest of passions: to learn.

Chapter 14 - Voice: Dominic

My name is Dominic Bandall. Today is Monday, March 4th, 2019. This is session number nine in my interview with Ms. Angela Grant.

Do you know what I find to be one of the strangest parts of my ability? By the age of eleven, I had, at least theoretically, unrestricted access to a firsthand account of all of history. This is the kind of extraordinary power reserved for the gods, for legends, for superheroes...and I was a mere boy. It is quite remarkable. There were simply no boundaries, then or now, to what I could retrieve through my dreams. My ability allows me to dig so deeply into the past, and with such precision, I can find answers to questions that even the greatest minds will never begin to formulate, let alone answer. The closest even the finest scholars can get to this data is by inference or deduction, both of which are, of course, prone to errors.

I had no idea if there were others like Giuseppe and me. Giuseppe had told me they were all dead, but who knew? What if he was wrong? And if so, where were they? Were they like Giuseppe, with minds full of extraordinary information that could be vital to humankind, but so tormented by lunacy that they were locked in a mental ward somewhere? Or, were they like me, perfectly positioned to make ground-breaking discoveries, but continuously threatened by the possibility of searching for a faux event that would finally destroy their body? These were questions that I constantly wondered about.

It was right around that time that I finally let go of my trepidation about seeking new moments. Curiosity got the better of me and I felt an urge to search beyond my familiar and happy moments. To protect myself as I embarked on this new journey, I decided to keep a list to remind myself of what I should do and, more important, what I must never attempt. It was basically a list of guidelines and rules for using my ability.

To do this, I got a brand-new composition book. It was a good idea and I'm still rather proud of myself for having thought of that. It also sheds some light on my frame of mind at the time. For one, it shows that I was optimistic...that I anticipated gathering so much information and accumulating so much wisdom that I would need a book of rules to corral them. Second, it shows that I was brazen enough to believe I would live long enough to fill all those pages. I did the math: fifty pages, ten one-inch lines per page. That gave me room for five hundred rules.

I opened the new book, and ran my hand down the first page before making my first rule, the rule that will always be burned into my memory:

1: Never go back to a time that didn't exist

I paused for a moment, thinking about nothing in particular, before I continued:

2: Never tell anyone

3: Never hurt people by looking into their life

4: Do I really want to know the answer?

5: What will I do with the information I get?

6: This killed Giuseppe

7: This killed Lizzy

8: Learn

I still keep the same journal with me. My rules, guidelines, notes, and scratch marks now fill nearly the whole book. The pages are worn and tattered. Obviously, some rules have seen revision over the years. I no longer need it to remember the rules, but I keep it with me at all times as proof...a physical reminder to myself that this is real. When we are done with our interviews, in addition to the recordings, I'd also like you to have my composition book, Angela.

<Angela: "Thank you, Dominic.">

Let me go back to Labor Day, September 5th, 1960, the day before school was going to start. We had a grand neighborhood barbecue. Cassius Clay won the Olympic gold medal in light heavyweight boxing, a moment I so much enjoy...the wide-eyed innocence of that eighteen-year-old kid who grew to become one of the greatest boxers ever.... But I don't want to stray off topic again.

I welcomed sixth grade with the kind of eagerness my teachers were not accustomed to. By the end of the second week, all the information in my textbooks had become part of my catalog of historical data. How can I explain what I did? I guess you could say I uploaded it. To create a moment for my dreams, I would mentally upload every bit of information in my books by using a visual image of each page which was, by then, securely logged in my brain. I guess I memorized the information, but remembering it—recalling the words, letters, numbers, and symbols—wasn't enough for me to fully understand it. My ability to process raw information into a bigger, more meaningful picture, was undeveloped.

In the second week of school, I failed both my mathematics and grammar quizzes. I asked my father for help. No matter the problem, when other measures failed, I could always rely on him to guide me. He never questioned my reasons, never tried to probe into whatever was bothering me. He just lent his support when I asked for it, answered my questions, and left me to figure out the rest on my own. I told him how much effort I had put into learning the material. I told him I had expected to be tested on what we had been assigned to read, and that was not what happened. My father explained the situation in a way I had not thought of. "Reading a textbook is not learning."

Dad then launched into one of his favorite rants about education. He said learning requires more than just memorization. It must also include extrapolation, interpretation, understanding, and practice. Then, he gave me examples. He said a math book might explain that one plus one equals two, and one plus two equals three, and that one plus four equals five, but if I cannot figure out that one plus three equals four, I will not have learned a thing. When I told him the answer, Dad explained that I had been able to figure it out because I understood the concept—the process. In the same way, a grammar book need not explain why a phrase like, "'I see,' said the blind man" makes sense because students will be able to understand what "see" means in that context. Or why a question like, "What's the weight of the weight?" requires interpretation of the words, not just the definition.

What my father said made sense. Well, it made sense to him, just like it does to you and me today. But I had been relying on memorization for so many years that my ability to think analytically was not as developed as it should have been, or as advanced as I thought it was. It isn't surprising that I thought memorization was the way to learn; when you're young, you're spoon-fed information and expected to just echo it. I remember the sinking feeling I had when I realized that learning was a lot harder than I expected.

After that, I had to adjust my process. Instead of merely memorizing everything I was taught, my goal was to understand it. If I was having a hard time, I reached out to my instructors, family, and friends. If I didn't understand something, we worked on it until I did. My teachers cared about me, just as they cared about all their students, so much...more than I understood. The list of people I am indebted to for that help and caring is sure to be longer than my list of rules. It indeed is amazing to think back on those days: learning was something that most kids did naturally through experience, yet I, a supposed child prodigy, finally had to learn how to learn.

I began to excel in all my classes. I grew to love learning and developing my mind. However, I soon discovered that my efforts in school, in addition to my continued education during the night, were severely taxing my mental and physical stamina. I felt so drained, it was as if I had nothing left. A new way of looking at things saved me: Could I maybe use my ability to do more than just learn? And if so, what could I use it for?

In the spring of 1961, our little part of the world was all abuzz over the first human spaceflight by an American. In class, we watched the live TV broadcast of astronaut Alan Shepard as he took off in the Mercury-Redstone 3 rocket. As we watched, instead of thinking about reliving the moment later in my dreams, I focused on where I was right at that moment, experiencing the incredible spaceflight with my friends.

Billy and I lived through the takeoff together. I leaned over and asked him if he ever wanted to go to space. I watched his eyes shine as he imagined blasting off, hurtling through the skies until there was no more sky to reach. We took turns wondering what Shepard was thinking. We mimicked impressions of what we thought his radio chatter sounded like. We talked about what the stars must look like so close to heaven.

Watching Alan Shepard's flight was a pivotal life experience for me; it was then that I learned to live my own life, not just moments of the past. I made a point of never experiencing the flight in my dreams. Instead, I have kept this adventure in the place I first experienced it: in my classroom, with my friends. I never wanted to change it for fear of losing the emotions I felt back then. I made myself a promise before falling asleep on May 5th, 1961. Some moments need to be untouched. Pure. I scribbled a new rule in my journal.

Rule Number 9: Live

Billy, a founding father of the original gang to which my loyalty was first and foremost, was responsible for expanding the scope of my learning. In 1961, at the end of the school year, Billy was struggling so much in math, science, and social studies, he was afraid he would have to repeat sixth grade. He asked for my help and proposed a barter system as a means of payment. His deal was simple: I help him pass his classes and he would ensure my social standing next year in middle school.

    My close group of friends in grade school was forged by fire. When Lizzy died—she was the one who brought me into the pack and declared me one of them—we vowed our bond would never be broken. In grade school, it was our group that ruled, but there would be a whole new crew of people when we transitioned to middle school. I didn't know how it would change things, but I was not afraid. Although my bad leg put me at a disadvantage, I knew my friends would always be there for me. I knew Billy's offer was less about an exchange of services and more a cry for help. Whatever the reason, I was there for him. We spent the next month working together.

    In September, Billy and I entered middle school, buoyed by our standings as the best stickball player in Pelham Bay (a title he claimed only after paying homage to Lizzy), and the smartest kid to ever walk the school halls. Billy exceeded his promise to be there for me in ways I could never have imagined. He remained my closest friend throughout the rest of our school days. I tutored him when he needed it. He made sure no one tried to use my disfigurement to degrade me. I hope my services were as valuable to him as his were to me.

The changes in my life allowed me to get past the constant feeling of dread about seeing and reliving the hard experiences of death, suffering, and loss. My school days were focused on learning, and I was diligent about it. My afternoons were spent absorbed in the perfect childhood mix of homework, tutorials, playtime, and socialization. I remained in that pattern for several years. It strengthened me physically, emotionally, and mentally.

* * *

By 1967, after sticking to my established rules and protocol, my use of my ability had been so well honed, I could learn and recall just about anything I wanted to. I was confident I had reached a level of control over my ability that even exceeded Giuseppe's. As my high school graduation approached, I began to worry about my future. Right then, things were predictable, and no matter what I learned and discovered in my dreams, there was nothing that threatened the physical security and comfort I was enjoying. Every step forward seemed fraught with danger: physical danger, emotional duress, and the nightly threat of the assault my mind might unleash on me. I had to figure out where I wanted to go and how I could safely get there.

On February 20th, while I sat in the living room with my closest confidant, my father, I asked him to help me figure out what to do with my life. Dad asked me if I would like to join him for a beer. He said I'd be eighteen soon enough (but not to tell Mother anyway). When he came back from the kitchen with two opened bottles, he warned me, "Be careful how many of these things you put away. They go straight to your head." When he joked how just two beers give him the most fantastic dreams, I politely declined his offer with the excuse—one that was not true—that I had a quiz in the morning. Dad didn't argue and placed both bottles next to himself. To this day, a drop of alcohol has never passed my lips.

I got up to get a glass of milk, and as I weaved through the tiny rooms of our downstairs, I told him I didn't know what the future held for me. I asked him the two questions I had: Where did I want to go? How could I safely arrive at my destination? Dad responded that my future was boundless. He told me not to concern myself with the upcoming requirement to register for the draft because he was sure I would be designated 4-F. He pointed out that I already had numerous early acceptance letters from universities. Several of those acceptance letters were from schools I didn't even apply to; they were merely sent by college recruiters who discovered high school students who seemed promising. Dad said he thought it was just a matter of what I wanted to do with my life.

That was all wonderful, except none of it addressed my questions, and I think Dad realized that because he leaned over and turned the sound up on the television. We were watching the news about J. Robert Oppenheimer's death the previous day. The report discussed the physicist's career, achievements, and his impact on the world. They kept showing photos and videos of mushroom clouds while the audio boasted of his remarkable scientific advances. The dichotomy wasn't lost on either of us. We watched the report in silence. When it was over, Dad turned off the television. I watched him work through an internal debate—I could see it playing out on his face—about how to best express what was in his head. Instead of the valuable advice I expected, all I got was random bits of trivia about Oppenheimer, the impact Oppenheimer had on Dad's life, and that the two of them had quite a bit in common. Dad was born less than a mile from where Oppenheimer grew up. Both were born in wealthy neighborhoods on the Upper West Side. Both lost a parent at a young age. Oppenheimer's mother died when he was a teenager. Where their lives differed, Dad proudly boasted that his own life had been far better. He praised Oppenheimer for giving him a chance. Dad was convinced that if the United States had not dropped the bombs on Hiroshima and Nagasaki, he would have died; he was part of the first wave of forces set to invade Japan. After surviving, after coming home, Dad saw everything as a gift, a gift to relish, a gift to learn and pass on to a new generation…a generation only in existence because of the work of Oppenheimer and others.

Dad then said that, though Oppenheimer was a flawed man, his intellect and passion for learning were extraordinary and this was something Dad thought I could relate to. In fact, he suggested that I try to model myself after this man who was learned in so many areas. Oppenheimer majored in chemistry at Harvard. He also studied history, literature, and math. He was well versed in English and French literature, and later obtained a doctorate in philosophy. He was also a vocal critic of the government and his political opinions, sometimes criticized, were well known.

Dad hoped I would try to learn everything I could, just like Oppenheimer had. He explained that in grade school, I was taught to do what my teachers told me to do and repeat what they told me to repeat. In high school, I learned how to learn, and in college, I would discover what I wanted and needed to learn.

Dad was right. Discovery was the next step. I asked him one last question: "When will I start to learn?" Dad assured me that, by the time I figured out the answer, I would have most of the information I needed committed to memory, and all I would have to do was wade through it.

"That," he told me, "will lead to bounties of discovery."

Chapter 15 - Voice: Dominic

My name is Dominic Bandall. Today is Monday, March 4th, 2019. This is session number ten in my interview with Ms. Angela Grant.

There are certain limitations to having access to infinite moments in history. The most serious limitation for me, ironically, is time. So far, I have had 25,348 opportunities to search moments in history, correct the historical record, uncover secrets of the past, and discover what is real and what is not in legends and lore. I have utilized a mere fraction of the time productively. It took me more than eleven percent of my life to discover I had my ability. When I finally figured it out, I used it recklessly, or at least carelessly. I used it to satisfy my curiosity and other personal needs, like that majestic Yankees-Dodgers game in 1949 and intrusions into the life of my best friend. Gradually, though, I began to dedicate some of my efforts to bettering the world. I now believe the good I have done rationalizes this gifted curse of mine.

I use most of my time to learn, not only about myself and about the past, but also how to survive the tribulations I face every day of my journey. You know, I have often wondered if I should have used my ability, my unique hindsight, differently. I thought perhaps I should have put my efforts into preventing moments yet to come—those we will wish had never occurred. That would have allowed me to save those I lost...Giuseppe, Lizzy, Sharon. But, I went on to understand that all the moments I've experienced have been necessary, for they ultimately shaped me into the man I am now...sitting here in front of you.

On March 3rd, 1969, my friend Billy died. In my dreams, I was able to be with him, in that world beyond life. I chose to return to life, but my friend left it, and me, forever. Billy, who was almost a year older than me, had registered for the draft before we even graduated from high school. In July 1967, when he was ordered to report for duty with the United States Marine Corps, he joked that he was almost relieved. He had no plans to go to college, nor were there many schools eager to recruit a hell of a stickball player with barely passing grades. He found there were few opportunities for work in 1967 and planned to join the Army. I pleaded with him not to enlist. There was constant media coverage of the war in Vietnam. I read about it every day in the newspapers and watched TV. I saw the video clips of US soldiers fighting. And of course, there were all the antiwar protests. I never searched for moments in Vietnam. By the time I was seventeen, I had already seen enough of the horrors of war. I had no taste for it.

Billy, on the other hand, looked forward to the opportunity to prove himself a warrior. We said we would write to each other often. I also promised not to look for Billy on the news. He promised to never appear on one of those clips. Ultimately, neither of us were able to keep our vows. I wrote to him while he was training for war at Parris Island and Camp Lejeune. Billy wrote when he could, though the intervals between his letters grew longer and longer. But, three months after he deployed overseas, he sent me a final note saying it was pointless to send him any more letters. His company rarely got mail and if it did, it was often several months old, by which time the intended recipients were either dead or had been rotated back to the States. I should not have listened to him. I should have continued to write.

Curiosity and concern for my friend forced me to make rash, poorly planned decisions about the moments I focused on. In 1968 and 1969, I spent many nights alongside Billy, I mean, Lance Corporal William Dossey—Rifleman, Second Platoon, Company M, Third Battalion, Ninth Marines—"Death in the Dark," while they conducted combat operations throughout the Quang Tri Province in Central Vietnam.

I was amazed by how Billy was able to fight with precision and, at the same time, with rage. I watched while he was on patrol, searching for the enemy, marking their movement by coordinating artillery with heartless precision. I was afraid for him when I watched him fight hand to hand. Unlike his fellow platoonmates, I could translate the look in his eyes after he gutted a PAVN soldier with his bayonet: it was the look of abject fear. His actions expressed skill and cold-hearted determination, but in his eyes, I saw a soldier scared of the firefight he was in, and afraid of being left behind when his friends moved on to the next mission.

During that time, I would spend my nights witnessing Billy at war and my days on schoolwork and planning for after graduation. After watching him in combat, thereby ignoring my fourth rule—Do I really want to know the answer?—I finally stopped watching that part of his life. Instead, I decided to join him while he was relaxing in the evenings at Vandegrift Combat Base and telling his friends about his exploits and victories. Billy told me he was very much at home as a marine and was considering reenlisting when that tour was finished.

On March 3rd, 1969, after completing a successful operation, Billy's unit was withdrawing from the Quang Tri Province and moving into Laos. As they were returning to their first support base, they ran into strong enemy resistance; a ferocious battle erupted. Surviving members of the platoon described receiving heavy machine gun fire from all sides. Grenade after grenade fell, hitting their targets with pinpoint accuracy. The last of the three bullets Billy took severed his spine. I am relieved to say I no longer saw fear in my friend's eyes. There was no pain. There was no longing for anything. As he lay on the ground of a once-lush jungle, Billy watched the battle as it raged around him. Then finally, he closed his eyes. There would be no more moments for my friend.

Before I fell asleep that night, March 3rd, 1969, I focused on how Billy spent that same evening in Vietnam. Of course, that meant I was searching for a moment that did not exist.

For that potentially fatal transgression, I spent the next two weeks in a coma at Lenox Hill Hospital. When I finally came out of it, I opened my eyes and saw my darling mother sitting by my bedside, keeping vigil. The first words out of my mouth were, "Is Billy dead?" Puzzled—it was the last thing she expected me to say—she ignored the question and told me to just relax. She straightened the edges of my pillow, then excused herself to find my father.

I heard the two of them speaking in whispers just outside my room. Dad kept saying, "Don't worry. Everything is going to be okay," and "He must have heard us talking while he was in the coma or coming out of it." The two of them walked into my room and Dad asked me how I felt. Did my leg hurt? Did I have feeling everywhere? I didn't care about any of that. I begged them to answer my question. Dad looked at me closely and asked if I had heard or seen something.

I closed my eyes and pictured death. I knew Billy was dead. Later, through military records, I found out he died on March 3rd, 1969, during a firefight near Fire Support Base Cunningham in Quang Tri Province, somewhere between 1400 and 1630 hours, local time. By the time the sun had set in Vietnam, at 1802 hours, Billy's body was already back at the FSB, documented as killed in action and awaiting transportation for additional processing elsewhere.

All accounts said my friend was dead, but I had seen something different when I visited him that evening. I watched as energy passed through Billy's body, slowly dissipating until no pulses remained. I watched as an ambient light seeped through the black fabric of his body bag, and then slowly faded as the moment slipped away. I listened as all the bustling sounds of the casualty collection point dimmed. It was not that I was losing grasp of the moment; I was losing my friend's energy. I reached out and found the moment in which he was dying. I held on to it while it lost strength and slowly faded into nonexistence. The moment never ended; it just reached a point in which I realized there was nothing there. I remained within this realm of nothingness for over two weeks. I could not explain to my parents why I was asking about Billy. I could only ask them again if he was dead. Dad finally confirmed that his body had been buried two days before I woke up from the coma.

The moment of Billy's death—a snapshot that lasted thirteen days for me—was troublesome. In the past, when I tried to access nonexistent moments, all I experienced was emptiness. No darkness, no eerie silence, no cold vacuum of space. All I felt was desolation. The physical consequences of meeting a void were the same as before, but there was something different about that moment with Billy. It was as if my mind and my ability were at odds with each other; I couldn't decide if the patterns of energy I was experiencing existed or not. My mind held on tight—it was as alert and clear as it always is when I am experiencing moments—and I felt physically strong when flashing lights and rumbling noises surrounded Billy. I could still feel this struggle as I tried to maintain a connection with a moment that did not want to exist. Ultimately, though, the overwhelming feeling of emptiness returned.

After coming out of the coma, I had to stay in the hospital for three more months while doctors tried to heal me. I did the physical therapy faithfully during the day, even though it was humiliating and painful. In the evening, I tried to understand what had happened. Was my coma a psychological reaction to the overwhelming experience I had witnessed? Had I tapped into an exact moment of death, when the last sparkle of energy in a body dissipates into the world beyond? Perhaps I had experienced the exact moment a soul leaves a body and begins its spiritual journey?

Angela, the journey to this crossroad left me unprepared to face the answers I so desperately sought.

* * *

It had been over two years since my conversation with Dad about my future. I took his advice and went to Hunter College in New York City. Hunter is a fine liberal arts institution with programs and curricula across a wide range of fields. It was there, I assured myself, that I would find myself and find a path for my future that included finding the true calling for my ability.

Although I was sad to leave my friends, I eagerly awaited the next phase of my life. I have never been a social person; I am unable to connect with people with simpler, less complicated lives than mine and I was unwilling to put myself in the vulnerable position of growing close to someone again. I did not allow myself to get distracted by the foolish thoughts of girls that typically overwhelm teenage boys. Even though my ability, and the prize of immense knowledge and insight that came with it, deprived me of a normal life, I never lamented. First Corinthians talks about love. It says, "But strive for the greater gifts...faith, hope, and love abide..." and "...the greatest of these is love." These words are true, but at that point, they meant little to me; I was still a child and would remain a child for many years to come. To me, the greatest gift was being cautious about my health and well-being. Except for fooling around with my friends, I did not engage in most of the things kids usually do. Yes, I realized I was missing out on a lot of the fun parts of childhood, but I was less afraid of moving on without my friends than I was of the danger that could very well be waiting for me.

I treated those last few months of high school as if they were a farewell tour of my childhood. My friends did too. Billy was happy to finally be free of schoolwork and boasted about his plans to either join the Army or go backpacking overseas. It's unfortunate that he never got the chance to live those dreams.

Dennis, Patrick, and Rich also served in Vietnam. Dennis and Rich were both killed in action. Patrick served in the military police. He was in one of the last groups to evacuate the DAO compound during the fall of Saigon on April 30th, 1975. Command Sergeant Major Patrick Jeffers retired after thirty-five years in uniform.

Karen accepted my invitation to escort her to our senior prom. Jimmy and Milt had been prodding me for weeks to ask her. She was a stunning beauty and I guaranteed them there was no chance she would go to prom with me. But they persisted, and eventually I felt obliged to at least act like I was a normal kid. When I asked Karen, she accepted immediately, wrapped her arms around me, and giggled with glee. For the second time in my life, I felt that pang of elation. Good god, that is a wonderfully frightening experience!

Karen tried to make everything easy for me because she knew how shy and awkward I was. She told me what to wear and what time to arrive at her house to pick her up. When we arrived at the prom, she hooked her arm through mine and told me to follow her lead. For the whole evening, she discreetly whispered what I should do and say. When we returned home, Karen gave me a soft kiss on my lips before thanking me for a wonderful evening. The next day, we picked back up as friends. I will never forget those kissable lips.

And speaking of my childhood friends, we all ended up taking different paths after high school. Jimmy and Laurie, for example, got married four days after they both graduated from Iona College. Jimmy moved back to the neighborhood and took over the local grocery store his father had opened years before. He soon became a respected member of the community. Now retired, the couple spends their time as loving grandparents and volunteers at our old church.

Bobby's calling was to the church. He says his proudest moments are conducting the baptisms, communions, weddings, and funerals he has performed for our friends and their relatives.

And Milt? He became a lawyer and went on to have an illustrious career as an assistant district attorney. We saw each other often during his time as ADA. Sometimes we argued cases together, sometimes we were opposing counsel. Never once did our work interfere with our personal relationship, nor did it rattle our bond. Milt was my best man when Sharon and I got married. In 1998, he happily agreed to come on board with our firm but refused to be a named partner. Milt was at work in his office when Flight 11 hit.

Last year, Patrick, Jimmy, Laurie, and Bobby spent a week with me here in Hawai'i. It was the smallest reunion we've had so far and our first without Karen. We reminisced about the old days and the great times we had had together, starting with the first time I stepped in during their stickball game. We talked a lot about Karen, who passed away a few years ago at the age of sixty-five. She was surrounded by her loving family: her husband of forty-six years, six children, and sixteen grandchildren including one adorable little infant granddaughter named Lizzy, in honor of my Lizzy...our Lizzy. We wondered if that little treasure was going to be anything like our Lizzy.

Saying goodbye at the end of their visit was a gloomy moment for all of us because we all suspected that by the next reunion, if we were going to have one, the herd would be thinner again. I had the same fear of letting go and moving on fifty-one years earlier, when there were still ten of us. But I had no choice. Taking Dad's advice, I set out to discover.

Chapter 16 - Voice: Dominic

My name is Dominic Bandall. Today is Monday, March 4th, 2019. This is session number eleven in my interview with Ms. Angela Grant.

  I moved into a single room in one of the Hunter dormitories downtown. Even though it was my mother's suggestion that I move there, she was worried that the commute to the main campus on 68th Street would be a lot for me—two trips a day, each requiring two subways and a bit of a walk. She even worried it would take time away from my studies. I'm sure my mother had an ulterior motive when she suggested I leave home and move to student housing: enhancing my pathetic social life.

  Whatever her reasons, she was sad to see me go. Dad told me she missed me terribly when I left. He told her she could so easily hop on the subway and visit me anytime, but she refused. She said she wanted to treat me like the grown man I was. She didn't want to drop in on me unannounced and would only meet me when we had planned it in advance. I took the hint from Dad and I made a point of calling her often and asking her to go on mother-son outings. She never told me she was missing me, and I deliberately did not press her to talk about it. I wanted to treat her with the same respect she gave me. Being sensitive to my mother's wants and needs was, I realized, the key to establishing a mature relationship with her. And, if that didn't work out so well, I would just have to rely on the old-fashioned way: listening to my father tell me what an ignorant blockhead I was and how to treat my mother better!

My new world at college felt far colder than my life in the Bronx, but I got to like the anonymity and isolation of living in the City. There are millions of people in Manhattan, but if you stay away from them, they stay away from you. It is an unspoken rule. Even in the dorm, when you passed a neighbor in the hallway, there was no need to speak; a simple nod was all that was needed. This was not, however, the case in the classroom. Even in the lecture halls with two or three hundred students, I would invariably sit next to the one with a big, wide-open personality. I found mine in the first minute, of the first class, of the first semester, of my first year. I knew immediately that Maria DiGiorgio was from Queens, specifically Jackson Heights, specifically 79th Street, just off Northern Boulevard. And...that English Composition was her first class, but she almost didn't take it because it started so early and she had to take the bus in and was worried about what time she had to get up, and she left the house at five o'clock just to make sure she was there on time. But, could I believe it? It took her only thirty-five minutes which left her with too much time, but there was a great diner just across the way.

Maria was exhausting. After that "conversation," the longest one we ever had, she knew my name was Dominic.

We had several classes together. Fortunately, she found out quickly I was not much of a talker, and eventually, she stopped trying to engage me. I was proud that I wasn't a talker. Funny how we change, isn't it?

I took as many of the required core courses as I could in the first few semesters. I had no idea what I wanted to major in, but the required classes were meant to prepare me for whatever I chose to focus on. My ability to quickly commit the material to memory and my lonely existence allowed me ample time to study. After the first three weeks, the only thing I had to do was participate in class and act engaged. Aside from occasional visits to Pelham Bay and going out with Mother, I spent my time "discovering," as my father put it, in the afternoons and weekends. I had no interest in making room for anything else.

Listing my options was step one and discovery was step two.

One day, early in the semester, I grabbed my composition book, now filled with a page and a half of wisdom, sat down at the desk, and pulled out the list of college programs and courses I had tucked in the back. I planned to take a systematic yet straightforward approach to choose what I was going to study. How ridiculous, I thought, that I, perhaps one of the most powerful minds in history, was about to determine my future by making a pros and cons list from a school brochure. My process was underwhelming, at best.

> Anthropology: I was, and am still, intrigued by the study of humans, humanity, societies, and cultures. That was a possibility.
>
> Archaeology: I saw this as a subset of anthropology, the study of human history through the study of physical remains. Possible.
>
> Art: Art can bring beauty into your life, and learning how to appreciate and understand it was something I thought I would enjoy.
>
> Biological Sciences: Intriguing! I put an asterisk next to this listing, mainly because it could be a way for me to understand Billy's fate.

Chemistry: I thought this might help me better understand my ability.

Economics: Immediately discounted. I struggled enough with the flawed concepts while in high school and wanted nothing more to do with it.

Education: I said no to this as well. The only reason I would ever consider teaching was so that, on the unlikely chance I would ever meet someone with my ability, I could teach them like Giuseppe had taught me. Also, I was having enough trouble myself learning about the moments I discovered.

English: I had no love for the art of language, written or spoken. I already struggled with my need to artfully craft my words to conceal the information my ability afforded me. In other words, I couldn't just speak or write naturally.

Language: I pushed French, German, Italian, Russian, Spanish, and Latin to the wayside.

Geography: I didn't know much about this field of study, nor did I understand how my ability would impact my understanding of the nature and relative arrangement of dirt.

History: I shuddered just thinking about being fed the bastardizations of history most of the world accepts as fact. And to have to spout it back! No! I was so repulsed at the thought, I hastily scratched off anthropology and archaeology too.

Home Economics: I chuckled at what I saw as the frivolousness of some studies. This was one of the subjects I would rely on heavily in later life.

Mathematics: With all the information about math from the beginning of time already at my fingertips, I saw no value in the abstract study of mathematical concepts.

Philosophy: Much like religion, I considered this as a fallback option should I be unable to develop a tangible cause and effect.

Physical Education: I looked down at the brace and chuckled again.

Political Science: Much like history, I found no appeal in trying to convince people that the facts they believe so profoundly are irrelevant or wrong.

Psychology: The thought of analyzing the mental status of others, especially when based on a limited understanding of a person's past and present state of mind, was offensive. I thought of the way people had analyzed Giuseppe's psychological state, and the understanding of Mr. Strauss as a loving, compassionate father, and feared the day when someone peered into me.

Of twenty-two offered courses of study, all but art, chemistry, and biological sciences seemed impractical for me, not to mention distasteful or irrelevant. Trust me when I say that the irony of passing on many of these courses of study in 1967 is not lost on me today.

I made an appointment to meet the chair of the department of art and art history, Professor Davet Beussier, who asked his students to call him by his first name. He was an odd little fellow who relished influencing the impressionable young minds of incoming freshmen. He told me why I should major in art and began explaining the two different areas of study within an art major—study of art and history of art. As soon as he launched into the wonders of becoming an artist, I interrupted him and explained I had no artistic talent and had no plans to become an artist. Instead, I was interested in the history of art and how it had impacted cultures throughout history. When you look at a painting, there is no dispute that the painting was indeed created. When you look at the *Adoration of the Magi,* there is no deniability as to its creation. Machu Picchu, Stonehenge, Ta Prohm...those sites exist. The appreciation of their beauty and the interpretation of their impact are points to debate and discuss. There is no set answer, and this is what fascinated me. In my naivete, I failed to consider that the actual origin of many famous works of art is not known. I didn't yet realize that art was another victim of our reinterpretation of history. I asked Davet to tell me more about the art history program.

He took me to the department lecture hall. Inside, preparations were underway for the creation of a large model, a replica, of the ancient city of Rome. He told me he got the idea for having his senior class build the model while he and his wife were touring Rome last summer; specifically, while standing among the ruins of the Colosseum. Over the next semester, Davet explained, he would guide them through the architectural development of the city from 509 BC to 330 AD. He hoped that by creating a scale model of ancient Rome—the walls, gates, roads and aqueducts, etcetera—his students would learn about that fine example of grand architecture. And, that by learning about the many materials and processes the Romans used—marble, painting, mosaic, gems, silver and bronze work, terra-cotta—his students would obtain a deeper understanding of all art, not just Roman art.

He then asked me to envision walking around Rome, just as he and his wife had, just as people have for millennia...to imagine the grand coliseums, bathhouses, gardens, porticoes, and theaters the city once had. That night, I did precisely that; I shared the same moments in Rome that Davet and Sophie Beussier had when he first got the idea to have his students build a model of the ancient city. I saw the sparkle in her eyes while she watched his passion and energy. He wanted to inspire his students, but I could see the incredible passion it inspired in him and his wife that day. My moment ended with the passionate kiss they shared at the base of the Colosseum.

I woke in the morning with a profound sense of sadness. What was the value of sharing someone else's past moment? I could see the same magic they saw, hear the same sounds of life they heard, and even though I could see their passion, I couldn't feel it. I realized that watching others and not living my own life would never be satisfying.

College, my new beginning, should have been the place I would discover my true passion in life...the place that would at least ignite the spark. Instead, I fell into a numbing depression. I put the search for my future on hold. I was drowning in dark visions and memories of the past. You know, in retrospect, I find it almost amusing. Fear, distrust, and a general lack of interest made me turn away from so many things that mean a lot to me now. Unsure of the future and afraid of the past, I focused on the present, especially my studies. I remembered what Dad told me: learn now and in time, my calling, my future, would surface. Back then, I never thought I would actually have a rewarding future, but I trusted my father implicitly and I didn't feel like I needed to second-guess him. I wondered if my own child would have the same kind of trust in me and follow my suggestions as readily as I did my father's.

The weekdays were focused on school. On the weekends, I spent time with family and friends, and had adventures. For the first time, I saw the City as a tourist. I wanted my own experiences and memories, not dreams and moments. I took the New York subway challenge and rode every subway line, all for twenty cents. Mother and Dad and I went to the grand opening of the new Madison Square Garden and we saw Bob Hope and Bing Crosby perform as part of the USO show. I was there during the April 4th riots when Dr. King was assassinated. Years later, I looked into James Earl Ray's eyes when he pulled the trigger.

That year, 1968, I felt the fear and anger that was gripping our city. There were the Columbia University protests by the Students for a Democratic Society (the SDS), the teachers strike, Bobby Kennedy...hell, if there was a reason to protest, we did it. Just before the violence between antiwar protesters and police broke out at the Democratic Convention in Chicago, my friend Billy shipped out to Vietnam. While my fondness for him increased after I watched him in my nighttime visits, so too did my hatred for the war. The days we shared while he was over there were particularly intense because Billy was like a brother; when I awoke from being in those moments, I felt the same fear, exhilaration, and rage my friend on the other side of the world felt.

* * *

When I woke up on the morning of March 16th, 1969, I decided the time had come to start a new journey. While in the hospital recovering from my dangerous foray into the nonexistent moment with Billy, I thought a lot about the two of us, and decided there had to be more to our connection than just an emotional bond. I thought I might learn more about this, about the relationship between our brains and the energy around us, by taking some biology classes.

Because I was going to be missing quite a bit of school, I asked my mother to contact the chair of the biological sciences department, Dr. Andrew Downing, to ask him if I could continue my studies remotely while I was recovering. He got my teachers to give me all the class work, homework, and texts. They were more than happy to oblige, perhaps because they saw me as a serious and promising student.

As soon as I realized those classes might help me discover more about my ability, I jumped into the material with such enthusiasm. Of most significant interest to me were the classes on learning and memory, microbial genetics, and animal physiology. I began to think about a project that might help me understand my ability: if I could recreate my unique ability in an animal, I would be on my way to understanding what I needed to discover. After I was discharged from the hospital, I met with Dr. Downing. He told me that if I graduated with a degree in the behavioral sciences, I should consider pursuing a graduate program that researched abnormalities and abnormal development in the animal brain.

I was scheduled to go back to school in the fall of 1969. By then, I had completed most of the required courses, and I planned to focus on the classes I thought might help me unlock the secret to my ability. I could hardly contain my enthusiasm and spent most of my days researching at the library. I kept mulling over the need to better control this thing. If I could, I thought that maybe someday I could close my eyes without being afraid that my own thoughts might destroy me.

Admittedly, from the moment I first woke up in the hospital, I had been pushing myself hard, but I still lacked endurance and tired quickly. One afternoon, while I was in the library reading an article entitled *Perceptual Illusions and Brain Models,* my eyes grew weary, but I kept reading. To create a definitive image that I could experience in my dreams and commit to memory, I continued to flip through the pages. As I worked through the last few pages—an analysis of cerebral functions—I was startled by a voice from behind me.

"You know, that article would be a lot better if you actually read the words." I turned around and saw the most beautiful woman imaginable. She had a stack of books in her arms and a slight, almost indifferent grin on her face. I noticed she had subtle beads of sweat on her forehead. It was still warm. Summer was refusing to let go of its last few days, and I reached in my pocket and offered her my handkerchief.

As I was about to stand up to assist her with the books she was carrying, I stammered, "They've got every fan in the building blowing, but it's still a scorcher in here." I remained seated, however, for my leg provided no assistance and my left hand was curled inward, resting lifelessly in a sling across my chest. Instead, I asked her to join me and sit down. "You look a little worn out there." She was stunning. I couldn't take my eyes off her as she drifted around the table. She was wearing a simple yellow linen dress that was just above the knee, and low-heeled sandals in the same striking yellow. When she walked, I saw the slight definition of muscles flexing in her calves. When she sat, I locked on her beautiful gray eyes—a sharp contrast to the brightness of her wardrobe. I nervously extended my hand and introduced myself.

"My name's Sharon...Sharon Peers," she responded. "It's a pleasure to meet you, Dominic. Would you care to explain which of your classes requires flipping through the pages of a journal? Most of my teachers require that we actually read the words, understand them, and occasionally, even remember them."

Suddenly, I felt rather foolish. I made a mental note to add Rule Number 78 to my list: Be careful not to display my ability around others. No sooner did I think that than I violated it: "I just can remember what I read, no matter how fast I do it." Years later, on our tenth anniversary, we relived our first moment together, laughing at the effect my exaggerated sense of self-importance had on others.

From that moment on, I assumed a role with Sharon that I would never escape: I could never tell her anything but the complete truth about anything, and that included what I saw in my dreams, what I felt in my heart, and whatever was in my head. A filter is a wonderful, often essential, skill to use when conversing, but I never could curtail or modify anything I shared with her. I later realized that being graceful with my words and using the right tone were the best tactics, eventually excelling in those areas. Over the years, we reminisced about our first meeting. Sharon's way of telling it was far better than mine. She said she had first seen me from across the library as I was mindlessly turning the pages of a journal. She said she knew immediately that I was special—everything about me intrigued her. To get a closer look at me, she quietly wound her way across the library. Then, after checking me out, she moved in and introduced herself. I would have said her motive was curiosity and interest in an oddity; Sharon said it was fascination and a desire to know more about me.

"No, that's not it," she said, more to herself than to me. "You weren't thinking about the book you were reading. You were somewhere else...you were thinking about someone else." My blush confirmed her guess. She continued, "From the look on your face, and your reaction just now, you were thinking of someone close to you. Did you think you'd find your answer in those books? When did you realize the answer was not there?"

I was dumbstruck. Somehow, a total stranger had homed in on my innermost thoughts. It was just unimaginable, yet I had encountered the unthinkable once before in a girl. I might have pressed her for more information, but I was too surprised to speak. I watched her eyes as she scanned the scene: my leg locked straight in its brace, my arm hanging across my body, surrounded by stacks of scientific books and journals. After absorbing all she needed, Sharon looked at me and with a swipe of her finger, she pushed a lock of blonde hair that had fallen across her face back into her short-layered bob. "I've seen that look before," she said. "It is the look of loss…of a friend, a family member, a loved one. Have you lived through such a loss? And if so, I am sorry. You're sitting here in the library on a day when the temperature is expected to be almost one hundred degrees, and here you are with a heavy brace on your leg and a sling around your arm. That must not be comfortable on the coolest of days. There must be an important reason for you to be here, but judging from the way I saw you reading, I don't think that is the case. I've been watching for some time. You seem to have lost interest, or perhaps you already found what you were looking for. Based on your reaction, I assume it is the former."

    That was the first time Ms. Sharon Peers impressed the hell out of me. It surely wasn't the last. For the next four hours, we played an uninterrupted game of *quid pro quo*. I told her I was indeed looking for something—concerning my friend's death—that I was trying to figure out what happens to the energy in a life when life ends.

Sharon had questions, but it was my turn. She told me she was a freshman at John Jay College and planned to attend law school after graduating. She explained that reading people and trying to imagine their story was her way of practicing the art of interrogation and cross-examination. It was her turn, so I answered her question about what had happened to Billy.

I told her I was also a CUNY student at Hunter College and was in the process of figuring out what to study...what to do with my life. I told her a bit about my family, my childhood, my attacks of cerebral hypoxia. Obviously, I didn't say a word about my ability. Sharon told me about her life growing up in Connecticut with her parents and sister. She told me her whole family—her mother, father, and little sister, Allison—had been killed by a drunk driver. The driver was charged with vehicular homicide and had received only a sixteen-month prison sentence. She had moved to New York three years earlier and had been living with her grandparents ever since. I also talked about loss—Giuseppe, Lizzy, and Billy—and of my admittedly inexplicable need to find answers about their deaths. But our conversation became morose, so I changed the subject with one more question: "Do you like Italian food?"

Chapter 17 - Voice: Dominic

My name is Dominic J. Bandall, and this is session number twelve in my interview with Angela Grant.

Sharon and I were engaged forty-eight years ago today, on March 5th, 1971. It was a beautiful day in Rome...but, I don't want to get ahead of myself. So much happened between the first time I met her—the love of my life—and the day we got engaged.

Our "first date" ended up lasting six incredible nights.

Sharon took me up on my offer for dinner. We left the library and took the subway to Little Italy to eat at my favorite restaurant, Paolucci's. On the way downtown, I boasted about how great their food was, but she seemed unimpressed, as are most New Yorkers when you claim to know of a restaurant that is better than their favorite. She voted for Lombardi's and assured me that I just had to try their to-die-for hot antipasto. I guaranteed her she would love my pick better—neither of us was willing to budge. Once we got out of the subway, she asked, "Will you be alright walking all the way to Mulberry Street? Will your leg be okay?" I assured her it would. Heck, with how I was feeling, I could've floated there!

As we walked, I told her, "My father fought in Germany alongside the owner, Dominick Paolucci."

Sharon looked at me and winked. "Dominic?"

I smiled. "Dominick-with a 'k'. Dominick has extended a standing invitation to my family to come anytime. He always tells me, 'If it's a special occasion, I will make sure it is extra delicious.' I eat here pretty regularly, just about once a week, but those are not special occasions—not like tonight is." My focus at the time was on maintaining my balance, but when I first revisited that moment, I noticed the corners of Sharon's mouth curling ever so slightly as she fought to suppress her smile.

When we walked into the restaurant, I was promptly greeted by Dominick and his wife Frances, who gave me warm hugs and kisses. Frances became emotional when she saw my leg brace and sling. I realized I had not been there since my last hospitalization. Dominick said I looked strong, but Frances thought I looked too skinny...then again, she always thought I looked too skinny. Then, when she realized the beautiful woman who had walked in just before me was my date, she greeted Sharon warmly and jumped into action. Frances made us feel like the most important customers in the restaurant; she even asked the couple at her best table if they would mind moving. She did it with such diplomacy and decorum, although they were definitely going to move.

Once we were seated, Dominick gave us menus. He knew I would have my usual, the chicken parmesan, but presented a menu nonetheless. I always loved their chicken parm. Sharon perused the menu and asked me about some of their entrées. I was impressed when she pronounced each of them with a beautiful accent. She spoke fluent Italian! It was charming, hearing her speak it with her New York accent, with those low guttural tones. She asked Dominick, in his native language, if the *perciatelli al filetto di pomodoro* was prepared at the time of each order or if it had been made earlier, because she didn't like it when the onions were overcooked and sat too long. Dominick assured her every meal was made to order, and that the onions could be cooked to whatever translucency she wanted. He also recommended the broiled sea bass, although he made a point of telling us it had lots of garlic. Sharon looked at me and winked. "I don't think that will be a problem tonight."

After we placed our orders, I looked over at Sharon. She had just come from a day at the library but couldn't have looked more beautiful had she spent hours getting ready. She was radiant...just a natural beauty. Sharon wore no makeup, yet her lips were rosy and her cheeks blushed pink. Her fingernails were neither long nor painted. She was not wearing any jewelry. Any pendant or string would only have detracted from the gentle curves of her neck. She didn't seem to mind my stare—my obvious admiration—but she would not tolerate any prolonged pauses in our conversation. "From the way Frances is fawning all over us, I bet she's going to call your mother with a detailed report." She grinned at the humor of her insight. Whatever she imagined Frances might say, it did not appear to bother or embarrass her.

"I'm sure that call is happening right now. Speaking of my mother, would you care to join me for dinner Saturday...in the Bronx, with my parents?"

"I think I am already going to be invited."

We had a fine meal. When I noticed she didn't order wine, I asked if it had something to do with the incident with her family. Sharon replied, "It wasn't an incident. It was murder." She had no objection to alcohol; in fact, she loved having a glass of good wine. But that night, when the waiter nor I asked if she wanted wine, she decided to refrain since the omission was most likely deliberate. Even then, before she honed her skills to a fine art, Sharon could read people with alarming accuracy. God, that woman was smart. I confirmed her hypothesis; alcohol had never touched my lips, and I saw no reason it ever would.

I also asked if her decision to study law had anything to do with her family. She told me, "Yes, it did, but only in part. I truly believe in a just and fair world, and what happened to my family only increased that belief in the need for justice. When I was a child, I was taught everything happens because it is God's will. I was also taught that, 'For justice will prevail, and all the morally upright will be vindicated,' but now I know that justice doesn't happen simply because it is God's will; to be vindicated, vindication must be deliberately sought. The Bible is often contradictory, but many of the stories have value and speak the truth."

For the first time, our ideologies seemed to be at odds. I had to interject: "History as we know it is rarely based on authenticity. Often the stories we accept as factual are only one version of a truth. They have been revised, edited, and polished to present a specific message." My comment seemed to strike a nerve with Sharon—this young woman who would later become our lead trial lawyer. Both of us dug in our heels. What ensued was a most heated, but enjoyable, discussion in which we both tried to impress the other with our smarts. We were comically brazen in our approaches.

"I'll agree with that, Dominic, to a point. It is our responsibility as fair and honest people to eradicate inaccuracies and falsehoods from the records, and to work with only facts and truths. Remember the Warren Commission after Kennedy's assassination? I followed the progress of that investigation for nearly ten months while they were researching the facts, rumors, and accusations. I was riveted to the news and so inspired when they finally got to the truth. It was during that time that I decided I wanted to be a lawyer. I believe in justice and seeking it at all costs. You know, I have a bound copy of the thousand-plus-page Warren Report on my bookshelf because it reminds me every day what can be done in the name of justice."

"You're assuming the report contains the truth about what happened," I rebutted. "I have firsthand knowledge—so-called, that is—of Kennedy's assassination and know that while most of the report is accurate, there are many small discrepancies. Despite the errors, it is considered to be the final and accurate version of the assassination. From a historian's perspective, it's their Gettysburg Address."

Sharon looked confused. She started her reply with, "What the fuck...?" but changed her mind midcourse and chose a softer response. "What do you mean 'their Gettysburg Address'?"

I began a carefully constructed explanation of my analogy. Of course, neither of us disputed the enormous significance of Lincoln's speech that day on the battlefield, but then I told her about a version of events that differed from the historically accepted facts: Lincoln actually wrote the document typically recognized as the actual Gettysburg Address while he was on the train traveling back to Washington, hours after he had delivered the speech. I told her about the other versions of the speech, all of which are still in existence, and all of which are considered imperfect reproductions of that original document.

"What if," I proposed, "the original copy, with the original wording, is no longer in existence, or lost to a private collector? What if the original speech as Lincoln delivered it that day was never put on paper and instead what we have are merely his own edited versions of the address?" I thought it best to introduce some ambiguity into the day's actual events.

Sharon conceded. "That's an interesting idea. Maybe there is value in considering the existence of alternate versions, but what if the difference between the versions is something as minor as different punctuation? That would not change the message intended by President Lincoln."

"I agree, but let's take it one step further. What if the difference is something more important than punctuation? Let's imagine the speech was never given. Even more extreme, let's imagine Lincoln's declamation was originally intended to express further dissent with the actions of the Confederate states. That would have created a much different legacy for Mr. Lincoln." There was no rebuttal, no confirmation, no need for clarification. Sharon just wanted to see how far down that rabbit hole I was willing to go. It felt safe for me to keep going.

"I am using the Gettysburg Address as a metaphor. History as it is generally presented, as it is taught in school, as it is written in books, is rarely accurate. Instead, it is often the agreed-upon message the people choose to present, or at least, the majority of people.

Sometimes that message justifies what it is we think is right. Sometimes, it is presented in a way intended to remove ambiguities. Even other times the history as it is presented is intended to increase certainty among a class of people, reinforcing our collective need for 'faith.'"

Sharon leaned back and pushed her plate forward slightly, promising to return to her remaining piece of fish. Taking her time, slowly dabbing the corners of her mouth, she finally responded, "Okay, Dominic. I've been trying to figure you out, but I have to admit, I'm stumped. Since you are now aware of the extent of my deductive skills, what are your limitations? I know you have a disability, have had it since you were a child, and it's getting worse. You are very intelligent, possibly one of the smartest people I have met. You can do—can be—whatever you want. The problem, as I see it, is that you have an overwhelming need to do something, but you are just not sure what it is. You have been through tragedies and felt a lot of pain, more than anyone should have to experience. You seem to care for others deeply, but are hesitant to establish significant connections. Some might see this as shyness; others would call it arrogance. But there is something else that I can't quite identify. It is something I've never experienced before, but for some strange reason, I want to. What is it about you, Dominic Bandall? What is it you are hiding from everyone?"

I froze, unsure of whether there was any safe response. Thankfully, Sharon did not leave me in that uncomfortable state for long. She waved her hand, "Never mind. I don't want to put you on the spot like this. You can just think about an answer, and maybe we can discuss it in the morning."

If she intended that comment to lessen my anxiety, she failed miserably. "In the morning?" My mind ran wild. Did she think we would spend the night together? Did she intend for me to go home with her? I had no idea where she lived, who she lived with or if she lived alone. Maybe she still lived with her grandparents. I didn't think they'd be pleased if some random guy slept at their house, in their granddaughter's bed. I scrambled to consider every possibility. We could go to my dorm room, but were we allowed to have guests? If not, was it enforced? After all, I thought, there was a guy down the hall from me whose girlfriend slept with him almost every night. But did Sharon consider me her boyfriend? Even though it was the '60s, the age of "free sex," I was a very sheltered young man. Did she expect me to have sex with her? I had no idea if I could go through with it, or even what I was supposed to do. In fact, that one kiss with Karen was the extent of my sexual experience. I had seen people have sex in my dreams. I saw some photographs in magazines when I was thirteen and I fell asleep wondering what had happened when those photos were taken. I didn't think I could do any of that with my leg brace on, or with my arm problems. I was sure something would go wrong...that she would be turned off or frightened...that the magic I had felt all day would dissipate in a flash. I thought about what it would look like to see her, what it would feel like to hold her. It had been so long since I had felt that kind of interest in a girl. It had been so long since I had watched Lizzy in my dreams. Oh, Lizzy! I panicked. I thought about the beautiful idea of spending a night with Sharon and compared it to the horrid decimation of Lizzy's life. I had no idea what to do.

 Never noticing my grueling moments of agony, Sharon just continued rambling on, with hardly a pause between sentences. "I hope you don't mind if I crash in your room. Nothing weird or anything, but I don't want to go all the way out to Staten Island this late. Besides, I'm having a great time. How about you?"

I nonchalantly shot back, "Yeah, that sounds cool." I hoped to god my flushed face didn't give me away. Years later, Sharon loved it when I retold her that story. I knew everything that happened that night, but not what Sharon had been thinking. I asked her many times about it...if she thought anything was going to happen between us, if she wanted me to make an advance. Over the next thirty-three years, every time I asked her, she would only say: "I'll take that to the grave with me." But as always, it was accompanied by her wink. It was endearing.

I fought to put away my devilish thoughts, and we continued the evening. After I paid the bill, we headed out into the night. The City had cooled, and I felt energized. I recommended walking back to my dorm room, but Sharon, always my caretaker, suggested a taxi...her treat.

I offered her modest, if not oversized, sleepwear and told her to take the bed. I would sleep on the floor. Sharon thought it would be nice for us to share the covers but, she said, only if I could "continue to be a gentleman."

Before we fell asleep that night, Sharon thanked me for a stimulating day. She said, "I can't wait to see what kind of amazement tomorrow brings." She held my face and gave me a passionate kiss. I wanted the moment to never end. I dozed off with the realization that, fortunately, it never would.

    That was the day I met Sharon Peers. Thursday, August 28th, 1969.

Chapter 18 - Voice: Dominic

Today is March 5th, 2019. My name is Dominic J. Bandall, and this is session number thirteen in my interview with Angela Grant.

I woke the next morning unsure if the night before had even occurred. I was so afraid it hadn't, I couldn't even look over to the other side of the bed. Instead, I just lay there and let out a deep sigh.

"Good morning." That beautiful voice let me know everything was still perfect in my world. Those treasured moments from yesterday, so crisp in my mind—what I felt, what I saw, heard, and smelled—all of it had happened. It was real. If I'd had only that one day, it would have been enough for me, but knowing I would have another...well, I felt a surge of excitement and glee.

"Good morning to you!"

Six hours of cramped slumber had only made her more beautiful. When I saw her grin, I could tell there was something on her mind. "Have you ever seen yourself sleeping? Wait, hah! Never mind...of course you haven't. I've been watching you sleep for the better part of an hour now and it's the most amazing sight. You never moved. Not your head, not your arms or hands, or your legs. If it weren't for your faint breaths and the gentle beating of your heart, you would have made a great corpse. I counted: thirty-two beats per minute. That's incredible."

"I guess my body was expending energy elsewhere," I replied and quickly changed the subject. "Are you hungry? There is a great bagel shop on the corner."

"No. I've got to get back home."

"Yeah, okay. Are your grandparents going to be upset that you stayed out all night?"

"No, man," she quipped, flashing the peace sign. "Free love!"

"Right. Well, I guess you've got to go home sometime." Sharon told me later that I looked at her with the saddest puppy-dog eyes she had ever seen.

"I just have to go home to take a bath and change my clothes. I don't want to spend the day with you looking like I was out partying all night." She smiled with that wink—oh god, that wink—before continuing, "Hey, are you still going to call your mother?"

"Yeah. If I don't, she'll probably be knocking on my door by noon." Sharon leaned in and planted a deep kiss on my mouth.

"That's a good idea."

I didn't want our time together to end, even if it was only a temporary interruption. "I have an appointment with my physical therapist at nine o'clock and then I'm free for the rest of the day. Do you want to come back to the City later and meet me?"

"Nine o'clock? I'm coming with you! After your appointment, we can go together to my grandparents'." That was not a suggestion or a question.

While hunting for her clothes in my tiny room, Sharon turned and looked at me, peering hard into my eyes. We had been playing this silly game of trying to read each other's intentions and desires. One thing I knew is that I was hooked. I was ready for anything she wanted to give me, but I had no idea what she was offering, what she wanted or, for that matter, what I needed. I could see her mind racing, perhaps trying to make the same determinations as me.

"There is only one unresolved matter," Sharon announced as she lifted my undershirt over her head and tossed it onto the floor. Assuming this would be something I didn't want to hear, I panicked. The girl knew she was in complete control at that moment, and paused before stepping into her dress and fastening the yellow buttons running down her midriff. Finally, she said, "What's the secret you have, Dominic? What didn't you tell me last night?"

Having a secret, especially holding on to one like mine, can be an enormous burden. For so long I had wanted—needed—to tell someone. My truth kept me isolated and secluded; I was sure that telling someone would finally free me and allow me to have a connection, a relationship with another person. Every day since the summer of 1957, I had needed to tell someone, but on August 29th, 1969, I no longer wanted to tell someone; I wanted to tell Sharon Peers! Nothing compares to the rush of exhilaration I felt about the prospect of discussing my ability. I had felt that same euphoria a few times when I thought I could trust someone enough to tell them, but it was only momentary, for I never could take the plunge. It was just as exhilarating as five days ago when I told you, Angela. That morning with Sharon was the first time I got so close to revealing my secret.

But there was not enough time just then. I tried to explain this to Sharon. I promised we'd discuss it later in the day. She refused. Sharon had no idea what she was stepping into. Her suggestion to "just tell me and we can talk about details later" was laughable. If she'd known what was coming her way, surely she wouldn't have kept persisting.

Then, suddenly, I threw caution to the wind. What the hell, I figured, and gave the poor girl precisely what she asked for. "I'm able to go back in time and relive moments from the past...any event in history...any person...any era. I experience those moments in my sleep. Now, I must go to the doctor, as my body is failing because of the sins of my mind."

Sharon didn't look at me strangely. She didn't ask me for clarification. I think that is the moment I fell in love with her. "Okay," she said. "You need to get dressed so we can grab some bagels before your appointment. We can talk about the details later." She responded just as she had promised.

All I wanted was to finally bare my soul and share secrets I had kept inside for too long. At that moment, having access to the entire history of the world was less important than the fact that I had just told Sharon about it, even if I hadn't revealed any details...details would come later, as she suggested. So, silently, I grabbed a wrinkled pair of khakis and a faded blue button-down shirt. Ah, college days! Looking back, Sharon had her work cut out for her if she wanted me to be part of her world. Here she was, rummaging around my little dorm room for yesterday's clothing, attire meant for nothing more than a day in the library, yet she was dressed to the nines...and then there was me...in my wrinkled dreary clothes. As much as I was floored by Sharon's beauty, I was more blown away by her behavior toward me, especially the things she did not do. She didn't say a word about my pitiful wardrobe. When I was wrestling my leg back into its brace, she didn't wince or turn away. And she kept her word by not pressing me for more information about my other world just then.

We changed the subject to last night's meal. When I asked her what she thought, Sharon praised the meal as fantastic, as good as her favorite Italian restaurant–that fact pained her to admit. Her concession speech was graceful. Sadly, years later, in 2013, Dominick and Frances died only weeks apart. I can still envision my dad up in heaven, laughing about their timing, "You never did have an original thought, Nick!"

Sharon rubbed her tummy in anticipation as she ordered a plain bagel with a schmear: cream cheese, garlic, and extra capers. Adam didn't need to take my order. The usual.

On the walk up Park Avenue and on the bus to Lenox Hill Hospital, she wouldn't talk about anything but my physical therapy. "What do they do exactly? Do they stretch you? Do you do exercises? Will it improve your strength? How long are the sessions? Will they do the same things to your arm?" I discovered she knew a lot more about physical therapy than I did—a byproduct of living with elderly grandparents. I told her what I knew, and she filled in the blanks for me. The whole time, I was dying for her to ask me about my revelation. *Goddamnit,* I screamed in my head. *Why won't you talk about it? Why don't you ask me?*

In the waiting room, Sharon asked if she could look at the treatment records I had brought with me. I had nothing to hide from her. I wondered what she thought as she read the cover of my file:

Bandall, Dominic J.

DOB: October 9, 1949

Age: 19

Height: 5'11"

Weight: 151 lbs.

Diagnosis: Cerebral Hypoxia - March 3, 1961

L arm

L leg

I watched her read through the notes. Nearly six months had passed since my last hospitalization. As an inpatient, I was having daily, sometimes twice-daily PT sessions, and now, as an outpatient, I had them four days a week. All those appointments generated a lot of paperwork. She didn't appear to be satisfied with the summaries; she pored through the daily notes. I just sat back and watched her read. I had already memorized the whole thing. Besides, I had a better way to spend my time.

The moments we shared the night before had filled my dreams with an intensity words cannot describe. I could recall every movement, the faint whimper she made when satisfied, the sweet smell of her skin pressed close to mine. I had experienced many intense moments in my dreams, but I realized there was something different about my dreams of her. It was an imperceptible difference that I suddenly understood. For the first time, I realized there were different kinds of moments. All are flashes of energy that anyone can see, but the moments that are first formed in your own mind contain emotions that can never be experienced by someone else. The satisfaction of your own awareness, the anticipation of the next instant, the intense realization a moment is yours....

I looked at the sandy-blonde hair that fell across her face. Every strand, bleached by the sun, was a slightly different shade. Her face and eyes were scrunched with intensity as she tried to envision the pain I had endured. Her breasts, rhythmically rising and falling with every shallow breath, became still when she came to the more intense parts of my report. Her lips, slightly pursed, curled up on one side when she noticed my stare. That grin! That moment existed only because of her, and only for me.

They called my name far too quickly.

For two hours, Sharon watched as I did my therapy. I struggled. I failed. I fell. As the therapist worked my two mangled limbs, I groaned, I screamed, and I cursed. Sharon never turned away. She did not look at me with pity. She just watched with an equal mixture of curiosity and concern. When I was done, and was struggling with the straps on my brace, she stood by my side, gently rubbing her hand across my shoulders.

"Better now?"

"Better," I replied.

She leaned down, said, "Good," and then kissed me on the cheek. As we were leaving, we discussed the best way to get to Staten Island. Sharon voted for the ferry, and although it was not the most efficient route, we both agreed we couldn't pass it up on that beautiful summer day. We chatted on the bus as we made our way downtown to the ferry terminal. Something about her set me at ease, emotionally and physically. She held my hand as we walked between the piers. That was one moment when her hands were not busy animating everything she said. She was always very expressive with her hands....

As we walked, she told me about her grandparents, Robert and Dorothy Peers. They came to the United States from their Dutch homeland, Robert in 1898 and Dot in 1903. Both were living in lower Manhattan when they met—they married a year later. Their commitment to family was a constant source of happiness for them, even during the Depression and going through two world wars. Tragedy struck when Dennis, their youngest son, and his family were killed in a car accident. Robert and Dot were shattered. They only discovered that their granddaughter, Sharon, was alive when she walked into their living room the next day. One little child's life went on. The heartbroken couple rejoiced. They took care of Sharon ever since that day. She was an angel who would always find her way.

Even though I would meet the Peers in less than an hour, I experienced so many emotions in that short period that I felt like I already knew so many moments of their lifetimes.

Sharon and I sat on a bench while we waited thirty minutes for the next ferry. She held my face in her hands and pressed her lips to mine, then leaned back so she could get a good look at me.

"What?" I asked nervously.

"I just want to look at you...a reminder that this is real." It was her way of connecting with me, of letting me know she was happy with our new friendship. I was on cloud nine.

And then, she changed the subject. "Explain to me what you said, that you can 'relive moments from the past.' What does that mean?" Angela, the explanation I offered Sharon was far less polished than the one I gave you on Thursday. I had never shared my secret with anyone, so it was crude and unfinished. For fifteen minutes, I explained my ability, how it worked, the scope of my access and reach into the past, and the physical consequences I faced when I did it incorrectly. She sat there silently and stoically while I delivered that mind-boggling confession. She did not look at me like I was crazy...the way you did. She remained quiet when I finished speaking. I couldn't tell if she believed me, pitied me because she thought I was deluded, or was angered that I thought she might fall for such a ridiculous claim. As she told me later, she felt all of the above; everything in her heart and soul told her I was telling her the truth, but everything in her brain told her to doubt me.

After getting on the ferry, we stood on the deck and watched New York Harbor disappear. We didn't talk. Finally, by the time the Statue of Liberty came into view, she said, "You know, I hope you realize how bizarre your story sounds, but, okay, okay. However, you are going to have to convince me. Convince me it's true." She rubbed the side of my face with her hand, and we walked across the bow toward the exit.

I spent the rest of the day convincing Sharon the only way I knew how: by telling her stories about what had happened in my life. I told her about my father and String Bean. I told her about the insane summer I was hospitalized, met Giuseppe, and met Lizzy. I told her about faraway adventures—on the battlefield in Gettysburg, in the forests of Germany, in ancient Egypt and Mesopotamia. I introduced her to Lizzy, and Billy, and the rest of the gang. I shared some of my exhilarating moments and my darkest nightmares. I described how I could so effortlessly learn and remember what I was taught and the difficulty of discovering that much of it was not accurate. I told her as much about my past as I could fit in before we arrived at her grandparents' home.

Life continued to unfold around us. I met Mr. and Mrs. Peers. We shared a lovely afternoon...lovely except for the thirty minutes of interrogation I was subjected to when Sharon excused herself to clean up. I even called Mother, who wasn't thrilled that I had disappeared for the day—she had already spoken with Frances—but was excited when I told her I was going to be bringing my new friend over on Saturday afternoon...a girl. We enjoyed an early supper and laughed. I told them about school and my classes. I was the perfect polite, quiet, interesting guest. Every time Sharon and I were alone, she pressed me for more stories, but there was never time to give me her reaction.

We left early in the evening. During the ferry ride, again, she asked for more stories, and more information about my ability. I told her about the blissful dream I had had revisiting our kiss the night before. When I stopped talking, she gave me a surprised look. "That's it?" she said. "You've skipped to last night already? How do you expect me to understand you when you condense twelve years of superpowers into eight hours?" I felt minimized and got defensive.

"Ability…I refer to it as my ability. I guess I did summarize a lot of it. Sorry if I bored you."

"I'm sorry. Ability. And, no, you did not bore me! It's just that yesterday, when you were telling me about your life, you were spirited and your eyes sparkled. It was so interesting, I hung on every word. Today, I saw my grandparents have the same response. You have such a fantastic affinity for storytelling, but I can't tell if these stories you animate are real, fable, delusion, or maybe just beyond my comprehension. Perhaps it is all of these….

"The way you explained your…ability—as you call it—was not particularly clear and there is something I don't trust. Today, at my grandparents', I listened to you tell them a clean, innocent—and untrue—version of our time last night, and when you did your words sounded forced. I also know how you sound when you talk about something you care for; you don't need to put any effort into making your point. The stories you told my grandparents were different. You rolled out some fantastic tales, and each of them sounded equally unbelievable." At the time, I didn't realize I had not yet developed a technique for articulating my moments. I was trying to convince her that my ability was real instead of just letting my stories, my words, make the case for me.

We walked in silence from the ferry to the bus stop. Sharon wanted to give me time to absorb her rejection. When she stopped to check the bus schedule, I kept walking up Water Street. It was lunacy for me to assume I could've walked four miles to my dorm, but there was no way I was going to stop and face further disgrace. Many years later, on our fifth wedding anniversary, Sharon told me she had considered letting me walk away. If she needed to, she could have stayed with her friends in Tribeca for the night.

Just before I turned the corner, she yelled, "Hey! What is your problem?" This, from the woman who had just discredited everything about me! I turned and stormed back in a fit of rage.

"You are my problem!" I yelled. "I finally found someone I wanted to share my secrets with, someone who, I thought, might understand a bit of the pain and loss I was facing every single day." I shouted that the knowledge I had from my ability, knowledge so far beyond her comprehension, was of little value since I was forced to keep it hidden. I cried as I told her about Giuseppe, and how I feared his fate would also be mine. As we stood face-to-face, I asked her why she had let me open up, only to spurn me.

Sharon needed no time to form an answer; she just needed a moment to give one. "Because you believe the stories are true. You feel they are true, and you want me to believe they are true." Of all the things I expected her to say, that wasn't one of 'em.

She explained, "When you have something to say, something you want to share, you are so good at expressing yourself. You can paint your emotions—your elation, your sadness—so eloquently. That's a rare quality, Dominic. But when you tell me about your ability, you're not merely sharing stories; you are trying so hard to convince me...and you want to convince me because I asked you to. It sounds as if you never had to convince anyone before. You have incredible recall, but your strength lies in repeating the facts, not persuading others of the implausible. Giuseppe already knew about your ability. You never told your friends about it, except maybe Elizabeth—Lizzy— but what you told her, she already knew. She couldn't handle sharing her pain. You've never had trouble convincing your father of your skills, although you have never tried to explain the truth behind them. Anyway, it kind of sounds like he already knows. I look forward to meeting him tomorrow, if I'm still invited." Before I could protest, she continued. "Don't worry. It's not my place to discuss your stories. When you talk about this with me, it is as if you are trying to win the case of *Your Perception v. Reality.* The problem is, dear, you're not very good at it. Maybe it is just that this was your first effort. As for me, I am convinced...convinced that you believe the stories are true. I just don't know if they are or if that is simply your impression."

Sharon did not need three more years of undergraduate school and an additional three of law school to prove she could win an argument. She set me up. She set me up, and I fell for it—hook, line, and sinker. "Simply your impression." That was a nice way of saying I may be insane, and it looked like she was convinced that was the case. Still, something made her decide not to give up on me. She seemed to be willing to risk my pain to get to the truth. To get there, she had to risk her own. I was at her mercy.

I reached out to her and asked her softly, "What else can I do?"

"Prove it!" she said as she grabbed my hands...my right clenched fist and my left immobilized hand. "Prove to me you can do what you claim. A parlor trick, if you will. Tell me something that will prove beyond a reasonable doubt your ability exists."

We didn't speak on the bus on our way uptown. Even in those early days, we were comfortable being together without talking. We respected each other's space. We got off at 25th Street, stopped off at Monte's for a nightcap, walked to my dorm, and got ready for bed—all of that with less than forty words spoken, and that included Sharon saying she'd need her own toothbrush if this were going to be a regular thing. In her rush to pack for the weekend, it was the one thing she forgot.

When we got into bed, before I could say a word, my new affection beat me to the punch; she put her finger on my lips and said, "Don't talk. I want you to tell me about the night my family died. What happened in that car?" I raised my eyebrows and sighed heavily as she continued.

"Look, Dominic, I understand exactly what I'm asking you to do. There's no need for us to discuss it anymore now. Don't talk to me; that's what tomorrow is for. Goodnight, dear." After planting a little kiss on my nose, she turned and pulled the bedsheet up to her shoulder.

No, Sharon didn't understand at all what she was asking me to do. To do what she wanted, I would have to violate my safeguards...disregard the rules that were designed to keep me safe. She was also asking me to stare into a moment of death...the demise of three souls. She was asking me to step into her world and witness hideous details that may have been better left buried. She wanted to find the truth...but it was a truth she may not have wanted to know. All that, without even allowing me the opportunity to respond or discuss it with her!

My last thought of the day was what she had asked of me.

I awoke to the warmth of midday sun burning into my skin. When I reached across to the other side of our tiny bed, I found it was empty. I felt a pang of loneliness. My sigh echoed off the walls.

"Good morning."

She was there! Sitting on my metal desk chair, one leg crossed over the other, she was sipping a steaming cup of coffee from a mug I recognized from the common room in my dorm. And I thought I was the only one who liked hot coffee on ninety-degree days! Sharon was effortlessly beautiful sitting there. Her hair, a perfect mess, was pulled back with a blue satin ribbon. She was wearing a watercolor-blue, tie-dye mini qipao. Even the simplest garments looked fabulous when wrapped around her figure. She still wore no makeup or nail polish. Her toenails, peeking out of turquoise wedge sandals, were also unpolished.

"I've been watching you sleep for a while." I looked at the clock on my desk. It was nearly ten. "You seemed so calm and peaceful, but I saw that you were crying...well, it was more like one tear." I felt embarrassed and checked to make sure my eyes were dry.

"No. Don't worry. It's okay." She came over and offered me her coffee. I sat up to drink it.

"Is this your first?" I asked, holding up the cup.

"Third. You keep it." Oh, bliss.

Sharon wasted no more time. She wanted to know if I had done what she had asked, and if so, what I had learned about that night. I nodded. "Don't just nod if you have something to say."

"I fell asleep last night focusing on the last car ride your father, mother, and sister took together. My journey last night was foolish, a dangerous gamble—I didn't have definitive proof those three ever took a car ride together. If what you told me about the event had been inaccurate, it would have plunged me into an abyss and my body would suffer the consequences. This one time, I decided it was worth the risk. Fortunately, you were accurate. They did take that drive. Sorry, 'fortunately' was a poor choice of words." She waved her hand, dismissing my apology.

"There was also a chance the accident never occurred or that that ride was not the last time they were in a car together. Their last trip in a vehicle could have been in an ambulance. I apologize if it sounds like I'm being flippant, Sharon. If I'm going to be completely honest and forthcoming, I must go through each step." Another rushed wave of dismissal.

"After dinner, your family left Carmichael's Restaurant in Stamford. Your dad was driving, your mom was in the passenger seat, and Allison was in the back. She was sitting in the middle because it allowed her to see out the front window and not just look at the backs of her parents' heads. Dennis hoped to make it back to Greenwich by 10:30. He was irritated and just wanted to get home.

"Sharon," I asked, "how much of this do you want to hear? You know you don't have—"

"Tell me every detail. Please be complete and honest, Dominic."

The facts and the accompanying details I see in my dreams can be so cruel, so raw, so brutal. However, as hard as it is to face facts, it is sometimes—and I do mean sometimes—better to know them than not. Sometimes, knowing the facts can bring closure, and that's what I wanted to do for Sharon: give her the opportunity to find closure on this tragedy. That moment was the greatest gift I ever offered to the love of my life.

So, I continued....

"Your mother was talking to your father. She said—and this is exactly what she said—'Dennis, for the love of Christ, can you just let it go? She's growing up, she's going to make stupid choices. Don't you remember what we were like at that age? Kids are more irresponsible these days than we were, but she'll grow up.'

"Sharon, it didn't take me long to realize they were talking about you. You had chosen to skip dinner with your family so that you could work with your boyfriend, Alex, on rolling out the first edition of the *East Village Other*." The *East Village Other* was a new newspaper dedicated to free speech and support of the underground movement it was inspiring.

"Your dad referred to Alex as 'that goddamn beatnik who's fucking my daughter.' It was not a good evening. Your mother was worried about you, your dad was furious, and Allison didn't say much but looked unnerved by the sharp words between your parents.

"Amanda wanted to take I-95, but Dennis refused. 'All these damn end-of-summer tourists will have that new road backed up all the way to Waterford.' He took US-1. Allison, exhausted from the stress of the evening, fell asleep in the backseat. Amanda sat quietly while keeping her eyes fixed on your father most of the time. Even though he was in such a bad mood, he didn't let it affect his driving. He was a good driver that night—he was cautious and careful, only taking his eyes off the road a few times to check on his wife and daughter.

"Just as their 1962 Ford Galaxie crossed the intersection at Fairfield Avenue, they were struck by a car that blew through a red light. No headlights. No attempt to slow down or even divert. I apologize for not having more information about the driver. Maybe someday, you'll want to know more about that moment. All I can tell you is what I searched for."

It pained me to watch Sharon suffer through my description. "The driver was going much too fast when he, or she—I don't know which—plowed through the intersection and hit your family's car broadside, on the passenger side. The force of the collision killed your mother instantly. Allison—the skin on her face and arms was literally sheared off—lived only a moment longer. Your father's legs were crushed and pinned by the undercarriage and his arms were fractured and bent back unnaturally. He lived for forty-six seconds after the impact during which time he was able to turn his head and see what had happened to your mother and Allison." Sharon, bent over with her hands clasped behind her head, struggled to hear me through the sound of her own sobs.

I kept going. "Your dad, apparently coming to grips with the devastation, smiled."

She lifted her head and looked at me.

"He smiled and whispered your name. The last words your father spoke were, 'Sharon...thank God....' As the energy expired from your father, the last car ride he, your mother, and your sister took ended."

As agonizing as it was for Sharon to listen to my story and to discover those gruesome details, it was all she had to connect her to her lost family. Unfortunately, once she knew what had happened, it didn't make her feel better or give her what she was looking for. "Sharon, your father's last thought was one of relief because you weren't in the car." Tears were streaming down her face, and her face was flushed.

"Did he suffer?"

"I don't think so. I know that being in shock is surprisingly effective at masking pain. He didn't look like he was suffering."

She leaned forward and fell into my arms and continued to cry. There was nothing I could say to console her. I held her—yes, I could only use my right arm—and rocked her gently when she calmed down and held her more tightly when she sobbed. I ran my fingers through her hair. Gradually, she relaxed. She moved her hand down my arm and interlocked her fingers with mine. She lifted our clasped hands to her cheek and kissed mine. With a weak voice, she said, "I have one question." I released her hand so we could face each other.

"What happened to my father after that? What happened to all of them?"

"That's two questions." Sarcasm was never my strong suit, but it worked. Sharon smiled and gave me a playful jab as she wiped her tears away.

"I don't know." And that was the truth. I tried to explain in more detail what I knew about my ability, including what Giuseppe had taught me, what I had learned on my own, and the assumptions I had made. I told her I can see the organization of energy that comprises moments in the past. I don't know where the energy comes from or how it arranges itself. I can experience everything in these moments—the visuals, the sounds, smells...my mind creates a sense of the emotions—without physically being there. I do not occupy a space in these moments. I have no interaction with anyone. I guess that somehow my mind can absorb, internalize, and translate the energy as it was in the past. I also told her I have no idea why or how I have my ability, or how many others also have it, or have had it.

I told her, "When I met you in the library, I was struggling with the thought that I would never be able to understand my strange ability. Every attempt to figure it out led nowhere. I realized nothing I read was going to help me. The problem was, I didn't know where else to look. Apparently, discovering a new path is something I am not good at."

She responded, "I am sure a lack of intellectual resources is not the problem."

But she was wrong, and I explained why. I successfully defended my position, which is something I guess I should be happy about.

"All right, I guess you are not as smart as everyone thinks you are, or as smart as you think you are." Kind of a backhanded victory, I guess.

I then told her about a concept I had often considered, one concerning light, darkness, energy, and death. "What if the cessation of life—life as we know it—is a dissolution of energy?" A quirky look, a subtle tilt of her head, and squinted eyes suggested confusion, but her silence invited me to continue. "When a moment in my dreams ends, there is nothing more. My mind is satisfied. When I reach for moments that don't exist, it ravages my body while all my mind embraces is darkness. But now I realize there must be something else, and I think it may have to do with light and darkness.

"In my dreams, when people have died—and I have watched that happen hundreds of times—I've noticed that as life left them, each person radiated a unique kind of light. For some, their light disappeared abruptly...instantaneously. Your mother and Lizzy died like that. In others, the light dissipated slowly. Allison...just that slightest flick. Your father, perhaps, fought a bit longer. Only when he realized you were safe did he succumb, causing his light to fade. Billy's light burned longer."

"Do you think Billy was fighting death?"

I couldn't answer that question, and it bothered me. I didn't know how Billy could have fought death, even for a short time, because his injuries were much too significant. He was already dead...he had been for hours.

"What did you see? You said it was light. Light's just another form of energy, isn't it?" Sharon asked.

I concurred.

"I think you're asking, what is this energy and where does it go, right?"

Again, I concurred. I put my faith in this smart, insightful, challenging, emotional, beautiful woman. I asked her, "What do you think it was?"

"Perhaps, the last release from a body isn't light but the final transition of the soul."

I had never thought of that. I was not as smart as I'd thought. So many questions bubbled to the surface, but what came out was, "Whoa! I think I need to have an extended conversation with Father O'Malley the next time I'm up in Pelham Bay.

"Shit! Pelham Bay! We're going to be late."

We rushed to get ready. After grabbing my dirty laundry—a present for my mother—we flew out the door and raced to the subway. I asked Sharon one more time if she was ready to meet my family.

"That's the only thing I have been waiting for all morning." Smartass.

Sharon never told me whether I proved my claim or not. I never asked.

Chapter 19 - Voice: Dominic

Today is March 5th, 2019. My name is Dominic J. Bandall, and this is session number fourteen in my interview with Angela Grant.

Have you ever seen a woman radiate? Devoid of all sensuality, her warmth is instead a consequence of surroundings. Her world is presented in a brand-new context; a picturesque scene once thought unimaginable, suddenly becomes the new standard for magnificence; dulled sensations bound by loss are swiftly dismissed in favor of new creations; no longer fearful of what may come, she waits with eager expectation for what will emerge next. I've had the opportunity to witness this phenomenon several times in my life, but the first such occasion was on Saturday, August 30th, 1969, when Sharon Peers met my mother, May Bandall.

Beyond her polished presentation—impeccable manners, gracious and polite—I could tell my mother was indeed happy, singularly proud of her son and excited for his future, yet suddenly amazed by the woman standing beside him. No one was good enough for her baby boy, until then.

After kisses and hugs at the front door, when the introductions were complete and the laundry bags had been set aside, my mother and Sharon went upstairs to begin a tour of the home. First stop, of course, was my old bedroom. When the ladies were out of sight, my dad walked out onto the porch. "Dominic," he snickered, "good to see you. Why don't you come on in? I think they're going to be a while."

I updated Dad on my rehab while Sharon and Mother walked around the house and the backyard. Sharon told me later that within forty minutes, she knew every high point of my childhood. She saw my report cards and achievement awards from kindergarten through my interrupted second year at Hunter, and a display of every leg brace I had worn over the years. She was also apprised of Mother's decorating style and heard all about the brand-new GE Filter Flo that washes, agitates, and spins. Except for the occasional oohs and aahs, Sharon listened quietly throughout the tour.

"But enough of this," I heard Mother say from the top of the stairs. "It is getting late and I have to finish making supper. We are having grilled steaks served with salad from my garden."

The evening was wonderful. We all joined in the conversation as Mother prepared dinner. There was a nonstop flow of chatter. There was also a lot of focus on Sharon, who navigated the evening beautifully. She modified her behavior as necessary: sometimes she was the meek girlfriend, eager to be polite and pleasant, other times she was more relaxed, bold, and open. She asked questions about family pictures and pieces of furniture she had seen around the house. Mother happily offered up every detail she could squeeze into the conversation. Sharon called my mother "ma'am" only once. Mother put an end to that immediately and asked her to please call them Tony and May. When my mother asked us to go get my laundry, Sharon said, "That's all right, May. Dominic and I can do his laundry." I never did laundry before that day. Everything she said and did only seemed to make my parents more fond of her. I'm not sure how far ahead Mother's imagination traveled that day, but she probably made it at least as far as her second grandchild.

Once we sat down at the picnic table for supper, Sharon's interview began. She handled herself beautifully. She talked about her studies at John Jay and her plans to become a lawyer. Dad asked what she wanted to specialize in. "My goal is to seek justice. I want to fight for justice. Wherever it's needed, in whatever form it takes, that's what I will focus on. Right now, I am discovering what to learn." Dad shot a glance at me and said, "That's very admirable. Exactly what college is for." I had to chuckle. Subtle, Dad, subtle.

Mother mentioned that Bobby was home from seminary school for two weeks, and said she was sure that he and our other friends would love to meet Sharon. "Oh, I don't think I'll be able to do that today, May. I have to leave soon to get back to my grandparents in Staten Island." Sharon looked over at me and winked.

Mother said she didn't think it was safe for a young woman to ride the subway and the bus so late and insisted we stay overnight. Sharon, she said, could sleep in my bedroom, and I would sleep on the couch downstairs. She also wanted us to join them at church the next day, where Bobby would be assisting Father O'Malley in the mass. She told Sharon she would lend her something to wear, something from her younger days...considering they were about the same height and size. Dad knew better than to say a word. There were no two ways about it; we would not be able to leave until after Sunday breakfast at the diner.

After dinner, as Sharon and I walked through my old neighborhood, I told her about the places we passed and about the people I grew up with. In front of Lizzy's house, I told her I could so clearly remember our conversations, our stickball games, thousands of tire tracks rubbed into the asphalt. Of course, the family that had moved into the Strausses' old house had no idea of the horror perpetrated there. At the stairs to the subway, I pointed up and said, "This is where Lizzy's mother took her life and where Lizzy, years later, would do the same thing. This is also the spot where I first met Giuseppe. He would take this subway downtown every day to warn people in City Hall about the demons who were destroying his neighborhood." It was now the spot where Sharon had gotten off the train with me earlier in the day and entered my world...no longer a place that frightened me.

"And that, over there, is where those demons exacted their revenge."

As we walked down the Avenue, Sharon said, "So, tell me, what's it like...to see the past?" I tried to describe how my ability was akin to a dream with such clarity about events to which I had no physical connection or presence. I tried to describe how it felt to remember details of my dreams so sharply that it felt like I actually lived them. I tried to explain what it was like to have that kind of recall of a moment, of every pointed aspect but one: I wasn't there.

"In a word, Sharon, lonely. This incredible gift leaves my heart lonely and desolate. What is the sense of having memories that don't belong to me...memories about things I was not a part of and concern no one I care about? What is the purpose of experiencing incredible moments when no one knows anything about your discoveries—nor would they be able to even comprehend them?

"Do you remember our kiss on Thursday night?"

Sharon winked. "Do I remember? Of course, silly! I was there!"

"That dark, musty air in my room. God, it was so hot, but the warmth of your body felt sensational. I felt that tenderness we shared. Your lips, flush and moist as they pressed against mine, your tongue gently touching mine. I have beautiful memories of that night because I was there. When I see moments in my dreams that I haven't been a part of, it just makes me feel sad. Some of the moments I recall are so utterly fantastic, but because I was never a part of them, they just remind me I will never truly share in the deserved bliss."

"So why don't you try to create your own fantastic experiences? Use your ability to learn and broaden your understanding of life, not to replace it." She pulled my arm around her waist. "And as far as those fantastic experiences, if what you know and can learn will make our world better, by all means, share them! Share them through stories. Express them as legends. Or maybe you can find a way to present them as fact." Sharon paused and looked at me. "And next time you experience something so utterly sensational, share it with someone who deserves the same sensations." She pulled me in for a kiss. The little boy in me hoped someone on the Avenue was watching. I wanted people to know what the "Bandall kid" was doing that Saturday night. I felt so alive, I wanted the whole world to know!

When we finally broke apart, Sharon grabbed my hands and looked up to the sky. "Take me up there." Just a month before, Neil Armstrong and Buzz Aldrin had walked on the moon. "I want to feel what it's like to walk on the moon. I know you say you don't feel as if you are physically present in the moments you dream, but what I want to know is, how close can you get? How close can you get to Armstrong? And, how close can you bring me?" I looked at Sharon in surprise. That pixie-haired dream was right; I could absolutely share my dreams with her.

"Tomorrow morning," I promised her, "I will take you to the stars."

I was drained and I'm sure the day's events had been taxing for Sharon as well. We stopped talking and walked for an hour, hand in hand, arm in arm. I told her no more stories, she posed no more challenges. It was pure euphoria. When we got back, I reluctantly relaxed my grasp of her hand as she ascended to her residence for the evening. I lay down and covered myself. Then, as I have done so many times before, I asked my mind to care for me while it showed me secrets of the universe.

On the table beside our couch—my bunk for the evening—was a black pen. With the tip up, I wrapped my fingers around the base as it staked claim to my stomach, authenticating the reality of my body before I succumbed to the fate of my mind. After that one final exercise, I was pulled into slumber.

Moments later, my mind flashes to a time in the past. I hear a voice saying, "There you go." One man appears in my field of vision: an astronaut. He is hidden inside a spacesuit designed to protect him, although he does not appear to be in any danger as nothing around him looks menacing. It's easy for me to focus on the figure as there is no one else in sight. Other than the spacecraft and the ladder leading down to the surface, nothing even looks earthly. He climbs down the ladder, then hesitates to take the last step to the ground. He climbs back up a few rungs toward the safety of the spacecraft. He is describing every action he is taking to another man. I hear their radio chatter. The other man is inside the craft, watching him, guiding him, and getting ready to join him. The images I am seeing feel...maybe like something before life began or perhaps after it was extinguished. There is nothing but gray, and brown, and dullness. Nothing moves on the surface. Nothing moves through the air. There is no sound except the echoey voices of the two astronauts. The surface is void of life until the man jumps onto it. There is...nothing...only firm ground below his feet and a powdery light flow of dust into which his boot makes a print.

"That's one small step for man, one giant leap for mankind."

The images I am seeing feel familiar somehow. But there is no indication of life—just gentle, rolling terrain, dust, and sand that moves only minuscule distances, pushed by the sun or pulled by some other force traveling through space. As the men conduct their preplanned tasks, there is no emotion in their eyes. No emotion because there is nothing to react to. The land is dead. There is no reason to be there other than to tell others later, "We stood upon death and returned to tell you about it." Maybe someday the astronauts will recognize the enormity of their feat, but for now, they are focused only on their mission.

I woke up suddenly and looked around. Everything was just as it had been when I fell asleep, including the pen—unmoved. I put it back on the table, then got up and scurried upstairs. Sharon would still be sound asleep, but my exhilaration couldn't wait until morning. I just had to ask her to join me on the amazing trip I had just taken, not considering the sheer lunacy of it. I mean, have you ever had someone wake you from a sound sleep to ask you to take a trip to the moon? Unwilling to give her time to wake up or a chance to respond, I just launched full speed into my adventure. It took a second for Sharon to understand what was going on, but once she did, her eyes lit up. I described the moon's surface and the lonely vacuum of space, but all she heard was the extraordinariness of the space adventure. As I described footsteps pressing into fine grains of dust, she saw the first impressions of a new era. While I described the methodical procedures of two trained space navigators, Sharon pictured adventurers blazing a new trail for humanity.

Mother was not happy when she woke up a few hours later to find me in my old room with Sharon. I was still a kid in her eyes. Actually, I was still a kid, although it didn't feel like it at the time. My assurances that we were just talking did not convince her. "Mass starts at nine o'clock. I expect you two to shine." That meant I was to dress in my Sunday best.

I was already downstairs, dressed and ready, when Sharon came into the dining room. She was wearing a red-and-white polka-dot halter dress with a white patent-leather belt cinched tightly around her waist, and peep-toe pumps to match her dress. Her blonde hair had a slight wave in the front; the ends were turned under in a soft roll on the sides. She was wearing a white bead necklace and matching bracelet, accented by a matching red hat with a red silk flower on the side. Sharon walked toward me while pulling lipstick and a small mirror from her white bag. It was the first time I had seen her with makeup on. She was wearing black liner that enhanced her eyes. Soft pink blush highlighted her cheekbones. I could smell a faint hint of perfume. Oh, I knew the guys would be jealous when they saw me walk in with this gorgeous girl on my arm!

"Your mother's back-in-the-day style is choice!"

I quickly pushed away the thought of my mother wearing the same outfit and stammered, "You look absolutely beautiful."

She slipped on a red bolero jacket to cover her bare shoulders and returned the compliment, "Not too bad yourself, Mr. Handsome! We will be the talk of the neighborhood. Now let's go. I want to meet Karen."

"Maybe I told you too much, too soon," I grumbled as we walked outside, my arm around her waist.

And she was correct. Every set of eyes gazed at us. Friends were overjoyed to see me looking so happy and healthy after my recent hospitalization. They praised me for fighting my way back. I struggled to keep my balance as I was hugged, and punched, and pinched. With the perfect blend of sarcasm, admiration, and awe, my friends showered me with their love.

After the service, I sat in the back pew with Bobby and we got a chance to catch up. He told me about seminary and said he was growing more and more fond of his profession. I told him about school and my time in the hospital and, of course, I went on about Sharon. Bobby told me he could understand why I liked her so much, and indulged me as I sang her praises for far too long. I asked him if he would be allowed to hear my confession. "No, you need to see Father O'Malley for that." And then he repeated Canon Law 965: "A priest alone is the minister of the sacrament of penance.

"Have you committed a sin?"

"I don't know, Bobby. I don't know."

As soon as I asked about confession, I changed my mind. Maybe it was either that I couldn't imagine revealing my secrets, knowing some of the horrors the church had committed in the name of righteousness, or because of the tenets it held to that I knew were false. Maybe it was all of the above. Whatever it was, I quickly backpedaled and assured Bobby it was nothing. In doing so, I had closed the door to using religion to understand my ability, just like I had with various fields of study at school.

By the time we left for Manhattan, Sharon had a lot of admirers. Yes, I had had my fifteen minutes of fame, but for the rest of the time, it was Sharon everyone was fawning over. Sharon and Mother said goodbye. They promised to get together again soon, and often. Dad tapped me on the shoulder and whispered, "Maybe next time you guys come, we can leave Sharon with your mother and catch a Yankees game." With our hands in our pockets, we struck the same pose and smiled. But then, still smiling, Dad leaned in and said quietly, "Just be sure, Dominic. Don't open up completely unless you're sure."

I didn't ask him what he meant. I just responded, "Oh, I'm sure."

"Then don't hold anything back." I had already decided to do that, but Dad's affirmation meant the world to me. After our final goodbyes, Sharon and I stepped back into our own world. On the subway ride, I watched and listened as she talked about how lucky I was to have such a remarkable life. She was impressed by everything she had witnessed, and enjoyed everyone she'd met, especially Karen. "Is there a reason you two never became a couple? Did you ever think you would end up with one of your old friends?"

As soon as the words were out of her mouth, she retreated, "Oh, I'm so sorry, Dominic." She quickly changed the subject. "What you told me about the moon landing...it was extraordinary. The way you described it made me feel like I was there."

Just then, I realized something had changed in my life. I had actually shared a moment I experienced in my sleep with someone else—well, someone other than Giuseppe. My role had suddenly changed from that of a lonely, third-party interloper to the keeper of a magical world that I could finally experience with another. There was no need to let go of my restraint—it no longer existed.

"I promise you, if I can find a way to get there, I will take you anywhere you want to go."

For the next three days—actually, for the rest of our life together—we shared the most extraordinary moments of the universe. Sharon would tell me what she longed to explore. If I had been there before, I would take her, and if not, we traveled together the next day...all through my descriptions of the moments.

We roamed the plains of Asia before civilization existed. We took those first cautious steps onto the shores of Plymouth Rock. We fought as soldiers on the battlefield at Gettysburg and later listened to Lincoln's speech. We landed at Normandy, fought the Battle of Caporetto, and watched Alexander the Great destroy Thebes. We took the first flight with Orville Wright in 1903. We watched and listened as the first transplanted heart beat life into another body. We hoisted the pillars at Stonehenge, went down with Amelia Earhart. We walked down the aisle with Sharon's parents on their wedding day and experienced the moment of her birth.

Sharon taught me how to interpret and describe the details I knew to be true. I told her of the constraints binding my reach, holding me to define moments of reality and nothing more.

During our solitude, Sharon offered herself to me. She offered the foundation of her life, welcoming me to share every moment in her past. She offered her soul, pledging her love for me for as long as I remained willing to accept it. She offered her body. I was awkward, shy, and hesitant to receive the gift of her existence. Sharon, as always, guided me and welcomed me into our new life. I only hope I offered at least a fraction in return.

Alas, our beautiful days of togetherness in our own little world were soon to end. The fall semester was about to start for both of us. Even though our schools were close to each other—back then, John Jay was in the Police Academy on East 20th Street—neither of us liked the idea of spending time apart. Sharon surprised me when she blurted out, "Dominic, I have an idea! Why don't you join me and go to law school as well?"

I wasn't in pursuit of a trade. "My destiny lies in uncovering the secret behind my ability," I said, trying to sound like I knew what I was talking about. Sharon was prepared for that conversation and laid out salient points to consider. "Let's look at the merits of that undertaking. What would you gain from uncovering this secret and what's the possibility that you'll even find it? What are the consequences of failing? Moreover, wouldn't being in possession of the truth," she posited, "be much more valuable if you weren't the only one aware of it? It should affect more than just you. That's what the law is all about.

"It was only after I lost my family, lost everything that mattered to me, that I realized what truly matters in the world. What matters is justice, the simple due process of what is right and what is wrong. With your ability, you can find and correct the untruths that are festering in and polluting our world. You can do that right now."

My thoughts grew dark. "I know all about justice! The injustices I have seen in my life—Giuseppe's murder, Lizzy's desecration, even Gino—the people responsible got the justice they deserved."

"With Gino, that wasn't justice. That was a matter of circumstance."

I brought up Lizzy again. At that moment, four years of guilt and sorrow crested. On the same day Sharon's world as she knew it ended with a horrible act of injustice, Stephen Strauss's world also ended. I will live with that sin for the rest of my life. I was relieved I had not shared it with Bobby, but now I was desperate to release my burden to Sharon. I told her what I had said to Stephen Strauss in our final meeting. I told her I had kept my word to him—that I would exact justice for Lizzy's rape. She didn't denounce me.

"That was not justice; that was vengeance. Dominic, I've given a lot of thought to the difference between justice and revenge, retribution, retaliation, and vengeance. There is no simple distinction. I wish there was."

I felt tears begin to well up in my eyes. I was so confused. "What do I do now?" It was the same question I had asked my father, and Giuseppe. It sounds like such a simple question, but the burden I placed on Sharon was enormous.

"Discover the answer with me. Let's do it together."

Chapter 20 - Voice: Dominic

Today is March 5th, 2019. My name is Dominic J. Bandall, and this is session number fifteen in my interview with Angela Grant.

Transferring from Hunter to John Jay College, both CUNY schools, was not difficult. It required two visits to the admissions department, arranging for Hunter to send them my transcripts, and an interview with the dean of students. The transfer was only minorly disruptive, and I was happy to be enrolled in my new school.

Our "first date" ended six days after we met, on Wednesday, September 3rd, 1969, when Sharon and I walked into class together, beginning our sophomore year as members of the class of 1972. For the next six years, our lives were a routine of drudgery. Weekdays were for academics, discovering, learning, and applying our skills. It was a time we often wished for a merciful end to, yet one we would never trade away.

We perfectly complemented each other in many ways. While Sharon didn't have my memory, she was a better speaker, and was more eloquent and clever than I ever hoped to be, and this would serve her well as a civil litigator. I too planned to focus on civil litigation, but my trajectory was different. My knowledge of substantive and procedural law complemented her ability to skillfully apply and debate legal tenets. She helped me improve my interpersonal skills and showed me how to act more like a professional and less like an awkward kid. Even though my ability to obtain, absorb, and remember information obviously gave me an advantage over Sharon, it was not much of one. God, her ability to remember details was remarkable. As one of the highest testing members of Mensa International, to say her intelligence was in any way inferior to mine would be a laughable, baseless claim. I often relied on her to tutor me! She showed me how to see the world in a different light...to notice and appreciate the things that so often go unnoticed by others.

The time we spent outside of school was magical. I took Sharon to distant lands and ancient ages. We shared a mutual passion for our own adventure and travel, but with limited time and resources, our experiences were confined mainly to the northeast and, often, to our own city. When we walked the beaches of New York Harbor, I painted a picture of the City as it was long ago. Even though every New Yorker is, by birthright, an expert on the history of their city, Sharon and I were able to discover many things about it that few, if any, knew.

New York was always a land of abundance. Long before Native Americans first settled on the island, it was rich with wildlife, herbs, and other vegetation. The first humans to settle there lived near the river shoreline. This gave them access to the many waterways, all the fish and shellfish they needed, as well as needed protection from the harsh environment of the ocean. We explored the island with the European settlers, Verrazano, Henry Hudson, Kieft, and Minuit. We fought against the Dutch, then the British. We watched our city transform from quiet rolling hills, green forests, and a bounty of wildlife, to a place teeming with settlers, then slaves, then immigrants. With every new addition, our city grew larger, more diverse, increasingly exciting. We welcomed the Irish, Germans, Jews, Italians, and others from across the ocean and from throughout the country. We lived through the disturbances caused by Union and Confederacy sympathizers, the draft riots in 1863, Prohibition, the Black Panthers, and Young Lords. We lived through the consolidation of the city into the five boroughs we know today. We watched as the tunnels were dug, and tracks were laid. We experienced the evolution of lower Manhattan...a magnificent creation of man. We watched the construction of the grandest New York skyscrapers: the Singer

Building, the Metlife Tower, the Woolworth Building, 40 Wall Street, the Chrysler Building. Sharon was horrified when I described in lurid detail the day in 1945 when a B-25 crashed into the Empire State Building.

"Can you imagine if that happened today? If a plane crashed into one of our skyscrapers, like the new World Trade Center towers they're building?"

Honestly, at the time, I could not.

<Long pause>

<Angela: "Do you want to stop for now?">

No, dear. Of course not. We have a tight schedule to adhere to, and I'm afraid I've already taken too many liberties with it. Where were we? Ah, yes...our travels and adventures.

Our first actual vacation was in 1971. Sharon knew how I yearned to explore other worlds—in my own reality, not through moments created for others. I remembered the story Davet Beussier told me about walking through the streets of Rome, hand in hand with his wife, Sophie. Davet's knowledge of ancient Rome allowed him to bring to life the glorious past of that city. Sophie and Davet were lovers, able to experience the splendor and beauty of a forgotten past together, just like Sharon and I. Maybe because of that bond, this was one of Sharon's favorite stories.

As a surprise, as a gift, I arranged a trip to Rome so I could bring the ancient city to life in the same way Davet had. She was overjoyed. For two months, I researched ancient Rome...a world that had been dead for two millennia. I studied the architecture and the culture, I learned the language, both written and spoken, and I witnessed the documented calamities that had struck Rome. I saw the city at its grandest, as well as its most unfortunate times.

By the time we arrived in Rome, I was thoroughly immersed in its ancient history.

As we walked across the city, I would animate life as it had been. While we sat along the banks of the Tiber River, I described the story of Romulus and Remus just as it was told to the children of the first settlers in Rome. I read aloud the first papers documenting the founding of the Republic of Rome. I showed her places in the city where battles had raged and where victorious armies had gathered before marching off to conquer other forces in other worlds. I described the ancient monuments that used to dot the city. We stood among the arches and aqueducts, marveled at the hydraulic engineering of the Baths of Caracalla, and relived some of the most violent and ferocious events that had occurred in the Colosseum. I recreated the noisy and colorful marketplaces, the grand attire worn by Roman senators, and the simple clothes of common citizens. Slaves were sold next to slabs of meat and barrels of olives. I acted out, in Italian as it was spoken then, the bartering and arguing between merchants and customers that could be heard across the plaza.

At times in my life, it was difficult for me to separate the past and the present. Sometimes, I didn't even want to leave the worlds created by my moments, which to me felt like peace, bliss, victory, beauty, and utopia.

I often wondered if this is how it begins. Why choose the unpredictable nature of today and tomorrow when I could forgo that, in favor of the safe worlds of the past? Of course, time immemorial is full of pain, danger, and frightening events, but none of that is able to hurt me, for what once was can no longer create. Only the present can damage me and create new opportunities for pain.

But Sharon was not a part of the past I experienced. She was always the reason I came back.

I never did share any of my turmoil with Sharon. Still, she was there for me...to talk to, to teach, to learn from, to love. She, alone, made me want to continue. As we sat in our hotel room late one afternoon, while I was gazing out the window and grappling with my thoughts, I noticed that she was watching me—for how long, I did not know. She came over and sat by my side, took my face in her hands, and softly caressed my scruffy beard. She placed a tender kiss on my lips and whispered, "I love you." Those brief periods of time, and opportunities for more, were my only reasons to keep going on with the present and into the future.

On our final day in Rome, we visited the basilicas. For two law students, the buildings that once housed those ancient courts were beyond fascinating. As we walked through the rubble of the Roman Forum, I recreated its former beauty for Sharon. I showed her where the Basilica Porcia used to stand and described every stone placed, every cloth hung. We marveled at this detailed vision of a world that had not been seen in nearly two thousand years. Then, in my poor attempt at their ancient language, I presented Sharon with an argument formatted according to the rules of the tribunals in 75 BC. Sharon's eyes sparkled and she smiled as she listened to me tell my tale with an intensity she had never before experienced. When I finished, she clapped her hands and bounced up and down on the balls of her feet. "That was wonderful! A very impressive argument, sir. What was your proposal?"

I reached in my pocket for the ring. My proposal was for her to become my wife. That was March 5th, 1971, forty-eight years ago today. From that day forward, we loved each other, and we continued to grow together. Professionally, we were eager to begin practicing law.

Chapter 21 - Voice: Angela

We sat in silence for a bit. I had grown accustomed to the look on Dominic's face when he was trying to figure out how to say something difficult. Maybe it was his age, or possibly his fragile state, that caused him to let his guard down and be so transparent. Maybe he felt intimidated by me—a strong, young woman—just as he had been by Lizzy so many years before, and by Sharon when he first met her. And yes, I liked to think of myself as strong. It's the way I always tried to present myself to everyone, whether family, friends, or colleagues. But, good lord, with all the things Dominic had told me about Sharon, I realized comparing myself to a woman of that caliber put me at a distinct disadvantage. Did I even come close? I wonder that even now. I would have loved to have met her.

Dominic broke the silence. "Angela, I'm not sure our conversation is going to go the way you hope it will." I wasn't sure what he meant. "You may turn on your recorder if you wish."

"Thank you, Dominic. I want you to know I am incredibly interested in your story, your personal life, and your career as a lawyer."

He told me, "I'm not going to talk about my career."

I couldn't believe it! What the hell was I going to bring back to school? Chronicles of an old man's superpowers? But I had already invested six days and I wanted to hear whatever he chose to tell me, so I decided not to respond. I turned on my recorder and he began to speak.

> "I'm not going to talk about the cases I've handled as an attorney, my investigations, or the unique methods I used to substantiate my claims. Nothing I have done can be considered illegal because there is no law against my unusual method of obtaining evidence. And, that is what I did. I used my ability to uncover the truth when the absence of that truth prevented deserving men and women from obtaining justice.
>
> "The first case I took—Sharon and I took—was that of a vagrant named Justin Franco who I used to see rummaging through trash and scavenging in the Pelham Bay landfill. Everyone in my old neighborhood knew him and considered him harmless. He didn't bother us, so we didn't bother

him. I know...it's hardly a shining example of how to care for those who are homeless and mentally disabled.

"One day, in search of quality restaurant scraps and a warm place to sleep, Justin walked across the bridge to City Island. When he turned the corner into the parking lot, he came across a dead man, later identified as Thomas Chippoli. Justin, who didn't think he was doing anything wrong, walked up to the body to see if there was anything of value on it. Just as he crouched down to dig through the man's pockets, a group of people leaving the Marina Restaurant spotted him. Instinctively, Justin ran. Forty-five minutes later, he was apprehended by the police and arrested. Chippoli's body had three gunshot wounds that had been inflicted at close range. The victim's blood was on Justin's coat. Six witnesses swore they saw Justin shoot Mr. Chippoli in cold blood.

Justin was charged with armed robbery and second-degree murder.

"I heard what happened to Justin from my mother. Sharon and I had just opened our practice. Because I knew who he was, because he seemed like a gentle soul who was struggling, I decided to investigate his case. When I discovered he was going to be arraigned the next day, I did what many brand-new attorneys do: sniff everything, examine everything, talk to everyone. I raced around and spoke to the first responding officers and several of the witnesses. I got permission to see Mr. Chippoli's body. After confirming his death, Sharon and I determined the best way to approach discovery. We knew we had to approach it as simply a death, because we didn't know for certain that Chippoli had been murdered. We also established it had to be the death of an individual, not Thomas Chippoli, because using a person's name can elicit flawed results. I went to sleep that night thinking about the moment of the death at the Marina Restaurant on October 28th, 1972.

"At the arraignment on Thursday morning, Sharon relieved the assigned legal aid attorney of his client, and we took on Justin Franco's case. Justin entered a plea of not guilty to all of the charges. Bail was denied and a trial date was set for mid-January. We assured Justin he would be okay, then formed our strategy. On November 1st, Sharon organized a group of volunteers from Pelham Bay into teams and gave each group specific instructions to search the areas by the golf course and the landfill. She instructed one of the teams to search a specific place in the landfill. To avoid the appearance of bias, for that team, we deliberately chose people who did not know Sharon, me, or the defendant.

"A pistol found under the Parkway was a ballistic match to a bullet found in Thomas Chippoli's body. Fingerprints on the gun belonged to a guy named Eli Knaack, a criminal with a long record of petty theft and assault charges. Chippoli's wallet and wedding ring were found in Knaack's apartment.

"We got Justin Franco off. After his release, while the neighbors who helped prove his innocence never thought about him again, Sharon and I did. We helped him get admitted to the VA hospital for inpatient treatment and psychosocial rehabilitation. Since his medical discharge from the Army in 1955, Private First Class Franco had been homeless and roaming the streets of New York with nothing but nightmares from the Chosin Reservoir flooding his mind, and a Distinguished Service Cross medal pinned to his chest."

"I don't understand. Why are you telling me this amazing story now, when all I have is the voice recorder? Why didn't you tell it to me when we were filming?"

"Justin Franco is dead, Angela. He was buried with honors in Calverton National Cemetery. Over the course of twenty-nine years, Sharon and I changed the trajectory of thousands of cases of innocent victims that could have so easily gone the wrong way. We were well known for only taking on cases for which we knew we could get justice. If we rejected someone's request for representation, it was because we were quite certain they were guilty. When opposing counsel found out it was Bandall and Bandall they were up against, they generally settled fast."

In my first year of law school, there was a class called Civil Procedure in the American Legal System that focused on the execution of contracts and torts, standards and structures of suits, motions, and pleas, and rules that govern procedure in the courts. One of the things we learned about was a litmus test called the Bandall Principle that helps lawyers determine whether there is anything out there that could completely tank their case. An absolute like that will trump the most solid information, the most believable witnesses, and foolproof evidence. Regardless of where in a case a lawyer is, if a potentially fatal piece of information like that is discovered, it is prudent to drop everything and settle in the most expeditious manner possible.

> "My ability gave me access to information that was critical in the discovery phase of lawsuits. Nothing we did was illegal. We ensured that when we used information from my 'inside' knowledge, it was unimpeachable. In fact, the evidence we presented went unchallenged 99.6 percent of the time. However, my methods were, of course, without precedent. If we had been challenged and unable to fend off charges of improper conduct, claiming we had used alternate practices to obtain information would, I'm afraid, have led to the dismissal of many of our findings. Because I am no longer a member of the New York State Bar, any discredit would not affect my standing, but the possible legal action would be significant...for my

clients, for myself, and for the estate of Sharon Bandall."

"Yes, of course, I understand. That makes sense."

"Nothing I've done as a lawyer was illegal or immoral. Ethically, under the limited understanding we have, I may be in somewhat of a gray area. But, never have I broken the law, except for one time."

"But what about before, when you were not an attorney? What about Stephen Strauss? Heck, you weren't even in law school then."

I waited to hear what Dominic was going to tell me about those ethically gray areas, and about the one time he had broken the law. I knew a lot about his complicated life, but none of it led me to believe he had the capacity to inflict harm on another or to go through with an act of vengeance.

"If I live through this, Angela, I will give you the interview you deserve. No questions will be off-limits."

"If? I don't understand what you're talking about, Dominic."

"Until the day comes, all I can offer you is the words I have prepared. Everything I have told you so far has been essential. You needed to understand what I was capable of before you could understand what I have done...."

Dominic drifted off once more. I was confused by so many things that had happened in the past few days, but I was certain of one thing: now was not the time to conclude our discussions. I had long since given up trying to determine what was coming next or what the outcome would be.

"You have my full attention."

"Thank you for your vote of confidence. Let's resume our dialogue in the morning."

Chapter 22 - Voice: Dominic

Today is Wednesday, March 6th, 2019. My name is Dominic J. Bandall. This is session number sixteen in my interview with Angela Grant.

Sharon and I had been waiting until we finished law school to get married, so on September 29th, 1975, when we received notice that we had both passed the New York State Bar exam, our moment had arrived. We were relieved. Our families were elated. We began making wedding plans. We did not go through Pre-Cana since Father O'Malley thought it unnecessary in our case; he had watched us as we grew closer and closer over the years. He simply offered us the church for our wedding. We picked Sunday, October 5th as the date.

Dates...calendars...they are such an imprecise way to keep track of time. Calendars are merely an attempt by humankind to correlate their existence with celestial observations or long-abandoned cultural events. Our Julian calendar is but one more attempt to improve upon the one ancient Egyptians introduced more than five thousand years ago. I myself much prefer the ancient Mesopotamian Gezer calendar, for the Canaanites subdivided their years into predictable events...which I prefer to refer to as moments. Anyhow, I don't know if the day we chose for our wedding, October 5th, was predestined, charmed, or just random, but whatever it was, I used it to give gifts to my loved ones as a way to celebrate the special event.

For Sharon, my wedding gift was to take her back to the Women's March on Versailles on October 5th in 1789. The October March, as it was called, helped ignite the first sparks of the French Revolution. I had witnessed what Sharon—just one woman—was capable of doing when someone she cared for was in danger and I wanted her to know what a large group of women—1,114, to be exact—did to protect their loved ones who had been threatened.

I presented Dad with a baseball program from October 5th, 1912, when the New York Highlanders beat the Washington Senators eight to six. It was their last game at Hilltop Park and their last game as the Highlanders. After a dismal season, the team began 1913 at the Polo Grounds as the New York Yankees. The program was signed by Hal Chase and Jack Lelivelt—both of whom homered in the game—the brothers Homer and Tommy Thompson, and the winning pitcher, Bugs Raymond. The scorecard was completely filled in. Dad asked me if I would tell him about the details of the game sometime. "You know, a story like the ones you used to make up when you were a kid," is what he said. I happily kept my promise, and that program became a most cherished treasure of his.

My gift to Mother was more personal. I presented her with a vision of her child with a functional set of legs. Sharon, who never thought the damage to my legs and arms had been caused by my episodes of cerebral hypoxia, was determined to help me get better. We had been working together for almost six years to overcome my disabilities. When she decided I wasn't making enough progress at Lenox Hill, she developed a home healthcare program for me. We increased the frequency and intensity of my physical therapy sessions. The pain and anguish I experienced at Lenox Hill didn't compare to the torture I experienced at the hands of Ms. Sharon Peers. The power of her tiny body was remarkable. As my strength and flexibility improved, I gained the ability to walk without assistance. Until that day, we hadn't shared the full extent of my progress with anyone.

On our wedding day, while the groomsmen were seating guests, Mother found me sitting in the narthex waiting for my tasks to begin. You should've seen the look on her face when I stood up and walked to her...with neither a brace nor cane. I took her arm and escorted her to the front pew, then took my position. Except for my parents and a few of their older friends, no one in the church had ever seen me walk without a brace, and even that had been a long time ago. I saw heads turning to look at me. I heard my mother whisper that Sharon was largely responsible for my improvement. I watched as word of her magic spread throughout the pews until Sharon appeared in the entranceway. A curtain of silence fell.

Artists would describe Sharon as the absolute rendition of desire. Upon her entrance into any room, half the audience wanted to be with her, the other half wanted to be her. The most contentious souls were put at ease by her virtuous manner; her wielding of words could soothe the quarrelsome as fast as they panicked adversaries. Sharon's beauty complemented her ferocity, intensity enhanced grace. From the afternoon we met until the morning we said goodbye, and for the 14,988 days in between, my heart momentarily stopped every time I looked at her. I was never sure what it was. A sharp pang of fear that it might be the last time I would ever lay eyes upon her face? A crushing desire to embrace her and savor her lips?

That day, when I saw her at the far end of the church, the reason my heart stopped was obvious; it was no longer possible for her to be any more beautiful. Her wedding dress, which clung tightly down the length of her body, flared at the bottom into a magnificent chapel train. It had a modest curved neckline and graceful capped sleeves. As beautiful as she looked that day, however, every day after she was even more and more alluring.

What would have happened to had Sharon not approached me that day in the library? How long would I have muddled through, trying to find a path forward? No matter how much I knew, how much data and information I accumulated, I still couldn't figure out what the purpose of my life was. What does uncertainty do to a person when it lingers for too long? When do you stop searching? When do you realize there is nothing more to explore? Or worse, does the knowledge you have accumulated merely become the insignificant moments of your own existence? Meeting Sharon saved me.

But, no, she saved me from much more than just that. From the day we met, she gave me the focus and direction to keep my demons at bay. I never once had an attack of cerebral hypoxia while we were together. She did everything possible to ensure that my dreams did not cause further harm. Instead of venturing into dangerous territory during my sleep, I searched for moments that were crafted by our yearning to discover, moments targeted by her curiosity and desire to expand our worlds, moments that were found because of the wonder of her energy, mind, beauty, and passion.

Sharon saved my life—she swears I saved hers. Beneath her confident and strong exterior, there was an immeasurable load of turmoil and confusion; she was unable, or possibly unwilling, to explore what caused her suffering. When we met, the poor girl was searching for a purpose she could not define, could not describe, and would never find on her own. When she met me, she found someone with the power to do the very few things she could not: I could see everything she saw, yet I could do so objectively, without her preconceptions. I was able to help her uncover the truth in her life and allay her fears. Before we met, she was just waiting for something to happen that would push her to insanity or self-destruction. All that, she said, disappeared on August 28th, 1969, the day we met.

* * *

When Sharon asked me the day after we met to dream about the night her family was killed, I knew I was entering potentially dangerous territory and was frightened. I felt that way each time she asked me to reach into her past—and trust me, I was careful to venture there only upon her request because of the torturous lessons I learned with Lizzy. I warned her I might uncover things she never knew or didn't want to know. I told her I could not control, nor would I agree to filter, the events I experienced. What I discovered...that's what I would tell her. Still, she wanted me to discover her life.

It was while describing to Sharon what I learned about her past that I began to master the art of presenting and articulating information, disclosing only what I understood to be facts. In many cases, the past I discovered differed significantly from the one she remembered, whether her version of events was caused by faded childhood recollections, incomplete understanding of what had been going on at the time, or an emotional reaction that misinterpreted reality. In telling Sharon about her past, I learned to paint an objective picture that was free of the agitations that can muddy one's recollection or emotions, coloring the facts. I was merely an objective observer. I described scenes with such clarity, it was as if the listener was right there when the event occurred. When litigating, my storytelling skills, the vivid details and facts I was able to provide, helped me win many cases. For Sharon, this helped her become the woman she had wanted to someday be.

A city kid like me, Sharon grew up in the Bronx, in Morris Park, not far from where we lived. Her life was full of turmoil and anxiety from the day she was born. On September 15th, 1951, her mother, Amanda, was scared and alone when she gave birth to her eight-week-premature daughter at Peters VA Medical Center. At that moment, Private Dennis Peers, her husband of four months, was advancing north toward Hill 931 as the North Korean People's Army prepared for their counterattack of Heartbreak Ridge. Dennis was drafted into the Army on January 7th, 1951. On the night before he left, he and Amanda, the innocent young girl he was dating, spent one night together, saying goodbye.

Just days before Dennis was about to ship out for Korea—he was going to be fresh backfill following the ill-fated "Home by Christmas" offensive—Amanda discovered she was pregnant. Captain Williams, the commander of Dennis's training unit, gave the private a forty-eight-hour pass to go home and marry his pregnant girlfriend. Marriage would at least give Amanda the basic benefits of her husband's military service. After a quick wedding, which did not include any kind of celebration, Dennis had to turn around and go right back to base. Along with 150 other new soldiers, he was sent by train to Fort Lewis, Washington, from where he was shipped out and then integrated into the Ninth Infantry Division on the Korean Peninsula. After arriving in-country on September 10th, Dennis's unit was almost immediately rotated into combat. By the time they arrived, the intense fighting across the peninsula had settled primarily along the thirty-eighth parallel. Dennis's military service was short-lived and ferocious. For three days, his unit fought some of the bloodiest battles of the war on Hills 894, 931, and 851.

After giving birth to her daughter, Sharon, Amanda was allowed one restless night in the hospital before being discharged. This nineteen-year-old mother, a child herself, faced the daunting task of having to raise a little girl without her husband. Frightened and anxious, she returned to the only home she had ever known—her parents' house. Amanda's parents resented being forced to help care for their new grandchild, and for their own child. That was how they saw their daughter...she was a child who had made irresponsible, foolish decisions. Feeling unwelcome and like a burden, Amanda was unequipped to quell her own feelings of resentment.

On September 16th, just at the moment his daughter was born on the other side of the world, Private Peers was hit by a barrage of machine-gun fire in the opening volley of North Korea's counterattack. He spent five months rotating through field hospitals in Korea and Japan before returning to the United States. On February 18th, 1952, Dennis cried as he held his daughter for the first time.

Because Sharon wanted to learn more about the first year of her life, in the early days of our relationship I spent many nights visiting Dennis and Amanda. Until I dreamed about it, Sharon never knew why her dad always celebrated a special father-daughter day on February 18th. It was the day the two of them met. When Sharon learned about her parents' past, she understood. "It all makes so much sense now. Their intolerance of my recklessness when I was a teenager, my lack of focus, things I put them through...it must have been hard to let me go through those mistakes. They never shared their pain or spoke of these stories. I wish they had told me what they had been through instead of trying to direct me. I think I would have been a lot less resistant to their guidance and a lot less rebellious.

"Promise me, Dominic, when we have a child, we will be as open and honest with them as your father is with you." Her comment caught me off guard. I had intended to share with Sharon unfiltered stories about her father; her mention of a child unnerved me. I wanted to spend the rest of my life with Sharon, and I prayed she could somehow feel the same way, but until then, I never imagined it would actually happen. Suddenly, not only was she talking about building a life with me, but children were also part of her plan. How could I raise a child? What if he or she was like me? How could I keep a child safe from darkness? Dad managed to keep me safe, but I have no idea if he was even aware of what he did.

For the time being, I buried my concerns. Sharon was my priority. She needed someone to care for her, to soothe her fears, to safeguard her soul. Her care would forever be my priority. I kissed her brow. "I promise, my love."

While Sharon's father was recovering from his war injuries at Walter Reed, her grandfather—her mother's father—passed away. He was young when he died, but he had a long history of poor work conditions and poor nutrition, as well as an unhealthy love of whiskey. Her grandmother blamed his death on the stress of having to take care of their grandchild, Sharon, who she saw as a product of Amanda's sinful ways. Dennis's military pay, and later his disability compensation, did little to placate her.

After Dennis's medical discharge from the Army and his release from Walter Reed, the three of them—Dennis, Amanda, and Sharon—were finally together, living in Amanda's parents' house, in Amanda's childhood bedroom. Dennis worked hard to recover from his injuries. The machine-gun fire had torn large chunks of muscle, tissue, and bone from his body. For hours after the battle, no one expected him to make it off the hill alive; for weeks after evacuation, no one expected him to ever meet his daughter or see his wife again; for months after repatriation, no one expected him to leave the hospital; for years to follow, no one expected him to walk. Both legs were immobile for well over a year and his arms were terribly weak. Yet, Dennis was determined to recover; with the help of his wife and young daughter, he did just that.

Sharon may have honed her nursing skills while living with her paternal grandparents, but it was during those early years with her father that she first learned about physical therapy and being a caregiver. By the time she was four, Sharon was helping her father with his physical therapy exercises, knew how to care for some of his less-serious wounds, and portioned out his medications.

Dennis grew stronger every month, and every year. Using his GI benefits, he went to college to study economics, eventually becoming a CPA. Being an accountant suited him. His broken body was ill-equipped for any physical job.

In 1956, Amanda's mother died. Some believed she died of a broken heart. Once again, blame for her death was placed on the young couple. Amanda felt shame for her joyous relief that neither of her parents would ever again be able to levy guilt on her or her husband.

Amanda and Dennis's youthful mistake may have burdened Amanda's parents, but it also weighed on the young couple themselves and influenced the way they raised their daughter. Sharon's childhood was regimented and carefully controlled. Her parents worried that they weren't adequately preparing her to navigate through inevitable difficulties and as a result, they could never enjoy the life they created for their family. They didn't want their daughter to end up like them; they wanted her to live the life they should have had.

Sharon always tried to win her parents' approval. She wanted to make them proud, to assure them she had a good head on her shoulders and was and always would be careful. Despite having the same ultimate goal, both sides would continue to clash.

Pop Pop and Grandma Dot, Sharon's paternal grandparents, lived close by—only two blocks away—and showered her with love. They were a bright spot in her life. From them, Sharon learned what love could be. Both had emigrated from their England to experience the wondrous riches of the world. Their bond was based on the mutual desire to realize happiness. They thanked God's love for bringing them together. To them, raising four young boys during the Depression was not a hardship, but a labor of love. Dennis adored his parents dearly, but found their blissful, dreamy approach to life naive and irresponsible.

Before Dennis's war injury, the Peers family had already suffered the deaths of two of their children. Eric, their oldest boy, was in the Navy when World War II erupted. He was killed at Pearl Harbor on December 7th of '41. Michel died on October 24th, 1944 aboard the USS Princeton. I once told Sharon the story of her uncle's heroic efforts during the Battle of the Sibuyan Sea in the Leyte Gulf. He saved the lives of six sailors when a bomb pierced the light carrier.

In 1958, Sharon's little sister, Allison, was born. Sharon loved the idea of being a big sister, but the new addition meant the Peers had to move, a concept Sharon was not at all happy about. Her parents, on the other hand, were delighted about leaving that dingy two-bedroom house, for too much heartache and sorrow lived there. They finally could afford to move, as Dennis was doing well with his accounting business. They chose Waterford, Connecticut as the place where they would start anew and raise their girls safely and comfortably. Pop Pop and Grandma Dot were terribly saddened that there would be such a distance between them and their granddaughters. Oh, how they adored those little girls! Both promised Sharon they would visit often. Sharon remembers thinking back then that they were almost sickeningly positive. She was upset and angry about the move. It ripped her from the only people she truly loved and forced her to live in a new place that had nothing she cared about.

The rage Sharon felt never subsided, at least not until after her parents passed away. She had no regrets about anything in her life except for the anger she felt toward her mother and father. Some of the stories I told her—moments in which her parents' strictness proved to be only a show of love—offered her some consolation, but not enough.

Sharon grew up smart and strong. God, that girl was smart. One of the things that helped her was her confidence—a quality I sorely lack, even now. In addition to extraordinary retention, her ability to rationalize concepts and extrapolate relational causes in mathematics earned her the title "Little Miss Einstein" in a 1963 article written by a professor at MIT. She loved math. It was fun and easy for her, as well as a great escape from the mundane aspects of the suburban life she so despised.

When Sharon was a teenager, she was introduced to the concepts of good and evil, right and wrong, and oppression and justice. That was during the political turmoil in the 1960s.

Like most of us, she was glued to the TV when the events of Kennedy's assassination played out on November 22nd, 1963.

She was watching the live broadcast when Jack Ruby gave Oswald, as she put it, "exactly what he deserved" when he shot him in the abdomen at point-blank range. Even after I shared the truth about that tumultuous time in our nation's history, Sharon stood by her satisfaction—she just wished the rest could have been held accountable as well.

She lived through President Johnson's escalation of the war in Vietnam. She researched international treaties, military structure and organization, and cultural and historical developments in other countries as well as in the United States. This helped her learn vital concepts and allowed her to discuss them knowledgeably and rationally with others. She never blindly believed the news, wanting instead to get to the truth of what transpired: proof of action and intent. Her father called this her "communist hippie talk."

Sharon's response to her father's mocking and disparagement of her interests was to rebel and seek out the "communist hippies" that her father hated and everyone was supposed to fear. At first, her parents didn't notice her trips into the City. Then on May 2nd, 1964, Sharon joined City University students at a rally calling for the withdrawal of troops from Vietnam and an end to US military aid. The protest was peaceful, but when officers noticed a tiny twelve-year-old protester in the crowd, they pulled her aside.

Sharon's father was infuriated by the phone call that interrupted his workday processing late tax filings. His daughter's trip to Manhattan to protest with a crowd of angry students presented a danger that was utterly incomprehensible to him. While driving his little girl home from the police station, he asked her how she could do something so stupid. That little girl's reply makes me so proud. She screamed out in a fury, "How in god's name can you accuse me of stupidity? Do you have any idea how smart I am? This...this...academy you enrolled me in is nothing more than an overpriced nursery. I spend my days confined within their walls because you tell me I must. I do the work they assign because I am told that's what I must do. The work is agonizingly simple. When I complete their tasks for the day, I feel as if I have actually lost knowledge. So, I sit in the classroom and I read. I read books I doubt my teachers even know exist and if they do, I doubt they would understand them. If I am accused of not paying attention or if I am called on in class, I answer their questions knowledgeably. Fortunately, I still have four hours left of the day to maybe learn something. After school, I go to the library, or the hospital, or the police station. There, I feel alive.

"I go to the City almost every weekend. I spend time with Grandma Dot and Pop Pop. I miss them so much! We go on walks around the neighborhood and in the park. I always tell them that I hate living in Connecticut and ask if I can move back to the Bronx to live with them. Grandma Dot always tries to reassure me that you and Mom moved so Allison and I would have a better life. She's so wonderful, but I heard you say you wanted to move because you couldn't stand living another minute in that house. And that's the reason you took me away from the only people I have ever truly loved. I hate you for that."

Sharon sat in the car and boiled. She told me she wasn't sure how far to push her tirade but felt the need to hurt her father more. "Every time Pop Pop and I take a walk, he tells me he will buy me whatever I want. I usually pick a book, and it is often one you would never allow me to read...you know, like about the war, politics, or sex. Pop Pop doesn't judge me, and he doesn't say no to my choices. This is what he tells me: he says that both formal education and life experience are important, but they are very different. You can read about something all day long, but until you live it, you'll never truly understand. Of course, some experiences are too dangerous to be part of, and in those cases, I must first learn as much as I can. He says he hopes I never have to endure some of the experiences others have, but he still encourages me to read and understand them. I want to understand both extremes, and everything in between!

"Sometimes I choose a magazine as my treat. I know you think those periodicals are trash, but they give me information about the things that matter to me. I read about Columbia students who are organizing protests to fight for equal rights for black people and for women, and against this war we're creeping into. I go and meet with them. I sit and have coffee and listen to their speeches. Last weekend, I even gave my own speech on how the government is using fear to control its citizens. They loved it! They invited me to join a protest organized by the May 2nd committee. I've been preparing and looking forward to this for two weeks now. But you don't know any of this because you never ask about my day or what I am thinking or feeling. You never listen; all you want to do is keep me hidden away in Connecticut."

Dennis never wanted to keep Sharon hidden away; he just wanted to keep her safe from the danger and pain he had experienced in his own life. Unfortunately, he could never explain this to her and hated himself for his inability to connect with the daughter he loved so much. With my help, Sharon learned a lot about her father. She learned that on the night her father picked her up from the police station, he had told his wife how awful he felt about his inability to connect with his sweet girl. Through me, she heard the words she had so desperately needed.

After the police incident, Sharon's father had no other recourse but to ground his daughter indefinitely. Lasting only a few days, her home imprisonment ended for two reasons: Dennis was afraid to enforce it—Sharon's fiery opposition was too much for him—and more important, he didn't want to punish her. In his daughter, he saw the fire he used to have. When he looked at Sharon, he recalled his brighter days before the fear and pain began. He went to church often and prayed. He confessed to his priest that which he never could share with his family: he wanted Sharon to be free...carefree and untouched by the dark elements of life. He vowed he would curse God to hell if anything ever happened to her.

Of course, Sharon knew none of that. She didn't understand him and didn't realize how much he loved her. She continued to rebel and accelerated her protest in a most wonderful way: by excelling academically. Better grades allowed her father to worry less about her, and that made it easier for her to continue to follow her passions. Of course, being a good student did not mean everything was fine in the Peers household. Her parents would sometimes find her hidden underground publications, photographs of her in the East Village, a blue lace bra....

Sharon admitted to me with a smirk that the bra was not an accidental find; she wanted her parents to know she was growing up. At thirteen, in the spring of 1965, she was already a regular in the youth movement. She didn't look thirteen. She didn't dress, or act, or speak like a thirteen-year-old. Sharon was very much in control of herself. She didn't use drugs. She tried marijuana once but didn't like the numb feeling it gave her, and she knew about the dangers of LSD and other hallucinogens. For her, passing as a college student was easy. She had begun to blossom into womanhood.

At an antiwar meeting in June of '65, as Sharon was reading aloud an article about the Vietnam Day Committee, a newcomer walked into the room. Alex was an eighteen-year-old freshman at NYU. When the opportunity arose, Sharon quickly rifled through his wallet buried in his backpack. He was from the quiet middle-class town of Hamburg, New Jersey, and said he was having trouble adapting to city life. He told her he had come to the meeting because he had heard about a young girl who gave fascinating speeches and had interesting ideas. Sharon was immediately drawn to him.

After talking for a while, they went to a nearby coffee shop where Sharon showed him a copy of a magazine she loved: *Fuck You: A Magazine of the Arts.* She told him about William Burroughs, her favorite contributor to the magazine. Alex never asked her age and Sharon never offered it. He began to lay on more than his fair share of compliments. He praised her for her curiosity and for the energy she put into important issues. This did nothing to impress Sharon at all. In fact, she saw through his coyness and knew right away what he was after. She saw him staring at her while she was talking. Three times, she had to redirect his attention to her face. Alex apologized but he kept it up. Sharon finally had enough.

"Do you want to fuck me?" Her question had its desired effect.

"Huh? What?"

"I asked you a question. Do you want to fuck me?"

"No. Well, yes, but...." Sharon had the kid right where she wanted him. She always knew where, when, and how to inflict the perfect strike. She was just beginning to notice the effect her looks had on men, so she spelled it out for him.

"Listen, Alex, I think you're twitchin', but I only score with men who take this seriously...all this shit going on in the world."

"Hey, I take this real serious, I do. I mean, I'm doing what I can."

Sharon had the poor bastard on the ropes. What she said to him was true, at least partially. She considered social awareness an attractive, if not essential, quality and thought Alex was cute, but Sharon had no experience with men. The most she had done was kiss a guy one time on the day of her ill-fated marijuana experiment. Sharon told me that while she had recently started birth control pills to fit in with her peers, she had never given much thought to having sex...until the day she met Alex. All during their discussion about politics and the war, and even when she was hassling him for ogling her, it was all she could think about.

Sharon made a deal with Alex. It was the first negotiation she made that had a lasting impact on her life. "I don't believe you. I think you're only feigning interest in things that matter to me so you can get what you *really* want."

When Alex began to protest, Sharon raised her finger to demand his silence.

"I like you. I think you're cute and would be a lot of fun. If you can prove to me you seriously care about our efforts, I'll do it with you. If not, I'm outta here."

Alex insisted he was serious. He told her about a guy he knew who was starting an underground paper. "Y'know, they asked me to be part of it, but I wasn't sure. I'm kind of thinking I might, though."

That feigned nonchalance made it clear to Sharon he was nervous. She enjoyed being in control of the situation, but she was unnerved as well. She just hoped he was too naive to pick up on it.

In the end, however, after all the discourse, they reached a stalemate. It was getting late and she needed to take two trains to get to Connecticut for Sunday supper, or as Alex was told, she "needed to prepare for class tomorrow morning." When she stood up, Alex misjudged her timing and remained seated. Sharon put one hand on his shoulder, indicating he was to stay put, leaned in for a kiss while massaging his crotch with her other hand, and whispered, "Let's meet up again Saturday. Don't disappoint me, babe." Sharon stuffed the magazine into her knapsack and turned toward the door.

As she left the shop, I saw that her lips were slightly curled up at the corners, but her legs looked a little wobbly.

The first time I told Sharon what I witnessed when I visited her first meeting with Alex, she laughed so uncontrollably that tears were streaming down her face. "Oh my god," she shrieked, "I was such a bitch! Why in god's name did he even come back the following week?" With her arms softly nuzzled around her waist, she looked up at me and winked, "You have to tell me more! I want to know more."

When Alex returned to the coffee shop a week later, he proudly announced that he had gotten a job at the new underground newspaper, the *East Village Other*. He said he had joined the EVO as a favor to the paper's founding member, his good friend, his pal, Dan Rattiner. Alex didn't even know Rattiner; it was his classmate in English Lit who was the friend...of a friend of Rattiner's! Nevertheless, the two boys successfully landed jobs at the paper. Alex's role was to run copy from location to location. Hardly an exciting endeavor, but it earned him a notch on his belt...and I mean that quite literally. The logo was branded on his belt indicating he was an EVO courier. Rattiner and his colleagues had a hearty laugh after the two boys left. "I still say we should've branded them on the ass!" The story brought

Sharon to tears once again. She laughed until she fell backward onto our bed. She told me Alex perfectly suited her needs at the time: for experience, for passion, and for romance.

Sharon invited me to experience the moment they finally slept together. I declined. I was unwilling to intrude on her private experience. Sharon said she only wanted me to better understand her—that her past immature dalliances had no effect on what we had. Although Sharon and I had only been dating for a few weeks at that time, it felt as if we had been soulmates for years.

"That's not it," I explained. "You were only thirteen. A child. It doesn't matter if you looked older or that he didn't know your age. Other times when I visited you in your youth, I didn't see the beautiful woman you are now; I saw you as a child. If I witness your first experience of intimacy, it will be the same thing. I will see a young child. I also am afraid that I will connect the moment—I will connect you at that age—to Lizzy. I worry that if I see you are afraid—if I see that fear in your eyes like the fear I saw in Lizzy's—I will always look at you as someone who might suffer the same fate as my dear little friend. In my eyes, you would then become Lizzy, the girl I thought I was destined to be with, even though I was just a kid."

When she heard that, she pulled me down, and whispered softly in my ear, "This is what I want you to see when you dream tonight...." I seemed to be the one thing that would break Sharon free from her obsessive desire to expose every aspect of the truth.

Neither of us ever mentioned Alex again. I already knew a few things: they had sex twice; he bought her that blue bra; she spent the night with him when her family was killed on Friday, June 18th, 1965.

The morning following the accident, Sharon dropped in on her grandparents, as she often did. When she walked in the front door, her grandparents shrieked, jumped up, and wrapped their arms around her. Neither of them was able to form the words to tell her why.

Sharon never cried for her parents. Of course, she was horrified that they died, and in such a violent way, but she did not feel sorry for them. Even the empathy she felt when she found out about her parents' hardships did not make her remorseful for the choices she had made when she was growing up. She felt for her parents, but they had made their own choices. She did not feel this way about her sister, Allison. Sharon's greatest regret was not the time she lost with Allison; it was the time she threw away while her sister was alive. It warmed her heart to hear stories of Allison's happy childhood. She loved to hear that she was so close to their parents and had so many friends. Maybe Dennis and Amanda were committed to getting it right the second time around. I reassured Sharon that she too was part of a loving family. She did not scoff when I told her that. Instead, she was thankful her sister and parents had shared the kind of love she felt she never had.

While Sharon was grateful that her beloved grandparents took her in, she couldn't bear to live in her old neighborhood any longer. The good feelings she used to have were replaced by haunting memories. Her grandparents instantly committed to doing what was needed and within a month of the accident, they moved to Staten Island. Pop Pop took care of dissolving Dennis and Amanda's assets and Dennis's business. He put the proceeds into modest savings and investment accounts in Sharon's name. When she graduated from John Jay, they presented her with a tidy sum to help jumpstart her new life.

Sharon settled into her new life on Staten Island. That was her first year of high school and she wanted to go to public school, a "regular school," as she called it, because she was sick of "stuck-up" academies. She threw herself into academics and learning. She had no interest in "foolish games," as she called them, or even simple pleasures. This quality was reminiscent of Dennis and it concerned her grandmother. Pop Pop reassured her everything would work out. "The girl will find her way. There just needs to be a spark."

Sharon struggled to find a direction, to find what she should learn, and why she should continue to try, very much like I did. She explained it to me like this: "I struggled to understand the reason for going on, for taking the next step, when every step only led to more questions, more hurt, and more disappointment. My father understood this, stopped searching, and instead chose to stay put and work with what was within his reach. I wondered if that was going to happen to me too. If it didn't, why would I continue? If I went forward, how would I know when to stop because I had reached my destination?"

I asked her when it was that she decided there was more to life.

"After my family died, I stopped going to the protests all the time. I grew tired of the rallies against...well, against everything. There was nothing more for me to fight for or against. I liked the life Pop

Pop and Grandma Dot had—I could picture a life like that for myself someday, with someone...the one. My grandparents kept assuring me that I would find my calling in time. While that was a wonderful thought, I found it hard to believe it would happen."

She told me she finally found her calling on April 15th, 1967, the day she went to hear Dr. Martin Luther King speak at an antiwar protest. The protesters marched from Central Park to the United Nations on 42nd Street. She was in awe of Dr. King and had been following his trail of activism since the Albany Movement. Sharon told me about the experience she had that day while standing in the crowd outside the United Nations.

"I stood there in the pouring rain, Dominic, in a sea of humanity bearing no name, title, or race. Every person in the crowd of thousands shared one unified message: ending an unjust war. Near the end of his speech, Dr. King declared: '...I would suggest that there is, however, another kind of power that America can and should be. It is a moral power, a power harnessed to the service of peace and human beings.' I realized right then that the moral power he was talking about was justice. Social justice. Legal justice. Criminal justice. Moral justice. I have spent so much time considering the similarities between the many forms of justice and whether one has priority over another. It is the law that defines reasonable boundaries of our social, criminal, moral, and ethical actions. It is those actions, and the majority opinion that determine the tenets of our laws. I realized right then that if I were going to make an impact on the world, I would use the laws we have established as a government and a society."

And so, Ms. Sharon Peers began to learn about, and put together an understanding of, our complex legal system. She hoped to bring clarity to ambiguous laws, to protect those who were victims of the illegal enforcement or application of the law. While law school would give her the needed degree, how she was going to turn this goal into tangible action was a mystery to her...that is, until the day we met, August 28th, 1969. I was, as I explained to you earlier, in my own time of need just then.

<Angela: "She sounds incredible.">

Angela, she was indeed.

* * *

Well, let's pick up where we left off before all this talk of the distant past. Where were we? Yes, I believe we had just married. We moved to a modest walk-up on East 81st Street in Yorkville. It served as both our home and our office. We spent almost all our time working and building our new practice. Winning the Franco case attracted some unique attention. We began to draw a steady stream of indigent clients, small businesses, and others who were unable to afford more sophisticated—or really, any—legal representation. Sharon and I were in seventh heaven! Although we did not make much money in those early years, our expenses were low. The commute took less than a minute—it was about fifteen feet from our bedroom to the office. Most of our clients and most of the county courthouses were close by or readily accessible by bus or subway.

During this time, my darling wife kept me focused on my physical therapy. She did all she could to minimize my debilitating side effects: atrophy, edema, and arthritic joints. Occasionally, she would seek medical advice, but for the most part, Sharon developed my PT regimen herself and ensured I adhered to the schedule. Even when I cursed and begged her to let me stop, the torture continued. "The past may have broken you, but I'm not going to let it destroy your future." God, every time she claimed my care like that, I fell in love with her all over again.

Speaking of the past...the subject fascinated Sharon. Long before we met, she would often go to the Metropolitan Museum and pore over the exhibits. She would walk through the collections and imagine what the world was like when different works of art were created. I was happy to answer her questions. In 1977, I took her back three thousand years ago to a world when the Thracians advanced the Iron Age and enlightened the Greeks on architecture. I brought her back to the Middle Ages and the weaving of the Unicorn Tapestries. I told her about the delicate brushstrokes on the Japanese screens. My moments never replaced the personal experience of seeing these works, but they opened her mind and imagination in ways she never imagined.

Sharon's Pop Pop passed away in 1975. It happened shortly after our wedding in which he walked her down the aisle. Grandma Dot passed a year later, proving that souls destined to be together refuse to separate.

No longer close to most of her old friends, Sharon bonded with my friends and with my family. She met a woman named Barbara at the gym, and right away knew my old friend Milt would like her—they would hit it off. She told Barbara, "Have I got the perfect person for you! You absolutely have to meet him!" All of us went on a double date—Sharon's idea—and the two indeed hit it off splendidly...so much, they ended up married.

    The wedding, which took place on June 4th, 1977, was quite an event. Bobby, then an associate rector, officiated the ceremony. I was the best man and Sharon was matron of honor. There were so many people at the reception, they filled the hall and spilled out into the streets. As we sat at the head table, and I looked into the crowd, all I could observe was a sea of love. I begged for the tide to never recede. It reminded me of my parents' wedding. I watched Mother and Dad engaged in an animated conversation with Billy's parents and Patrick. Everyone was happy and full of life. However, I knew from my past moments that this one would not last. I looked at Billy's parents and wondered if they also missed their son and wished he were there with all of us. Soon enough, they too passed on; I will be forever horrified by the moment of their tragic accident. Seventeen people who attended the wedding would lose their lives on that fateful day in September 2001. I have relived those deaths hundreds of times. All I knew at the time was that there was sure to be many moments of sorrow and pain down the road that I would experience.

Instead of creating a morose atmosphere, it made me treasure that happy day even more.

I leaned over to Sharon and whispered, "This is the kind of wedding I always wanted to give you." Recognizing my tone, and knowing how I often fell into melancholy moods, she gave me a kiss, then jumped out of her seat. I watched her run over to my mother and whisper something to her that caused both of them to scream and hug each other tightly. Dad jumped at their gleeful outburst. Sharon stepped over to the microphone, winked at me, and motioned to the band to take a break. "Excuse me," she began. "I know it's traditional for the best man to make the first toast, but in case you haven't noticed, I don't do things by the book. Dominic, I assume you're okay with this?" Laughter erupted when I simulated the motion of tipping my cap in her direction.

"Thanks, babe. When I met Barb in dance class, all I could think was, 'Milton has to meet this bunny.' She was boogying to...do you remember the song, Babs?" Barbara wrinkled her nose in preparation for the embarrassment. "'The Hustle'! That was it! Anyway, I watched her dance and was mesmerized. The girl was graceful, sophisticated, and sultry. I must have stared a little too long because when 'Lady Marmalade' came on, she invited me to join in."

"Quit staring and get your scrawny ass in here!" Barbara's interjection made everyone laugh.

"Quit staring and get my scrawny ass in there. Barb wasn't afraid to tell it like it was. Forty-five minutes later, we were out sipping Manhattans. The second I laid eyes on her, I knew she was perfect for Milton. Convincing him, I knew, wouldn't be a problem. She is absolutely beautiful, and God, has so many exciting interests and hobbies! I thought about taking her for myself, but, alas, I am already married." I blushed as I looked over to gauge my mother's reaction. "Besides, I'm not sure Dominic is strong enough to handle two firecrackers like us." Laughing tempestuously, Mother buried her head into Dad's shoulder to hide her tears. "No, this woman was for Milton. It was the easiest argument I've ever had to make. I told her about this guy, a man I love dearly, a man who befriended me the day we met and made me his close friend. Thank you, Milt. I'm honored."

"Thank you for coming along, Shar."

"So, I told Barbara about this godsend. He was an angelic altar boy who became a jock in high school. He pitched his team to victory in the city championships. He worked at the grocery store and when he delivered food to older people, he would change light bulbs and sample their panforte. After college, he returned to New York to protect his neighborhood as a rising star in the DA's office. Barb, do you remember the only question you asked me?"

"Is he cute?"

The chuckles continued. Sharon popped the mic out of its stand and walked over to Milt and Barbara. Milt grabbed Sharon's hand and held it tightly. After a moment, Sharon placed Milt's hand on top of his new bride's, then turned to face the crowd and amplified, "Drop-dead gorgeous!" The crowd erupted as guests stood up, clapping and hollering. "Today is your day, and may every tomorrow be just as wonderful. Congratulations to you both!"

That was a hard speech to follow. My toast was basically a sophisticated equivalent of "Yeah, what she said." Sharon was unusually eloquent. In one moment, she could impassion a group to a fevered pitch, then in the next, she had them hanging on her words, even towards the most mundane subjects. As the bride and groom made their way to the center of the room for their first dance, I asked Sharon what she had said to my mother. Sharon whispered, "I couldn't hold it in any longer. I had to tell her I'm pregnant. But let's talk about that later. Today is their day."

I was overwhelmed by the dissonance of my emotions. I wasn't happy or sad or shocked. I couldn't even form a complete thought, as there was no room in my mind for the creation of additional awareness. I was in that numb state for twelve seconds, but I only realized that later when I relived the moment. There was a clock on the far side of the hall, just above the fire door. The world kept going on around me. Milt and Barbara got into position under the lights. Everyone was screaming and whistling in celebration. The band reassembled and began readying their instruments. I could only see that thin red clock arm violently thrusting time forward in twelve distinct pulses. There was no sound except for those twelve shots of cannon fire announcing the arrival of a new epoch for me. For twelve seconds, the world around me was frenzied chaos, yet all I found was a clock.

Sharon pulled my face close to hers. "I found out yesterday. I didn't want to tell you, or anyone else, for precisely this reason. This is their day and we can't upstage them. But, what you said about wanting to have given me a wedding like this, you made it sound like I've been deprived. No! I am the luckiest woman ever! I just needed to share our news momentarily. I wanted you to witness my joy, displayed as an expression you have never seen from me before. I love you so much, Dominic. Thank you for everything you've given me. All I ask right now is for you to let Barb and Milton have their day." She offered me her hand with a look that said she would repay me for my selflessness.

By that time, Sharon and I had managed to fill nearly half of my composition book. Her focus was on developing conservative rules to keep my mind secure and my body safe. We both developed valuable techniques for focusing concentration in studies. I learned how to effectively control Rule Number 241: how to pull your focus away from moments. Moments can distract with their awareness, they can overwhelm with their images, and they can destroy without ever existing. I surrendered to her will; the day was indeed for our friends.

What a fantastic evening! Everyone laughed, danced, and celebrated into the early hours. Sharon danced nonstop. That is something I could spend an eternity watching. I even mustered the strength to get out onto the floor, once with Barb, once with my darling mother, and the rest with the love of my life. I kept my word and didn't mention—didn't even think about—the child growing in her womb.

When the hall finally closed, we bid farewell, but only for a few hours. After church the next day, my parents were having a celebratory meal for the happy couple and thirty of their closest loved ones. I barely had the strength to return home and climb the steps to my old bedroom. Sharon nuzzled and lulled me to sleep, reinforcing visions of her body swaying across the dance floor. Then, she helped my mother and the rest of the work crew downstairs. I don't know how Mother accomplished everything. She had been one of the last to leave the reception and barely slept. On the way to mass the next morning, she greeted everyone as they dropped off food. Mother finally scurried off to church, but left immediately after communion.

The perfect weather made our brunch in the backyard a picturesque scene, reminiscent of our first year in the neighborhood. The party was a decadent topping to a momentous occasion, and I have such beautiful memories of it. Milt entertained us with a story about the anxiety he felt at the wedding. It only subsided, he said, when he saw Barbara walk down the aisle. Sharon playfully rapped him on the shoulder and told him he wasn't the only one who was emotional at the wedding. Milt quipped, "I guess I'd better start learning to take direction from the women in my life."

"Only one woman," Barbara added. "Only me."

When the party wound down and Milt and Barbara drove away amidst the clatter of the cheesy tin cans that had been tied to the rear bumper, I looked at my mother and saw the happy look on her face. Sharon put her arms around me and squeezed gently. "Well, I guess you better say something before your mom explodes." She held my arm as I rose. Grabbing a glass of orange juice, I stood, and I raised my glass to the departed newlyweds.

"Last night was a perfect example of love, not only between Barb and Milton but all of us who shared the day with them. I hope they will enjoy their time in the Caribbean, but we look forward to their return so they can once again brighten our world. To the Claytons!" Everyone raised their glasses, and there were whoops of "To the Claytons!" and "To Milt and Barbara!"

"One more thing: Sharon and I would be greatly appreciative if Barbara and Milt begin to grow their family soon because our little Bandall child is going to need a partner in crime."

The reaction was exquisite.

Mother was beside herself with excitement. She spent most of the day phoning friends and sharing our news. Milt, who called from the airport, was overjoyed as he cursed me for not letting them know before they left. Dad and I spent the day together. He told me the birth of a child is the most important event in a man's life. But I was frightened. With my issues, with my struggling leg and arm, I didn't know how I could care for a young life when, on many days, I could barely attend to myself.

"You're strong and determined, Dominic. You'll do as much as you can, then you'll do more. You have a lovely, caring wife. You have family and friends. As your practice grows, you'll have the resources to care for your family. There is nothing you can't accomplish."

I told Dad I didn't know how Sharon and I were going to manage all the changes we would have to make. Our apartment in Yorkville was too small for even the two of us. Would Sharon be able to continue working? Would she want to? I was sure I could not maintain our practice by myself.

"It will all work out, Dominic. Your mother and I fumbled around in the dark for years, but we always found our mark. Remain focused. You'll be fine."

I set my fears aside for a while. Dad and I sat in the living room, shades down and curtains were drawn to block out the sun, and watched the Yankees play a midday game in Chicago. In the top of the first inning, Thurman Munson blasted a towering home run into the right-field bleachers. "Yeah!" Dad burst. He tried to stay calm because there was still a lot of game left to play...although the importance of scoring first was never to be overlooked. He sat back in his chair to admire the instant replay. "Munson looks great. Have you ever seen a swing that beautiful?" Whether that was a rhetorical question or not, I don't know, but...yes, I had seen a swing much more beautiful than that clunky swat. Four swings, to be exact. Lou Gehrig. June 3rd, 1932. Philadelphia. Gehrig started the scoring with a two-run blast in the top of the first inning against the Philadelphia Athletics. In his next three at-bats, he notched another three home runs. After Gehrig grounded out in the eighth inning, Babe Ruth razzed him for leaving him stranded on second base until Chapman finally drove him home. As of the Babe made his way back to the dugout, he mocked Gehrig. "Couldn't get to five, could you?"

Gehrig was quick with a comeback. "I figured you needed a little exercise while rounding the bases."

Those were indeed the four most beautiful swings ever. Of course, Dad never got to see them. I remember thinking it was too bad that he would never know or understand some of the joys my ability gave me. For one fleeting moment, I wished I could pass my ability on to my child. Just as quickly, I cursed myself for that horrible, selfish thought. But I couldn't shake the idea. Would my child inherit my ability? Giuseppe's grandfather told him he had seen that happen. I never discovered whether my own grandfather had the gift. Sharon urged me to research that, but it was too daunting. I couldn't ask Dad; I don't know if he knew anything about it, and even if he did, maybe he would have been too uncomfortable to admit it...because of what it meant for me, and his grandchild. If, by some grace of God, he knew nothing of the power I possessed, I felt I had no right to introduce my absolute horror into his life.

The game was almost over when I broke out of my reverie. I looked at the man who had been there for me through every crisis. "Dad, how do I protect my child from danger? How can I ensure he or she will be safe?"

"You can't. If you think you can protect your child from every danger, get that foolishness out of your head right now. You can love her and guide her to the fullest of your capacity, but there will always be situations in which you can't do anything but hope...hope the direction and guidance you have instilled in her take root, hope outside forces don't overwhelm her, and hope our loving God finds a way to keep her safe. There will not be a damn thing you can do other than hope."

"Her?" Dad didn't reply. He was lost in baseball...or the grandchild!

The game ended with the Yankees taking the rubber match to win the series two to one. Dad picked up his two beer cans and shuffled over to the kitchen. He yelled, "That's my opinion anyway." I wanted to ask him more, but I felt it wasn't my place to push this sensitive subject.

During the pregnancy, Sharon and I often talked about what we would do if our child had my ability, and how we would deal with it. We didn't get far. In fact, the whole conversation was a joke: two lawyers trying to come up with a strategy for raising a uniquely gifted child, without input from anyone else, when they had never even raised any child before.

So, during the nights, I searched for clues. In as safe a manner as possible, I searched for others with my ability. I tried to learn about the moment when they discovered their ability. I found many souls. I watched many lives abruptly end. It was maddening. It was a fruitless hunt for hope in a sea of death. Sharon convinced me to call it off.

One day, while walking with Sharon in Central Park, she stopped on the path and looked at the pond. I was taken by her beauty. A simple sheath dress showed off her beautifully toned body. The bump on her stomach was the only indication she was pregnant. Summer was ending, and the temperature had begun to fade under the weight of a crisp September. She pulled my arms to her. "Feel me," she demanded. "Feel this life we have." My wife put her hands on mine as I pressed them to her stomach. "Do you feel that, Dominic? Do you feel that life inside me?" I sighed heavily to let her know how it moved me. "We created that life, we're caring for that life, but ultimately, that life is developing on its own. All we can do is provide every opportunity, then step back."

I'd like to say my anxiety lifted, but as her pregnancy advanced, so too did my fear and worry. Thankfully, though, my concerns were no longer about passing on my ability, but merely the task of being a father. It was absolutely the greatest class of tension I had ever experienced. We carefully considered where to live, where would be the best place for us and our new baby. Both of us wanted to live in a family-oriented community. We had our sights set on a few properties—two in Pelham Bay and one in Morris Park—but we had to wait until early springtime to move. It was of no matter to me, the delay that is. As long as I had all my loves under one roof, a few months in our cramped Yorkville apartment didn't matter.

Bandall and Bandall was beginning to hit its stride. In November of that year, we settled our first corporate case, against Dormall Pharmaceuticals. While the details of the final disposition are sealed as a condition of the settlement, I can tell you we won our clients more than $400 million, as well as medical expenses for the surviving victims. It was a contingency fee case, and our fee was significant. It was so much money, we almost felt guilty taking it.

Father Bobby set our minds at ease about the absurd amounts of money we began making. "Take your share, you two. Cleanse the blood money by using it for good purposes. Use it to give your child all the opportunities he or she will need to be part of the next generation of impact. Use it to contribute to the community. Be sure to reward yourselves for the important work you do, but also use it to help those who cannot protect themselves. Maybe one day, the people you champion will do the same for others. What's that quote? 'It takes money to make money'? I wouldn't know; our collection plates are entirely too empty..."

I agreed with my friend. "You are right, Bobby. That's it exactly." So, that was what we did. We used the money to make more money to help more people. We moved our office to a small commercial space—a shop front—one block away from our apartment and, by the end of 1977, we had two paralegals, one high-value corporate litigator, and four pro bono cases. We relished the waning days of our one-track minds: work.

In late January of 1978, after the close of the *Tully v. Qire Corporation* case, we decided to take a break to spend more time together during Sharon's last weeks of pregnancy. My expecting wife was the picture of beauty and health. Well into her ninth month, she was still leading tai chi classes and taking daily walks to the grocery store. In the evening, after dinner, I would talk to our unborn daughter. Sharon would lean against me as I spun brand-new tales, all exciting, all true. I told my child about my adventures growing up. I shared stories about playing stickball with my friends, about Lizzy and how she was the fastest runner I had ever seen...that is, until the day I first watched Sharon run. I told her about Sharon's escapades, her activism, and fighting for justice. I told her about all the amazing women in her family. I often spoke about how everyone was looking forward to her arrival.

Sharon, who very much wanted to fully experience the joy of motherhood and childbirth, decided to give birth at a nurse-midwifery center on the Upper East Side called the Childbearing Center. There, expectant mothers could give birth in a more natural way and in a nonhospital setting. It was quite a radical idea at the time—the second organization of its kind in the country and the first in an urban environment; they faced quite a bit of opposition. They were a client of ours, Sharon represented their purpose. As a show of solidarity and faith in what the center was doing, Sharon decided to give birth there.

Through no fault of the staff, the short, six-hour experience was a brutal one. Sharon's tiny frame seemed unprepared for the rigors of childbirth. Sharon insisted that, under no circumstances, was she to be administered any pain medication. She did not want her mind or her baby to be clouded by drugs. Interestingly, she remembered none of the pain, and later I couldn't even convince her it had occurred.

At 2:42, on the afternoon of February 1st, 1978, Allison May Bandall came into the world.

From the moment I laid eyes on her, she was the most beautiful creation I ever laid eyes upon. Even to this day, her angelic face warms my heart. I hold this picture close wherever I go. I've done so since the day it was taken. It's our only picture as a family. Dad took it when he and Mother were finally allowed in the room. What a glorious day to celebrate life.

We lived a lifetime in that single day. Sharon gazed down with love at our daughter as she nursed. Dad and I savored the sight of three generations: daughter, mother, and grandmother. I held my little girl as she fell asleep on my chest. I prayed for dreams to keep her safe. When she woke up and cried from hunger, wanting nothing more than her mother's milk, I sighed a breath of relief. Finally, that night, the nurse took little Allison to the nursery so that all of us could rest.

Late at night, or rather, early in the morning, Sharon and I were woken up by a somber-looking attendant. Allison May, she told us, had died in her sleep. They had tried to resuscitate her, but it seemed as if her crib death was sudden and immediate. They reassured us she did not suffer.

Sharon didn't speak. She did not move. She did not blink. I was unable to reach her. That catastrophic moment was exactly the terminus I had feared. I had been afraid something would go terribly wrong. I had felt such relief when Allison opened her eyes and cried while I was cradling her in my arms. In that instant, all my fear had disappeared. I felt betrayed...betrayed by my own unguarded frivolity and betrayed by Allison. I needed my wife to console me and assure me I was not at fault. I reached out to hold her.

"Get off of me!" she screamed. "This is your fucking fault! I hate you. Get the fuck away from me!"

She began hitting my face and swinging at my arms and chest. My dazed reaction was immediate. I wrapped my arms around her and rocked us back and forth. I was frantic. I cried, "I love you" over and over again. In an avalanche of grief and tears, she pounded her fists on my back.

She couldn't stop whimpering, "I hate you."

When her energy faded, her assault slowed and her crying softened. I maintained my grip on my wife until I felt her body go limp in my arms, and gently eased her back and watched as she slept. I whispered that I would be there when she woke up. I stayed awake and watched her struggle for every breath, determined to fulfill my promise of being there, afraid to fall asleep and give my ability the opportunity to take yet another life. Sharon eventually surrendered to exhaustion and slept without moving for nine hours.

When she opened her eyes, she saw me there, holding her hand and smiling. In that lonely room, where our most troublesome nightmare unfolded, I fell in love with Sharon a thousand times over.

She later told me my depleted expression only assured her everything would be all right.

"Was it a dream?" was her grasp at the impossible.

"No, my love. It happened. She's dead."

Neither of us cried. It was not a time for tears. Instead, both of us were lost in our own thoughts of what the hell to do next. I reassured my wife that I would use my ability to determine what had gone wrong. I started to tell her my plan: I would experience Allison May's moments, see what she saw and heard, and maybe that would help us find out what happened. Sharon put her hand on my cheek and subdued, "Hush now." She knew that it was far too dangerous for me to attempt a blind search to find if pieces and parts existed, and if they were connected. Rule Number 247: Never search for a moment to prove it exists.

Sharon and I recovered. We were severely wounded, but we learned to live with our scarred trauma. We would learn that new lesson in due time. Mother and Dad handled the arrangements for Allison May. A funeral was too much for us to bear. Father Bobby assured us she was not in limbo, instead had been entrusted "to the abundant mercy of God, that our beloved child may find a home in his kingdom." Sharon wanted to have her cremated; we spread her ashes at tender places known only to the two of us. She took her memories to the grave, as will I.

We kept nothing of our daughter's short life. Within a week, every trace of her was gone. Dad purged our apartment before we returned.

We tried to keep busy with various business matters and other personal affairs. The doors of our law office remained closed. With little notice to our family and friends, we fled the City we once held so close to our hearts.

We arrived at the tropical paradise of Hawai'i on February 8th, 1977. One of our past clients, Janice Kamaka, a complainant in the Dormall case, had been asking us for months to come to visit her and her family on the Big Island. She thought it was exactly what we needed to make Sharon's pregnancy restful and rewarding. By February, Hawai'i was exactly what we needed to make the whole thing go away.

Janice had purchased a sizable piece of property just outside her husband's childhood home—now that he was dead there was nothing left in New York that she cherished. Janice and her family welcomed us with open arms. A driver met us at the airport to collect our bags and take us to Papaaloa, as the community was designated at the time. Tadeas, though he insisted we call him Tad, give us a quick tour on the way. "By the way, Pāpaʻaloa," he said with the correct pronunciation, "is the true Hawaiian name given to our home. Dan, Janice's late husband, and I grew up there together. Janice is restoring the church in which they were married. Anyway, we've always referred to our community as Pāpaʻaloa, but the white man, no offense, tried to remove the Polynesian from our culture. They renamed it Papaaloa."

There was a distinct change of atmosphere in the car. It didn't matter to me; I was too busy falling in love with the incredible scenery. But not Sharon. "Oh, that's horrible, Tad! Isn't that a terrible way to treat a native culture, Mr. Bandall?" She softened her dig with a smile...then winked at me. Oh god, how I missed her charm! My wife had finally returned. She nuzzled against my chest and continued. "We absolutely must lend a hand to do something about that." Sharon kept her word and later headed an effort to petition the US Board on Geographic Names to officially change the name back to its original: Pāpaʻaloa. It took twenty-three years, but they got it done…a few months before Sharon died.

Janice and her family welcomed us to the Big Island with an incredible luau. Sharon loved it. Not once did I see her frown or even look sad. She fell in love with Hawaiʻi immediately; the culture, music, and food were unlike anything she ever experienced. After the luau, she was exhausted and a little bit tipsy. Drain beyond all imagination, yet before we fell asleep, Sharon focused my mind, as she always did. "Dominic, thank you for making my dreams come true. Thank you for using your visions to ease my soul. I can't do this without you. Please guide me somewhere."

Only within the privacy of our relationship was Sharon able to be so vulnerable. She appeared strong to everyone else—a flawless example of success in every way—but I knew she was damaged, scarred, and beaten. That only strengthened her. The strongest steel is not forged in the hottest fire, but rather by the constant beating, pounding, and deforming of its mass. If the mass doesn't break, it's folded over and pounded more. Eventually, after repeated folds, it takes the form it was always meant to be, then, finally, polished.

Sharon was that steel, that foundation strengthening rebar, that blade sharpened to a razor's edge.

When she woke the next morning, I was holding her hand. She looked at me quizzically—she always woke up before me. I assured her I had slept well and was just taking advantage of waking up first. Eager to give her a glimpse of the Island and its culture, I told her about a dream of the first people who came ashore there. They were seafarers from another land who arrived in vessels unlike anything I had ever seen. They spoke a strange language. Their weathered skin and the condition of their clothing made it clear they had been on the ocean for a long time. I did not know where they had come from. They began to scour the Island in search of potable water. "That was it, my love," I told her. "That was all I saw in my moment. I have no idea when those men came ashore. It will be interesting to hear stories from some of the locals on the Island."

Sharon popped up, squeaked with glee, and ran to the dining room to find the feast of vegetables and pastries Janice had prepared for breakfast. As the ladies ate, they made plans to explore the Big Island. Sharon invited me to come sit with them. "We absolutely must learn about this incredible culture." I understood the not-so-subtle cue and asked Janice if she had any literature on the history of Hawai'i.

"No, but if you want to know the true history, there is a wonderful library in Hilo. We can check it out on the way to the airport."

Do you remember the helicopter ride when you first arrived, Angela?

<Angela: "Yes. It was amazing.">

I stole that trick from Janice. She arranged for us to tour the Island by air. I know how you felt, for I too had that experience. Our guide took us around the Island's perimeter and atop each of its five volcanoes. As we rounded the southeast corner, Sharon cinched her fingers around my arm and exhaled a guttural "Whoa...." The beauty of Honu'apo jumped through the mist and fog. Even though it had been decimated by a tsunami a few years before—the cycle of growth and destruction continued, as it had for thousands of years—Honu'apo retained its beauty. Before our tour concluded, we both had fallen in love with Honu'apo and its surroundings.

We loved Hawai'i so much, we decided to purchase a parcel of land just beyond the Whittington Beach County Park in Ka'ū,

Honuʻapo. "This will be a lovely place for a new home, a new start," I told Sharon on the day we signed the title and transfer documents. Hawaiʻi had welcomed us in our time of need. It cleansed Sharon of sorrow and heartache—purged the pain of years of death and loss. The land was perfect for me, as well. The Polynesian air surely made a big difference to my health. I improved beyond any of our expectations. Picking up loose change, thumbing through a legal brief, taking a walk to enjoy the sights and the fragrance of fresh blossoms…it's these seemingly inconsequential things in life you long for most when you are deprived of them. On the Island, we had no limitations.

We decided to relocate our firm to Hawaiʻi. Until we passed the Hawaiʻi State Bar, we would fill our time with mediation, estate administration, and probate work. Sharon and I entered into a legal arrangement with the residents of Kaʻū to fund reclamation efforts to maintain the sanctity of the land. We traveled throughout the islands whenever we could find the time, savoring the unique beauty of each. We enjoyed the food, music, and culture of the native population. Although my ability allowed me to learn the language fast, Sharon's proficiency in each of the unique dialects seriously impressed some of the elders. I dreamed about moments to help both of us learn the ancient language.

Sadly, just four months after we stepped into paradise, we had to leave. I got a call from Milt who told me the DA's office had refused to bring charges in the death of Joe Ferrer, and thought our "investigative litigation" might help the Ferrer family get justice. How could I break the news to Sharon that I wanted to return to New York? When I told her about Milt's call, I didn't get the fight I expected. "Justice is so much more than the fair and impartial administration of the law. It's the determination of rights according to that law, according to rules of equity. It's a set of principles defining what is right and impartial. Long before a specific law applies, there needs to be conformity to truth, fact, or reason. Only then can law take form, but long before that law, there is still a need for justice. Do you think you can find the truth, Dominic? I will help you decide how to do it. We can search together."

In two nights, I was able to get an outline of the truth about what had happened in the Ferrer case. Milt was surprised when we called him back. "I thought the mountain air might've numbed your desire," he joked.

Sharon found his New Yorker attitude entertaining. "It's the *tropical* air, Milton. Tropical air."

"Whatever. So, when can I expect you?"

We returned to New York two days later. It was late June, and the summer was already gearing up to be a scorcher. Because we had given up our apartment on East 81st Street, we stayed in the Bronx with my parents for two months before moving back downtown. Not only did we need easier access to the courthouses, but we wanted to avoid falling into any mental or emotional traps of our past. Picking up where we left off with the practice was easy. Shanda White, who we had kept on the payroll while we were in Hawai'i, had been maintaining our open accounts.

In mid-August, Sharon and I closed on an apartment on West 50th Street. At that time, Hell's Kitchen was kind of a grimy place, rife with gang violence and other less-desirable aspects of city life. Sharon saw something different. Everything she wanted was there: proximity to courthouses, libraries, and our beloved John Jay was ideal for research. Everything in Manhattan—the theaters, piers, parks— delighted Sharon. Our nineteenth-floor apartment had an incredible view south to the World Trade Center and east, across the Hudson

River. Dad and I sometimes gazed through the plate-glass windows and talked about the days when he worked on those magnificent buildings.

It didn't take us long to become fully immersed in New York life again. We were engrossed in our practice and continued strengthening our roots in the Bronx while making new connections in Hell's Kitchen.

However, we always considered Honuʻapo our real home and returned often. We also spent every February there to celebrate Allison May's birthday. Our house on the Island was modest; we had no need for excess. We also respected and made every effort to help maintain that sanctity our land instilled in us by the native population. We began researching the history of the Island. I would uncover moments in my sleep about what had actually transpired; together we would weave a tapestry that slowly took form as a historical map of the Islands, strengthening our connection.

* * *

On Sharon's final visit to Honuʻapo in February of 2001, we hosted a luau for our closest friends and invited respected elders from throughout the Islands. Sharon and I spoke to the elders in fluent

ʻŌlelo Hawaiʻi, their native tongue, and told them about the history of their Polynesian paradise. We described life in Oʻahu, in Maui, in Molokaʻi, Lānaʻi, Kauaʻi, Niʻihau, and Hawaiʻi before the white man first arrived. We told them about the time before it was a state, before it was a US territory. We talked with the elders about the Kingdom of Hawaiʻi and how the chiefdoms unified under King Kamehameha. They loved hearing those rarely told stories. They laughed at the simplicity of kauwā commoners and marveled at the power the kahuna possessed as high priests of the chiefdoms. A quarrel broke out when we told them the correct order in which the Tahitian explorers had actually conquered the Polynesian settlements.

The crowd became silent when I started speaking an ancient language not uttered for 2,900 years. Sharon translated as I told the story of the first settlers to land on the shores of Kohala. They were searching the seas for their god, Hiʻūakūū. This word, which our guests had never heard, was Sharon's best phonetic translation of the "god beyond the sea, emerging from the sea." This group of 120 men, women, and children arrived on the land that would later be called Hawaiʻi in an armada of fifteen highly unusual seafaring vessels, the likes of which had, and have still, never been seen in our time. For generations, they had traveled the ocean, from islands far west to islands far east, in search of Hiʻūakūū. Their commitment was absolute. When their efforts were unsuccessful in one location, the tribal leader would announce that it was time to move to the next. Each time they moved on, they would merely plunge ahead without a plan or scouting party.

When they arrived on Kohala, they found a verdant land of luscious and bountiful vegetation next to barren terrain created by lava flows. They settled there and named their land Hiʻūakūū. Over the course of two hundred years, families thrived, communities were established, and they formed a complex hierarchal government. When the volcano of Hualālai erupted, as it often did, their religious leaders would gather the children to watch Hiʻūakūū emerging from the sea.

The elders were fascinated as I continued to share that story and they begged me to tell them what happened to the people of Hiʻūakūū.

This is what I told them.

"Your earliest people worshipped the land and shared the earth with their god long before my god sent his son to us. When the children asked if they would ever meet their creator, the priests told them their god would come when they were pure.

"Eventually, the women became barren—for twenty years, no children were born. They saw this as a sign of the coming. One day, Hualālai erupted with a ferocity unlike ever before. The volcano spewed lava in the air as far as the Forbidden Isle of Ni'ihau. The flow quickly extruded down the mountainside and the people of Hi'ūakūū were suddenly overcome by the god they prayed to. There were no screams of anguish, for the lava flow took them far too quickly. There was no fear, for every soul welcomed this union with their creator."

The next day we led an excursion of our friends and the elders to an area near Palihae Gulch on the northwest part of the Island. I told them that, buried far beneath that earth, were the remains of the Island's first inhabitants. We bound our research on the true history of Hawai'i into books and gave the elders several copies. Our research and our stories portrayed a past very different from the history they knew. There is no way to prove what I discovered in my dreams, and to most, the book is considered a fantastic tale of fiction.

To the elders, however, the possibility that what we told them was a revelation into their land exceeds any value man may define.

It wasn't until 1993—fifteen years after we first went to Hawai'i—that I found out Sharon had been documenting the history of the Island as I told it to her. She never told me she was writing it down because she wanted me to describe my moments purely, as I experienced them. She didn't want me to express them in a way that was calculated for documentation. Only when she needed to ask me questions—to better understand my descriptions or clarify inconsistencies—did she finally disclose her undertaking.

* * *

Yes, Sharon is defined by the impact she had on so many people. Her curriculum vitae, which lists one thousand one hundred and seventeen litigation and class-action cases, ninety-three criminal defense cases, and legal support for twenty-three other criminal proceedings, is only the smallest part of her full accomplishments.

On August 30th, 1969, when Sharon came with me to Pelham Bay, she inadvertently helped heal a neighborhood. The community had experienced far too much loss—Billy, Rich, Dennis, Lizzy and Rebecca Strauss—it was far too painful to talk about, yet no one had ever forgotten them. She asked questions which forced answers, sparking stories, creating laughter and smiles. Also, through Sharon, people remembered Lizzy; Sharon had the same exuberance and energy. Without knowing it, she helped us regain a bit of faith that life does get better. Not only did she heal me, but my recovery gave the community a modicum of hope. Sharon brought life itself with her, and life begat fortune. When Barbara Clayton announced her pregnancy, shortly after the birth and death of Allison May, it was a source of joy for the neighborhood and for our family. Even though my mother knew she was never going to have another grandchild of her own, she received the news with joy. Sharon's efforts to heal our extended family weren't lauded, but they did not go unnoticed.

When we lost Allison May, Pop Pop, and Grandma Dot, and when we would later lose Dad and Mother, and all the others, we heard one message: Weep now, child, for your body needs to. Tomorrow is the day to frolic together in the bounty you have reaped, to once again sow, and to continue nourishing your fields.

Another thing Sharon did was to fight tirelessly to improve Hell's Kitchen. Although we lived in a tower complex, we were still within the boundaries of the Preservation Area, under which specific zoning rules of the Special Clinton District were put in place to limit commercialization and maintain the low-rise character of the neighborhood. Sharon helped with the maintenance, revision, and enforcement of zoning laws. One of the cases she was very proud of was her work on the Windermere apartments. Whenever she heard someone mention the Windermere, her lips would curl into a smug little grin. "That's where I got my first death threat," she would tell anyone within earshot. Sharon would expound on the elegant building's construction in 1881, its transition from a residence for families to flophouse, to home of struggling artists, to basically a single-room occupancy building. After the building was sold in 1980, the new owner tried to force the tenants out of their rent-controlled apartments by ransacking the building and deliberately moving in prostitutes. Burglaries in the building, violence, and death threats to tenants were commonplace until 1985, when Sharon managed to, as she so eloquently worded it, "help put those scum buckets who managed the building in jail." Oh, how I hope she is looking down and can see the Windermere now! What a victory she won.

    That was Sharon. At any point in her life, she gave priority to those in need at the expense of her own well-being. Whenever necessary, she fought for justice. When someone praised her bravery and fortitude, she would quote Agesilaus II, king of ancient Sparta: "Courage is of no value unless accompanied by justice; yet if all men became just, there would be no need for courage." Sharon loved these words for they are as accurate now as they were 2,400 years ago.

Sharon never took her quest for justice to the next level, and for that, I am to blame. She declined three different mayoral appointments for a judgeship. She refused suggestions that she run for state and federal representative seats. The reasons she gave for not pursuing these positions were a lack of interest and distaste for the political side of the law, but I knew it was because of me. My secret would be a severe liability in all of those roles, not only because if anyone found out, it would damage her reputation, but because taking a job like that might compromise the most important job she already treasured: keeping me safe. "It's out of the question," she told me each time. "I won't risk exposing your ability to the world. You know the rules, Dominic: never tell anyone, remain cautious around others, don't reveal your ability. Our faces on the front page of the *Daily News* is not a particularly good way to keep out of sight."

Despite her grand intentions, we did end up on the front page of the *Daily News*, twice. First, in December 1980, after we took down Amalgamated Carbon. The second time was in 1983, when we moved our firm to the World Trade Center. As we were entering the North Tower on our first official day, a photographer yelled to catch our attention. The next day, there was the photo of us, with the headline "Brains, Beauty & the Beast." The caption read, "Sharon and Dominic Bandall to stand guard over New York City from atop the World Trade Center." I found the whole thing flattering, theatrics notwithstanding. Sharon suggested bringing a defamation lawsuit against the paper, but I convinced her the caption only reinforced our branding: a powerhouse legal team fighting for justice. "Besides," I added, "have you seen what I look like trying to navigate these city streets? I think 'beast' is entirely appropriate." We ended up hanging a framed copy of that *Daily News* front page, signed by the photographer, in the waiting room of our office.

There were several reasons for relocating our office to the World Trade Center. The first was captured perfectly by that snapshot. We always wanted to be guardians of our fair city, to fight for those whom justice had forsaken. Also, we had become successful enough by then that we needed a more formal space. We often held pretrial and mediation meetings to give our opposing counsel a chance to settle, especially if they didn't want any of the embarrassing evidence we uncovered to become public. Also, our address just looked impressive and gave us some bragging rights with other firms: One World Trade Center, 94th floor, Suite 105, New York, NY 10048. We deliberately did not use the office for client meetings because we wanted them to feel comfortable and not out of place in a world that was, in most cases, far grander than what they were used to. Usually we went to their house, a restaurant, or some other convenient location. However, when we wanted to notify our clients of a successful outcome to a case, whether it was a settlement or judgment in our favor, we had a driver bring them to Tower One. For the pain, suffering, and humiliation they often endured, we felt it was appropriate.

Dad was so proud when we moved into the North Tower. At the time, he was working nearby, overseeing the planning and construction of Building 7. We had lunch together often...usually just a dog with relish. Dad told me the challenges of the current work crews were nothing compared to the difficulties they faced when they broke ground on our building in 1968. Sharon loved listening to Dad's stories and always tried to keep him talking. "Why did they decide to build this tower first? You also did the demolition of Radio Row? So, what was it like looking out the window the first time? Do you think they'll construct a Building 8?" She had asked him all those questions before and already knew every answer. She wasn't just trying to boost his ego; she loved to hear him talk about it and was fascinated whenever he shared another adventure.

We were indeed on the top of the world, but we were hardly a colossal presence. After Milt joined the firm in 1998, we only had three lawyers, five paralegals, and three administrative assistants. Sharon wanted to remain small to reduce the risk of exposing me. Bringing in Milt was more of a necessity than a personal outreach. As our focus shifted toward unjust charges, incarcerations, and criminal proceedings against disadvantaged populations, his in-depth expertise on criminal code in jurisdictions from coast to coast made him an asset. We labored over whether to share my ability with Milt. After contemplating and debating every aspect of this risky proposition for nearly three years, we finally decided to do it. He had shown us he could separate his personal and professional opinions. We planned to invite Milt and Barbara to join us in Hawai'i in February 2002. That would give us time to thoroughly unravel an incredible story that spanned fifty-one years.

What you now know, Angela, exceeds any dossier on Sharon Peers Bandall. She would proudly stand here today and own all the decisions she made and the actions she took throughout her life, both good and bad. This was the woman who saved me, as well as thousands of other people. She was one of the central architects of the movement for women to empower themselves. She was emotional, tender, and loyal. Sharon fought for the City and held everyone to one standard: Justice.

<Extended pause>

But, the Sharon I know of is so much more than that. So often, we comforted each other over one problem or another. She would cry, and I was there to console her. I would cry, and she was there to hold me. Whatever the reason, before we were done, we would decide to move on together. As much as she pushed my body to its limits, she did the same to herself. She had the character of a thousand warrior princesses. Sharon ran her first New York City Marathon in 1991 as a backlash against an arbitrary plateau: her fortieth birthday. She had no problem with the race and was as strong and graceful as she was the day I met her.

<Pause>

Sharon was committed to holding me to the level of excellence she noticed in me so many years before. Her unqualified perfection was fascinating, not just in her actions, which I had grown accustomed to, but rather by how she was able to remain morally virtuous. I wanted to celebrate her deity, not her accomplishments. Saturday the 15th of September was going to be a night to remember in Hell's Kitchen. It would have been Sharon's fiftieth birthday. An army of four hundred family members and friends were eager to celebrate with us at the B.B. King Blues Club. I had spent the previous twenty-three months planning the party. Sharon had thrown me a surprise party on my fiftieth, but there was no way I would have succeeded at catching her unexpected—she would've picked up on it instantly. Instead, I tantalized her with the details. The invitation list. The venue. The food. The musical headliner.

On the morning of September 1st, when Sharon woke up and saw I was already out of bed, she sat up in a startled frenzy. It was still rare that she slept later than me. I walked out of our closet with a beautiful, sequined, black silk midi dress I had just bought for her. "I thought you might like to wear this to your party."

She jumped right up, yanked her nightgown over her head, and shrieked, "Oh, I have to try this on right away!" With her back to me, she paused. For a moment, I was nineteen years old again—from across my dorm room I was staring at the most beautiful creature I could imagine. Sharon had become only more alluring over the years; her youthful exuberance, athleticism, and sophistication were tantalizing. She turned slowly, pivoting on the ball of her foot as I approached with the dress. I couldn't stop staring at her and she stood in silence, savoring the time until her motion broke me from my trance. Sharon had an immobilizing effect on me.

She winked. Oh, god, that wink. Sharon never did try on that dress.

<Extended pause>

There were just a few things left for me to do before Saturday's party. On Tuesday morning, before work, I had to go pick up her birthday gift—a diamond-encrusted, eighteen-karat, white-gold choker necklace. I talked to Sharon before she left in the morning, telling her that I would be in a little late because I had some last-minute party planning to do. We both checked our calendars, then made plans for an early dinner—just the two of us. I gave her a tender kiss and said goodbye to my love.

My driver dropped me off on Greenwich and Warren shortly before the jeweler opened. I was going to walk to the office from there. The City is a marvel. In the dead of night, it comes alive with energy. In the morning rush hour, its incredible silhouette against a backdrop of bright blue sky is mesmerizing. I looked up at the Tower and wondered if—hoped that—Sharon was looking down at me, an insignificant speck far below her. I never heard the rumblings of the engines. I never saw panic in the street. I only looked up in peace, only to see my life, my Sharon, disappear in an instant.

<Extended pause>

Chapter 23 - Voice: Angela

After a seemingly endless silence, I began to grow concerned. "Dominic? Dominic, are you okay?" I called his name again and again, but he didn't respond. His head was down, his eyes were closed, shoulders sagged. His sobs turned to whimpers. Between shallow breaths, there was an occasional heave of his chest. "Dominic? Do you want to stop for the evening?"

He was asleep. The great Dominic Bandall had fallen asleep in the middle of his argument. The picture of this little old man sawing logs in his chair might have been amusing if I had not just heard the extraordinary story he told me. I was frightened.

I suddenly wondered how this man, immensely vulnerable and delicate, had survived for as long as he did. I tried to imagine the torment of watching so many lives, so much love, suffer and die over and over again as he did. In the days since the stories of his life and career first flashed before me, so many years ago, it darn near overtook me on more than one occasion.

I didn't know what to do. I was afraid to touch him. Did Sharon ever wake Dominic while he was dreaming? I didn't recall him telling me about that. Would something bad happen to him? It was a risk I was not prepared to take.

Instead, I left the room and went to the kitchen. Hy'ing was waiting there, just as she stood by every night. I told her about the scene in the office. "Oh, don't worry. He does that a lot," she reassured me. "I'll go put a blanket over his legs and let him be. He will wake up in an hour or so and go to bed. I will take care of him." She suggested I eat something before I retired. I grabbed a power bar and drank the juice she had just pressed for me.

"You two were in there for a long time."

I looked at the clock. Wow! It was already 11:30. We had been in the office for over fifteen hours—an uninterrupted monologue. I have never seen someone have that kind of focus, able to maintain a monologue like that for so long. He didn't even seem to struggle. It looked like it was easier for him than for me, and I was just observing! When I needed to use the bathroom—he saw me squirm—he motioned to the facilities, only extending a mid-sentence pause while I rushed out of the room. He never stopped to use the bathroom himself—he had a catheter drainage bag hidden in the leg of his pants. Dominic never ate and only took occasional sips of water. I told Hy'ing, "It was amazing! What stamina! He just kept on talking, never broke his stride or lost his train of thought. It seemed as if he knew exactly what he wanted to say—well, he told me it was a script he had written ahead of time—but it was so well rehearsed, he simply spilled it out with hardly a pause. For the most part, he spoke with little emotion, that is until he started to tell me about the day Sharon..."

Hy'ing cut me off. I could tell she wanted to know more about her employer, her friend, but apparently her loyalty was stronger than any curiosity. In fact, she cut our whole conversation short and hurried me on my way. "It is late, and I know Dominic expects you at 8:30 tomorrow morning in his office."

I was drained. Given the opportunity, I probably would have fallen asleep before Dominic did. I had done nothing physical to justify my exhaustion—all I did was sit there and listen—but his tale was so hard to hear. Despite my depleted state, I couldn't fall asleep. I kept thinking about the story Dominic had told me. It was beautiful and moving, but so tragic. The question that kept rolling through my brain was: Was it even true?

I thought about all he had told me and compared it to other information I had on him and Sharon. I knew about their professional lives—there was a lot of documentation written by others, as well as papers Sharon and Dominic had written—but I had also read biographies on both of them. I knew Dominic was a highly respected lawyer—confident, articulate, persuasive and, most of all, a ruthless adversary who expected nothing less than complete victory in the courtroom. Much had also been written about their firm and its successes. One thing always stressed in those articles was that their protocol, in their investigations and in the courtroom, left very little room for error or misinterpretation. The man I had been listening to for the past week described himself as meek, unsure, and afraid. The way he depicted a sad, scared boy in need of someone to care for and save him from his demons simply didn't jibe with the reputation he had. I could not connect the two sides of him.

And Sharon? Dominic's account confirmed she was very much the woman I had heard about and always had profound admiration for. She was as strong and confident as everyone said. The stories he told me of her youth seemed plausible...raised in adversity yet able to turn her life into something truly remarkable. She was an inspiration, and after what Dominic told me, I realized my desire to model my career after hers had been the right decision.

Then I went back to the question that had been on my mind from the minute I got Dominic's invitation to Hawaii: Why me? What was Dominic after? Did he see me as a stand-in for the daughter he never got a chance to know? Did he want to pass on the values he and Sharon were not able to give to their daughter? It occurred to me that if I straightened and dyed my hair, I could probably pass for Sharon in her younger years, so maybe he thought I looked like his daughter would have at my age. That would be understandable...a man of advancing years, in declining health, searching for a deserving lawyer to whom he could bequeath his wife's legacy. But if that were the case, I couldn't figure out why then, after so many years? Those taunting thoughts and questions kept me awake for a long time. I finally decided I had to confront him. The mystery of it all had gone on long enough.

I would later come to understand that Dominic was both people. He was the confident and assertive lawyer who, with authority, precision, and the blunt force of the truth, put fear in others. His counterpart lived his life in fear—fear of the beast inside him that could explode at any moment, and fear of having to witness the torment of the souls whose lives he dreamed of. The only support he ever had came from his mother and father, Sharon, and Giuseppe. By the time we met, almost eighteen years had passed since he lost the final piece of this blessed trinity. How did he last so long before the beast proved triumphant?

As I said, that revelation came only much later. On that morning, March 7th, 2019, I was resolute, angry, and ready to pounce on Dominic's self-description as a wounded fawn. At 8:28, I walked into his office. I found him waiting for our session to begin, impeccably dressed in a three-piece suit, with a fresh haircut, clean shave, and a steaming cup of black coffee on his side table. He looked up at me, smiled, and struggled to stand up. Mr. Bandall nodded politely as he greeted me. "Good morning, Angela. Please accept my sincere apologies for yesterday's transgression. If you will allow, I am eager to begin today's discussion."

Chapter 24 - Voice: Dominic

Today is Thursday, March 7th, 2019. My name is Dominic J. Bandall. This is session number seventeen of my interview with Ms. Angela Grant.

"At his best, man is the noblest of all animals; separated from law and justice, he is the worst." This interpretation of Aristotle's is sufficient for the purposes of our discussion. On 9/11, I bore witness to the worst. We all did. We lived through a complete separation of the populace from natural law. To save humankind from itself, I have devoted my life to the application of justice ever since that day.

For you to understand what occurred after September 11th, 2001, I must take you back to my own experience on that horrific day. To be clear, I am not a survivor, nor was I a responder; I was a witness to murder. I am also a victim; I am a grieving husband, a grieving friend, and a grieving employer. Of course, I am just one of many who went through moments of unimaginable terror.

This is how the day first unfolded before me, just as so many others' countless experiences of terror were created, before the clarity of its revelation in my dreams. This was my moment.

In response to the massive first explosion, my leg gave out and I fell to the ground, dropping my cane and briefcase. I lay on the sidewalk as the thunder continued to roar in one extended avalanche of destruction. I looked up at the World Trade Center and saw that a gaping hole had been torn into the upper part of the North Tower. Plumes of white and sickly yellow smoke poured from the black gouge. Within seconds, fiery orange flames burst through the undersides of the mushrooming clouds. The flames diffused in every direction...then returned, reformed, and tried to escape once again. The smoke turned dark...black. When the fires retreated, pausing to take their first breath, I saw what they left behind: nothing.

The spot where Sharon had been sitting was hollow. Empty. She was due in court that morning and had gone in early to do some last-minute preparation. Surely, Sharon had been sitting at her desk at that moment. For a second, I considered other possibilities. Maybe she had gone to refill her water bottle as she often did early in the morning. Perhaps she was talking with Jessica, the paralegal who was helping her with pretrial disclosure paperwork for the Select Instruments case. Maybe she went to use the restroom.

But, none of that mattered; I could see everything was gone. All that remained was a blackened void through which fire continued to push ash and smoke. I knew Sharon was gone. I screamed her name at the top of my lungs, then sat on the concrete and cried for her, begging for it not to be true. I could hear sounds all around me.

"Oh, my god!"

"Holy shit!"

"What was that?"

"Oh, my god!"

"Hurry."

"Come on! Come on!"

"It was a plane!"

Sirens wailed, alarms shrieked, and the building continued to roar.

I cried out Sharon's name over and over. A man rushed to help me. He put his arm around my shoulders and said, "All right, buddy. It's all right. I'm sure she's okay." But I knew the awful truth.

Anita, my driver, was suddenly by my side. She had been waiting at the end of the block to make sure I got into the building okay. She picked up my things, tucked her head under my arm and walked me over to the car. As we stumbled down the street, I strained to look back at the burning tower. I told her to drive to the entrance of our building, the North Tower, but she refused. "We have to leave now! Look what's happening! It is much too dangerous. We have to leave!" By then, fire trucks, police cars, and ambulances were pouring into lower Manhattan. Debris and ash were raining down on everything and everyone. People were running away. Others were too numb and shocked to move. Anita wanted to take me up to the Bronx. I refused. As a compromise, I had her drive to our apartment in Hell's Kitchen—my apartment...the apartment—where she insisted on staying with me. "It's going to take me hours to get home to Tribeca." Even though we had no idea what was going on, I knew "hours" was gloriously optimistic. Anita never tried to make me feel better or offer words of encouragement. Both of us had come to the same conclusion: everyone in the office was dead.

As chaos erupted around us, we sat in the living room and watched the catastrophe unfold on TV. Our repeated attempts to call family and friends were unsuccessful—the phone grid had buckled under the millions of calls flooding in and out of the City. I was able to connect to Sharon's phone seven times, each with the same result:

"Hello, you have reached Sharon P. Bandall. Please leave your name, number, and a brief message and I will return your call as soon as possible. Thanks, and have a great day!" I never left a voicemail. I knew she was gone. I was calling because I needed to hear her voice.

For me, the nightmare of September 11th was a familiar feeling. Like the moments I experienced in so many others' worst day, there was incomprehensible horror all around me, yet nothing I could do to influence any of it. I was forced to hear, see, and smell that which I could not touch. My city screamed at me as its heart was pierced, but it refused to acknowledge when I screamed back because I was not part of its suffering...I was not in the tower with my family.

Instead, I watched from my comfortable armchair miles away as Armageddon unfolded. I watched the second plane, flying low, strike through the belly of the South Tower. I watched the building fall into a cloud of pulverized remains. Then the North Tower fell. I felt no sorrow for my beloved as the structure came down because I knew she was no longer inside. Slowly, a wind cleared the view and what seemed like a dream was now a ghostly reality. The towers that had adorned our skyline that morning now lay in ruins at our feet.

New York was in chaos; I didn't know what was happening elsewhere in the world. All I knew was what I saw on TV, and that wasn't very helpful. Everyone was just trying to figure out what had happened. I needed to know details and began to make a plan to focus my thoughts for my dream.

When our president spoke, I felt as if he were speaking to me. "Make no mistake: The United States will hunt down and punish those responsible for these cowardly acts." As he continued to talk, I scrawled across the top of my legal pad: JUSTICE. When he finished speaking, I looked down at my notes.

JUSTICE?

Before New York City peered out through the grime, as responders climbed hissing volcanoes of rubble in search of survivors, I was busy preparing a quest for justice. This was a task I had done so many times before. Define my search. Find the events I know occurred. Identify traps, holes, uncertainties. Then I wrote down the rules that applied to that situation. Rule Number 401: There is no emotion. This rule was a recent addition that I had added at Sharon's insistence when I became nostalgic about a moment. She told me, "Dominic, there can be no emotion in the game we are playing.

Emotion will cloud your mind. Emotion will kill you." She traced her finger across the next empty line and tapped the spot. "401: There is no emotion."

That was when I realized I had lost my Sharon forever. I don't care to describe the torrent of pain I surrendered to, though I am not ashamed about my grief. On that day, I was one of millions mourning the loss of loved ones. Anita and I held each other and cried. She was there for me and did what she could to draw the pain out of me. I knew she was there, I felt her there, I heard her soothing voice, but none of that mattered. All I heard were mutterings and wails of anguish.

Over and over again I bellowed, "There *is* emotion! Goddamnit, there is and you're not here to stop it. It *will* cloud my mind! It *will* kill me!" I cursed Sharon for leaving me. For the first time in nearly twenty-six years, she would not be by the side of her pitiful, wounded pet when my body finally succumbs to sleep. I began to wonder if that day was a precursor to my long-overdue departure from this earth. Was I destined to soon follow my soulmate in the same way I have witnessed other true loves rejoin for the final act of their togetherness?

There I sat in my multimillion-dollar condominium, looking down on a myriad of creatures, dead and dying—observing a disaster that would undoubtedly destroy countless more—and I feared for my own safety. It was in those hours where I lost the right to ever pity myself again, for every hour after my awakening is burdened with that shame.

On Tuesday, September 11th, 2001, however, as blue fought to regain its rightful place in the sky before surrendering to nightfall, I felt floods of emotion and fear. I spent the night staring into emptiness, watching people scrambling to save the suffering.

I thought about Pop Pop and Grandma Dot when they realized Sharon had not been in the fatal car accident, and how their lives had been instantly resurrected when she told them, "I'm okay." I longed to hear my wife speak those words...not in my moments, but right then. I longed to see her beautiful smile. I wanted to feel the grip of her embrace, the taste of her lips, her breath on my face as she whispered the words, "I'm okay." I offered my life to God in exchange for those words. But of course, I knew my wish would never be fulfilled, and any longing would cloud my mind before ultimately killing me. The thing is, I wanted nothing else but that.

I don't remember eating or drinking. I can recall no activity other than staring at the destruction as gray plumes turned black from the night, then ash again with the morning sun. September 12th. The majestic backdrop...still wasted.

I have never revisited the time I spent in our apartment after the attack. There is nothing I care to recall. Until early evening, all I was doing was avoiding my destiny. Finally, unable to fight my slumber anymore, I drifted off, aching for Sharon.

I wondered how my love spent the night of September 11th, 2001.

Chapter 25 - Voice: Dominic

Today is Thursday, March 7th, 2019. My name is Dominic J. Bandall. This is session number eighteen in my interview with Angela Grant.

"Justice is merely incidental to law and order." I'm sure it would be no surprise to J. Edgar Hoover to know our focus has been on maintaining the illusion of one under the pretext of the other.

When I finally opened my eyes, the sun was blurring the images around me into a single form, and shades of fantastic colors were trying to erupt out of the smudged background. I was relieved to see Anita's face, depleted though it was, come into focus because it assured me that reality still existed and that meant everything would be all right.

Making one last grasp at the impossible, I asked, "Was it all a dream?"

"No, Dominic. It happened."

Anita's declaration was unnecessary. I knew what had happened—in fact, more so than anyone else—as I had already felt 2,843 beloved souls perish at the World Trade Center.

Many were identified and received a proper farewell. In time, others would be recognized for their compelled martyrdom. Some people's deaths have gone unnoticed; they may never even be missed. Before opening my eyes that day, I had accumulated more than three thousand moments of 9/11. Between each moment, where life normally takes focus, was nothing. I strained my mind against the boundaries of its concentration to remember what had happened, but all I got were fragments of sound. My other senses gave me nothing. What cruelty! Even Joe Bonham had his mind and could feel the delicate touch of his caretaker. What was I left with? Scraps. An occasional word. And of course, the harrowing final moments of so many. I was so confused about what had happened before the coma and the "reality" I woke up to, I momentarily considered that maybe none of it—the devastating loss of life and now my broken body—had even happened. Had the whole thing been a dream? Had Anita lied to me? Was it possible that I actually had a bit of optimism left in me?

No, I told myself. It was not a dream. Was I still asleep?

To confirm either my hypothesis or my dementia, I asked Anita a series of questions.

"What is today's date?"

"Wednesday, November 14th."

I fought to maintain my composure. *Dammit, Dominic*, I scolded myself. *Stay focused. Find your factual stakes. Search for traps, holes, and uncertainties.*

"2001?"

"Yes, it's still 2001," she said with a slight grin.

My god, that kid was amazing. Anita joined my pool of drivers in early 2000, while working her way through night school. Her confidence and poise in every situation, her exuberance for the most mundane tasks, caught my attention. I soon began asking for advice and using her as my sounding board, not on legal matters, but on a variety of other topics—guidance on how to appear normal. It seems I was self-assured only in my role as a lawyer.

Although Anita had been to my apartment hundreds of times, I had no idea where she lived. I remembered from the day of the attacks—it was Tribeca. I knew she was going to school, but I never bothered to learn more about her or ask about her interests, goals, or family. It is embarrassing, especially considering how much Anita knew about me...and my unique physical problems.

When I fell asleep on the evening of September 12th, Anita stood guard over me. She always carried a copy of the guidelines for my care that Sharon had given her in case something went wrong. Apparently, Sharon had trained most of our staff for these kinds of emergencies. When I began to show signs of distress, Anita immediately initiated the procedures that undoubtedly saved my life.

"You fell asleep at 7:50 p.m. Shortly after ten, you had a seizure. You were convulsing quite violently. I had already retrieved your medical kit, with your mouth guard and the oxygen mask. I got you on the floor, laid you on your side, put a pillow under your head, and called 911. I didn't know who else to call because I was already sure everyone on the list was dead. When I finally got through to the 911 operator—it took forever—I told him you were having a grand mal seizure, just like Sharon instructed me to do. I have no idea how the ambulance got there so quickly with everything else that was going on that night. They were amazing.

"The paramedics said they'd never seen anything like it before. You just continued to cycle between tonic and clonic phases. You never relaxed. And once you got to the hospital, even though they sedated you heavily, you kept seizing. You should have been catatonic."

"That's it? Until today?"

"That is it, Dominic. Despite the drugs, you continued to have seizures—sometimes hundreds of times a day. I called your lawyer because Sharon told me he had power of attorney if she was not there." Anita was sitting beside me, holding my hand as she talked to me. Oh, how I cherished the comfort.

"It seems you know an awful lot about my care," I told her. She squeezed my hand tighter and turned her head away. I could see she was trying to hide a tear that had spilled down her cheek. She took a minute to regain her composure and turned back to me.

"I've had plenty of time to brush up on all the terminology! The doctors encouraged me to visit you as often as possible. It seems my voice comforted you. Mr. Emmanuelle has arranged for me to stay on the payroll with the firm. This morning, I received a call from your doctor who told me you didn't have any seizures last night. I rushed down here. Oh, I'm so glad you've come back, Dominic!"

I had so many questions about what happened...so many holes to fill in. Gathering those details was my second step. First was correcting one of my past shortcomings. "Anita, how is your schoolwork progressing?" I learned she had graduated with a bachelor's degree in the spring and was working toward an MBA from Columbia Business School. Later, after she graduated, she joined our firm as an accountant and I'm proud to say that today, Anita is my senior advisor at Durant Hodgson Private Wealth Management.

In an attempt to curb my seizures, the doctors put me into a medically induced coma for two months. So much changed after I woke from the coma, although it didn't compare to the changes that occurred in the world while I slept. My tube was removed the day my seizures subsided. The doctors and nurses were astonished that I showed no signs of mental or cognitive impairment. I scored perfectly on the speech, memory, and logic evaluations. Shayna, my attending nurse, bubbled with pride, almost as if I were her own child and my first spoken words were lines from a Shakespearean sonnet. Physically, I did not fare so well. I was listless from the neck down. Doctors were cautiously optimistic and said they expected me to regain my strength, slowly but steadily. I was less assured. I told them, "It worsens with each episode. This was long overdue and for that delay, I shall suffer." No one paid attention to what I said.

While the nurses quietly continued to examine me, I was left alone with my thoughts. I was trying to understand what had occurred before the coma and what I had experienced in my dreams. It is an amazing disunion of concepts: I had this tremendous amount of information, organized and categorized in my brain to afford me instant access, yet I was unaware I had that knowledge until it was something I tried to recall. And when I did that—when I interrogated my own subconscious—the answers chilled my bones.

What happened? Two planes hit the Twin Towers. The buildings burned, crumbled, and fell.

How many victims died in the World Trade Center? There were 2,843—140 in the planes, although 13 were already dead, and 2,716 in and around the buildings. Ten murderers were responsible for all the devastation.

What were their names? The answer was intolerable. I grimaced as every name flashed before me. No one reacted to my pained expressions, for my hospital room was empty. I saw Anita standing in the doorway, talking with the neurologist. "Let's not talk too much about the attack. Dominic doesn't know the full scale of what happened and he's in a fragile state right now. Let's focus on healing, not adding more trauma."

I was no longer in the "fragile state" they assumed. I had already been there and back after trying to retrieve a moment in time that did not exist. Sharon did not exist in any physical sense on the evening of September 11th. When I searched, I found only a void, the intensity of which was more significant than any I ever experienced. I repeatedly fought against the sin of omission. I kept searching for a better truth, but it only made me fall further into that uninhabited zone until I became so despondent, I finally searched for the moment Sharon died.

Sharon had an incredible view of the City from her office. She never closed her curtains; I used to wonder if she thought the majestic skyline might disappear if she did. Bandall and Bandall occupied a small space—three modest offices, an administrative area, and one conference room—on the 94th floor of the North Tower. We had neither the personnel nor the bankroll for a corner suite. Sharon placed her desk facing into the office because she knew the extraordinary view would be too distracting. It did not, however, stop her from getting up often and gazing out...which is exactly what she was doing when I first found her in my dream.

What I wouldn't give to know the song running through her mind as she stood by the window, gently swaying, one arm pulled across her body, taking the lead to a sensual rhythm. Her once-blonde hair, a glimmering array of shades of gray, was pulled back into a sleek knot. She had gone into work dressed for court in perfect lawyer attire: muted gray skirt and matching jacket, gray patent-leather wedge pumps, and white blouse. When she got into the office, she hung her suit jacket on the door, took off her shoes, and opened the top three buttons of her blouse.

Sharon popped out of her trance and returned to the large pile of legal documents on her desk. I could tell my love was distracted because after only twelve minutes, she stopped working and opened the mail server. The last e-mail she wrote was intended for me.

Babe,

I'm so excited to spend some quiet time with you tonight. I don't think we'll get too many breaks this weekend! Don't worry, I'll make sure you have just as much fun as I will.

I just want you to know th

I have spent so many of my waking hours thinking of what Sharon wanted me to know. The possibilities are endless. So too is my sinful imagination! There is nothing she could have said that would bother me—nothing that I would not adore—if only she would have uttered the words. Alas, I will never know the truth while I am still in this world.

Like everyone else, Sharon was unaware of what was tearing through her majestic view at that moment. Instead, my love was grinning as she was typing the message to me. Suddenly interrupted by the frenzy outside her office—the muffled sounds and screams—she looked up. When Sharon saw Melissa, Michael Girard's mother, at her door, her grin faded fast and I saw her mouth the word "What?"

I have visited this moment more times than I want to admit. Each time, I longed to find a sign of hope that she was okay. I never found it. There was never a light...no sign her soul was trying to hold on to this physical world. In an instant, ours was no longer a world for my wife. Finally, many years ago, I made peace with this. Sharon's death is no longer a moment I care to visit...in any way, for any purpose. But for the sake of our conversation, and to ensure we stay within our allotted time, I allowed myself the latitude to do so now, although I had to do it briefly because we only have limited time.

<Angela: "Thank you.">

When our interviews are completed, I will be able to think about better moments than this.

As far as I can tell, I ended up in the hospital because I violated my rules when I searched for Sharon shortly after the attack. I forged ahead and searched for her, only to step headlong into a desolate void...headlong into a moment that never was and never will be. I have no idea how long I cycled through the torment and anticipation of finding her. I do not understand why I accepted as a fact that Sharon was dead and why I decided to search for other moments in the way I did. I did not let emotion play a part in my search; my wife was the only factual stake I needed.

When I woke up after the coma, the events surrounding her death were clear.

While in my coma, Sharon's lessons became muscle memory. I used my disciplined approach to form the moment I wanted to find in my dream. Define my search. Determine the factual stakes that will form the right moment. Identify traps, holes, uncertainties. And, of course, Rule Number 401: There is no emotion.

Every moment I experienced from 9/11 was crisp and vivid. When I searched for the first death at the World Trade Center, it was my beloved Sharon who claimed that dubious honor. Then I searched for the last person to die at the World Trade Center. I didn't learn the poor man's name, but I saw him fade away, without even a whimper. He was scared and alone, struggling to breathe, underneath massive blocks of rubble. His light, the essence of his existence, continued to burn until, released by rays of the sun, it was no longer needed.

I then searched for the second person to die, then the third, then the fourth, until finally I once again found the last man to die, my unnamed friend. Like at Hiroshima, death was instantaneous for many. I had the honor of reliving excruciating details of each loss of life, including the thirteen passengers who were already deceased when the planes hit. Only when every death was accounted for did I return to my human existence.

My caretakers at the hospital carefully tended to my every need. I felt so much gratitude as they fed me, cared for and worked my muscles, joints, and skin, then bathed and dressed me. Anita visited often and would sit beside my bed. When I was being cared for, she turned her attention to school work. "I have nowhere else to go. Besides, Dominic, you're still paying me, so I figured I should do something to earn my salary."

"You need a raise," I announced with an assured nod of my head. "I'll reach out to Alexander today."

Even though she lowered her head and tried to hide her face, I could see that something made her cheeks flush. "What is it, Anita?" I asked. "What do you want to say?"

I rarely asked that question because I was often unsure of the answer and fearful of the possibilities. Had the poor child been told I would never walk again? Had she overheard the word "quadriplegic" concerning my prognosis? Did she suspect I had something like cancer, heart disease, or worse? Did she fear I was about to join my dead coworkers?

Anita was clearly desperate to talk, but she couldn't get the words out. Perhaps she wasn't sure if she had the courage. It was painful to watch. I so much wanted to unburden her from being the one to tell me about the catastrophic loss of our Bandall and Bandall family, yet I couldn't tell her that I already knew; I was unable to breach my own pact. Rule Number 2: Never tell anyone.

Vibrant expression of coherent speech is a skill I am often accused of having perfected, but on that occasion, I was at a loss...a condition I hoped was as temporary as I prayed my paralysis would be.

Finally, I thought *fuck it* and blurted out, "Anita, I know. Jessica, Radcliffe, Jacinta, Cade, Jack, Melissa, Rebecca, Amy...yes, I know they are all dead." As I rattled off the roster, Anita's expression shifted from frightened and anxious to surprised and confused. Then I softly uttered "Sharon" and her eyes welled up. She burst into tears when I said, "Milt, Barbara, Adam, Maria, Dennis...."

"How do you know?"

Rule Number 2: Never tell anyone.

"Hospital room chatter." I blamed it on visitors and friends who had inadvertently discussed the attacks in my room, perhaps not knowing I could hear them.

The morning of 9/11, Adam and Maria—they were Milt and Barbara's son and daughter-in-law—brought their baby, Dennis, to the firm for his first visit. I was not there when they arrived, and because I hadn't told anyone I was going to the jewelers, no one knew where I was. After showing off Dennis, Barbara announced: "I'll hang around for ten more minutes. I'd sure hate for Dominic to miss meeting this little guy, but we need to leave soon, Milton. What if I—"

* * *

I do not like to think about the months I was in the hospital. I left the building only twice in the six weeks after I came out of my coma. The first was when I went to a memorial mass at our church in the Bronx. Father Bobby held a service for the families in our firm as well as six Bronx neighbors that died on 9/11. The second time was to attend a memorial service for Amy at a Baptist church in Queens.

I had no intention of ever returning to our apartment again, and had asked my lawyer, Alexander, and our financial advisor, Quentin, to handle everything for me. On March 5th, 2002, I asked Anita, "What do you think I should do now?" She took my hand in hers. With wisdom beyond her years, and love more fabulous than I could comprehend, Anita set me free.

"You need to follow your heart, your body, and the rules you've set for yourself. What will feed all three? It seems to me you've already identified the answer. Never doubt yourself. Never underestimate what you have already done."

Anita held me as I wept. My tears were not for Sharon, or for my family, or for the pain I felt and the hardships I knew were yet to come. The tears I shed were for everything I knew I had to lose. On Thursday, March 7th, 2002, I finally departed the hospital. Celebrating my release with me were my lawyer, my accountant, and my driver. They were the people closest to me. They cared for me and shared my sorrow for one more night in the city I loved, far from the city I knew.

The next day, for the second time in my life, I fled New York City. Before leaving, I asked Anita to take me for a ride. Although I had regained some movement in my hands and arms, I was frail—my legs were still immobile. After I was helped into the back seat and we were finally alone, Anita turned around and said, "All right, Dominic, what's the secret? Where are we going?"

"Just drive," I told her. "I will tell you where to go."

We meandered through the city streets that meant so much to me. We drove past Sharon's and my home in Hell's Kitchen, our residences when we were at John Jay, up to Hunter College, over to Yorkville, up into the Bronx, Sharon's old home in Morris Park, through Parkchester, then finally to Pelham Bay. So many memories, so many moments of love and suffering, joy and devastation. Father Bobby was waiting outside the rectory when we pulled up. He hopped into the back seat with me and we meandered the streets of Pelham Bay, just as we had so many times before.

"Do you remember that day, Dominic? Right over there?"

We were on my old block. "I sure do. Man, the fun we had on this street."

"No," he corrected, "I mean there, the sewer cap. I was standing right there, on second base, when I first caught sight of you. Lizzy was giving you the lay of the land. When I looked at her, I knew she liked the dopey boy who had just moved in. I was just a kid, but I could tell she had fallen for you that quickly. Did Sharon have the same look when she saw that dopey boy in the library? God, I wish I could go back and relive that day with Lizzy. Her expression was truly a wonderful and inspiring display of her childhood crush…and probably love."

We both sat quietly with our own thoughts: Bobby wishing he could go back in time and me realizing I had been too lost in my infatuation with little Elizabeth Strauss to notice what he saw, even though I had revisited that day so many times in my dreams. I closed my eyes, and with Bobby's voice describing the moment, replayed the interaction that had occurred forty-four years earlier.

I had to agree with Bobby. "My god! She was incredible."

"There is still more love for you here if you stay. Please understand, my friend, if you decide to leave us, our love will follow you. 'Let love be without dissimulation. Abhor that which is evil; cleave to that which is good.' Your goodness makes us want to reveal our love. For that, I thank you, my brother."

I assured Bobby that I treasured him, I loved him, and I loved the extended family I was leaving behind. There was nothing left in New York for me but painful reminders of empty voids. I asked Bobby for forgiveness "for what I have done and for what I have left undone." He smiled, because to him I suppose it sounded absurd. Then he laid his hands on my head and absolved me of my sins.

That was Friday, March 8th, 2002, the day I left New York forever.

Chapter 26 - Voice: Dominic

Today is Thursday, March 7th, 2019. My name is Dominic Bandall. This is session number nineteen in my interview with Ms. Angela Grant.

As Haile Selassie said in 1963, "Throughout history, it has been the inaction of those who could have acted; the indifference of those who should have known better; the silence of the voice of justice when it mattered most; that has made it possible for evil to triumph."

On March 8th, 2002, I left behind the shattered remnants of a world I loved but no longer favored. The memories of people I cherished—Mother and Dad, Sharon and Allison May, Milt and Barbara, Lizzy, Giuseppe, and so many others—were forever here, in my heart, and here, in my mind. The homes, buildings, parks, and streets were physical reminders of their absence. They stood strong despite my loss. They lay in rubble as my condition improved. When I boarded the plane, I left my agony on the tarmac.

* * *

On November 15th, 2001, the day after I woke from my slumber, two men—one from the CIA and one from the FBI—entered my hospital room and asked me if I would consider working with them as an intelligence analyst on the 9/11 terrorist attacks.

The FBI director spoke with me by phone. "Mr. Bandall, we are impressed with the cases you have handled. We are especially curious about your ability to obtain evidence no one else seems able to find. In fact, we often wonder how and where you find it. There's been a consideration to investigate the matter for some time, but honestly, at this point we don't care. All we know is that we need your assistance. What do you say? For your wife?"

That these two ghosts had the nerve to intrude on me, especially when I had just come out of a coma and had suffered such a debilitating loss...it took every ounce of strength to keep myself from cursing and telling them to "get the hell out of my room and leave me alone for good." But I quickly realized they had a point: finding the truth behind the attacks, finding those ultimately responsible, holding them to account, and ensuring the security of our nation and its allies...well, for that, I decided to overlook their misstep.

"Gentlemen, first, never again use my wife or anyone else I love as a bargaining chip. I will help you, but if you ever do something like that again, I guarantee you will regret it." Then I told them what my requirements were: unfettered access to any and all information the FBI and CIA had on the terrorists and their attacks or anything else they had that might help me. If they needed to obtain top-level security clearance for me to review classified information, then that's what they would have to do. I was prepared for them to refuse, but they were in such dire need of my help, there was no hesitation.

So began my sixteen-year stint working with the CIA's National Resources Division. I was listed as one of their lawyers and an investigator. Later, I was instrumental in the trial and conviction of Zacarias Moussaoui and Khalid Sheikh Mohammed, and my research led to the capture and killing of Osama bin Laden. But those cases came later. In terms of finding justice for the events of 9/11, it is not what I did, but what I failed to do.

I began a slow and careful investigation into the events that led up to the attacks, but I was in no condition to search for new information just then. I had to temporarily put off researching essential questions such as, "Are there any more attacks planned?" and "Who was the mastermind behind 9/11?" It was just too dangerous for me. To do it safely—in a way that wouldn't land me right back in the hospital, or worse—I had to wait until my faculties were fully restored. I knew I had to stay focused on my rules, so I made these my priority:

> 1: Never go back to a time that didn't exist
>
> 7: This killed Lizzy
>
> 8: Learn
>
> 247: Never search for a moment just to prove it exists
>
> 401: There is no emotion

Were I to attempt another foolhardy shortcut, the consequences were sure to be extreme, if not fatal. While I still lay in the hospital bed, I made a solemn vow to my wife.

"I will not allow the unintended byproduct of my ability to destroy me. When we meet again, my love, it will be of my own free will."

When I first regained consciousness, I did not know enough of my surroundings to safely attempt searching for novel information. I committed to making no attempt until my condition was improved. For two days, I drifted into sleep throughout the day, satiated by soothing moments of Sharon and of Lizzy. Visions of their boundless energy and play were essential tools in my basket of tricks, guaranteed to soften my heart and comfort any otherwise uncontrollable anguish.

Slowly, in the daylight hours, my plan took form. Before I opened up to Anita, one reminder loomed above everything:

Rule Number 2: Never tell anyone

I had no other choice. On November 18th, I asked Anita to retrieve two items from the apartment: Sharon's physical therapy protocol for me and my green composition book.

Later that day, she walked into my room with a box of files, on top of which was my composition book. She greeted me with her always-pleasant smile. "Don't you want to know the story behind this?" I asked as I thumbed through the well-worn pages.

"I don't know what it is, but it's entirely up to you, Dominic."

For her loyalty, and of course, for saving my life, I am so indebted to Anita. I smiled at the innocent beauty of her face. "Come," I said while patting the spot next to me on the side of the bed. "Sit here with me for a minute." I opened to the last page of my composition book, handed it to her, and asked her to write down my three final entries:

402: Define my search

403: Determine the factual stakes from which moments will form

404: Identify traps, holes, uncertainties

"Anita, this book contains a list of 404 rules I use to guide me through a world that most people could not begin to understand." I spent the rest of the day telling her stories of my past, my ability, and the incessant search for justice that continued to elude me. I answered her questions with the unfiltered truth, as I understood it. She wanted to hear more stories about Sharon, and about Lizzy. I painted pictures of them, describing their poised confidence. I told her, "These women are good role models for you. You could learn a lot from them about how to effectively confront challenges in life." Anita listened intently, laying her head on my shoulder, amazed by my words and comforted by my reassuring confidence in her.

I sometimes wonder how I would have told Allison May about myself and my ability; I wonder how she would have reacted to my stories. She and Anita would have been close in age. Perhaps there was a bit of transference on my part. Maybe one of the reasons I grew so fond of Anita—beyond all her amazing qualities—is because I saw her as a daughter. But not until that day, as she sat next to me, did I finally find my little love.

* * *

Under the guise of the current client portfolio of Bandall and Bandall, I met with the NRD regularly during the three months I spent in the hospital. No records were kept, no recordings of our meetings were made.

Because I didn't have any feeling in my arms and legs, and I couldn't use them, Anita did everything for me. She cared for me, she fed me, and she helped me with the intelligence reports I was given. She helped me review and catalog thousands of documents and audio and video tapes so that later, in my dreams, I could search through their hidden moments.

After quickly absorbing the information the agencies gave me, I realized they didn't have much; few connections had been made and fewer conclusions had been drawn. Also, because I didn't know Arabic, Farsi, Pashto, Darī, or Urdu, nor did I understand the culture, I was at a disadvantage. So at first, I had to rely on the NRD translations, but I knew that to truly understand any of the intelligence we had, and to make sense of the moments I found at night, I would have to learn these languages. Every moment—on each of the four planes, the conversations in the hotel rooms before the attacks, at the training camps near Kandahar—was clouded until I could break the language barrier.

Such was the world I thrust myself into on March 9th, 2002. From the time I arrived on the Big Island until today, I struggled to become the man you see before you. The only way I can describe the events to you is to tell you about the few places where life still existed for me: my health, my home, and my search for justice.

Chapter 27 - Voice: Dominic

Today is Thursday, March 7th, 2019. My name is Dominic J. Bandall. This is session number twenty in my interview with Ms. Angela Grant.

I arrived in Hawai'i a paraplegic. It has taken me the better part of sixteen years to turn myself into the weakened specimen of physical prowess sitting before you today.

<Dominic chuckles.>

The fact is, I'm an old man who has pushed his body past the limit. My doctors are astonished at my fortitude. Except for the damage caused by the cerebral hypoxia, my health has been excellent. That's what they say every time I see them. "I'm a New Yorker," I tell them. "What the hell am I supposed to do? Quit?"

I've undergone many tests and had various procedures to treat my condition, but I always resist their efforts to identify the cause of my illness. I know they think I'm just an angry old man who has no good reason for refusing care. What they don't understand is that I have a very good reason: I already know the cause of my episodes. In every case, it was ignorance, or stupidity, or a broken heart. I know there is no way doctors can prevent another episode; that is my responsibility alone. If I get sick again, it will be because I allow it to happen.

The only treatments I've rejected are those that involve some kind of manipulation of my mind; for example, electroconvulsive therapy, deep brain stimulation, transcranial magnetic stimulation, psychosurgery, and psilocybin. These "treatments" sound more like something from a damn horror movie than real medical procedures. Although my frustration got the better of me on more than one occasion, I tried to understand their thinking. Apparently, they decided that some kind of underlying psychological issue had caused my last episode, or perhaps the last episode was aggravated by a psychological problem. I assured them I had committed no crime, so there was no need to declare me *doli incapax*, or to treat me as such.

My eyesight, speech, touch, taste, and smell have all diminished to varying degrees, but my mind—my ability to think clearly—is the one thing that has not been affected. Shortly after I came out of the coma, I worked hard to prove that I was of sound mind and therefore competent to make decisions about my own healthcare. I invited anyone who asserted the opposite to prove it by providing explicit evidence and not merely conjecture.

No one took me up on the challenge.

I focused on a strict regimen of physical therapy. I was able to eat by myself in less than three weeks. In six months, I took the first timid steps on my own. In another two months, I was able to go to the bathroom without assistance.

I haven't made any progress in over a year and will not get any better than I am now. They say I have plateaued. As I age, the laws of nature will overtake my stubbornness. I'm okay with this. I am relatively mobile; I have adequate use of my arms and legs; I can enjoy the sights, sounds, and smells of the Island. To make up for my physical shortcomings, I have the best technology in the world: adaptive tools for writing, for I can no longer use a pen or keyboard; mobility options allow me the freedom to explore the beauty of Hawai'i on my own; an oxygen concentrator keeps me safely nourished day and night. I have never been concerned about my lost ability to function as a man, nor have I ever felt a need to try to address it.

For everything else, for rehabilitation and sustainment of the body, mind, and heart, I have the most amazing family here...in this, my beloved home.

Chapter 28 - Voice: Dominic

My name is Dominic Bandall. This is session number twenty-one in my interview with Ms. Angela Grant.

Every time Sharon and I came' to Hawai'i, we swore we would never leave. But there was always something that took us back to New York City. All those reasons died on 9/11. When I came back, of course, Janice Kamaka again welcomed me into her house for the six weeks it took to renovate our—my— Ka'ū residence. As you can see, our dream of building a quaint little residence never quite happened.

When I finally moved into this house, we increased the level and scope of my physical therapy. Surgery was not, and still is not, an option for me, so physical therapy is what I have...and I am committed to it. I continue to base my regimen on the programs Sharon created. I have access to the best doctors, trainers, and equipment available to supplement the work she started.

Bringing all those people and corporations to justice has made me a wealthy man. Insurance settlements, the sale of my real estate holdings, and sound financial advice further increased my wealth. While I am by no means parsimonious, I am very careful about where and how I spend my money. Caring for myself, both physically and emotionally, has turned out to be very expensive. But I listened to what Father Bobby recommended regarding the money we made. I worked hard for justice—to bring positive change to things that matter to us—and that gave me the resources to make a difference in the world. I hope that one day, those I have helped might do the same for others. Alexander and Quentin have been controlling my assets for some time. They have exceeded all my expectations regarding my personal and business matters. They have never let me down and I never give their decisions a second thought. Some may consider that too trusting, foolhardy, or ignorant, but I made the right decision to trust them.

In addition to continuing my goal of realizing justice for Sharon and the others who died because of hate and anger, I focus on my new family. I lost my first family on that terrible day, but from their ashes, this new one grew. It grew from the families of my work colleagues at Bandall and Bandall: Jessica Tidwell, Radcliffe Takemoto, Jacinta and Cade Wei, Jack Vandermark, Melissa Larson, Rebecca Sparozic, and Amy Pelayo. These amazing people, each of whom died because they worked at our law firm, left behind loved ones who lost so much. I share what I have with them, without hesitation.

You met Melissa Girard's son, Michael, in New York. He is an impressive young man who has worked hard for everything he's earned. He refused my assistance in getting him a scholarship for college because he considered it a "handout." Instead, he paid for his last two years of college with money from his mother's life insurance. He is one of my most valued confidants and my link to New York, a place he refuses to leave. He does various jobs for me there, including managing a few of my remaining properties.

You have also met Sage, Kalena, Hy'ing, Robert, and Wen. Most of them were born in New York, but after the tragedy, they moved here to Hawai'i, the home of their parents.

Robert was only an infant when Rebecca, his mother, died. Robert's father asked me if his son could come here to work for me after graduating from high school. Of course, I welcomed him with open arms.

Sage, who lost his father, Radcliffe, moved to the Island to work for me and care for his mother who has been suffering crippling anxiety and depression ever since her husband died seventeen-and-a-half years ago.

After 9/11, Wen went to live with her grandparents, then served five years in the US Army. Now she wants to work here for a couple of years to save up money and travel the world.

Sisters Kalena and Hy'ing lost everything when both of their parents, Jacinta and Cade, were killed. The little girls, then only six and ten years old, were found alone in their apartment four days after the Towers fell. The City was going to put both girls into foster care, but Alexander intervened, and after gaining temporary custody of both girls, he arranged for their uncle to adopt them. Later, both sisters moved here to work for me.

Amy's parents wanted nothing to do with me after she died, although, thankfully, they did let me attend her memorial service. I have, of course, respected their wishes and pray someday they will forgive me for taking away their only daughter.

After accompanying me to Hawai'i after I got out of the hospital, and staying with me for a week, Anita went back to New York to continue with school. She is married now. Her husband, Charles, and their beautiful daughter, Allison May, spent a week with us over this past Christmas break. I cried at the sight of that beautiful seven-year-old angel! All she wanted to do was run through the tall grass in the open fields so she could drop to her knees and hide. I am amazed by what Anita has accomplished in her life and remain forever in her debt.

Janice died peacefully in her sleep on June 15th, 2007. She willed her property to the residents of Pāpaʻaloa. I intend to follow her lead by bequeathing them my ranch. Of course, I also intend to uphold the agreement Sharon and I made to fund reclamation efforts for the land in Kaʻū. Everything else will go to my family.

Before I continue, we must rest. Try to build up your physical and emotional strength, Angela. I expect you to be in prime condition tomorrow. Good night, my dear.

<Angela: *"Good night, Dominic."*>

Chapter 29 - Voice: Angela

"Thank you very much, Dominic," I said. I hadn't even thought about turning on my recorder until Dominic gestured for me to do so.

"Not at all, Angela. I'm sure by now you are confused and have lots of questions."

"I'm trying not to question you or think ahead. I guess you could say I learned that lesson the hard way on our first day. I don't think I could have handled all of this except by locking my brain into receive-only mode."

"That is very smart of you. I consider myself an excellent judge of character. Had you not shown yourself to be the strong soul you are, I doubt our conversation would have reached this point."

"What point is that, Dominic? You told me if I kept my part of the bargain, you would turn the recordings over to me when we were done. But what am I supposed to do with them?"

"Whatever you deem appropriate."

"What does that mean?"

"What it means is my history will be yours to share, hold on to, or dismiss. You determine if my stories live up to my claims or if they are merely inconsequential ramblings of a condemned man."

"But why me? Why am I responsible for deciding what to do with your legacy? While your story is an incredible one, it will hardly affect me one way or the other. Have we spent eight days together simply to establish a bond? Have you done something since you arrived in Hawaii that you feel the need to confess to? If so, why tell me?"

"Your frustration is justifiable. I commend you for allowing me to venture so deeply into my tale, and for listening instead of reacting. All I ask is for you to give me one more day—one more day—before you decide to believe or dismiss my story. I will not ask you again to wait before I tell you the full story. I will not delay it any longer. I will give each question you ask a total and unfiltered response.

You cannot understand what I have done until you hear the complete tale. This is not fair, I know, but positing a solution before I have presented the full equation is also unfair. This is the only way I know how to do it.

"Tomorrow I will tell you about my discovery of justice. I told you about my health—my disability, treatments, setbacks, years of pain and suffering—and about my new family and my home, so they wouldn't be a distraction to my findings."

There was no point in arguing with him. I knew nothing I could say would change his mind and could only have aggravated me further. I turned off my recorder and collected my things to leave his office. Neither of us said a word. Honestly, I wasn't sure what would have come out of my mouth if I had—a curse, a scream, or a cry. I don't know what was going on in Dominic's head as I left. Did he regret inviting me? The thought of him running across the office to apologize and plead for my forgiveness made me smile. For so many reasons, that would never happen....

Hy'ing was in the kitchen when I walked in. "Dominic said this is your last night in Honuʻapo. I thought you'd enjoy some local delicacies."

"Pupu!" I laughed. It was one of my favorite Hawaiian meals. I felt lighthearted for the first time all day.

Hy'ing laughed too and invited me to sit while she served me the cubed ahi, pulled kalua pork, glazed shrimp, green onions, pickled ginger, wasabi, cilantro, carrots, almonds, pea shoots, and edamame. I don't need a photographic memory to remember every angelic detail of that meal. As Hy'ing was sprinkling balsamic vinaigrette on my fish, I caught her looking at me. It occurred to me that it might be a good time to interview her. I took out my recorder and pressed record.

"Tell me about your parents, Jacinta and Cade."

I could see she wasn't sure how to respond. She knew Dominic must have told me their names, yet also knew that what we said in our meetings was off-limits to the staff.

"I don't really remember much about my parents. I was only six when they died. Kalena would know more."

I wondered if she was trying to see if Dominic had told me Kalena was her sister.

> "Most of what I remember about Mom and Dad comes from photos and stories Dominic used to tell us when we were young. We could tell he liked Kalena and me. His eyes would light up when he saw us. To be honest, I think he still feels that way. He just seems happy when we are around.
>
> "When I was a child, Dominic called me Mālai, which he said means 'to live with haste.' That's what my ancestors would have called me instead of Hy'ing. He told us the most incredible stories...so much imagination and creativity! He took us away to wonderful worlds when ours felt unbearable. Kalena never liked his stories much. She would say, 'That's not true!' and 'Prove it!' I think she liked teasing him almost as much as he enjoyed her teasing.

"I was born in New York, Kalena was born in Hawai'i, before our parents moved. After they died—after we became orphans—we were raised by family members. We moved here with our uncle, my father's brother. He was born in China. I guess that makes me some sort of Chinese/Hawaiian/New Yorker. I'm not sure what the hell I am, but my mother's side of the family doesn't care for the mix. Mom and Dad had moved to New York to work for the Bandalls. My grandmother always felt Dominic was responsible for my mom's death. Whatever. I think Dominic blames himself a bit as well. Maybe that's why he takes such good care of us."

"No, that's not it, Hy'ing. I am certain his affection for and care of you has nothing to do with pity or penance. Don't worry, I am not going to go into what Dominic and I discussed, but I can tell you this: he considers you family. Every time he mentions you and the rest of his 'children,' he gets that look of happiness you mentioned. And, by the way, your attitude shows you are clearly a New Yorker!"

"Hell, who knows? Maybe I'll find out tomorrow that I'm Dominic's illegitimate child!"

Hy'ing's loyalty to Dominic was obvious.

"Don't worry. I'll be a good boss when this is all mine."

We both giggled.

Then I turned off the recorder so we could enjoy our last evening together.

Oddly, that night I had the most peaceful sleep I'd had since my arrival. I stopped thinking about what was coming next and put aside all expectations. Instead, I savored the time I had spent there. I vowed, whatever the outcome, to cherish meeting the great Dominic J. Bandall.

The next morning began rather abruptly as soon as I entered Dominic's office.

Chapter 30 - Voice: Dominic

My name is Dominic Bandall, and this is the twenty-second and final session in my interview with Angela Grant. Today is March 8th, 2019. It is the seventeenth anniversary of the day I arrived in Hawai'i.

Good morning, Angela! You're late. I almost started without you.

<Angela: "I'm sorry, Dominic.">

Don't give it a second thought. Anyway, I love the serenity of the early morning. But we must stay on schedule today.

Today is March 8th, seventeen years to the day that I arrived on the Island to begin a new chapter of my life. When I think about it, I'm amazed how much time has elapsed since 9/11. It's only a few years less than my life before Sharon, yet it seems like an eternity. I have all those moments, all my memories with her, yet I would gladly give all of that away if I could just hold her in my arms one more time. I long for the days I would curl myself against her body when we were in bed. I have access to millions of moments throughout all of history, yet the most precious are those when I would think to myself: *This is happening right now. Whatever will happen in the next moment has not yet occurred. The energy for that moment has not yet received direction on how to assemble. When it does, how it does, is within my control.* At those points, we were energy—raw energy stimulating new moments. I miss those days of eager anticipation, wondering who would move first and create a splendid disruption. Now, every day when I wake, I feel neither anticipation nor excitement about what is in store for me...no readiness for surprises at the turn of a corner. I know everything that is going to happen throughout my day—there is nothing more I want to discover. I miss that slow, tantalizing unfurling of new moments. That was something Sharon taught me to love.

Those happy feelings have been gone for more than seventeen years now. What I am left with is the painful burn of complete immersion in loss. When I woke up from the coma on November 14th, 2001, I already knew firsthand about the horror experienced by every one of those 2,856 innocent souls who had died above, below, and on the streets of New York City. Later, I experienced the horror that their brothers and sisters in DC and Pennsylvania experienced. At that time, I knew everything about the attacks except why they were committed and who issued the decree to carry them out.

Even before I learned the foreign languages and could understand what those men were saying, I had observed much. I saw the man known as Mohamed Atta. He was not dispassionate; he was determined. Angry. He seemed to despise every person on Flight 11, including his four accomplices. To him, they were boys who didn't know what they were doing or why they were doing it. There were few words shared between the conspirators; they were engaged in a well-scripted act, and they knew exactly what was going to happen every single moment, from the beginning to the end. They followed their leader, Atta, without hesitation and without question. At first, I wondered if Atta orchestrated all the attacks, but then I saw that each plane—Flight 175, Flight 77, then Flight 93—had its own leader and that each leader had total control of his subordinates.

With the basic information I had received from the NRD, I visited the moment when Atta sat at Osama bin Laden's feet with an impish look on his face. I saw that everyone cowered when they were in the presence of their master, bin Laden. They crowed and boasted about their accomplishments to try to gain his favor. I didn't need to understand the language they were speaking to understand what was going on.

I knew it would take more than my ability to succeed in my research on 9/11. Unlike my studies into the strange languages and culture of the ancient settlers of Hi'ūakūū, where most of the information was lost to the modern world, now I had a wealth of resources. I had books, audiocassettes, and recorded lectures to help me learn. There were teachers and subject-matter experts on the religions, the cultures, and the history of hostilities in the Middle East. Most importantly, I could depose witnesses, participate in interrogations, and conduct interviews. Physically interacting with the people whose moments I explored in my dreams gave me an extraordinary advantage.

For a moment, I was seven years old again; I saw Giuseppe standing in front of me, his hand gently resting on my shoulder as he guided me. "Go and learn. In time, we will fight for justice together. For now, you have to find the truth yourself." I saw Dad guiding me in 1967, when I was preparing to graduate high school, and this was the same guidance and direction I needed as a fifty-two-year-old man. The moment I looked into my father's eyes, I knew what he was going to say: I was taught how to receive instruction in school. I was taught how to learn from Sharon. I had to discover what to learn, and when I figured that out, all I had to do was wade through the harvest of information I had reaped. That would lead me to bounties of discovery. My instructions were clear.

When I first got here to the Island, I was still recovering from my illness. There was little I could do for myself. I was as helpless as a small child. My caregivers fed me, bathed me, and attended to all my needs. My so-called friends at the NRD saw me as a shattered man who was trying to rehabilitate himself, but who was isolated, alone, and had retreated from the world. For the most part, this is the way they have viewed me for the last seventeen years. I prefer it that way.

Rule Number 2: Never tell anyone

It was essential for me to understand the foreign languages in my moments, both written and spoken. I decided to make Arabic my first discovery. I started by watching videos made for children and reading grade-school books that taught the classical Arabic language, Arabiyya. Then, I moved on to high school- and college-level lecture tapes. I discovered a recording of Dr. Zahra Al-Shakar, a professor in the Arabic and Islamic Studies Department at the University of Bahrain, giving a lecture to her class. I was impressed with her passion and the way she breathed vitality into a language that is considered everlasting and pure and unchanged since it was handed down by

Allah. It was refreshing that she didn't discuss jihad and that her passion had nothing to do with conflict.

In early 2003, just as the United States took its war on terror into Iraq, I invited Zahra to Hawai'i to teach me about Arabic culture and the Arab-Islamic civilization. I told her, "I have little interest in the political agenda of my country. Instead, I would like to better understand the culture that gave rise to the atrocities of my wife's death and the events that have occurred since then."

What I actually wanted was to learn more about the moments I had already experienced and those I would seek out later. To Zahra, I was a lonely old man with nothing but free time and money, destined to spend my remaining days wallowing in pity over something I did not understand. "Careful, Mr. Dominic," Zahra warned. "Depending on the culture, there is a big difference between what we consider justified actions on our part and what you interpret as atrocities against you, and vice versa." She agreed to come—within a month, all the arrangements were finalized. Zahra took up residence in the staff quarters adjacent to my house.

By the time she moved in, I was already proficient in Arabiyya. There's a beauty in the purity of the language. Most Muslim scholars believe it is the only language in which the Qur'an can be rightfully and accurately expressed. All other translations, they believe, misrepresent the word of Allah as it was given to the Prophet Mohammed.

Zahra shared a children's song her mother used to sing to her when she was a child.

<Dominic singing in Arabic>

> *Gargee'an and Gargee'an*
>
> *May God give you babies*
>
> *May God bless the homeowners*
>
> *We come, knocking the rock by our feet*
>
> *A dish of pearls, dish of pearls*
>
> *A dish of coral, dish of coral*
>
> *Transfigures the king's face*
>
> *You give to us or we give to you?*
>
> *We take you to Mecca*
>
> *This Mecca the universe*
>
> *Built from plaster and light*
>
> *Hey those who are on the roof*
>
> *Give us sweets or should we leave?*

When Zahra was a baby, her mother would cradle and rock her. She would continue to hum the tune long after the lyrics had expired. That made me remember Mother singing me to sleep when I was a child. I imagined Sharon doing the same for Allison May. I longed to experience that moment with Zahra and her mother. I thought if I could witness that just once, maybe it would somehow lessen the pain I felt over never having such a moment with my own family. My desire was never fulfilled.

Rule Number 3: Never hurt people by looking into their life

Under Zahra's tutelage, I became quite fluent in Arabiyya, Pashto, Fārsī-ye Darī, Kurdish, and Urdu. While Zahra was impressed with my ability to learn so quickly, she soon became frustrated with my evasiveness and constant requests for information about particular areas in Afghanistan and Iraq and the tribal dialects spoken there.

Our lessons would extend from dawn till dusk, but my education continued throughout the night; I would go to sleep and truly learn what she had taught me. I would sometimes pause our lessons for days, sometimes for weeks, while I worked on other matters, instructing my staff to tell her which regions and cultures I wanted to discuss the next time we met. Usually, she wouldn't know when we were going to start up again. I would contact her the day before I was ready. I never explained these interruptions to Zahra.

On December 30th, 2006, after Zahra, like the rest of the world, watched the execution of Saddam Hussein, she demanded to speak to me. When I met her in the atrium, she threw her notes and textbooks, strewing them across the floor and under my wheelchair.

"You played a role in this!" she yelled.

I sat in silence. It was an emotion I'd seen so many times: anger, loathing, and hate of those with different ideologies. There are Sunnis who hate Shi'as for bastardizing Islam, Shi'as who want to punish Sunnis for not practicing true Islam. Both unleash havoc on anyone—regardless of whether they are Kurds, Christians, or Yazidi—who stands in their way or disagrees with them. Many Westerners despise anyone who is Muslim. Whenever I have seen that hate, whether in an Afghan training camp, on board a hijacked airplane, or in a guard tower in Abu Ghraib, I recognized the mindset: there was no interest in understanding that which is different, only a desire to destroy the repugnant.

"Is this what you want to learn? Is this the justice you hope to achieve with the help of my instruction? Well, there is no need for you to interpret Saddam Hussein's message because it is so clear: 'Long live our great struggling people. Long live Iraq, long live Iraq. Long live Palestine. Long live jihad and the mujahideen.'"

I said nothing. Zahra continued her accusations, her facts. She was correct. As I listened to her repeat Hussein's words, I was transported back to the moment in my dream when I heard him speak them. We had not created a martyr—we merely gave our enemies justification for their actions. We became the infidels they were convinced we were, thereby handing them a reason to fight us. My silence was a clear indication of my complicity and Zahra had every right to voice her rage. She sympathized with her brothers and sisters who were fighting the evils of the West. Although she was not a violent person, her frustration over the injustices committed by the West during the previous three-and-a-half years made her side with the mujahideen. The guilt she felt was pronounced...guilt for living a soft life, appeasing the whims of a sad, angry old man in Hawai'i, while war raged on the other side of the world without her.

A few weeks after we discussed the Turkmen population who live in northern Iraq, Saddam Hussein was captured in Ad-Dawr. Shortly after Zahra and I began working on Urdu, the United States took action in Pakistan. This pattern continued—again and again—in Samarra, Fallujah, Mosul, Tal Afar, and North Waziristan.

In April of 2006, Zahra's cousin, Sami al-Juburi, was killed in Iraq, in a battle near Yusufiyah. She said he was an innocent victim, a farmer, mowed down mercilessly when American soldiers swept through his town. al-Juburi was not an innocent victim; he was killed while engaging in combat with British SAS forces. It was not my role to challenge her, so I let her believe what she wanted. Actually, I had little pity for Zahra or her friends and family in Iraq. We both had our reasons for entering our arrangement. I needed to better understand the language and culture of those I saw as criminals. She wanted to escape the danger of her turbulent homeland. Once we had both fulfilled our needs, it was time for us to part ways. There was nothing more she could teach me because my ability far exceeded her knowledge and personal experiences. Zahra knew she had to go back to Iraq, but struggled with the finality. However, on December 30th, with the killing of Saddam Hussein, her decision was made.

Zahra had said the mujahideen were starting a jihad and she was right. My goal was to bring those who were still alive and responsible for 9/11 to justice. Of course, the five men who killed Sharon and all those others in the World Trade Center were dead, but my search for justice went beyond their hands. Osama bin Laden had claimed sole responsibility for the attack, but I intended to find the others who also took part in the crime.

Our government's overarching concern, according to the NRD, was to determine if more attacks were being planned and what the next step in the jihad would be. Managing our often-conflicting agendas was at times a challenge. The agency wanted bin Laden. For some time, I successfully deflected efforts to pinpoint his location. I knew that if you cut off the head, thousands of tentacles would grow in its place, and so my plan was to understand the networks, and provide the NRD with enough intelligence to infiltrate, inject poison, and kill the entire body. I was convinced that the poison came in the form of justice.

International laws and treaties designed to inspire peace among warring nations, and religious law—be it the canon, sharia, or halakha—all have the common goal of protecting the righteous from the evil of transgressors. We obtain justice by finding those responsible for evil and trying them in a court of law.

Since Zahra's departure, I have had forty-three teachers, clerics, and tribesmen from a wide range of professions and trades visit me to teach me about their culture and heritage. Though I no longer let anyone stay with me for more than one month, I treasure the information they shared.

Even though I was making excellent progress understanding the complexities of the Middle Eastern languages and cultures, I still couldn't understand how our enemies applied their system of beliefs. The first moments I experienced in my dreams were strange and difficult to comprehend. It was alarming to see those young men respond with cheers when Atta appointed them to go on a mission that would lead them straight to their own death, and to see Atta beam with pride when bin Laden chose him to lead the suicide mission. I watched in horror as anger and hate were drilled into their impressionable minds.

Many of the terrorists were educated and lived comfortable lives. Mohamed Atta, like many others who trained in the Afghan military camps, like Khalden and al Farouq, went to college. We all know that bin Laden was born into a very wealthy Saudi family and was highly educated. Atta's father was a prominent lawyer in Egypt who specialized in both sharia and civil law.

Slowly, I expanded my search to include the people who planned the 9/11 attacks. Each morning, I documented the moments I experienced to see if I could find any patterns or triggering events that had led them to their ideology. I was always thinking about what could be done to somehow reverse all that hate and killing. What led them to twist the minds of so many young men? Could this be corrected? Cured?

My fascination with the Afghan and Iraqi cultures grew to a feverish pitch. The way they live is so different from what we are used to in the West. I'll try not to stray too far off topic, but I began having trouble navigating through my waking and dreaming worlds. While awake, I was imprisoned in a sterilized world designed to keep me safe. Even with the greatest technological advantages and conveniences at my fingertips, and an endless supply of the most delicious and nourishing foods, I felt stifled. My life had lost its savor. I found myself longing to sleep so I could discover the next grand palace, or sedentary rural village speckled with qal'ahs—lovely structures made of stone and mud-brick. The communal living in these villages lends itself to wonderful social interaction. The women congregate in the courtyard to share food and the chores of raising their families while the men gather on the flat roofs to pray and await guidance from their mujahideen leaders. These were the kinds of people who bin Laden recruited in the early 1980s to form a militant terrorist network, intent on expelling the Soviet Union from Afghanistan once and for all. Later, these same groups would turn their attention to what they saw as the menacing threat of the United States and its allies.

Janice inspired me to surround myself with things I need to feel alive, and to not ever settle for the world I have or am supposed to have. I chose to live in—immerse myself in—the worlds of the moments I traveled to. Until two weeks ago, I furnished my house to look like the Middle Eastern ones I've grown to love so dearly. From time to time, when my moments moved to different regions, I remodeled. My home reflected images I had pulled from history itself. My instructions to the remodelers and interior designers were sometimes painstakingly detailed. On other occasions, if the designers were familiar with the region, I would give them carte blanche to surprise me. I never touched this office; I want it to be the sole connection to my former life. This is where I do most of my work and where I documented my research and determined who I was going to invite next.

What a marvel it was to wake up and see my visions become a reality! This glory was no longer confined to my dreams. I was able to step on the dusty clay floors and feel the texture of the dried mud walls as I ran my hand along them. Nailed to the walls were beautifully painted tapestries with details so fine, I would continue to find new splendor on the second, or fifth, or thirty-fifth time I looked.

I delighted in my daily routine of sitting at my little table and eating the fantastic Middle Eastern food. Oh, the food! I have never tasted so many glorious dishes...my sincere apologies to the people of Hawai'i and New York City. I could talk about the food for days, but fear not! My culinary delights are well documented in my notes. You absolutely must try saji kabab! And the osh pyozee—stuffed onions—are the perfect complement to the goat and sheep kebabs. Heaven!

There is so much I adore about how the people in Iraq, Pakistan, and Afghanistan live. I love how powerful the bonds are within families and within the tribes, the loyalty they have to God and the law. I also love the way they furnish their homes, the intricate patterns, the azure and ochre colors, the simplicity of lines and forms, the carpets!

I wept as I watched these people's lives torn apart over and over again. One group destroyed in the name of God. The other destroyed in the name of peace, freedom, and justice. It was this perception of justice that compelled me to hold responsible the people whose actions led to 9/11. But, as I continued my research, I realized the tension between the United States, our allies, and the Middle East was not clear cut. Can I hold accountable our allies, even ourselves, for feeding the hate and providing justification for retaliation? We supported and armed bin Laden's al-Qaeda soldiers when they were considered "the enemy of my enemy."

Still, I persisted in my search. I wanted revenge for every individual directly responsible for Sharon's death. Every person who encouraged and supported Atta so he could fly a jet into the 94th floor of One World Trade Center needed to pay for the crime.

I have seen this war from many different angles. I have witnessed horror so grotesque you cannot even imagine. Incredibly brave young men and women are routinely thrust in harm's way to fight the enemy. They are confronted by vile predators and led by incompetent leaders. This is the horror of war for every person and every group that is involved: American soldiers, our allies' soldiers, ISIS, al-Qaeda, insurgent groups, and indigenous populations.

They are not seeking peace or a peaceful resolution. At one time, they merely wanted the United States and the Soviet Union to get out of their countries and leave them alone, but the goal changed to "destroy the infidel." And then, gradually, the United States stopped seeking "justice" and the war became a fight against evil. Our goal is not to let their good prosper, or to introduce our vision of a virtuous civilization; our purpose is to destroy.

When I could no longer bear the research, I began feeding information to the NRD that would help them locate and capture Osama bin Laden. With my help, they killed bin Laden. I watched the moment many times that month. I wanted to see justice delivered. I also wanted to experience the delicious satisfaction of my own vengeance.

I watched as those hard men executed their jobs. They moved through the mission systematically. Taking a life, killing the despised...these acts elicited no emotion from them. They simply got revenge for us. Then, I watched as sailors, marines, and soldiers buried bin Laden at sea. That time, I did see emotions...an avalanche of them. They wept for the thousands lost. They wept in joy for what this ended and in fear of what they started. Mostly, they wept in horror that anyone had to be killed and buried at all. No soul should ever have had to be there, but the job needed to be done. They wept for having become an instrument of justice...justice that was now buried beneath a mountain of mistakes and misdirection. Vengeance, true vengeance, does not weep. Revenge does not feel regret. Justice was blind that day. Those brave men and women performed their task without passion, the way they were trained, but when Justice removes her blindfold to witness the carnage caused by her actions, she weeps.

As for personal satisfaction, I never found it. After the day bin Laden was killed, May 2nd, 2011, I never again wanted vengeance or revenge. Instead, I wanted to understand how that kind of hatred and violence happened in the first place and what continues to nourish it today. I researched international law and sharia law to see if that would help me discover the true purpose of their jihad. What do they hope to achieve by destroying their beautiful land and harming so many people?

February 1st, 2017 would have been Allison May's thirty-ninth birthday. I rolled through the tall grass in my motorized wheelchair. It's a path I have traveled many times before. Every year on her birthday—on her first, fifth, and her sweet sixteenth—Sharon and I would walk around the grounds. We would talk about our beautiful baby girl and celebrate another remarkable year of the life Allison May should have lived. Sharon's fantastic stories were so exquisite, they rivaled the best realistic accounts I could ever tell.

Sharon and I used to tell each other stories about our past birthdays. In 2001, we laughed about our twenty-third birthdays. We were both in law school, feeding our hungry minds as we prepared ourselves for a world of endless possibilities. As we walked hand in hand, Sharon told me the story of a confident twenty-three-year-old girl named Allison May who was struggling with the overwhelming workload of her first year in medical school. She then rushed home to her mother and daddy to celebrate her birthday. We shed tears and said goodbye to Allison May...once again. Those moments of retrospection and sorrow were fuel for us; they gave us an opportunity to evaluate our lives and recommit to that which bonded us together: our love, our faith, and our commitment to justice.

In 1990, when Sharon turned thirty-nine, a coalition of forces led by the United States was beginning the troop buildup for the invasion of Kuwait in the first Gulf War. They never left.

While the United States exacted its version of justice for the crimes of 9/11, we were never able to fully understand why the attacks occurred. We destroyed numerous threats to the safety and sovereignty of our country and our way of life, and we undoubtedly saved many innocent people from persecution, but in doing so, we gave rise and validity to many organizations whose intent seems to be to destroy our existence and way of life. The United States' long-term strategy expands and recoils without a realistic understanding of its end goal. Original objectives are soon forgotten or are utterly unachievable.

One night, two years ago, on February 1st, 2017, I decided to reenergize my goal of documenting the true facts and causes of 9/11. I went back and reviewed my journals and the notes I had been keeping for fifteen years. I had been toiling most of the day trying to understand the actual cause and meaning of this fight for justice. Late in the evening, I concluded this was all the Gettysburg Address. We had hunted down and killed the man directly responsible for the events of 9/11, but we used our version of the facts as justification for our actions, or fodder to use as blame for the world's predicaments.

As my Dad explained to me, and I to Sharon, the Gettysburg Address is merely a metaphor. Our documented history is rarely accurate or factual. Instead, it is often the agreed-upon message we want or need to share. Sometimes that message rationalizes what we think is just; on other occasions we feel a need to remove ambiguity from events; on still more occasions we choose to arbitrarily increase conclusiveness by reinforcing our collective need for "faith." When our administration again changed political parties after the 2016 election, the agreed-upon message was rewritten once more. The original meaning has long been forgotten.

To many, my goal of documenting the facts and causes of 9/11 may no longer seem relevant. To others, it may seem traitorous or blasphemous to even think about assigning blame to anyone or anything other than that elusive group known as "the enemy." But to me, it is essential. For some, a profound sense of serenity comes with understanding the truth in all aspects. Much like the ancient inhabitants of Hiʻūakūū, the full reality will never be substantiated.

Some may find peace in this truth and knowledge...should you, Angela, choose to share it.

Chapter 31 - Voice: Angela

As soon as Dominic turned off the camera, I grabbed my recorder and turned it on. I sat there in silence.

> "Are you still with me, Angela?"

> "What do you mean by 'should I choose to share it'?"

> "My story is now yours. We agreed that if you participated in this interview, according to my conditions, I would give you the recordings. You have satisfied your portion of the arrangement, and so shall I."

I was dumbfounded. I'd spent the entire week listening to this fantastic story and it all led up to an ending which laid claim to nothing! All he gave me was "most people won't believe it, so it's up to you if you want to share it." That was it?

> "So, what do I do now?"

I assumed he had thought that part out as well.

"You go back to school and get ready for graduation. You will make an excellent attorney. I have the utmost confidence in you. I've spoken directly with the dean of students at New York Law School and assured her I have thoroughly vetted your academic abilities and qualifications for becoming a lawyer. I probably came off as an eccentric and crazy old man who has been keeping you captive for the week while I told you back-in-the-day stories. Her sympathy for you and my generous donation will preclude the need for you to write a paper rationalizing the time we spent together.

"I've arranged to have all the videos, all of my writings, and some of my personal belongings placed into a long-term storage facility to which you alone will have access. Everything in there will be your property. Alexander will contact you with the details.

> "Go home and live the incredible life meant for you. Though I have had an absolutely magical time finally making your acquaintance, I'm sure this will be the last time we see each other.
>
> "As for me, after you depart this afternoon, I have a date with a beautiful woman. From her last trip to the mainland, Hy'ing brought me a wonderful pinot noir from her favorite winery in the Yamhill-Carlton AVA. Oh, Sharon also loved the smell and flavor of the wines from that region. I'm going to enjoy a glass in her honor, maybe two, then relive the moment we danced at the B.B. King Blues Club on her fiftieth birthday."

I wept as I listened to Dominic announce the administration of his own death warrant.

> "Should I wake from the bliss of that moment, I'll visit the stories Sharon told me of the beautiful life Allison May has lived. The mere anticipation of experiencing those moments is quite exhilarating."

"Dominic, why should I be the one to tell your story? Why did you choose me?"

"Because I don't want you to fear this ability. My dad never feared it. And, that is one fact I do not need to validate. I never visited his moments to determine if he knew about my ability, nor do I ever plan to. I can still see the wisdom in his eyes. He saw flashes of the suffering his own father endured. He believed his father's visions and wept when they overtook the man's hold on reality. I wonder how long he feared the same fate for himself...and then for me.

"If Dad believed I had this curse, it never overwhelmed him. He shielded me from flights of fancy. Keeping me grounded in reality saved my life. His face would glow with delight whenever he watched me discover the might of my gift—well, that's what I assume he was responding to. I never had a chance to rescue Allison May, to teach her the wonders of our ability, or to save her from the dangers of her imagination.

"Your great-grandmother never realized her husband's true ability. All she could see was a man whose mental state was declining rapidly and that it was dangerous for their daughter, your grandmother, to remain near him. To protect both her daughter and herself, in the throes Giuseppe's psychosis, your great-grandmother abandoned her home and fled the Bronx. She was ashamed of her actions and didn't want anyone to know what she had done. She told everyone her Joseph had died in the war. Her daughter did not seem to want to learn more, nor did your mother. Knowledge of your family gift died with Madeleine in 1974. Your child, or theirs, will surely carry on this beatified curse."

<Extended pause>

"Hopefully you will be able to guide them. We would like to watch that from heaven."

Chapter 32 - Saturday, October 9, 2024

Angela paced across the room, tears streaming from her eyes, a child nuzzled securely in her arms. Though not yet two months old, Dominic's piercing blue eyes were fixed on his mother as she told a most fantastic story.

"Dominic Bandall died in his sleep early that Saturday morning in March of 2019, just hours after I left Hawaii. His doctor said he died peacefully, without any struggle or pain. Today would have been his seventy-fifth birthday.

"Alexander Emmanuelle met me at the airport when I arrived in New York and gave me the news. Arrangements were made according to Dominic's wishes."

Little Dominic cooed gently. It will be years before Angela knows if her son has the same ability as Dominic and Giuseppe. Until then, whenever her child closes his eyes, she will wonder about it and worry what will happen next. It's a concern she is willing to cope with, for the magic of seeing him open his eyes wide and purse his mouth into a smile eases whatever suffering she may have endured.

"I can't protect you from every danger in the world. Dominic taught me that lesson. I do promise, however, to give you my love and support. Should you need our assistance, your father and I will guide you with the wisdom passed on by Tony Bandall and Sharon Peers Bandall, two people who did not have the ability but learned how to care for those who did."

Angela gently rocked Dominic in her arms and softly sang him a lullaby. She imagined her mother smiling as they both reassured Dominic, "you belong to me...."

Angela laid her son in his bassinet. The little boy closed his eyes and soon drifted off to sleep. She reorganized her digital library of audio and video recordings and began to gather the keepsakes used while telling her story. Before returning them to a tattered footlocker, her mind flooded with the memories of moments she had now revisited thousands of times when she listened to the recorded voice of her mentor.

- A faded baseball dated October 9th, 1949
- Military medals, a rusted German bayonet, and dog tags from World War II
- A New York Highlanders baseball program from 1912

- A grainy photograph of Dominic, Sharon, and little Allison May
- A bound volume entitled *The True History of Hawai'i*
- Journals labeled *The True War on Terror*
- A well-worn stickball bat
- A diamond-encrusted, eighteen-karat, white-gold choker necklace
- Finally, a green composition book

Angela opened the book to the last page. Just below three entries in Anita's handwriting, she wrote in one final comment.

405: This killed Dominic

About the Author

Kevin was born and raised in New York City. A graduate of the United States Military Academy at West Point, he was diagnosed with multiple sclerosis (MS) in 1999, while serving overseas in command of a US Army Air Cavalry Troop. He is now medically retired and lives in Portland, Oregon with his daughter, Eleanor.

Kevin devotes much of his time and energy toward overcoming the challenges of his own MS, so he can fight for others. He began writing and blogging in 2010, for the Department of Veterans Affairs, the National MS Society, and then NEVER STOP NEVER QUIT, a charitable foundation he co-formed to further expand his fundraising and advocacy in the fight against MS.

"...fantastic stories, where I'm limited only by my imagination, not by the confines of this stupid disease."

NMSS Leadership Conference
Denver, CO
November 2016

Acknowledgments

Symphony

Original French Words by Andre Tabet and Roger Bernstein

English Words by Jack Lawrence

Music by Alstone

© Renewed 1973 MPL MUSIC PUBLISHING, INC.

All Rights Reserved

Reprinted by Permission of Hal Leonard LLC

Task Force Baum and the Hammelburg Raid

www.taskforcebaum.de/index1.html

© 2002 Peter Domes

Gargee'an and Gargee'an / Children's Song / (English)

Songs & Rhymes from Iran, Mama Lisa's World, February 21, 2017

https://www.mamalisa.com/?t=es&p=4561

© 2019 Lisa Yannucci

About the Author Photograph

© 2018 Keith Carlsen

KeithCarlsen.com

Moments

© 2019 Kevin Byrne

Published 2019 by
NEVER STOP NEVER QUIT, Portland, OR

NeverStopNeverQuit.com

All rights reserved. No part of this publication may be reproduced in any form or by any electronic or mechanical means, including information storage and retrieval systems, without permission in writing from the publisher, except by a reviewer who may quote brief passages in a review.

Never Stop... Never Quit...
Registered, U.S. Patent and Trademark Office

Paperback Edition
ISBN: 978-1-7324106-7-1

The Condemned Man Series

Inspired by *The Ramblings of a Condemned Man* collection, Kevin translates his personal version of the "chaotic, horrific, and truly burdensome" for his readers. The stories in this series are complete works of fiction. Every story, every character, however, experiences their own chaos and condemnation in a way that's somewhat familiar and comfortable to the author.

The Condemned Man series list of works include:

- *...in abeyance*
  First Published November 2018

- *Annie Flynn - first row, second desk*
  First Published December 2018

- *Moments*
  First Published April 2019

- Additional titles coming soon!

CPSIA information can be obtained
at www.ICGtesting.com
Printed in the USA
LVHW040748100619
620693LV00001B/49

9 781732 410671